# ANNA KASHINA

# *Assassin Queen*

## THE MAJAT CODE
## BOOK III

ANGRY
ROBOT

ANGRY ROBOT
An imprint of Watkins Media Ltd

Unit 11, Shepperton House
89 Shepperton Road
London N1 3DF
UK

www.angryrobotbooks.com
twitter.com/angryrobotbooks
The final cut

An Angry Robot paperback original 2016

Cover by Alejandro Colucci
Maps by Steve Luxton
Set in Meridien by Epub Services

ISBN 978 0 85766 606 2
Ebook ISBN 978 0 85766 607 9

Printed and bound in the United Kingdom by 4Edge Limited

9 8 7 6 5 4 3 2

*To VKB*

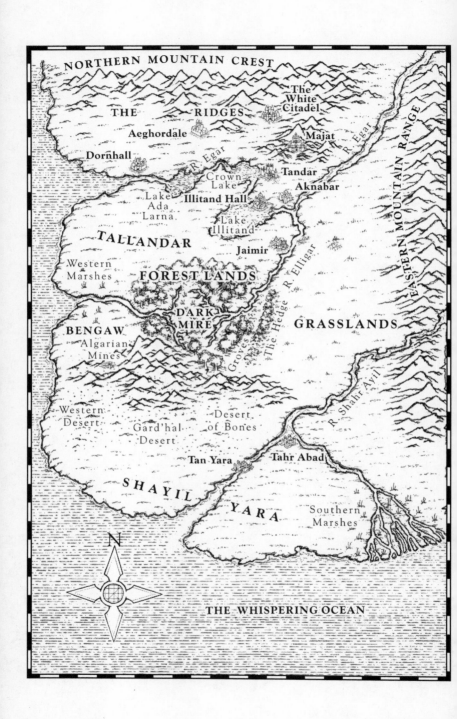

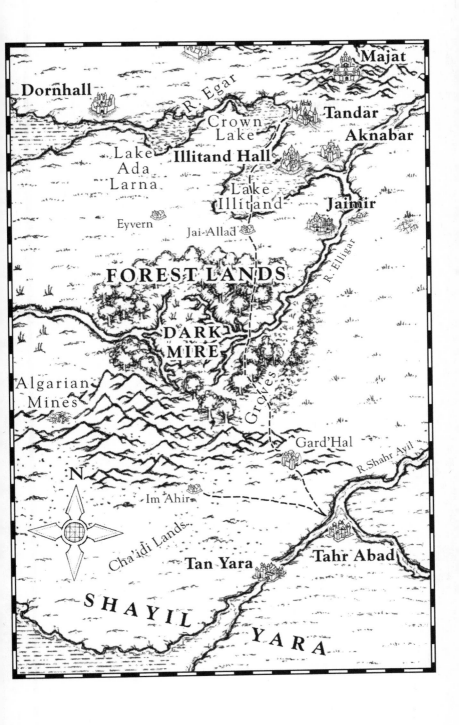

Majat

Dornhall

R. Egar

Crown
Lake

Tandar

Aknabar

Lake
Ada
Larna

Illitand Hall

Lake
Illitand

Eyvern

Jaimir

Jai-Allad

FOREST LANDS

R. Elligar

DARK
MIRE

Algarian
Mines

Groves

Gard'Hal

N

R. Shahr Ayil

Im Ahir

Cha'idi Lands

Tan Yara

Tahr Abad

S H A Y I L

Y A R A

# 1
# EMPATHY

Kaddim Nimos rushed through the stone hallway, staggering under the weight of his dying comrade. Xados, draped over his side, grew heavier by the minute. Sharp smells of blood and poisoned flesh pulsed from the man's injured shoulder in sickening waves, a stark reminder that his injury was no ordinary battle wound. Nimos grasped tighter, his comrade's moans mixing with the rasp of his own labored breath. Their only hope lay in speed, just a few more steps down the long hallway, through the gaping doorway at the far end. And then... Nimos shut his mind to the thought as he pulled on.

The large chamber greeted them with a familiar chill, sending relief through Nimos's exhausted body. His eyes fixed on the Reincarnate's cloaked shape, rising from the massive throne-like chair at the end of the room. The Kaddim leader's gaunt face darkened, his bony hand briskly gesturing to a low platform at the center of the room. Power charged the air around it, a nearly palpable aura that evoked an unsettling mix of dread and reassurance. Nimos staggered forward and lowered Xados onto the stone slab. *Please, let it not be too late.*

The Reincarnate's upward glance pinned him like a saber point.

"This looks like a spider bite, Kaddim Nimos. One of Lady Ayalla's."

Nimos swallowed. The Reincarnate's voice hinted accusation, as if Nimos was personally responsible for the wound. He needed to explain, but talking required steady breathing he couldn't yet manage after the crazy run. He bowed his agreement instead, his eyes trailing to the mess of Xados's shoulder.

It seemed unthinkable that this kind of destruction could be caused by a mere bite from such a small creature, even if scary enough to bring shiver at the memory. How could the little buggers possibly be so deadly? Nimos had wasted no time pulling Xados out of the battle and bringing him through the time vortex to the Kaddim's hidden stronghold. Yet, even back then he knew for certain that all this haste would not help to save Xados's life. And now, as he laid his eyes on the sickening sight, he wondered if it was too late to save anything at all.

The Reincarnate kept his hands steady as his fingers worked invisible lines in the air around the wound. Nimos watched Xados tremble under the touch of the magic that, he knew, had nothing to do with healing. He could almost see the traces of power left by the Reincarnate's movements – like a net, holding the disintegrating body together. Prolonging the agony just enough to... to...

"How did it happen?" the Reincarnate asked.

Nimos heaved a breath, wishing he didn't feel so exhausted.

"The Majat. Their new Guildmaster, Mai, is a problem."

"How so?"

Nimos struggled to steady his voice. "He sided with Prince Kythar Dorn, who rendered the Majat warriors immune to our control. We cannot stand up to the Majat's Gem-ranked warriors if our magic is ineffective." *Especially the ones of their top, Diamond rank.* Nimos shivered. Prince Kythar – Kyth, to his friends – possessed an inborn gift of elemental magic, one that could destroy their entire brotherhood if the Prince had succeeded in mastering it fully. And now, his alliance with the Majat created an additional problem. The Majat Guildmaster, Mai, leading his elite Gem-ranked fighters under Kyth's protection, was an obstacle the Kaddim hadn't counted on when they started this war.

The Reincarnate frowned. "Haven't you seeded a rivalry between Mai and the Prince, Kaddim Nimos?"

Nimos shrugged. He did. In fact, he hardly had to try. Kyth and Mai were in love with the same woman. Even a fool could work off this advantage to make sure the two could barely stand each other. Who would have known that Kyth and Mai would be able to put aside this kind of a disagreement and march together into battle? "Clearly I failed, Cursed Master."

"Still. The Majat don't form alliances."

Nimos looked away. They didn't, not in the known history of the kingdoms. Perhaps it was indeed his own fault for trying to do more than he could handle. Through his scheming, the Kaddim's strike against the Majat had landed too close to home, with Xados at the center of the action – as well as the ensuing chaos. And now the Majat were up in arms, and the Kaddim didn't have enough power to withstand them. If Mai and Kyth were to discover the location of this stronghold and descend on the Kaddim in full force…

He caught the Reincarnate's gaze, belatedly remembering that the Cursed Master's own magic made Nimos as transparent as an open book. He bowed his head, part in submission, part out of exhaustion.

"Besides, this still doesn't explain the spiders," the Reincarnate said.

Nimos kept his eyes on an oozing yellow streak soaking into the folds of Xados's robe. Even the Reincarnate's magic, which, he knew, was now working through his comrade's body to stabilize it, couldn't halt the process for long.

"The spiders come from Prince Kythar's side," he said. "His foster brother, Alder, is Lady Ayalla's favorite."

The Reincarnate's lips twitched. "She has many favorites, Kaddim. I heard she beds nearly every man who passes through her realm. What makes this one different enough to control the spiders?"

*Perhaps his sexual prowess?* Nimos bit back the sarcasm. "I am not certain, Cursed Master. Alder is completely ungifted when it comes to magic." *But he can control the spiders. Three, to be exact.* He looked away. How hard could it possibly have been for the Kaddim fighters to keep away *three*?

His heart sank as he raised his eyes to meet the Reincarnate's deep, dark stare.

"It's time, Kaddim Nimos. The magic is stable now, but it won't be for long. Do what you can."

Nimos's heart skipped a beat as he stepped toward the dying man. Xados's frame, partially hidden by the pus-soaked robe clinging to his body, seemed much

frailer than he remembered – not large enough for this
formidable swordsman and one of the Brotherhood's
best warriors. The man's injured shoulder looked a
mess, bones showing through the peeling flesh, the
smells of decay and poison palpable in the still air.
Nimos blocked his mind to it as he knelt by Xados's
side.

An unbidden memory rose in his mind. Two young
Kaddim initiates on a kitchen duty, showing off their
mind control by forcing rats out of their holes into the
cooking fire. Xados's rats always escaped in the end,
even if badly burned, but Nimos's magic was stronger.
From time to time he could force a rat into absolute
stillness, unable even to squeak as the fire consumed it
alive. Later on Nimos, the first of his peers, had learned
to do this to humans, feeding on their despair and pain.
And now, he was about to experience the same kind of
pain firsthand, by blending his mind with a man in his
dying agony.

He needed this last conversation with Xados, possible
only with the help of the Reincarnate's magic that could
hold back the poison long enough to share Xados's
thoughts. He was the only one in their Brotherhood
whose mind magic was strong enough to pull it off.

He hated himself for it as he reached down and put
his palms on the sides of Xados's face.

The pain lashed out like a raging flame, instantly
igniting every nerve in his body. The Reincarnate's
chamber fell away, sounds from outside so faint they
seemed surreal. Voices, screaming – or was it his own?

He willed himself to maintain the bond. Xados's
mind was still there, nearly intact. As the pain settled
in, he started feeling the thought flow, echoing like

words spoken aloud. *Our last conversation.*

*Get the bastards, Nimos. Make them pay for what they've done to me.*

*I will.* Nimos felt Xados's rage envelop him too, so strong that for a moment it numbed the worst of the pain. Images streamed in like a flood pouring through a breach in a dam. The recent battle with the Majat, their Diamonds spearheading the attack, breaking into the Kaddim's ring, hacking left and right. The sting of the spider bite. Rapidly flashing disbelief mixing with fear and anger. The dark furry shape scurrying away into the wall of fighters.

*I am dying, brother. Damn them all.*

*Show me what you know, Xados. Help us defeat them.*

The image that burst into his consciousness in response was not what he expected, so intense that he nearly broke the link. A slim, boyish warrior with pale blond hair, dressed in dashing black. Mai, the young Guildmaster. His movements seemed flawless as he advanced, his weapon – a double-bladed staff – descending so fast that Nimos heard a whistle of the parting air and the touch of wind on his skin. Nimos gaped, his own memory of being struck by Mai's staff still too fresh in his mind. The man was not only an inspiring leader. He was a fighting machine. How could they ever defeat him?

*Mai is faultless,* Xados said. *The most dangerous man alive... I'll show you what I know about his fighting style... He and his men...*

More fighting erupted, the images so real that Nimos felt, once again, drawn into the battle they just left. He didn't try to analyze it at all. Xados had spent years at the Majat Guild studying their styles, and he was now pouring out all this knowledge in a matter of minutes. Nimos did his best to absorb the information, move after flawless move, weapon upon exotic weapon, the fighting styles of every Diamond on the Majat force. Twelve Diamonds in active service, flipping in front of him like pages of a burning book.

The pain was scorching, shredding him like a thousand blades. He could no longer tell what was real, the Majat attacking him from all sides, the spiders – gray shadows, each nearly as big as a man's hand – rushing through the Kaddim ring...

*Nimos... Stay with me.*

*I don't know if I can.* Yet, Nimos's mind sprang back to alertness as a new image loomed ahead. A woman, slowly taking shape against the surrounding haze.

*Watch. She is the key... to defeating Mai.*

Nimos gasped as he looked on, gathering all his strength. The image was vivid now, a slim nineteen year-old, all slender curves and wiry muscle, her smooth dark skin accented by pale golden hair. *Kara.* He felt warmth briefly wash over him at her sight, followed by a surge of pain that left him gasping.

*She is Mai's weakness.*

Nimos was no longer certain which one of them had this thought. It hardly mattered. Kara had been the focus of his own plotting for so long. He knew everything about her, including the love she and Mai had for each other, yet the knowledge hadn't helped at all during their recent battle. Kara's fighting skill equaled Mai's, making her nearly as undefeatable.

*Don't think, Nimos. Just watch.*

Once again, Nimos stood in the center of the battle, the deafening clashing of steel pierced by occasional screams. Smell of wounded flesh hit his nostrils – or was it coming from within this chamber?

He was Xados now, Kara fighting another man right next to him as he reached forward to brush his fingers against the skin of her forearm, bared by her ripped sleeve. The jolt of magic that flew off his fingers pierced her like a needle. She started and nearly missed a blow, then recovered and moved on.

Nimos stared at the contact point, his mind magic detecting a blade of crackling power worming its way into her arm.

*I… marked her. She's yours now, Nimos. My… gift to you, brother.*

Nimos trembled, for a moment forgetting the pain.

*Take her now, while I'm still here.*

Nimos focused, summoning the last of his strength, his magic blending with Xados's, pulling through immeasurable distance to trigger the link. He felt a pull in response, holding on with all he had, sealing the bond, tugging it like an invisible leash that spanned time and space.

*Got it.*

A sigh echoed through Xados, like a tight string giving way. The pain eased – or was it because there wasn't enough body left to feel? Xados's thoughts were losing coherence, flooding from every corner in a jumble no longer possible to understand.

Kara's image became the last thread Nimos could cling to, the memory Xados held together that acquired so much more substance now that the link was activated. *She is mine.* The thought hovered in front of him like a lifeline as he shared his dying comrade's agony.

He did not catch the exact moment when the pain stopped, like a flicker of a candle blown out. His hands holding Xados's head sank into a wet sponge-like mass, Xados's body melting away like a patch of spring ice.

Nimos wasn't sure how much time passed before he felt the Reincarnate's hands on him, pulling him away, turning him over, laying him on the floor. Shadows loomed over him, but he couldn't comprehend them, grasping on to the memory that had carried him through.

*Kara.*

The mark Xados had implanted into her on the battlefield belonged to him now, bonding him to Kara for eternity. With this bond, he now had the power to change her. She would resist him, no doubt, but she could not possibly resist him forever.

Thanks to Xados, the Kaddim now had the means of defeating the Majat. Even better, they could do it in a way that hurt their enemies the most. In time, Kara would serve the Brotherhood, taking the place of the formidable warrior they just lost.

2

# SPIDERS

Kara leaned against the railing, watching the arriving
Majat warriors down in the castle courtyard. From
the balcony, sinking into the deep stone niche above
the castle entrance, she could get a good view without
making her presence obvious to the people below.
Their voices blended into an indistinct hum, accented
by the neighs of horses and clanking of the gear as the
riders dismounted, lining along the wall.

The smoothly hewn pillar by her side felt pleasantly
cool to her exercise-warmed skin. A breeze, fragrant
with the smells of lake water and apple orchards, shifted
her hair. Her chest swelled with a surreal feeling of
happiness as she watched Mai, standing in the center of
the command group. He looked so perfect, his powerful
stance charging the air around him with a force that
seemed to resonate in every corner of the courtyard,
reflecting in the expectant faces of his subordinates. His
mere presence spelled confidence. Yet looking at the
scene Kara simply couldn't get rid of a nagging sense
of foreboding.

A rustle of footsteps echoed in the passage behind.

Kara turned to see a young woman wearing a white cloak over a plain brown dress. Ellah, the King's truthseer – no doubt drawn to this perfect vantage point by her curiosity about the Majat's arrival. Kara greeted her with a brief nod, edging sideways to make room by the railing.

"Aren't you supposed to be down there with Mai?" Ellah asked.

"I'm not a Guild member." Kara couldn't quite manage to keep the edge out of her voice. The Majat affairs were complicated. A relationship with the Guildmaster made it impossible for her to maintain any formal connection to the Guild – or any other political ties whatsoever. She was fine with it, normally, but at times all these restrictions tended to get on her nerves.

"Who is that older man?" Ellah asked, pointing to a wiry man in his mid-fifties, his graying shoulder-length hair wavering in the breeze.

"Aghat Seldon. He's an older Diamond. Retired."

"Retired? Why's he here then?"

"Damned if I know." This was the question Kara had been asking herself ever since Seldon rode in through the gate at the head of the reinforcements and she saw Mai's frown of surprise. As one of the Guild's top-ranked seniors, Seldon belonged to the elite group that had the power to challenge the Guildmaster's authority – or even remove him from command, if warranted. Worse, Kara heard that Seldon had been after the post of the Majat Guildmaster for quite a while. The fact that he arrived on the brink of a war, apparently without Mai's prior knowledge, couldn't possibly be good.

"He's hiding something," Ellah said.

*Damn.* "Are you sure?"

Ellah nodded. "I can't hear the words, but the signs are clear enough. At least half of what he said to Mai was a lie. He's telling the truth now, though."

Kara swallowed. Down below, Seldon was speaking at length, pointing to the assembled troops. She guessed the discussion must be related to their upcoming march. But what could he possibly lie about? She wished she could overhear at least some of the conversation, but no matter how hard she strained her ears, from this distance she couldn't possibly catch the words.

She froze as her heightened senses caught a barely perceptible high-pitched rustle from the hallway behind. She spun around, feeling the color drain from her face.

Three spiders, each as large as a man's hand, emerged from the doorway and skidded to a halt in front of her.

Kara kept still, only half-registering Ellah's gasp beside her. These spiders, bestowed upon this castle by the mysterious Ayalla the Forest Mother, were fast and agile like no other creature she had ever seen. Their venom could dissolve a man with one bite. She had seen it happen to their enemies. She would never be able to forget the screams.

She slid her hand to the throwing daggers at her belt. The spiders edged forward and raised their front legs threateningly. As she stopped the movement, they stopped too, tense as if ready to leap.

A shiver crept down Kara's spine. Even from a few feet away she could see the way the spiders' hairy bodies glistened as they shifted, the movement of tiny claw-like appendages at the sides of their mouths. *Their venom.* They were honing in on her, leaving her very little room to act.

She glanced at the death-pale Ellah, pressing against the railing by her side.

"Try to move," she said quietly.

Ellah frowned. "Why?"

"I want to see what they'll do."

Ellah's eyes darted to the spiders, her knuckles white as she clenched the railing at her back. "What if they launch at me?"

"They won't, if you move just a little bit."

"How do you know?"

Kara sighed. She didn't know, not for certain. In fact, nothing she knew about these spiders could possibly help them out of their current predicament.

"I need to know which one of us they're after."

Ellah's jaw tightened. "Fine. You move then. I'm staying right here. Just let me know when you're done experimenting."

Kara turned away. By now she should be used to the fact that Ellah never did as told. She shifted her weight, freezing again as the spiders rose, as if bracing for a leap. *Damn.*

"Look, they're not letting me move at all. I think they're after me, not you, but we can't tell for sure unless you move. Away from me. Please?"

Ellah looked at her in indecision.

"If I'm right, you would be safer this way," Kara said.

"And if you're wrong?"

"Just bloody do it."

Ellah shuffled sideways. The spiders showed no reaction.

Kara felt an unpleasant hollowness in the pit of her stomach. She forced it down, knowing how important it was to keep calm.

"Now," she said. "Try to get off the balcony. Slowly. See if they have any objections."

Ellah hesitated. "And if they do?"

"You freeze. Simple."

Ellah's eyes darted to the balcony doorway. She edged toward it, moving slowly and keeping her eyes on the spiders all the time.

When she reached the doorway, Kara let out a sigh. "Now, get the hell out of here."

Ellah stepped through the doorway, then paused. "What about you?"

"I'll think of something."

"I'll get help."

"Thanks." *Whatever. Just get as far away as possible, please*. It wasn't going to look pretty if the spiders attacked. If Kara had any hope to survive she needed to act quickly, and she couldn't possibly do it until Ellah was out of the way.

It would be good if she could first figure out why the spiders were after her. Perhaps they'd lost their minds?

Ellah's feet skidded on the smoothly hewn stone as she darted down the hallway. The spiders showed no interest as they continued to watch Kara with their dark, beady eyes. *Dear Shal Addim, they're bigger than some mice I've seen in the palace kitchens.* Kara kept her fear in check, relaxing her muscles, receding into the background to appear inanimate – a trick that came with her Majat-trained stealth.

After a moment the spiders retreated an inch, but didn't change their attack posture. Clearly, whatever was triggering their aggression had to do with more than her actions – a thought that felt both comforting and frightening at the same time.

She judged the distance. With her skill, throwing three daggers at once wasn't a difficult task. Even from this close, she could probably kill all three spiders before they reached her. Probably. But a miss would most certainly seal her death warrant. Worse, if she succeeded in killing any of these creatures, she would violate the hard-earned trust of Lady Ayalla the Forest Mother, a key ally in their war against the Kaddim. Was she willing to risk bringing on the wrath of such a powerful being, putting everyone in danger to defend her own life?

Kara's mind raced. She was never fond of wildlife, especially the deadly kind that couldn't be trained or tamed. Still, she had seen the way Alder, the emissary of the Forest Mother at the King's court, took care of his deadly pets. He treated them like sentient beings, whispering to them, listening to their response. He seemed to believe he could reason with them. To her knowledge, he could make them attack on command – or hold them back – by saying the right words. Perhaps she, too, could find a way to communicate with them.

Very slowly, she lowered down to a crouch and placed her daggers on the floor.

"I mean you no harm," she said.

The spiders appeared to hesitate, shifting their hairy feet and retreating another inch or so.

She put more calmness into her voice. "You have no reason to attack me."

The spiders surveyed her intently.

"This is a mistake," Kara said softly, soothingly. "I am not your enemy."

The spiders flexed their legs in indecision. Kara forced herself to keep relaxed. She knew all animals could sense fear, and she needed to control hers, even if the thoughts of what could happen if the spiders changed their mind were hard to ignore.

She reached forward with her hand, palm open.

"Here," she said. "You can climb on me, and I'll take you back to Alder. This way, you'll be in control the whole way. If you decide to bite me, nothing could possibly stop you."

She waited, emptying her mind of any emotions or thoughts. A distant part of her screamed in terror as she felt the touch of a hairy spider leg, but she forced that part deeper down, relaxing to welcome the tingling sensation as the spiders filed up her arm. She could sense their weight as they settled on her shoulder, doing her best not to think of them at all.

"See?" she said. "It's called trust. I trust you with my life. I hope you trust me too."

Rapid footsteps clanged in the hallway outside. She sensed the spiders stiffen and forcibly kept her stomach from lurching. *When this is over I'm going to go where no one can hear and have a nice long scream.*

A tall, broad-shouldered young man rushed in, with Ellah close on his heels. *Alder.* Kara met his eyes, momentarily overwhelmed. *Will they listen to him?*

*Will his presence trigger them to do something rash?*

"What's happening?" Alder asked.

Kara forced a smile. She hated to admit how her body was beginning to feel sore from the effort of keeping still. This would not do at all. Not for someone of her training. "Nothing. We're just making friends, that's all."

"Ellah said they threatened you."

"Yes, they did."

"Why?"

Kara thought of shrugging, but quickly decided against it. No way of telling what the spiders would do if she moved her shoulder just now.

"No idea. I was going to ask you the same question, actually."

Alder's eyes briefly darted to the daggers on the floor, then to Kara's forehead which, she knew, must be glistening with sweat. His lips parted in a hissing sound. *Talking. He's talking to them.* She watched wide-eyed as the spiders leapt from her shoulder onto Alder's sleeve and pattered up his arm.

She flexed her muscles, surprised at how stiff she felt. *Bloody hell.*

"They're fine now," Alder said. "I don't think they will threaten you again."

"Thanks," she said.

"No problem. You did well, by the way."

Kara shrugged, a bad habit as she was now beginning to realize. "I didn't bloody do anything."

"You calmed them down." He glanced at the daggers on the floor again. "I know your instinct must have been to attack them."

"It's what they expected, isn't it?"

"Yes. Like I said, you did well."

She nodded, feeling the tension slowly leave her body, replaced by a weakness she normally experienced only after a very strenuous fight. More footsteps echoed down the hallway, the newcomers crowding into the doorway. Kyth, the Crown Prince. His dark blue eyes widened in alarm, then softened as he saw that Kara was out of danger. Her brief smile in response faded as she saw the red-haired lady step up to the Prince's side.

Lady Celana Illitand, a young and highly intelligent noblewoman, took a special interest in the Prince and wasn't a person Kara ever wanted to mess with. She kept her face impassive as Celana glanced at her with displeasure before fixing her eyes on the spiders.

"I think everything's fine now," Kara said. She picked up her daggers and sheathed them at her belt.

"I left them in the gardens hunting this morning," Alder said. "They did seem agitated, now that I think about it. I assumed they were hungry."

*Hunting.* Kara swallowed. The spiders were like small predators, doing marvels at keeping down the castle's population of mice and rats. Come to think of it, it was fortunate they didn't normally go after anything larger than that.

Footsteps and clanging of weapons signaled the arrival of reinforcements. *Dear Shal Addim, did Ellah alert the whole castle?* The thought faded instantly at the sight of Mai, the hallway behind him filled with armed Majat. She felt warm inside as she met his concerned gaze.

"What happened?" Mai's eyes briefly darted to Alder's shoulder before settling on Kara again. His frown deepened as he glanced over her sweaty hair, the weary set of her shoulders, the strain that she knew must be plainly visible on her face.

*Damn it, get a grip.* Mai knew her well, and she knew how fast his temper could flare if he believed she was in danger. The way his eyes kept returning to Alder filled her with unease. The last thing they needed right now was a confrontation between a member of the King's household and the Majat.

"I'm fine," she said, hoping that she sounded convincing.

Mai's expression told her she hadn't succeeded at all. His glare forced Alder to take a step back.

"Why did your spiders threaten Kara?" Mai demanded.

Alder shook his head. "I had nothing to do with it. I wasn't even here."

"It's your bloody job to keep them under control."

"Look…" Alder squared his shoulders. "I don't know what happened, but I–"

"I think *I* know," Kyth suddenly said.

Kara's skin prickled as she saw the Prince's grim look, the way his eyes bore into her with a mix of regret and disbelief. What the hell was going on?

"It's the Kaddim magic," Kyth said. "I sense it on Kara. I assume the spiders did as well."

Kara's eyes widened. Kyth's gift enabled him not only to resist the Kaddim and protect others from their magic, but also to sense it when it was used nearby. The fear she saw in his eyes echoed with hollowness in her chest.

"How is it possible?" Her voice came out as a near-whisper.

Kyth's gaze wavered. "I'm not sure. Their magic is faint on you, but I sense it exactly the way I do when the Kaddim apply their power."

"Maybe there is a Kaddim Brother in the vicinity, Your Highness?" Lady Celana asked.

Everyone exchanged glances. The idea seemed unlikely, since the Majat's recent strike had sent the Kaddim's magic-wielding leaders far away into their secret stronghold, where, as everyone assumed, they were now organizing their defense. Kara knew Kyth's father and Mai were preparing an attack that would hopefully destroy the Brotherhood once and for all. But if Kyth's words were true, more was at play than they all realized.

Kyth shook his head again. "No. It's coming from Kara, I'm certain of it."

Kara stared. She knew Kyth wouldn't lie. He used to love her, and he still cared for her deeply, even though she had given her heart to another. He was also a man of integrity. He would never accuse anyone unfairly, or speak of something like this unless he was absolutely certain.

In the ensuing silence, Mai crossed the small space of the balcony and took Kara's arm. She clung to him as he led her through, grateful for the support, wishing his closeness could make her feel safe, like it always did before.

She didn't trust herself to speak, or even do anything right now. Too many emotions welled inside her, threatening to overpower her. Fear, confusion, shock – and anger. So much anger.

How did it happen that the spiders, bestowed on this castle for protection, could have attacked and threatened her, one of the key defenders and top warriors on their force? Why couldn't Alder keep a better control on them? And worse, how was it possible that she had become the source of Kaddim magic?

She kept herself in check, just like she did with the spiders, releasing Mai's supporting arm to join the Diamonds of his Majat escort. She knew she should be the one speaking right now, but she was afraid to open her mouth for fear of saying something she would regret. Besides, Mai's reaction was already bad enough, his anger flaming out of every pore as he glared at the spiders perched on Alder's shoulder.

"Keep the beasts under control, Alder," he said. "Or I'll be forced to kill them."

"You can't," Alder protested, backing away. "The Forest Mother…"

Mai's short glance stopped him. "Just do your best, so that I don't feel tempted."

Kara flinched as she saw the furry shapes raise their legs threateningly again, as if they could actually understand Mai's words. Perhaps they could. Or maybe they acted this way because she was close to them again. She hastily stepped away, the Diamonds crowding around her protectively.

Mai ran his eyes around the gathering. "It's almost time for the King's council. Most of us are headed there, so we can perhaps continue this discussion – and hopefully make sure something like this doesn't bloody happen again?"

# 3

# MIND LINK

The King's council chamber was designed for noble gatherings, each of the chairs set around it in an even circle massive enough to accommodate all the essential ornaments and heraldry signs even for the highest born. Now that she claimed control of her emotions, Kara couldn't escape the feeling she didn't belong. She had to remind herself that she, like everyone else here, had been invited for a reason – in her case, her familiarity with the enemy, even if that familiarity had just become a bit too close for comfort.

She envied Mai's ability to instantly settle into any environment. Now, with the additional aura of power his Guildmaster status had given him, he became the natural focus of the gathering as soon as he stepped into the room. Perhaps part of it was due to the fact that the six Diamonds he brought with him easily outpowered any warrior force this chamber had ever seen, including the King's own hired Majat guards. If nothing else, this alone was bound to make this gathering historic, an unprecedented occasion of hosting the Majat Guildmaster and his very best warriors at the King's war council.

Kara glanced at Kyth, seated at the King's right. In the past few months he had matured so much, from the young idealistic boy who looked up to everyone around him, into a young man in his own right, fit one day to assume the throne. She felt guilty that part of this maturity was undoubtedly caused by the heartbreak he suffered when she professed her love for Mai. And now, seeing him next to Celana filled her with new hope. The royal lady looked so good by his side, her beauty and wit a match for the Prince in every way. With luck, and Lady Celana's persistence, the wound Kara had inflicted on the Prince's heart would heal – and soon.

Her eyes inadvertently slid to the spiders perched on Alder's shoulder. The creatures were motionless now. It was easy in this state to mistake them for an elaborate shoulder ornament, but after her recent ordeal she would never be able to look at them the same way. Her stomach clenched at the memory of their weight on her shoulder, the high-pitched crackling sound they emanated when they moved.

She glanced away to the last two members of the gathering, representing the two spiritual powers of the realm. The white-robed Keeper, Magister Egey Bashi, looked bulky and muscular, his warrior appearance so unbefitting the scholarly mission of his Order, or the superb healing skills Kara knew him to possess. The black-clad Father Bartholomeos, the head of the Holy Church, was nearly the exact opposite, thin and frail, his large gray eyes surveying the gathering with unease. His gaze hovered over Mai with a pained expression as the priest likely remembered the ruckus the Majat had caused at the Holy Monastery during the last battle with the Kaddim. Kara had no doubt the Holy Father would remember Mai and his men for a very long time.

"Thank you all for responding to my invitation for this council," the King said after everyone was seated. "I will get straight to the pressing matters at hand. As I'm sure you are all aware, despite Aghat Mai's and Prince Kythar's victory over the Kaddim two weeks ago, their five top men escaped. We can only presume that they have now reunited with the rest of the Kaddim leaders and are likely expecting our attack."

"Four top men, Your Majesty," Egey Bashi said. "The fifth was bitten by the spiders." He glanced at Alder's shoulder, and Kara inadvertently followed his gaze. "The venom would have liquefied his body, placing him beyond healing – or the resurrection the Kaddim are known for."

"Do we know this for certain?" the King asked.

"Yes," Kara said.

Her skin prickled at the memory. When the Kaddim had cornered her and tried to drag her into their time vortex, the spiders launched at one of her hooded attackers before the vortex swallowed them all. She stiffened as the images flowed in her mind. Cobblestones, collapsing around her. Fingers brushing her arm. The pulling sensation as she – very briefly – felt as if her body was being sucked away through the gaping hole that, for all she knew, spanned thousands of miles. It had been too close. And now, she couldn't get rid of a nagging feeling that she hadn't really escaped at all.

She glanced up into Kyth's widening eyes. *The Kaddim power. Is he sensing it again?* Her heart skipped a beat as she saw the answer in his face even before he spoke.

"It's back," Kyth said. "Sorry."

Kara jumped up, edging away from the table.

All the Majat around her were instantly on their feet, Mai darting to her side so fast that his shape blurred. His eyes sought hers questioningly as he planted himself between her and the door.

She wondered at the panic she felt at his interference, at her urge to pull away from him. This was Mai, the man she loved. His closeness always made her feel safe, protected. Why did she feel as if she'd rather be anywhere but here right now?

"I need to leave," she said.

Mai frowned. "Why?"

Why indeed? It felt as if the voice in her head wasn't exactly her own. "Mai, please. I–"

"What the hell is going on?" Magister Egey Bashi demanded.

"It's getting stronger," Kyth said.

"What, Your Highness?"

"The Kaddim power."

The Keeper's eyes widened.

"My spiders threatened Kara just before the council," Alder explained hastily. "Back then, Kyth sensed something strange. But then the spiders calmed down, so we all thought…"

Kara swallowed. Unbidden, the memory of the Kaddim attack stirred up again, now even more real than before. No – not the attack. The touch. Fingers brushing against her skin. The brief, caress-like movement felt pleasant at first, then so horrifying that it nearly disabled her. How could she have forgotten it so completely?

Kara's shoulders shook. She looked at Mai, still

standing between her and the door.

"Let me go," she pleaded.

His eyes narrowed. "Not without knowing exactly what's happening to you."

"But..." She paused, her eyes drawn to the spiders again. They were rising on Adler's shoulder, their front legs waving threateningly in the air.

Mai slid an arm around her waist, both gentle and firm, his flexing muscle showing her that it would be nearly impossible for her to break free. Despite everything, his closeness did feel soothing once she lent herself to it. She did her best to relax into his hold. Hell, only a short time ago she couldn't think of anything she wanted more than having his arms around her. Why was she suddenly so keen on getting away?

She tried to tell herself that her sudden urge to leave the room had nothing to do with the anxiety caused by the strange pulling sensation building inside her. Her reasons were entirely rational, she told herself firmly. If she could somehow give out Kaddim magic, she shouldn't be anywhere near the council chamber where the King and his allies were discussing ways to dispose of the Kaddim Brotherhood once and for all. It made sense. And yet, she couldn't escape the feeling that the pull that urged her to try to leave the room was much stronger than rational thought.

She took a deep breath, forcing the feeling away as she relaxed into Mai's embrace. He never held her this way at a formal gathering, not with the ongoing Guild's inquiry into her lineage that would determine the possibility of their marriage. If anyone still had any doubt about their relationship, they wouldn't from now on – and that made his intentions toward her official, irrevocable, barring some unforeseen problems on the side of the Guild. Why couldn't she just focus on that? She did, and the pull weakened. Sounds slowly returned, making her aware of the conversation going on around her.

"I think I read something like this in the old chronicles," Lady Celana said in her clear voice. "The Kaddim Brothers – or some of them at least – could place a mark on their victim, somewhat like the magic used for their brand mark. One text said it could bend a person to the Kaddim's will, even though the wording was not very specific. I assume, if such a thing is truly possible, the affected person would likely emanate Kaddim-like power." She glanced at Kara.

Magister Egey Bashi nodded thoughtfully. "You may be more right than you know, my lady. The Kaddim leaders are capable of what's known as a mind link – a very difficult form of magic to master." He turned to Kara. "Try to remember. During your last fight, did any of them touch you?"

"Other than when trying to kill her, you mean?" Mai asked.

The Keeper frowned. "I believe the touch I am speaking about should be memorable in a different way. Wasn't it?"

*Memorable in a different way.* Images flowed through her mind, their intensity making her gasp. The Kaddim Brothers, surrounding her in a tight ring as they tried to pull her into their vortex. Sabers, dancing around her in terrifying unity, preventing her escape. Mai, breaking through their line and pulling her out at the very last moment. Fingers brushing over her arm... *The touch.* "I... I believe so, yes."

The Keeper's lips briefly pressed into a stern line. "I feared this."

Kara glanced around, feeling like a trapped animal at the end of a hunt. It was all her fault. The Kaddim had been aware that both men leading the attack, Kyth and Mai, were in love with her. Targeting her made perfect sense.

"The Kaddim's mind control doesn't work on me, Magister," she said. "Remember?"

"True," Egey Bashi said. "But the mind link is different. Even with your ability to resist their regular power, it would be impossible to block off the link. It's at a much higher level of magic. To my knowledge, even among the Kaddim leaders only a few would be able to make full use of it. Unfortunately, there is at least one whose power is definitely strong enough. Kaddim Nimos."

*Nimos.* Kara swallowed. Nimos's scheming had nearly cost her and Mai their lives. She hoped they were rid of him, at least for a while. But if he was the one behind the link...

"What can this mind link do, exactly?" she asked.

Egey Bashi sighed. "What Lady Celana just mentioned is correct. Their goal is to gain control over you."

"*Control?*"

"Yes. To take over your will, so that they can use your knowledge, and your abilities, to their end."

"My abilities?" *Dear Shal Addim. My fighting skill. They can't touch that, can they?*

"I'm afraid so."

"How?"

The Keeper threw an uneasy glance at Mai. "The

man who placed the link will work to develop it over time, to achieve a... a closeness with you. It's much like an emotional attachment between two people," he looked at Mai again, "but all induced entirely by magic."

Kara's lips twitched. The explanation seemed ridiculous. "They hope to make me feel emotionally attached to one of them?"

Egey Bashi shrugged. "Given your resistance to the Kaddim's magic in the first place, I am not certain what will happen in your case. But yes, if they get their chance to explore the link to the full, this would likely happen, at least in some form."

"Can this link be removed?" Mai asked.

"To the best of my knowledge, Aghat Mai, only death can sever this link."

"Death." For a brief moment Mai's face contorted into a frightening mask.

"Yes."

"Then," Mai said, "I see no choice but to speed up our plans. We must find the Kaddim's hidden fortress and destroy the man who did this – along with the rest of them – once and for all."

He spoke calmly, as if discussing a regular matter. It took close knowledge to detect the edge behind the calmness, the one that made Mai such a dangerous man to cross. *Emotionally attached.* She felt nauseated at the thought.

"I must assume," she said, "that if they indeed have this kind of a power over me, the last thing you want is to keep me around the council chamber where you've all gathered to discuss battle plans."

Egey Bashi shook his head. "It doesn't happen this

fast, Aghat Kara. For all we know, there may be a way to counter this magic, so that none of it will ever happen at all."

"Not good enough, I'm afraid." She glanced at Mai. His glassy expression made her want to cry. *Emotionally attached. Not bloody possible.* "I should leave. I can't be allowed to hear the rest. The planning of this campaign is too important to take any risks."

Mai slowly released his hold. As he stepped away, she shivered at the emptiness left behind, his absence making her feel unprotected, vulnerable. She turned away for fear that he might catch her expression.

"I don't think you should be alone right now," Mai said.

She hesitated. She wanted to be alone, but given that no one knew for sure what was happening with her, it might indeed be a bad idea. "You're right."

Mai turned to his suite. "Aghat Raishan, go with Kara and stay by her side until I replace you."

Raishan saluted with a fist to his chest. His slanted gray eyes slid over to Kara, his lips creasing with a brief smile of encouragement. She smiled back, his air of calm efficiency making her feel instantly at ease.

Mai stepped to the door and pushed it open. An Emerald guard appeared in front of the open doorway.

"Jahib Lenart," Mai said. "You will accompany Aghat Raishan and Kara. Bring two of your men. Follow Aghat Raishan's orders at all times. If anything unusual happens, send a man to report to me at once."

Kara darted toward the exit, feeling everyone's eyes on her, relieved to hear the thud of the closed door behind her. Her decision to leave the council as soon as possible was probably for the best. Yet it felt strange to see Mai place her under guard, as if no longer sure whether she was a friend or an enemy. This unwelcome thought brought a pang of pain, immediately followed by anger. Surely thinking like this played right into the Kaddim's hands. In fact, they could well have planted the distrust into her head.

*Only death could sever the link.* If Mai's plan to seek out the Kaddim's secret stronghold and destroy the Brotherhood could not be realized in time, would she have to be the one to die to free everyone from the Kaddim? Was this the only way to ensure she didn't become an enemy? She forced down the thought as she strode down the hallway, holding her head high.

# 4
# THE COUNCIL

Kyth settled into his chair at the council table, fighting a sinking feeling in his heart. Kara's face when he told her about the Kaddim's magic continued to haunt him. He had never seen her look so defeated.

Knowing that he had lost her to Mai had been shattering, but he couldn't help also feeling rewarded at how happy she seemed these days. And now, thinking of her falling victim to the Kaddim's magic made Kyth boil with barely contained fury. He could see a similar fury reflected in Mai's face as the Majat lowered himself back into his seat across the table. In a strange way, this feeling bonded Kyth to this man, his successful rival, whose boyish looks and dazzling, iconic beauty were so deceiving. At heart, Mai was a ruthless killer who would not stop at anything to get his way – and Kyth seemed to be the only one to see him at face value.

"What else do you all know about the Kaddim mind link?" King Evan asked.

Egey Bashi briefly glanced at Mai. "While I would prefer to do some more reading on the subject first, Your Majesty, I do know that the consequences of such a link could be drastic. We have every reason to be alarmed."

Kyth bit his lip. He knew the Magister's tendency for understatements. He thought back to the way he had reacted to Kara back on the balcony, the warmth and excitement he always felt in her presence tainted with the bitter taste of the Kaddim magic. The memory of her trapped, helpless look wrenched his gut.

"According to my information," Magister Egey Bashi went on, "among the consequences of the link, control is by far not the worst that can happen in Kara's case."

Mai glanced up sharply. "Not the worst?"

"Do you remember the time the Kaddim tried to capture you and Prince Kythar, Aghat Mai?"

Mai briefly glanced in Kyth's direction. Kyth shivered, remembering. Back then, he and Mai had barely escaped with their lives. Mai would have died from his wounds, if Egey Bashi had not conjured some of the darkest Keepers' remedies to bring him back. It still seemed like a miracle that they both survived.

"From what I know," Egey Bashi went on, "the Kaddim's reason for capturing both of you that time was to try and take over your gifts: Prince Kythar's command of the elements, and Aghat Mai's Diamond-level fighting skill."

Mai's gaze wavered.

"The mark the Kaddim placed on Kara," Egey Bashi said, "could, among other things, serve the same purpose. To capture her skill, which equals that of Aghat Mai. The process is slower over a distance, but no less certain, if the mark is placed correctly."

"Capture her skill? What does this mean?" the King asked.

"I'm speaking of the worst possibility, Your Majesty, but if I'm right, this means that when our forces march against the Kaddim, we may potentially be facing an army of warriors, each of them fighting with the skill of a Diamond Majat."

Silence greeted his words as everyone at the table exchanged stunned glances. Kyth's heart quivered. Up until now they had been successfully defeating the Kaddim by using the Majat fighting force protected by Kyth's magic. Mai put a lot of effort into training Kyth to defend larger groups of warriors. Kyth had come to believe their main challenge lay in his ability to keep up. But if all the enemy's warriors – or even a few of them – could fight like Diamonds, all would be surely lost. Mai's reinforcements brought their total number of Diamond-skilled warriors up to eight, which included the retired Seldon – no longer in top shape – and Kara, whose gift could potentially be in jeopardy. Added to the Rubies, Emeralds, and Jades, it seemed like overkill only this morning. Was the Kaddim link going to upset this balance and all their plans?

"An army like that could destroy the world," the King said. "It would be useless for us to even try to stand up to them."

Egey Bashi nodded. "Unfortunately, yes. However, even if they can truly capture Kara's skill, they'd need to amplify it too, and then transfer it to their warriors one by one. It would take considerable time."

"How long?" Mai asked.

Egey Bashi shook his head. "I can't tell for sure, not without doing much more research. But if I were to guess – months, perhaps?"

What will happen to Kara in the meantime?"

"Like I said, Aghat Mai, I need time to give you full answers. I am fairly certain, however, that using her skill would make her more vulnerable to these attempts. She must refrain from any fighting, even in practice."

Mai exchanged quick glances with the other Diamonds. Kyth could guess the thoughts behind their grim expressions. For someone of their skill, fighting was as natural as breathing. Like the rest of them, Kara spent hours on the practice range. If she was deprived of this, on top of everything else…

Egey Bashi sighed. "I know it won't be easy. And even if she manages to be completely idle all the time, they will still be pulling at her, slowly. Speaking in military terms, it works much like a siege."

"Then," Mai said, "we must not lose any time. Now that the Majat reinforcements have arrived, we must move out right away."

The Keeper shook his head. "We don't even know the exact location of the Kaddim stronghold. All we know is that it's somewhere in the mountains on the northern border of the kingdom of Shayil Yara."

Mai shrugged. "Close enough. Once we get there, I'm sure we'd have no trouble finding some locals who–"

"It's a *desert* out there, Aghat. The only locals in those parts are the Cha'idi – the Desert Wanderers. They are nomadic people, very militant. They don't take kindly to strangers."

"It's all right," Mai said. "The Majat don't take kindly to strangers either. I'd say, with the right leverage we should get along splendidly with the Cha'idi people."

Kyth shifted in his seat, noting Father Bartholomeos's

hunted look. The Majat's version of "getting along splendidly" usually meant having their way without razing the place to the ground, just like they did recently at the Holy Monastery to rid it of the Kaddim. The priests had been compliant, even if scared out of their wits, but somehow he doubted that the Majat would be able to pull off the same trick with militant desert tribes.

"I'm afraid it's not that simple, Aghat Mai," the King said. "The Desert Wanderers have a seat on the royal council of Shayil Yara. The kind of diplomacy you are suggesting could easily be considered an act of war. Even with your formidable military force, you wouldn't want that, I'm sure."

"Fine, then. We can do it the nice way and ask for Queen Rajmella's support."

"*If* she provides it."

"Queen Rajmella is a vassal of Tallan Dar," Father Bartholomeos protested. "Surely Your Majesty's request would be enough?"

The King shook his head. "I did not negotiate the original agreement with Shayil Yara after the Holy Wars, but I couldn't help noticing how unfavorable it may seem to the Queen. Not only does it make Shayil Yara formally inferior to a male-dominated kingdom, but it also includes keeping the Queen's firstborn daughter, the heiress to the Southern Throne, hostage at our court."

Kyth bit his lip. Princess Aljbeda, the five year-old daughter of the Shayil Yaran Queen, was being raised in Tandar as the King's ward, to ensure Queen Rajmella's full cooperation in all affairs. He could see how this alone would make the Queen feel less than helpful, especially when it came to such subtleties as the allegiance of unruly desert tribes.

Mai tossed his head impatiently. "None of this would apply if I talk to her myself. The Majat Guild has no allegiance with anyone, and we are not keeping hostages from any kingdom. She shouldn't have any issues with me, should she?"

Egey Bashi glanced at him sideways. "She may have an issue of a different kind in your case, Aghat Mai. You are a man – and an attractive one, if you forgive me saying this."

Mai let out a short laugh. "You can't be serious, Magister."

"Unfortunately, I am."

"I assume men – even attractive ones – are still allowed at Shayil Yaran court, are they?"

"Oh, yes." Egey Bashi measured Mai with a meaningful glance. "I'm certain you and your men would receive a warm welcome. But would the Queen take your request seriously enough to negotiate with you?"

"I guess she'll just have to make a bloody exception this time."

"It's a gut reaction on their part, Aghat Mai. Please forgive me for saying that your looks, and those of many of your men, won't make it any easier to reach neutral ground."

Mai laughed. "Are you suggesting we all wear masks – or better yet, find someone old and infirm to lead the negotiations, Magister?"

"I have a suggestion, my lords," Lady Celana suddenly said.

All heads turned her way. Kyth's skin prickled. Her

expression was calm, but he knew her well enough to see the special gleam in her eyes. He was willing to bet that she likely harbored a very devious thought. Despite her youth, Lady Celana was one of the smartest people he knew. And now, he found himself eagerly waiting for what she had to say.

"I've studied Shayil Yaran customs in some detail," the royal lady said. "I was curious about the fact that they, a female-dominated land, always send men to Tallan Dar as their ambassadors."

Kyth nodded. He never questioned this before, but now that she mentioned it, it did seem unusual.

"And what did you find, my lady?" Mai asked.

Her cheeks flushed under his direct gaze. "They are well aware of our northern customs, Aghat Mai, so they actually take the effort to train men for any diplomatic missions related to Tallan Dar. In return, they normally expect us to do a similar thing and send a woman to their court for any serious negotiations. Sending a man is certainly allowed, but they would see it as unwillingness to abide by their customs. In my humble opinion, this may be one of the reasons for the failure of so many diplomatic missions to Shayil Yaran court… even though it is not my place to tell, of course." She briefly glanced at the King, who responded with a grave stare.

Kyth thought back to the way Celana's father had recently fallen out of favor, after reportedly conspiring with the Shayil Yaran ambassador. Was this why the royal lady felt compelled to do this research?

Mai shifted in his seat. "You suggest we find a woman to lead the negotiations, my lady?"

"Not just any woman," Celana said firmly. "Kara."

"Kara?"

"Yes."

Mai frowned. "With everything she is already going through, wouldn't it be best to leave her out of this?"

Egey Bashi leaned forward. "If I may intervene, Aghat Mai, I believe this is a brilliant idea. Kara would be perfect for the role. She is an Olivian by blood. By her looks, she could have been born in Shayil Yara. She is also a powerful woman. Everyone at Queen Rajmella's court would easily relate to her. They respect women of power."

"What about her mind link?" Mai asked.

"Even if the link takes hold, it should not affect her mind directly. Not for a while. Besides, we may be able to find a remedy that would at least partially counter the effects of the link. I, for one, will put every effort into this research." He turned to Lady Celana. "Well done, my lady."

Her cheeks were crimson now that everyone stared at her. Kyth smiled inwardly. It was hard to remember that someone as smart as Celana was also so young, barely seventeen. He never ceased to feel fascinated at such a mix of confidence and vulnerability in someone who was probably one of the smartest politicians in this room.

"They really don't think much of men in Shayil Yara, do they?" Mai said.

Egey Bashi grinned. "Oh, they do like men, Aghat Mai. You might find yourself surprised."

Mai's eyes slid over him with interest, but he did not question these statements. Kyth, on the other hand, felt more and more intrigued. He couldn't imagine what things were like at Shayil Yaran court, but Lady

Celana's deepening blush and the way the Diamonds in Mai's suite exchanged amused looks made him wonder.

"I am not fully convinced," the King said. "It may be dangerous to rely on Kara in a serious negotiation while she carries the Kaddim mark."

Mai lifted his head. "I will stay by her side, Your Majesty, and will make sure I participate in all the conversations. I am not letting Kara out of my sight. Not until I personally dispose of the man who placed the bloody mark on her."

"I hope you don't plan to take your entire Majat force to the Olivian court, Aghat Mai. They might think you are leading an invasion."

"Or an entertainment troupe," Egey Bashi muttered under his breath.

Mai shrugged.

"I feel obliged to caution you, Aghat Mai," Egey Bashi said. "The Kaddim have targeted Kara precisely because they expected this kind of a reaction from you. They are counting on you – and Prince Kythar – going after them as soon as possible to set things right. We must assume they have a plan to use the mind link to their advantage once you do."

Mai heaved a deep sigh. "My reaction changes nothing, Magister. The original purpose of this gathering has always been to come up with a plan to destroy the Kaddim. This is exactly what we're discussing, isn't it?"

"So far," the Keeper said, "we have discussed only the plans of finding their stronghold."

"That's because we already know what to do once we find them." Mai's eyes met Kyth's from across the table. "If Kyth can protect my men from the Kaddim's magic, I'm sure we will have no trouble defeating them."

Kyth swallowed. It was odd to see the way Mai placed so much faith in his gift, while also acting so demeaning toward him in every one-on-one conversation. He supposed it was inevitable, given the fact that until recently they both thought Kara was in love with Kyth. The reversal of roles came too quickly on the heels of their last Kaddim battle. Would they ever be able to put their rivalry aside and truly work together in the upcoming campaign?

Egey Bashi shook his head. "You forget. There is a distinct chance that by the time you arrive there, the Kaddim warriors will acquire at least a part of Kara's fighting skill. You mustn't ignore this possibility, Aghat Mai."

"I'm not, I assure you."

"Still. I feel obliged to discuss the alternatives." Egey Bashi glanced around the gathering.

Kyth held his breath as he watched the way Mai's face went still like a mask.

"Alternatives, Magister?"

Egey Bashi stiffened. "I believe you know what I mean, Aghat."

"I'm sure if I don't, you'll tell me." Mai's hand resting on the tabletop clenched into a fist. Kyth marveled at the way Egey Bashi didn't flinch under Mai's gaze.

"No need to get emotional, Aghat."

Mai slowly relaxed his shoulders.

"It must have occurred to you," Egey Bashi went on, "that the only sure way to prevent the Kaddim from capturing Kara's gift is to ensure, definitively, that her gift is not available for the taking."

*Death.* Kyth felt blood draining from his face. He kept his eyes on Mai, praying that the Majat would not entertain this possibility. Mai was the most ruthless man he knew. Did he love Kara enough not to feel the temptation?

Mai leaned forward. "I'd like to settle this once and for all, Magister. Kara's protection is my priority. No one will threaten her life, as long as I am in command. Is this understood?" He spoke slowly, his voice hypnotizing like that of a snake charmer.

Entranced, Kyth watched Egey Bashi recede into his chair.

"Understood, Aghat Mai," the Keeper said. "No need to get apprehensive. I was only talking about possibilities. This particular one, by the way, comes with serious complications, which takes it off the table anyway, at least for the moment. I just felt the need to make it clear, while we're on the topic."

Mai kept very still, watching him.

"In a normal case," Egey Bashi went on, "having Kara killed would have solved the problem. However, from what I know about the Kaddim, this action carries a chance of an opposite effect."

"Opposite, how?"

"The Kaddim link is a true bondage. The man who controls it shares her soul, even if Kara is not aware of it yet. If done the wrong way, her death could potentially complete the blend, releasing her power to the Kaddim all at once."

"Done the wrong way?" Mai's voice sent a shiver down Kyth's spine.

The Keeper nodded. "Yes. This is what I need to research before this option can be discussed any further, Aghat Mai."

Mai's jaw knotted. "I'm done discussing it, Magister.

I must also inform you that if I catch you discussing it with anyone else, Kara included, I will take a personal issue with it."

"Is it wise, Aghat Mai?"

"It's the way it is, Magister."

The two men paused, glaring at each other, the air around them charged as if crackling with an impending thunderstorm.

"How about another option, then," Egey Bashi said. "We could give Kara potions that would induce dreamless sleep for the majority of our journey."

"You are proposing to drug her?"

"Effectively, yes."

Mai briefly glanced down at the table top as he unclenched his hand. "I will not let anything be forced on her."

Egey Bashi sighed. "This way of thinking is playing right into Kaddim's hands, Aghat Mai. You can trust that they counted on precisely this reaction from you when they targeted Kara. You wouldn't react the same if someone else carried the link instead, would you?"

For the first time in this conversation Kyth saw Mai look uncomfortable. His stomach clenched with worry. Was the Diamond going to give in?

Mai heaved a breath. "My reaction would be the same if it came to any of my warriors, Magister. Before considering these 'options' as you call them, I have to be convinced that we have no other choice. The fact that it's Kara does make the whole thing more personal for me, but it doesn't change a thing."

"I hope this is indeed the case, Aghat Mai."

A brief smile slid over Mai's face, his amused expression harboring a hidden edge. "I'm letting this slide, Magister, because I'm sure it wasn't your intention just now to doubt my word in this public gathering."

The Keeper receded into his chair. "Please forgive me, Aghat Mai. I spoke rashly. I know you are a man of your word. It's just that I couldn't help worrying, given how closely this situation has affected you. I wouldn't want to see our enemies succeed."

Mai kept his gaze, the smile playing on his lips more frightening than an outburst of anger. "Neither would I, Magister, believe me. That's why we must act quickly, isn't it?"

Kyth's skin prickled. Knowing Mai well, he was aware of how close this conversation had come to an explosion. He was relieved to see Mai's resolve to protect Kara at all cost, but he was also aware how Egey Bashi's words could have seeded doubt in anyone less involved. The solutions mentioned by the Keeper would indeed make sense to an impartial observer. If Kara's fighting skill could threaten their military operation, drugging or killing her seemed like the only way to prevent it for certain. One life was not a high price to pay for the outcome of a war.

He prayed no one in their force would ever challenge Mai's command.

# 5
# PRACTICE FIGHT

Kara strode unseeingly through the castle hallways, only half aware of the clanging of weapons and gear of her Gem-ranked escort. Or was it her guard? She knew Mai had been considerate by charging Raishan, a close friend, with the task, but this didn't change the big picture. She was a threat. Knowingly or unknowingly, she might be used to betray them to the enemy.

Worse, she couldn't get rid of the pulling sensation that had enveloped her in the council chamber and for some reason refused to go away. As if she was back at their last fight with the Kaddim, where their leaders had surrounded her and tried to pull her with them through the time vortex. She could almost sense the wind on her cheek, the smells of stone and blood, the clanging of the dying battle. A hand, brushing her forearm in a near-intimate caress that felt so alien in the heat of the melee. She stiffened at the memory. *The touch.*

She hastily pulled up her sleeve as she walked, staring at her smooth, unblemished skin. No mark of any kind. She should feel reassured, yet all she could think of was that feeling, fingers brushing over her skin in a brief gesture that seemed too slow and deliberate to come from an opponent in a battle. *Bloody hell.*

Her footsteps raised an echo in the long castle hallway, the clatter of boots behind her more and more rapid, until she realized she was running, with Raishan keeping up beside her.

She came to an abrupt halt and spun around to face Raishan. The Diamond's face remained impassive, his eyes studying her calmly. Looking at him, she forced her breathing to relax, regaining her composure. Raishan had seen her through many ups and downs. She had no need to pretend around him, or to act tougher than she felt.

"Sorry," she said. "I didn't mean to run like that."

A brief smile touched Raishan's face. "No need to apologize. Are you all right?"

She threw a restrained glance at the Emeralds, hovering a few steps behind. Raishan guessed her feelings correctly, signaling for the men to retreat to the end of the hallway, out of earshot.

Kara forced a smile. "Thanks. I…" She let out a sigh. "Everything's been going so well. Or, so I thought. And now…"

He shook his head. "Nothing's changed."

"How can you say that?"

"We're still facing the same enemy, and our plan of dealing a quick and final strike remains the same. This mark is no more than a jab from the Kaddim's side, driven by desperation. They think they can weaken you, because they don't know you."

Her smile came out easier this time. "And you think you do?"

His eyes slid over her with warm affection. "You are one of our best warriors, and no Kaddim magic – or whatever else they try – could ever change that."

She held his gaze, feeling a sting of tears rising into her eyes. *Dear Shal Addim, what's wrong with me?* She took a deep breath. If only she could be as clear and solid about everything as Raishan.

"They're trying to force Mai's hand," she said quietly. "They know if they target me, he will react as fast as he possibly can to stop them. They're trying to make me their bloody *tool* against him." She clenched her fists, the pain of fingernails digging into her skin bringing only marginal comfort.

Raishan placed a hand on her arm. "You should know as well as I do that Aghat Mai would never do anything foolish. He is very level-headed – and very resourceful. Many enemies have made a mistake of underestimating him before. The Kaddim are making it too."

Kara paused to control a brief twitch in her lips. "I'm his weak spot. The Kaddim know it. They took many risks to target me, and no one else."

"You're also his strength. I'm sure you know it as well as the rest of us do."

She looked at him, against reason captivated by these simple words. She never expected to hear something like this from Raishan. She never even realized anyone could possibly think of her this way. And yet, it was true. She knew Mai's closeness made her stronger, and she had no doubt he felt the same. No matter what the Kaddim had planned, her place was next to Mai, and she would fight by his side as long as she lived.

"Surely," Raishan said, "you must have noticed the

joy we all felt seeing you together. The two of you are meant for each other. I believe nearly everyone in the Guild shares this feeling. When we return to the Majat Fortress you will be greeted like a queen."

She looked away. Being expelled from the Guild, having to pretend in the last weeks that she had nothing to do with the Majat, did tend to make her feel like an outsider. Yet, Raishan's words held the truth. She was raised and trained at the Majat Fortress to become one of their best. Both she and Mai were well loved, and many people would indeed be glad to see them together. Besides, the Majat Guildmaster did have the status and authority of a king, both in the Guild and in the surrounding lands. Marrying Mai *would* make her equal to a queen. It was just that no other Guildmaster's wife, to her knowledge, had ever evoked such an approval among the Majat. In fact, records of all the other Guildmasters' marriages had been hidden away so deep in the archives that up until recently she hadn't even realized his post allowed it at all.

Of course, no other Guildmaster's wife had ever been trained and ranked as a Diamond and then freed of all obligations to the Guild. Her situation was unprecedented in so many ways that even the chronicles would have trouble dealing with the information. Not that she cared. Up until now, her and Mai's happiness together had been her only consideration. And now, after Raishan's words, she realized anew how good her life could be if the dark shadow of the Kaddim magic wasn't looming over her.

"Mai has this effect on people, doesn't he?" she said quietly. "Whatever he does, people just... approve."

Raishan smiled. "An essential quality for a great

leader, don't you think?"

She raised her face to him. "What about Aghat Seldon?"

"What about him?"

"I couldn't help noticing a bit of tension when he arrived this morning."

Raishan shrugged. "Despite any regrets Seldon might harbor about losing his chances for the Guildmaster's post, he does realize he's no match for Aghat Mai. He would never stand in the way of the Guild's decisions."

"Why is he here then?"

Raishan frowned. "Not because of the orders he received from Aghat Mai, for sure. Seldon arrived unexpectedly, with a somewhat unsatisfactory explanation. He claims he was sent by the Guild's seniors, but he wouldn't clearly say why."

*The lie Ellah detected.* Kara's heart quivered. "Seldon may prove to be a problem."

Raishan smiled. "We both know Aghat Mai can handle it."

"I hope so." She looked away. Without the support of the senior Majat, Mai would never have been able to achieve his command. Seldon was, technically, one of them. Even if to the best of her knowledge he hadn't expressed any open hostility, she simply couldn't get past the fact that Seldon represented the group of people who had the power to remove Mai from his post – or worse.

Was an opposition to Mai brewing in the heart of the Majat Guild? Or, did Seldon come here with an agenda of his own?

Raishan reached forward and briefly touched her shoulder. "You really shouldn't worry so much. Our

Guild is in good hands. Everyone knows it, regardless of the personal ambitions they may harbor. Seldon's heart is in the right place. He would never do anything to jeopardize Aghat Mai's command in a war."

*It must be true, if the Guild has been setting their sights on Seldon as a potential leader, at least at some point.* Yet, Kara also knew that Mai's predecessor, while having the Majat's best interests at heart, had almost let the Guild fall into the Kaddim's hands.

She sighed. However much these thoughts bothered her, this wasn't something they would be able to solve in a short conversation.

"Thank you, Aghat Raishan," she said. "I know this kind of talk goes beyond your duty of guarding me, but you did make me feel a whole lot better just now."

Raishan grinned. "Guarding you has many sides to it, Aghat. We both know Aghat Mai's choice to charge me with this task wasn't incidental. And... I'm glad I helped."

Warmth filled her as she kept his gaze. She was surprised to realize how much Raishan's approval, everything he said to her just now, meant to her. She felt stronger from this short conversation, ready to do her best to put the whole situation behind her.

"I expect the King's council will probably last for a while," she said. "How about passing the time on the training grounds until they're done?"

Raishan nodded. "Sounds like a good idea."

They turned and resumed their walk along the corridor side by side, the clanking of Emeralds' feet echoing behind them.

The large courtyard at the back of the palace, normally dedicated entirely to the training of the King's five Gem-ranked Majat bodyguards, was packed. Mai's attack force flooded it from wall to wall, the activity resembling the lower market plaza on a busy day.

Men paused in their tasks and stepped aside, letting her and Raishan through to the elevated training platform at the far end. Kara strode up to the weapons stand beside it and chose a long staff from the back row – too heavy for her build, but appropriate for an intense workout she had in mind.

"Will you practice with me, Aghat Raishan?" she asked.

Raishan grinned. "If you're certain that's what you want." He picked the staff nearest to him, weighting it in his hands. Bigger and heavier than Kara, he could use any of them for an effective practice. Standing up to him with the heavy staff she chose would be an extra challenge – exactly what she needed just now.

She stepped onto the floor, half aware of the men pausing in their tasks to watch. Diamonds rarely had the opportunity to face each other. Seeing her and Raishan spar with heavy staffs was bound to be a sight not to be forgotten in a hurry.

The staff was heavy, but well balanced. She enjoyed the strain in her muscle as she parried Raishan's blows, the polished wood singing in her hands. His head-on attack was forceful and she enjoyed it too as she twisted out of his locks, spinning around, aiming for the peripheral spots. A quick smile slid over Raishan's face as he changed his tactics to match.

She waited until he was committed to the new attack and unexpectedly dropped to a crouch, sweeping low. His eyes widened as he jumped over her staff, his shape becoming a blur as he picked up speed. She kept ahead of him, aware of the silence around them, the crowd of top ranked warriors watching in awe as she and Raishan circled around the small practice space. She was now fighting at her full power and she could tell he was too. She stilled her mind, focusing on his moves, anticipating...

The pulling sensation wafted over her skin like a cold draft. She wavered as she parried Raishan's attack and clenched her teeth, recomposing. Her muscles were beginning to feel sore. Staffs were not choice weapons for both of them, and the need to wield a heavier one than she normally would pick was beginning to take its toll.

She could tell Raishan was tiring too, but the knowledge didn't help much. He was going to keep it up until she stopped, and, despite the sweat breaking on her forehead, she was not ready to do so just yet.

A sting at the back of her head made her stumble. For a moment, the boards under her feet felt uneven, like quicksand. Images of being nearly pulled into the Kaddim's vortex floated up into her head. The cobbles of the pavement, bucking. The ground caving in, pulling her down. The Kaddim Brother nearest to her brushing his hand over her skin. This time she felt the invasion all the way in, the touch like a needle piercing her skin. *The mark. A piece of their magic, inside me. A bridge to their minds...*

*Dear Shal Addim,* that's *how it works.*

She felt like she did back then, a force sweeping her, trying to pull her away. Her feet were still here, grasping the firmness of the training floor, but her balance shifted, as if she wasn't fully present on solid ground. Her hand wavered. The tip of her staff, raised for the block, dipped downward. She could see the horror in Raishan's eyes as his weapon came through, hitting her on the head.

Her vision darkened as she dropped her staff and sank to the floor, half-aware of Raishan rushing to her side. He caught her as she fell, and she saw his pale face very close.

"Damn it," he snapped. "Jahib Lenart, get Aghat Mai, quick!"

The pulling became stronger, drawing her into a void as she passed out in Raishan's arms.

Gradually, she started hearing sounds again, aware of the conversation going on beside her.

"I'm not sure what happened, Aghat Mai. She blocked me, and then, at the very last moment, she just tilted her staff away."

Her eyelids fluttered open. The midday sun hit her eyes with brightness that made her wince. *Damn it, did I just let Raishan knock me out in a practice fight?* Her eyes slowly focused on Mai's face leaning over her. She saw his shoulders relax as he met her gaze.

"Are you all right?"

She could hear the relief in his voice. *Damn it, how long was I out?*

"Sorry," she said. "It was entirely my fault."

"I'd say so. What were you thinking, picking a staff of this weight against an opponent of his skill?"

She shook her head, ignoring the throbbing in her head that felt worse from the movement. "No, not that. I wanted a good workout. It's..." She paused. *It's the Kaddim. They can disable me in a fight.* There was no way in hell she was going to say this out loud. If she did, it would make it all true. Worse, the feeling of relief she felt at the fact that she hadn't actually been pulled anywhere as it initially seemed, made it all even more unsettling.

Could the mark she carried enable the Kaddim to whisk her away through their time vortex? She shivered, clenching Mai's arm, his muscle reassuringly hard under the silky sleeve of his shirt.

Mai's gaze darkened. She knew he understood her without words. Seeing his expression, a mix of anger and concern, made her want to cry. Did she have to give up everything, including her fighting skill, because of the damned link?

"Are you feeling better?" Mai asked.

She nodded, using his hand for support to sit up. Her head ached. She winced as she felt around her temple. *Damn it, I must have a huge bruise.*

Raishan knelt in front of her, frowning with concern. "I'm so sorry. I should have done better. It was just so… unexpected."

She smiled. "It's all right, Aghat Raishan. No harm done."

His eyes hovered on the side of her head, suggesting otherwise. She took a breath as she rose to her feet, steadying herself against Mai's arm.

"Let's go inside," Mai said. "You need to have this bruise seen to."

She lowered her eyes as she followed him, sensing the unspoken words behind his brisk tone. He wanted to know how the hell it was possible for someone of her skill to get knocked out in a practice fight, even if she had been fighting a Diamond with a very heavy staff. She wanted to know that too, even if she probably wasn't going to like the answer. Worse, she couldn't escape a feeling there was something else he wasn't telling her, something they must have discussed in the council chamber after she left. Were things even more complicated than she already thought?

# 6
# CONTROL

The Keepers' quarters consisted of a long suite of rooms, opening into a large but cozy sitting area with tall armchairs arranged around the massive fireplace. Mai settled into one of these chairs, instantly receding into the background. His stillness made him appear nearly inanimate, but his alert eyes followed Kara's every move.

She winced as Magister Egey Bashi ran his fingers over her temple.

"I really think you shouldn't make such a big deal out of it," she said. "It's just a bruise. I've had those before."

The Keeper exchanged a look with Mai.

"The bone is intact," he said. "It's the concussion I am more worried about."

"I have no concussion, Magister. I would have noticed, wouldn't I?"

Another glance passed between the two men.

"How long were you out, Aghat Kara?" the Keeper asked.

She shrugged. "Fifteen minutes, at most. Right?"

She looked at Mai, who nodded. "Really, don't you think you are overreacting?"

"You were knocked out in a practice fight," Mai said. "I know Raishan did everything humanly possible to stop his hand. This makes the whole incident bloody disturbing, don't you think?"

She held his gaze. He was afraid, she realized. Perhaps he had reasons to be. If this happened in a real fight, against an enemy motivated to kill her rather than stay his hand to prevent injury, she would be dead. On the other hand, she would hardly expect to face anyone of Raishan's skill in a real battle, would she?

Egey Bashi let out a sigh. "Here, Aghat Kara, let me give you something to ease the swelling." He fumbled in his medicine pack.

Kara winced as his calloused fingers massaged the ointment into her skin. It stung, a coolness spreading over the affected area as the cure worked its course. She glanced into her reflection in the window pane. Her dark skin made the bruise nearly unnoticeable anyway. After the cure, she was certain no one could even tell she had been hit.

"You said you felt a pulling sensation as you were fighting?" Egey Bashi asked.

"Yes." Kara wondered at his frown, etched so deeply that it threatened to become permanent. "Why?"

Again, the two men exchanged a glance.

She sighed. "Can the two of you stop acting as if I'm not here?"

"Have you found anything else about the link, Magister?" Mai asked.

The Keeper gave him a dark look. "Nothing good, I'm afraid."

"Let's hear the bad, then."

"The fact that the sensation became obvious during a fight confirms what I said earlier. They are trying to use this link to pull away her gift. When she's using it, she becomes far more vulnerable."

Kara's eyes widened. "What?"

"Your fighting ability. They are trying to steal it and confer it to their warriors."

Kara felt the blood instantly drain out of her face. The throbbing in her temple eased. She felt cold, as if dropped into a pond of water. "Can they?"

"Yes."

"But..." She turned to Mai, vaguely aware of how desperate she must look.

He sprang out of the chair and stepped up to her side. His closeness felt reassuring, in sharp contrast with the frown that wouldn't leave his face.

"It will be all right," Mai said.

"How?"

"The Magister promised to come up with ways to neutralize this link."

The Keeper frowned. "Apart from sedating her, you mean?"

"Yes, apart from that."

"*Sedating* me?"

Mai shot her a quick glance. "That was one of the Magister's suggestions, before I told him what I think about that. I'm surprised it even came up this time."

She bit back a lump rising in her throat. She didn't want to be sedated. But if there was even a slightest chance that, because of her, their enemies might learn to fight like a Diamond Majat...

"I will consider it," she said

"I bloody hope not," Mai said. "You are instrumental to our plans. However, before we can even discuss them, we must be sure you are in full control of your own mind."

She stiffened as she noticed Mai's tightening jaw, the way his eyes darted to the Keeper again. She understood these looks, and her options, all too well. If stealing her gift was even a possibility, the only reasonable course of action would be to kill her. From the look in Mai's eyes she was certain the possibility had been discussed at the King's council after she left, even though she knew Mai would never entertain the thought. She wouldn't either, if their roles were reversed. She didn't want to die. But, given the alternatives, if sedation could help, it was definitely an option. If things remained as they were, she must at least bear this in mind. She forced a smile, aware of how both men were watching her now, as if evaluating her.

"What does it feel like when they use the link?" Egey Bashi asked.

She thought about it. "Like someone's touching me. Lightly, at first, but then it begins to feel as if I am being pulled. The reason I wavered when I fought Raishan was because it seemed as if the floor was disappearing from under my feet. And then... I... I realized exactly how they placed their link. When one of them touched me during the fight, it felt like a needle going in. Not painful at all. Just... cold." She paused, trying to control her trembling lips. She remembered what Egey Bashi had said in the council chamber about emotional attachment. The touch she remembered, the caress. Why couldn't she stop thinking about it?

"Where did they touch you?" Egey Bashi asked.

"On my arm. Here."

He reached forward and pulled up her sleeve. She kept still as both men examined the spot.

"I see nothing," Mai said at length.

Egey Bashi's rough, calloused hand massaged deeply into her skin. "Do you feel anything when I do that?"

"Pain. Just a little." She hesitated. She knew what Egey Bashi did should not have hurt at all.

"It works like their brand mark," Egey Bashi said. "Lighter, but with time it will probably become visible."

Mai placed a hand over her arm, pulling her sleeve into place. The gesture felt possessive – and intimate, sending a surge of warmth down her spine. Mai didn't normally dominate her at all. The fact that he was acting this way now showed how unsettled he was.

"When you fought Aghat Raishan just now, how did the sensation start?" Egey Bashi asked.

She swallowed. "It started as a memory. I thought of their vortex, what it felt like to be caught in it. And then it became too real, all too suddenly. As if I was caught in it again." She shivered. She would never forget the relief of waking up and seeing Mai's face leaning over her. "If you sedate me, would it prevent them from using the link?" *Would it stop these memories from coming back, again and again?*

Egey Bashi shook his head. "We cannot be certain. Not without learning more about it--which I am doing, as fast as I can." He pointed to a pile of books and scrolls on a table by the window. "In the meantime, it is imperative for you, Aghat Kara, to refrain from any dangerous activities that involve your Majat skill. Fighting included, I am sorry to say."

Kara quickly glanced at Mai. "I never though sparring

with Raishan on a practice range could be considered dangerous."

A quick grin slid over Mai's face. Normally, Diamonds were not permitted to fight each other, even in practice. Trainers always worried about needless injuries, especially when it came to the top Gem ranks. Of course, trainers couldn't possibly understand the ultimate pleasure of fighting a warrior whose skill matched yours. She knew Mai understood exactly how it felt, even if, as the Guildmaster, he was supposed to disapprove. To think that she may never be able to do it again…

"Have you tried to block this feeling when it arises?" Egey Bashi asked.

"Yes. By stilling my mind. I think this was why the spiders did not bite me. When I stilled my mind, they calmed down. Eventually." *Another memory I'd rather not dwell on.* She snuggled closer to Mai, reassured by his warmth, the firmness of his sculpted muscle against her leaning shoulder. At least for now, with only Mai and Egey Bashi present, she didn't need to pretend to be tougher than she felt.

"Stilling your mind?" Egey Bashi raised his eyebrows.

"It's a Majat training technique," she explained. "Clearing the mind of all emotions and thoughts. It's like focusing, but not quite. It also helps in fighting." She paused. Every Majat could do it, but it was so hard to explain the concept to the outsider.

The Keeper nodded slowly. "I think I know what you mean, Aghat. Keepers call it meditation – even though achieving the level you speak about is possible only for a few."

She shrugged. Her Diamond ranking required a lot of skills possible only to a few. It didn't surprise her that others tried and failed at a similar thing.

"Were you able to confirm if the Kaddim can use the link to hear us, or read my mind, Magister?"

"We are still not certain," Egey Bashi said. "That's why I have collected all these books."

Kara looked at him grimly. "Until you learn otherwise, Magister, we must assume that if I come to know anything about our plans, there will always be a danger that the Kaddim would be able to extort this information from my mind somehow. Which means you should probably keep this information from me, just in case."

Egey Bashi's gaze softened. "I hate for this to be happening, Aghat."

She briefly looked away. "Me too, Magister, believe me."

"I admire your spirit – and please be assured that I will do everything I possibly can to address this situation. However, barring another solution, for the time being you should probably develop a habit of always stilling your mind – if that's what you call it."

"I suppose I could try," she said. "In a way, it would somewhat resemble being sedated all the time, even if it would be less noticeable on the outside."

The Keeper exchanged a glance with Mai again. She shivered at the thought of the precarious position her situation was putting him into. As the attack leader, Mai had to drive all these decisions, hiding his plans from her, excluding her from every important conversation.

"Perhaps," Mai said, "we should take it one step at a time. Your participation in our plans would become critical only later on. Until then, you can travel with us without knowing any plans – and perhaps learn to control the link, so that by the time we need you to act, you can be confident you won't be giving anything away to the enemy."

"And if I can't?"

"Like any military campaign, it's all about taking risks. Just do your best, and we'll see how it goes."

She sighed. "I'll try."

Mai rose and held out a hand to her. "Come. I really think you should rest after that blow."

*The blow.* She had forgotten all about it. Surprised, she touched her temple, feeling no soreness at all. She smiled at Magister Egey Bashi gratefully. The Keepers had so many potent cures.

"Will you be traveling with us, Magister?" she asked.

Mai grinned. "Answering this question would be like giving away some of our plans, wouldn't it?" He took her hand. "Let's go."

She nodded, wondering. Could she handle this level of secrecy for a considerable part of their trip?

"Thank you for the cure, Magister," she said before stepping outside.

Mai led her all the way back into his room, which they now shared, and locked the door behind them. She stepped into his arms, inhaling his natural pine scent, relaxing into his hold. Even the Kaddim couldn't reach her here. She would be damned if she would let them invade her time with Mai.

His frown of concern dissolved into a smile as he looked down at her. Her breath caught at the tenderness in his gaze. When he looked at her like this, she felt complete. No matter what else happened to her, being with him made it all worth it.

"You really don't need to treat me like a child," she said. "I can take care of myself."

He shook his head. "Not after you took a hit on the head."

"You still believe I have a concussion?"

"I still believe you need some rest."

She hesitated. He was probably right. Yet, his closeness pushed the thought to the back of her mind, overpowered by another sort of desire. After all that happened today, couldn't they steal a moment of pleasure just for themselves?

"I can think of better things we could do right now," she whispered.

His eyes lit up with a tenderness that sent flutters into her stomach. "I can't touch you until I'm sure you are all right."

"I'm all right."

"You've been injured."

She grinned. "Fine. You don't have to touch me at all then. I'll do all the touching." She slid her hands into his hair and pulled him closer, sensing his smile as he leaned down to kiss her.

The fright and uncertainty of the past day receded to the back of her mind. She felt lightheaded from his closeness, from his strength that matched hers down to every bit. Only with him could she fully let herself go, without holding back, and she needed every bit of it now, when the recent events had nearly shattered her world.

She clung to him as if her life depended on it, their bodies so close they felt like one. As long as they had each other, nothing else mattered. No Kaddim's mind link could possibly rob her of the love she shared with him. He made her feel invincible. She would fight to her last breath to keep his love.

# 7
# RIVALS

Kyth entered the large audience hall at a fast walk. The vaulted space greeted him with an echo, amplified by the room's vast size. This was one of the older sections of the castle, its oppressive ceilings and massive arched columns designed, it seemed, to bear down on the room's visitors, to make them feel insignificant and small. A perfect match for the Majat Guildmaster, Kyth thought grimly as he made his way across. When the King had offered Mai the use of this hall as his personal audience chamber, Mai must have been elated.

Deep inside, Kyth admitted that he was perhaps being unfair to Mai. But it was true that the Majat seemed to enjoy flaunting his superiority in everyone's eyes – perhaps to compensate for the fact that he was by far the youngest in the known history to achieve his high post.

Or perhaps he reserved the worst of his attitude entirely for Kyth?

Mai sat in a tall chair at the far end of the chamber, the men in front of him engaged in what looked like a heated argument. They all stopped abruptly as the

Prince walked in, bowing exactly to the degree required by etiquette. Aghat Lance, a tall, cocky man with a dark tan and short, near-white hair, fixed Kyth with an unfriendly stare. The older Diamond, Seldon, greeted the Prince with a thin half-smile that touched only his lips. Kyth returned the smile, glancing at Seldon with curiosity.

In the days before Kyth's father assumed the throne, this man used to lead the King's Royal Pentade. From the limited information Kyth had gathered about the Majat Guild's affairs, this position made him the top candidate for the post of Guildmaster in due time, but now that Mai had snatched away the command, his youth and power made that route nearly impossible for Seldon. Kyth couldn't help wondering how the older Diamond was taking it.

The stern look of Seldon's narrowed eyes did not reassure him. Clearly, whatever was happening here before Kyth arrived, had upset everyone, even if Mai's serene expression could have fooled a more casual observer.

Mai did not rise to meet the Prince, nodding his head and waiting out Kyth's full bow down from the waist. Kyth knew that this form of greeting was warranted by etiquette, but he felt annoyed nonetheless. Mai seemed to be too bent on formalities and ranks. It surely wouldn't hurt to show some courtesy every once in a while, but even if Mai occasionally did it with others, these kinds of considerations didn't seem to apply in Kyth's case. Mai might have succeeded in winning the ultimate prize in their rivalry over Kara, but he didn't show any intention to be gracious about it.

"Aghat Mai," Kyth said stiffly, aware of everyone's

eyes fixed on him with impatience, as if he was interrupting something important.

"Prince Kythar." Mai continued to stare, his face showing no effort to appear friendly.

Kyth swallowed. "Please forgive the interruption. I hoped I could request a private audience."

Mai held still for a moment longer, then leaned back into his chair, turning to his companions. "Would you excuse us, please?"

The men bowed, saluting with their fists to their chests. Kyth watched them stride toward the door, so smoothly and noiselessly that it was hard to imagine they actually touched the floor with their feet.

"I assume this is important," Mai said when the door closed behind them.

*No, this is a bloody social call.* Kyth forced his face into a calm expression. It was useless to show displeasure or to initiate any disagreement. No matter what, Mai had a way of always coming up on top. Kyth relaxed his shoulders, reminding himself that despite the apparent impossibility of it, Mai was the man who made Kara happy.

"I am here because of Kara," he said.

Mai stiffened. He didn't respond as his eyes bore into Kyth with an unsettling mix of challenge and concern.

Kyth shifted from foot to foot. Now that he started the conversation, there seemed to be no easy way to say it. "I heard the way Magister Egey Bashi talked at the High Council. About sedating Kara or… or…"

*Killing her.* He knew Mai understood the unspoken words, just as he did back at the council. He prayed nothing that happened since could possibly change Mai's resolve.

Mai shrugged. "I think I made it clear where I stand. Besides, as the Magister himself said, the second option is not even on the list at the moment."

Kyth took a breath. "Yes. But if this ever changes, if he ever finds out that this could provide a solution after all, the men on your force… they might think similarly to the Magister. I know you have supreme authority among them," he continued hurriedly, seeing that Mai was about to interrupt. "I… I just thought it might help if I expressed my assurance that I am with you on that."

Mai's lips twitched, but Kyth refused to acknowledge the irony. By all rights, his support should mean a lot. Kyth's gift held a key to their victory. If Mai had any sense he would welcome this gesture – even if Kyth doubted the Majat would openly express his gratitude.

"I am important to this attack too," Kyth said. "And I wanted you to know that I will stand by your side against anyone who wishes her harm." He lifted his chin. "Since our attack plans depend on my ability to defend your men, I was hoping that this knowledge might give you additional leverage, in case any contrary arguments are ever raised."

He expected an objection, or at least mockery, both so common in his recent interactions with Mai. He felt alarmed when Mai merely nodded in response. Kyth looked closer, for the first time noticing the Diamond's drawn face, the dark circles under his eyes. Was this the strain of the preparations for the march, or was something else going on? Kyth's skin prickled. He had no idea what went into commanding an army that rivaled the combined forces of the Old Empire. It had to be a lot. Now that Kyth's temper cooled off, he couldn't help but admit that their hopes for victory depended most of all on Mai's well-being. Was Mai driving himself too hard?

"Since I made it very clear to the Magister that the subject is closed," Mai said, "I don't believe he will ever breach the question again. But thanks anyway." He pinched the bridge of his nose, the gesture making Kyth think of his father when he was tired.

"Are you all right?" Kyth asked.

Mai frowned, but the harsh retort Kyth was expecting never came. Instead, the Diamond's gaze wandered off to stare unseeingly into the depths of the room.

"Magister Egey Bashi was just here," Mai said.

"He was? Why?"

Mai heaved a sigh. "He believes that, given the imminent danger that our enemies might acquire at least a fraction of Kara's fighting skill, we need another addition to our force."

"Anyone in particular?"

"Oh, yes."

"Who?"

Mai measured him with his gaze, as if deciding if he was worthy of the information. "Lady Ayalla."

"The Forest Mother?" Kyth stared. "Is he serious?" Ayalla was a powerful sorceress who lived outside the boundaries of age and time, never interfering in the affairs outside her forest realm. While she did share their animosity for the Kaddim, asking her to march with them into battle seemed preposterous. Yet, Kyth reminded himself that under ordinary circumstances joining forces with the Majat seemed preposterous too. Yet here they were, planning an attack under the Majat Guildmaster's command.

"Apparently he is very serious," Mai said. "At least

about giving it a try. I was planning to discuss it with your foster brother. I understand he knows her like no other."

"He does." Alder knew Ayalla intimately. Yet, Kyth wasn't sure if this really gave Alder any advantage over the rest of them. Ayalla was rumored to be thousands of years old, even if she kept the appearance of a young girl. No one alive could possibly know her at all.

"Can he be trusted?" Mai asked.

Kyth's eyes widened. Was Mai asking him for advice?

"Alder is the most trustworthy man I know," he said earnestly.

"With your inclination to trust everyone–"

"Why ask me then?" Kyth blurted.

Mai sighed and pinched the bridge of his nose again. It occurred to Kyth that quite likely the Diamond hadn't had a good sleep in a very long time. He hoped it wasn't all because Kara now shared Mai's quarters – and presumably his bed. Kyth knew it was none of his business, but it was hard sometimes not to dwell on what was going on between these two.

"Why would you doubt Alder?" he asked.

Mai shrugged. "It's hard for him to be objective about a woman he's sleeping with, is it?"

*You know this firsthand, don't you?* Kyth bit his tongue before he could say anything he'd regret. If he and Mai were going to war together, he should learn to control his feelings, no matter how impossible it seemed.

"Alder can talk to the spiders," Kyth said. "Ayalla would never bestow this ability on him if she didn't trust him implicitly. This kind of a trust has to be worth some insight, doesn't it?"

"Yes." Mai's jaw tightened. "The spiders are the key, aren't they?"

*The spiders.* Ayalla had many at her command, enough to dissolve squadrons of enemy warriors and prevent them from ever coming back. "Is this why Magister Egey Bashi believes we need her help?"

Mai nodded. "If Ayalla joins our fight – or at least lends us more spiders, we won't have to depend so heavily on our fighting ability – or on your magic gift, for that matter. But then…"

Kyth felt the chill creep down his spine as he met Mai's gaze. He believed he now understood the Diamond's hesitation. *Kara.* The three spiders in the castle nearly killed her this morning. If they were to incorporate more spiders into their attack force…

"Perhaps it's best if Alder and I went to talk to Ayalla on our own," he said, "We both grew up in the Forestlands. We have been to her dwelling before." He shivered at the memory. Ayalla lived in the heart of the forest – the Dark Mire, the most frightening and mysterious area he had ever seen.

"It may be a good plan," Mai said. "No telling how she would take to a force of the Majat entering her lands." He pointed to a low table set out behind his throne, laid with maps and boxes of pins the Majat often used to plan their attacks.

Kyth leaned over the table with interest. The Majat Guild had secret means to obtain the most detailed maps of all the lands. This one not only showed the entire Forestlands in greater detail than Kyth had ever seen, but also had a clear layout of the Dark Mire, normally shown on maps only as a splotch of dark ink.

"How did you–" he began.

"Never mind that. Just look."

"At what?" Kyth stared at the rows of pins piercing

the precious map all the way across. The pin heads had different colors, and as he now realized they were mapping different routes from the King's castle where they now stood to the yellow line of the Southern Deserts.

"Your father will lend us barges to cross the lakes," Mai said. "We will use them to travel down Lake Illitand and land at Port Jai-Allad. From there, the Majat will bear east along the caravan roads leading to Shayil Yara. You and Alder, with a small party, will go to Ayalla. We'll meet again here." He pointed to a bigger pin, with converging lines for the green Grasslands, the yellow desert, and the blue of the River Shahr Ayil flowing down south. "The Gard'hal Outpost. This is where all caravans meet when traveling to Tahr Abad where the Queen's court resides most of the time."

"Are you taking your entire force to Shayil Yara then?"

"Haven't decided yet," Mai said. "Assuming we are aiming for a peaceful negotiation, it may be best to take only a few. The rest could wait at Gard'hal, or further south, until we complete our mission at the Queen's court."

Kyth nodded. The decision seemed too distant to dwell on – weeks of travel, even with the Majat's strenuous pace.

"Isn't there a better way to mark your maps without destroying them?" he asked.

Mai shrugged. "This is the best way to ensure the markings stay on, no matter what."

"But these maps... they must be worth a fortune!"

Mai's smile came out patronizing this time – or did Kyth only imagine it?

"We have our own cartographers," Mai said. "They draw a set of maps for each campaign."

Kyth looked away, hoping his surprise did not seem too obvious. Drawing maps for each campaign was a lavish expense no one could possibly afford. The fact that the Majat thought nothing of it only proved the point. The Majat Guild was as powerful as it came, from training undefeatable fighters down to the intricate details of getting precious maps custom-made for the march. With this kind of might on their side, defeating the Kaddim should have nothing to it. Why then couldn't he escape a sinking feeling in his chest?

# 8
# THE PORT

Kara narrowed her eyes as the gleaming width of the Crown Lake burst in front of her in its full glory. In the beams of the rising sun the water seemed to glow on its own, its molten smoothness haloed by the transparent haze of the dissipating morning mists. She inhaled a full breath of fresh wind, enjoying its fragrance and cooling touch, bathing her face in the tiny droplets of lake moisture.

The port stood empty at this hour, the only boats anchored in the harbor the flat, wide barges bristling with oars along their sides. Thick masts rising off their massive decks held square sails, designed to catch as much as possible of the scarce lake winds. The King's trade fleet. Kara counted twenty barges ready to sail, more than enough to take on their entire group with horses and gear. She nodded her approval. At this time of the year the winds blew steadily southward, enabling boats at full sail to cross from Tandar to the Southern Lakelands in no more than three days. Even if the winds did not cooperate, the complement of oarsmen on the lower decks would help to maintain the speed.

Up until now she had been thinking of a much slower route on horseback. She hoped, if the Kaddim could truly penetrate her thoughts, they had been fooled – not that it mattered now that the plan for the next leg of the trip had been laid out clearly in front of her.

She glanced at Mai, sitting on his horse a dozen yards away, seemingly idle as the activity erupted around him. Seldon jumped off the saddle, barking orders left and right. Not for the first time Kara thought about this marked difference in their command styles. If she was one of their Guild's seniors, she would do everything possible to keep Seldon away from any possibility of ordering people around. Unfortunately, such considerations hardly mattered here and now, when they were stuck with Seldon for the duration of the trip and even Mai's supreme authority could not keep him from giving orders to his inferiors without creating a major tension.

As she dismounted along with the others, she looked further to where the non-Majat – Kyth with his Kingsguard escort, Lady Celana, Egey Bashi, Alder, and Ellah – busied themselves with preparations of their own. Behind them, the semicircle of three-story buildings rose like a wall that separated the port and the adjoining plaza from the rest of the city, with only a few gateways for access. Looking at the jagged roofline, bathed in the gold of the rising sunlight, made her feel sad. She was about to leave the Crown City of Tandar – the place where she had spent so much time on assignments at the King's court, the place where she had found her love and made some of the most important decisions in her life.

Was she ever going to see this city again?

She ran her eyes along the endless rooflines paving the way up to the rising mass of the Royal Castle on the top of the distant hill. From here she could still see the small watchtower overlooking the lake, where she and Kyth used to sit in their days together watching the sunset, the wing housing the Majat quarters, one of them the room that she had shared with Mai during the past weeks. This castle held so many memories – most of them happy ones, until the Kaddim barged in, threatening to destroy everything she cherished.

Was she ever going to be this happy again?

A movement along the rooftops caught her gaze. She froze, peering at a side building flanking the edge of the port plaza. Did she imagine it? No, there it was again, a barely perceptible shift in the shadows behind a pointed protrusion of the roof.

Kara's skin prickled. She quickly glanced around, aware how everyone in sight was busy with loading up their gear and horses, all but ignorant of the empty plaza behind. Mai left no lookouts, confident that no intruder would ever dare to sneak up on the Majat army, so deadly despite its relatively small size. It would be suicidal for anyone to attempt an attack right now, with everyone in sight armed and battle-ready. Yet, as she peered into the shadows, she clearly saw a hooded figure creeping around the corner, a black-on-black crouching silhouette surveying the boarding party.

She couldn't see as well as she wanted against the blinding morning sky, but the space on the rooftop seemed big enough to hide several men. Assassins? Spies? Her hand slid to her knife belt in a gesture that she knew would look inconspicuous to an outsider while giving her quick access to her weapons.

Mai was away by the boats giving orders, and everyone around him looked preoccupied. If she had been allowed to participate in the preparations, rather than standing aside like an idle observer not privy to the plans, she would probably have been preoccupied too, giving the men on the roof a free run at executing their plan. Who could they possibly be? Not the Kaddim, she hoped. To the best of her knowledge all the Kaddim warriors on this side of the Lakes had been exterminated after their leaders' escape. Even if a few of them survived, it would be suicidal for a few men to attack a Majat force of this size. No, at worst these were men loyal to the Kaddim, gathering information in case a possibility arose to pass it along. The thought brought at least marginal reassurance. If the Kaddim had the need for spies, most likely they couldn't use the link they had with Kara for information. Or was it because of the way she had been so prominently removed from the command group?

The figure on the rooftop raised a hand, unfolding with a weapon that sprouted off his outstretched arm against the blinding sunlight. *A crossbow.* Kara whipped out her throwing daggers, sending them flying. She dove forward, guided by the low-pitched whistle of the bolt as she drew her sword and sliced it down in mid-air.

Her hand lowered as she peered up at the rooftop, squinting against the light. From this distance she could barely hear the grunts as her daggers reached their targets, followed by the louder screeches of the dislodged roof tiles and then, after a pause, the sight of three lifeless bodies rolling over the roof's edge and

folding down to the pavement below. Three. She had
thought so before the attack, but she couldn't tell for
sure. Just in case, she had sent eight daggers their way.
She'd need to retrieve all of them before the barges
set sail. *Did I get all of them?* She strained her senses,
but could detect no further movement on the rooftop.
Only three men. What were they thinking, trying to
attack a Majat army on the march?

Men filled the space around her, some sweeping past
to the wall and into the surrounding streets. Belatedly,
she reflected that she should have probably tried to
wound, rather than kill the mysterious attackers. If she
showed more finesse, the attackers could have been
questioned. The thought seemed strangely detached,
as if not entirely her own.

Mai rushed through the crowd toward her, the sight
of his narrowed eyes momentarily overwhelming her.
She was a fool, using her skill rather than alerting
others to the danger. Except that, when faced with
the attack, it was so hard not to act on instinct. And
now, it didn't seem to matter anymore. Worse, she
was beginning to feel sick. A pounding in her temples
erupted into a sudden, blinding headache. Her hand
wavered, dropping the sword. She swayed, feeling
Mai's hands on her, grasping on to him as she forced
her mind into stillness.

"I'm all right," she said.

He looked at her appraisingly, his deepening frown
telling her how unconvinced he was.

"What happened?"

"I… I'm not sure." She knew he wasn't asking about
the attack – a useless question when the attackers were
already dead and Mai's men were combing the plaza

and all the surrounding streets.

She felt so tired. Suddenly, just standing next to him seemed like an effort. She clenched her teeth, summoning all her strength. She knew it didn't come from physical exertion. She didn't do anything spectacular – nothing that a warrior of her rank could possibly sweat about. Why was she feeling so nauseated?

"They have the Kaddim brand marks, Aghat Mai," one of the Majat called out.

Mai's jaw tightened.

Someone tugged Kara's sleeve and she saw Magister Egey Bashi coming into view, with Kyth on his heels.

"The Prince is detecting the Kaddim magic on you," Egey Bashi said.

Kara let out a slow breath. "I do too. I think."

"When exactly did it start?" The Keeper's eyes bore into her with unsettling intensity.

"Just now. When I..." *When I used my skill.* She swallowed, seeing the way Kyth's eyes widened, the way Magister Egey Bashi's face folded into a grim expression. *My skill. Dear Shal Addim, they are trying to get me to use my skill.* The thought made her feel cold inside. The Kaddim had just sacrificed three men – not to target Mai, or anyone else in their group, which seemed impossible with so many Majat around – but simply to force Kara to use her skill. So that they could tap into it and transfer it to their warriors.

She felt nausea rising to her throat, no longer able to hide her weakness as she swayed and grasped Mai's arm for support.

"I... I am a danger," she said. "I shouldn't be here. Please, let me go."

"I'm not letting you out of my sight," Mai said. "If needed, I'll guard you personally, day and night. This way, if they try to force you to use weapons, I'll be right there to defend you."

*This way you will be a target too.* She bit back the thought, focusing instead on stilling her mind, blocking off the tugging sensation in her head, gathering strength to stay on her feet.

The scouts were returning with their reports – no suspicious activity nearby. Someone handed Kara her throwing daggers and she took them gratefully, sheathing them at her belt. Mai beckoned her as he turned back to giving orders and she slowly regained her composure, falling into stride by his side.

What he wanted to do could work – temporarily, provided she would not be hoaxed into using her skill again. But the Kaddim were clearly doing everything possible to try. They were willing to sacrifice lives, forcing their men into hopeless fights just so that Kara could be engaged.

With the march ahead of them, this was going to be a long haul. Sooner or later, the Kaddim would get what they wanted.

*I must do everything I can to sever the link. Even if I have to die.* She knew from Mai that the possibility had been brought up at the King's council, and dismissed because of the somewhat phantom dangers it harbored, of releasing her entire power to the Kaddim. It didn't seem plausible at all, not with the way she felt no connection to the Kaddim whatsoever. Deep inside she was convinced that Mai was just saying that to her so that she wouldn't feel tempted to facilitate this course of action.

As a warrior, she knew there was no avoiding the inevitable. She didn't want to die. But as long as she lived, everyone she loved could never feel safe.

She knew Mai would never let her take her own life. Neither would Kyth, or any of their other allies.

Which meant that, whatever the cost, she had to break away from them.

# 9

# ELEMENTAL MAGIC

Kyth's barge sailed last, putting ample distance between him and the Majat command group that included Mai and Kara. By now he was used to the fact that despite his outwardly important role as the leader of the King's force and the heir to the throne, he was being more or less removed from any daily decisions. He didn't even mind that much. Mai was definitely better than anyone he knew at handling the logistics of a military march. Besides, even if Kyth wasn't happy with the fact that he wouldn't see Kara for the duration of the trip across the lakes, he was glad to find himself in the company of Ellah and Alder, as well as Magister Egey Bashi, whose grounded, cynical wisdom helped everyone to keep a cool head. Lady Celana was also included in the party, and Kyth was surprised at how welcome he was finding the thought. While the lady's blushing and fidgeting whenever he showed up often made him feel embarrassed, once she was past her bouts of shyness she became an excellent storyteller whose wit and deep knowledge of the kingdom's affairs kept him in constant awe. Besides, he found it fascinating that she apparently considered him so attractive. It was a welcome change from the way everyone else treated him like a child.

In addition to the Kingsguards of Kyth's retinue, Mai left them an escort of two dozen Majat, several of them Ruby-ranked. Kyth was surprised Mai was willing to part with a few of his precious top Gems for such an extended time, especially since it seemed unlikely they would be attacked on the water. Still, the incident back at the port left everyone unsettled, wondering when and where to expect a next encounter.

Kyth and his friends were escorted into a roomy cabin in the aft section, where they were greeted by the barge's captain, a lean man in his early fifties who moved with the grace and agility of someone half his age. The man bowed low to the Prince, and exchanged elaborate court greetings with Lady Celana, before proclaiming that this cabin, and the entire barge, was at their full disposal for the duration of the trip. He then took his leave to give orders on deck, replaced by the stewards who served light refreshments, then left the travelers alone.

"We should probably have invited the Rubies to join us," Kyth reflected without enthusiasm.

Egey Bashi shrugged. "They would never leave the open space of the deck, Your Highness. Aghat Mai charged them with ensuring our safety. You know how seriously the Majat take it."

Kyth nodded. Here on the open water, with only the trusted men on board, the Majat's zeal seemed so excessive. He expected quiet time and smooth sailing. His father's men knew their jobs, especially when it came to navigating the lake waters.

"I was hoping, Prince Kythar," Egey Bashi went on, "that we could use this time to work on your gift. Despite how effective you were during the last battle, I keep feeling you are not using your full power. If our suspicions about the Kaddim plans are even partially true, we may need more from you."

"More?" Kyth heaved a slow sigh. With the recent turn of events, it did seem like a good idea to work on perfecting his skill. During the last weeks of preparation for the march everyone had been focusing so much on the Majat reinforcements that he didn't have a chance to even give this any thought.

He valued the opportunity to study with Magister Egey Bashi, one of the wisest teachers he knew, but he wasn't sure there was much more he could achieve. He looked at his companions, unsure how to discuss this in such a large group.

As if on cue, Lady Celana cleared her throat delicately. "With Your Highness's permission I'd like to take this opportunity to enjoy the view on deck. I heard in the fine weather like today one can see all the way to Castle Illitand."

"I will accompany you, my lady," Alder volunteered, hastily rising to his feet.

Kyth grinned at the way his foster brother offered his hand to Celana gallantly, like a born courtier. He knew it was much easier for Alder to wield an axe, the Forestland weapon he always wore in a strap at his back, than to engage in the subtleties of the court etiquette. It was nice to see him make the effort.

Ellah also rose, mumbling an equally superficial excuse as she followed them outside.

"Is there anything you believe you can teach me,

Magister?" Kyth asked when the door closed behind her.

Egey Bashi looked at him thoughtfully. "I cannot help hoping we can find a way to expand on your training, Your Highness. Perhaps Ellah's example could be our guide? She has been quite successful in training with me to use her truthsense."

Kyth looked away. His training so far had been vastly different from Ellah's. The girl spent her days talking to Egey Bash and learning to probe deeper into her own mind, while Kyth had to endure endless and strenuous Majat weapon exercises, designed to teach him to hold his ground against multiple opponents – as well as, it seemed, to humiliate him in front of everyone in sight. In battle, Kyth's sole purpose so far had been to keep attention on their attack force so that he could protect all of them from the Kaddim, and everyone believed weapon training was the best way to perfect this ability. However, during the past month Kyth had come to a painful realization that he would never become as good as the Majat expected him to be. By now, it seemed that the training hindered, rather than increased his magic ability.

It would be nice if the Keepers knew a better way, if only because it would give Kyth a much-needed break, but he doubted it was possible.

"I know about Ellah's training," Kyth said. "She sees colors in her mind, different when someone tells the truth or a lie. I don't think it applies to my gift at all."

"Do you even know exactly what your gift enables you to do?" Egey Bashi asked.

Kyth felt affronted. Of course he knew. His gift enabled him to control the elements, focusing their power to aid him – in swordplay, when needed, or, importantly for the upcoming battle, in focusing the elemental power to counteract the Kaddim's mind control. He could use the forces of wind, fire, or water and turn them into an invisible weapon that protected him and conferred the resistance to others. Didn't Magister Egey Bashi know it as well?

"I thought we went over it before, Magister," he said.

"We did, but I can't escape a feeling we are only scratching the surface. Try to think, Your Highness. Why do you think you can resist the Kaddim?"

Kyth sighed. "We discussed this too, many times. I can focus. When I do it, I imagine a blade that cuts through the blanket of mind power the Kaddim throw over their victims. This was why we decided on putting me through intensive blade training in the first place, isn't it?"

"I remember the way we arrived at the weapons analogy," the Keeper said. "And it did work well, for a while. But lately it seems to me that we've reached our limits with it."

"Perhaps this simply reflects the limits of my ability, Magister?"

Egey Bashi shook his head. "I don't think so, Prince Kythar. If I did, we wouldn't be having this conversation."

*Well, we have nothing better to do, have we?* Kyth bit back the retort. It wasn't Egey Bashi's fault that Kyth was sitting in this cabin when Kara was on another barge, half a mile ahead. She and Mai were probably given a separate cabin where they... they... Kyth's cheeks warmed under Egey Bashi's gaze.

"I'd like to train differently, Magister," he said. "But

I don't know how. Besides, Mai would never allow it, would he?" He paused. Mai thought he was in charge of everyone and everything. He would never let Kyth's training slip from under his control, if only because of the satisfaction Kyth's daily humiliations must be bringing him. Kyth was vaguely aware that he was probably being unfair, yet hard as he tried he couldn't find a flaw in this line of thinking. Mai used every opportunity to put Kyth down. And Kyth had no choice but to go along with it, given that the Majat were the only force that could guarantee their victory.

"Aghat Mai would never stand in the way of your progress," Egey Bashi said. "Surely you must know this, Prince Kythar."

"I doubt he cares. The only thing he cares about is his superiority." *And making me look bad in front of Kara – as if taking her away from me wasn't enough.*

The Keeper frowned. "You should stop this kind of thinking right now, Prince Kythar."

"Why, Magister?" Kyth blurted. "It's true, isn't it?"

Egey Bashi sighed. "We both know you are biased when it comes to Aghat Mai. I saw the way you looked at Kara when she boarded her barge. I can also see the way you look at Aghat Mai every time he is around. You feel upset right now, simply because you cannot stop thinking about them being together. Am I wrong?"

Kyth averted his gaze.

Egey Bashi nodded. "I thought so. And, I must tell you one thing. Kara is no longer a part of your life. She has made her choice, of her own free will. If you want our mission to succeed, you must accept this, and move on."

Kyth clenched his fists, then slowly relaxed under

the Keeper's intent gaze. He knew, however much it
pained him to admit it, that Egey Bashi was telling the
truth. Kyth was acting like a child, not a future leader
to his people. He could not allow his broken heart to
jeopardize their chances of victory.

"You are right, Magister," he said.

Egey Bashi reached forward and patted his arm.
"I know this isn't easy for you, Your Highness. For
whatever it's worth, I hope you can find comfort in the
knowledge that this kind of pain gets better with time.
It always does."

Kyth looked away again. He knew people liked to
say that, but it wasn't working at all in his case, not so
far. The pain was as fresh as if his breakup with Kara
happened just yesterday. The fact that she left him for
Mai, Kyth's opposite in every way, made it worse. What
could this ruthless man possibly give her that Kyth
couldn't? He swallowed, forcing away these thoughts
under Egey Bashi's knowing gaze.

"Regarding my ability," he said, "I really don't know
if I can do more. What I did to protect the Majat last
time... it was already so hard."

"Just think again," Egey Bashi said. "You told me
once before that when you focus the elemental power
you feel like you are wielding a sword. When you
protect others, you sometimes think of balancing a
spearhead over each of them. In fact, as I remember,
before you started having any weapons training, vast
elemental powers tended to overwhelm you. Is this
correct?"

"Yes." Kyth tried to remember the feeling. Raised
in the Forestlands, he used to be afraid of open spaces
with too much wind, and he had always been terrified

getting near large quantities of water. Once he nearly drowned fording a river in a shallow place.

Today, after years of training, he no longer felt this way. In fact, even now, traveling on a barge over the lake so wide that he couldn't see the distant shore didn't seem to bother him at all.

"Actually," he said, "I always thought weapons training was what enabled me to get in touch with my gift. But I... It is not quite true, is it?"

"Very likely not," Egey Bashi said. "Weapons training did help, and probably sealed the analogy to a sword you tend to evoke when you use your power. But it is all images, no more. Think of Ellah's gift, for example. She thinks of colors when she detects a truth or a lie, but in reality there are no colors involved at all. It's an analogy, just like the one you use with weapons – and in your case it seems to have outlived its use. We need to find a different one."

Kyth frowned. He had been thinking of his skill as an extension of swordplay for so long that it seemed impossible to change the way he looked at it. In part, he always hoped that by following it through, by enabling his skill and weaponry to feed each other, he could eventually become as good as Mai. But that probably wasn't going to happen, was it?

Unexpectedly, Egey Bashi's words gave him hope. What if he could find a different way to train, one that didn't involve the Majat?

"If not a sword, then what could it be?" he asked.

The Keeper leaned back in his chair. "From what I know, Your Highness, your ability to command the elements is an ancient power attributed to your royal line. Legends tell of the Dorn kings turning the ocean tides and forcing wildfires ripping through the lands to fold onto themselves and die. This, to me, calls for something different from a sword or a spearhead you imagine wielding."

Kyth nodded. In their recent travels, Lady Celana also told him stories from the old chronicles about the deeds of his distant ancestors. And then there was a time, during one of their Kaddim battles, when he was able to turn the power of the entire Kaddim leaders onto themselves and force them to surrender and retreat. He could never figure out what he did that time, but he certainly wasn't thinking of wielding a sword.

Could he ever invoke this kind of ability again?

"To my knowledge," Egey Bashi said, "your power is, in many ways, the exact opposite to the Kaddim. Their ability is to smother, while yours is to activate, strengthen, and expand. They diffuse, where you have the unique power to focus. You tell me you always use mental images of cutting the blanket of Kaddim's power using swords and spearheads, right?"

"Right."

"Perhaps, Your Highness, if you think of your ability in more of the expansive terms, you may find a new aspect to it?"

Kyth hesitated. The Keeper's voice evoked a string of images in his mind. The power of the wind, the water, the fire, focused into an invisible blade – no, not a blade, a beam that could empower his weapon and make him stronger and more agile. But if he focused more, he could mold this image into other forms. A ball, hurling through the sky as if shot out of a cannon. A shield that could deflect an enemy's attack. A dome that could descend onto his entire group, protecting them from outside forces. In this form, it did not cut through the Kaddim power, but it could still counter it, force it down to the ground and to the darkest pits below…

He lifted his face. "I think I understand, Magister," he said. "My power… I can wield it in different ways. A blade is only one of them."

"Good." Egey Bashi reached forward and patted his arm. "You've just taken an essential first step."

"A first step?" Kyth felt affronted again. The Magister's words just made everything he learned before seem insignificant.

The Keeper looked at him levelly, as if oblivious to the emotion, but a sharp gleam in his eyes spoke otherwise. "I hope you forgive an old man, Prince Kythar, for telling you one more thing. To win this war, it will be very important for you to control your feelings. Your jealousy of Aghat Mai, your desire to prove yourself, they are all understandable, believe me. I was once young and idealistic myself. But what I learned over the years is that the big picture is always grander than all these petty emotions. We are facing an enemy much more vast and powerful than anything we ever encountered before. Only an equal or greater power can ever hope to overcome them. Believe me, it will take everything we have – and more. No matter how hard it may seem, it is absolutely essential for you to put your personal feelings aside."

Kyth sighed. He knew the Magister was right. It just seemed that every time he made an effort, Mai popped up into his way, mocking and devaluing everything he did.

"I will try," he said. "But Mai – he makes it so difficult sometimes."

Egey Bashi nodded. "Aghat Mai is older and more mature than you, but not by much. He is indeed prone to all the same faults. An effort on both of your sides would be important. Especially where Kara is concerned."

"Kara should be kept out of this, Magister. She's going through enough."

"If both of you continue to defend her no matter what, she will potentially become our downfall."

Kyth lifted his chin. "What are you saying, Magister?"

Egey Bashi let out a sigh. "You saw for yourself what happened at the port. This was only the beginning. If we don't put a stop to it, by the time we reach the Kaddim fortress every one of their warriors will potentially be able to fight like her. If this happens, we stand no chance. She must be disabled, one way or another, before it's too late."

"Disabled."

"Yes. Death might still be an option, once I complete my research. But since it appears too risky at the moment, she should at least be sedated. We can also explore ways to weaken her physically, so that her Majat ability – or at least her using it when provoked – would no longer be a threat."

Kyth pushed away from the table. He was not going to stand for this kind of talk. Worse, in the depth of his heart he knew that Egey Bashi was right. Yet, following this line of reasoning seemed unthinkable. For once, he felt glad that Kara was Mai's responsibility – if only the Diamond could be trusted not to change his mind.

He did not bother with a response as he stepped out of the cabin onto the broad deck. The leading barge was no more than a speck in the distance ahead. Even if he strained his eyes, he couldn't make out individual shapes among the groups of people on decks. He hoped Kara was safe among them. He hoped, at least for the time being, she was at peace.

# 10

# ESCAPE

Kara woke to the sound of running feet and voices outside. She lifted her head to see that Mai's place next to her on the bed was empty. He must have been called out early, and left quietly not to disturb her sleep.

The barge was no longer moving. Yet, the voices, while loud, did not seem alarmed. *Have we reached the shore already?* That seemed possible, even if a few hours ahead of schedule. The wind on the trip had been steady and strong, leaving the oarsmen very little to do.

Her skin crept with warmth as she thought of the last two days when she and Mai had the cabin all to themselves, with a lot of spare time to enjoy each other's company. The only time she could forget about her link, at least temporarily, was in Mai's arms. If she could be alone with him all the time, she wouldn't be too worried about the Kaddim stealing her gift. But on the march that awaited them they would have no privacy and nearly no opportunity to spend time with each other. Every minute she stayed alive put them all in danger. She was happy that she got to have the last two days, but her time was up. She had to act now, to save everyone else.

She quietly slipped on her clothes and gear and slid outside.

The gray light of the breaking dawn dissipated into the thick morning mists. The dark line of the shore loomed ahead, no more than two cable lengths away. She ran her eyes around the activity on the deck, men preparing their gear and horses for disembarking.

Mai was at the far end, engaged in an intense conversation with the barge's command crew. He smiled to her and she waved back, edging behind the stacks of crates and sail cloth piled in the aft section of the barge. She briefly considered getting her horse, tethered among the pack, but decided against it. If she took the horse, her absence would be noticed almost immediately, precluding her from carrying out her plan.

Of course, with the amount of weapons she carried, the fastest and most efficient way would be to slit her own throat, saving everyone a lot of trouble. But the Keepers had equipped Mai and his men with some advanced cures which could easily heal deadly wounds and were rumored to work even for a short time after death. With everything at stake she couldn't possibly risk it. She had to come ashore and travel far enough from her group to ensure she was absolutely alone before she tried anything, with no possibility of help arriving within a sufficiently long time.

She tried her best to stifle all regrets as she allowed herself a last glimpse of Mai. He was a natural focus of all activity – a born leader, a great warrior, and deep inside, the kindest soul she had ever known. Just knowing that he loved her, that they had a chance to be together, even if briefly, made her life worth living. Giving it up was the least she could do to make sure Mai's enemies did not destroy everything he fought for. She tried to tell herself that Mai would understand, that he wouldn't blame her later on for taking matters into her own hands, but quickly dismissed the thought. His understanding was not essential. There were greater things at stake.

She stepped further behind the crates and quietly slid overboard.

Kyth's barge was making way to the pier when he heard shouting and saw men running around on the shore. Their crowd fell away as Mai swept through, like a slim black-clad tornado that left havoc in its wake. His pale face was set into a contorted mask that looked frightening even from this distance.

Kyth's heart fell. Something terrible must have happened, just a short time ago. *Is Kara all right? Did more Kaddim envoys attack her?*

He jumped off the barge before the ropes were secured into place and ran toward the activity.

It took effort to break through the tight ring of the Majat top Gems. They stepped aside to let Kyth through as they recognized him, closing behind him with a grim finality that settled the Prince into a realization that things were far worse than he thought.

"Mai!" Kyth shouted as he finally caught sight of the Diamond. "What happened?"

The Majat turned an unseeing gaze toward him. It seemed to take Mai a moment to recognize him.

"Kara," Mai said. "She wasn't on board our barge when we arrived."

"What do you mean, she wasn't on board?"

Mai's eyes flared. "You have a hearing problem?"

Kyth stepped back. Arguing with Mai in this state was not only futile, but dangerous. Besides, if something indeed happened to Kara, it was best to leave Mai to handle it. But what could it possibly be? Did the Kaddim find a way to disable her and kidnap her from a Majat-filled barge? Not likely, especially given Mai's resolve not to let her out of sight. Was she swept away through the Kaddim vortex? But didn't Magister Egey Bashi say such a thing was not possible without a Kaddim leader working the vortex magic right next to her?

Mai was giving orders, many of them in the Majat language that seemingly consisted entirely of sharp consonants, not possible for a normal person to even pronounce, let alone understand. As Kyth watched, one of the men stepped forward with a writing set, holding it out while Mai quickly scribbled a note on a piece of parchment. Mesmerized, Kyth watched another man fold the parchment up, and hand it down the line to a tall warrior petting a large hooded hawk perched on his forearm.

"Mai, what are you doing?" he asked.

"None of your bloody business."

Kyth lifted his chin. "It *is* my bloody business, as you should well know. I am a part of our campaign too – and an important one, last time I checked!"

Mai's glance glinted like a blade, but before the argument could erupt, Egey Bashi stepped up between them.

"Really, Aghat Mai. Prince Kythar is right. This concerns all of us, doesn't it?"

The Diamond froze in mid-movement, his brief

glance forcing the Keeper back a few steps. Then, Mai's face softened, as if a switch had flipped inside to turn him into a more normal mode.

"You're right, Magister," he said. "Sorry, Kyth. I was preoccupied."

*That's a bloody understatement.* Kyth nodded his acceptance, knowing better than saying this out loud. The situation seemed explosive enough without it.

"I was with Kara until morning," Mai said. "Then I went on deck to organize the departure. I saw her briefly when she emerged from the cabin later on. Then, no one saw her again. We have at least an hour unaccounted for."

"What about her horse?" Egey Bash asked.

"Still here. As are all the other horses we brought. I'm certain she's not on horseback." Mai signaled to the bird handler and the man removed the hood, flinging the hawk high into the sky. It took off with a long screeching cry.

"What's this for?" Kyth asked.

Mai hesitated, as if deciding if he was worthy of an answer. "A message to the local lord. If she passes through his lands, they'll delay her long enough for our search parties to reach her."

Kyth stared. "Is this local lord loyal to the Majat Guild?"

"No. I'm calling in a personal favor."

*A personal favor? From a Lakeland Lord?* Kyth's mouth fell open. To his knowledge, these lands, south of the lakes between the Forestlands and the northern marshes of Bengaw, were nearly lawless, each small lord claiming as much authority as a king. The crown never bothered to go after them, leaving them to settle their feuds on their own. Personal favors meant nothing down here, if he studied his history right.

What could Mai have possibly done to count on one?

"Do you believe then that she left of her own accord?" Egey Bashi asked.

Mai's eyes darted between groups of warriors preparing for departure with speed and efficiency that made Kyth blink. "No one could have possibly forced her. Not on my barge."

*The Kaddim could.* The thought made Kyth feel cold inside. She may have thought she was acting of her own accord, but what if...

He exchanged a quick glance with Magister Egey Bashi, the Keeper's dark gaze echoing his worst fears.

"Do you think they may have found a way to control her, Magister?" he asked quietly.

The Keeper held a pause. "Let's hope Aghat Mai's efforts to find her bring a result. Then we can learn for sure." He turned and strode away.

Kyth turned to see Mai's intent gaze fixed on him. He had forgotten how sharp the Majat's hearing was. Trying to keep secrets around Mai was a bad idea, especially when something so dear to him was concerned.

He expected another verbal attack, but to his surprise Mai's gaze softened as he met Kyth's.

"I'll get her back." It seemed as if Mai was going to say something else, but at that moment a young Majat warrior led in his horse. Mai swept into the saddle in one fluid move, leaving the unsaid words hanging. His hand shot up, a signal that sent men into their saddles, throwing their horses into gallop, dissipating in different directions. In moments, all that was left of them on the port plaza was a light cloud of dust melting into the remains of the morning mist.

Kyth stood for a moment looking after them. Then he turned around and went to search for Magister Egey Bashi.

# 11

# AMBUSH

Kara chose the most secluded spot along the shore to emerge from the water. She avoided the reed thickets, which could give her away by the trail of broken stems she was bound to leave if she tried to walk through. She also stayed clear of the long, grassy stretches of shoreline that were clearly visible from the port city of Jai-Allad where the barges with the Majat had landed. Drifting with the soft undercurrent to avoid creating a wake stream that could be seen from afar, she threw a last glance at the rows of wooden sheds that flanked the docks, their flat rooftops gradually giving way to the thatched reed roofs that prevailed in the rest of the city.

Southern Lakelands had a murky history. Originally a disputed land between Illitand and Bengaw, the two rival powers that emerged after the fall of the Old Empire, they all fell into the newly formed kingdom of Tallan Dar in the wake of the Holy Wars, but allegiances and loyalties here remained mixed. Some of the Bengaw nobility settled here, paying tribute to the king across the lakes but otherwise enjoying a nearly free run of their domains. Further south, the lands stepped dangerously close to the Forestlands, which harbored the apex of the old magic forced down by the Church but by no means subdued. Kara suppressed a shiver remembering Ayalla, the Forest Mother, who reigned there and whose spiders had threatened her so recently at the King's court. Perhaps she should have provoked them back then and let them finish the job? If only one could be so smart in hindsight.

With slow underwater strokes she swam toward a low line of ivies, whose drooping branches created a perfect curtain over the water near the shore. Once inside their shade, she chose a flat piece of the bank and pulled herself onto it in one smooth move.

The water had been cooler than comfortable, but the fresh bite of the early morning breeze made her long for the lake's protective shelter. She flexed her muscles to warm up, quickly squeezing the water out of her clothes and hair, and checking her weapons in their numerous straps. Once dry, she should give them a good cleanup, she thought, then stopped herself. Someone else would clean her weapons before claiming them for their own. Very soon, none of this would matter anymore.

She knew Mai would mount a search party as soon as he noticed her absence, but she hoped with all the bustle associated with disembarking, she had enough of a head start. All she needed now was to get far enough from civilization so that she'd be unlikely to be found for a sufficiently long time. A quick stab to the heart would do the job, and with all her combat training she should have no trouble doing it. She knew the perfect spot where she could slide a blade between her ribs without much resistance.

She looked at the sky. The slant of the rising sunbeams told her she must have spent at least an hour swimming away from the barge, and probably another half hour finding the best place to come ashore. Mai should be in port now, probably getting the horses saddled for pursuit and giving hell to his men for missing her escape. He would ride as fast as he could. But without knowing where exactly to search for her, he would be too late.

She had to make sure of it.

She kept to the line of bushes as she ran away from the water, toward a deeper grove of Lakeland willows that swept the wind with delicate garlands of leaves and honeyed buds. Their drooping curtains provided a perfect shelter from any watchful eyes. No one would ever find her inside.

The willows greeted her with a fresh, sweet aroma that made her head swim. She inhaled deeply before diving into their shade. There. The gnarled, grotesquely woven trunk of the nearest tree had a cleft that could easily hide a body. If she climbed deeper between the roots, no one would find her for days. Not until it was too late.

She briefly wondered why she, a professional killer, was taking such excessive precautions for what should essentially be the easiest kill of all. She also wondered at the unsettling feeling every time she thought of the Keepers' cures and the many ways they had to bring the mortally wounded back to health. Was it because of the memory of the pain one of these cures caused when used on her own wounds? Or was it the Kaddim's hatred of the Keepers, seeping into her own consciousness drop by drop, like exquisite poison? *Am*

*I thinking like a Kaddim now?* The thought made her shudder and she hastened to cover the last few steps to her destination.

"Halt!" A voice at her back made her freeze. It was unfamiliar, young, with a pitch to it that suggested its bearer's nerves were on edge and he was about to do something rash. *Probably holding a loaded crossbow pointed at me.* She turned around slowly, keeping her hands in plain sight.

The newcomer wasn't alone. Four more men crowded at his back, holding the reins of their horses. Their livery looked unfamiliar, black with an embroidery of crossed sabers on the left sleeve. Bengaw heraldry? This far north? She narrowed her eyes, but found no other signs of distinction that could give her a clue.

They all looked young and fit, and all had crossbows pointing in her direction. As she watched, they quickly closed the distance, their faces set into expressions of grim resolve. *Damn it, how did they find me here? How could I miss their approach?* The willow branches and tall grass concealed sounds, but however stealthy, these newcomers must have made a ruckus riding in.

Unless they had been warned of her arrival and were waiting here in ambush.

Her skin prickled.

"That's far enough," she said, halting the group in their tracks. Their fear as they eyed her sparked her curiosity. *Do they know who I am?* It hardly seemed likely. She wore no Majat regalia, or any other signs of distinction that could connect her to the Guild. Yet, their entranced looks as they watched her every move, the tense set of their bodies, told her they were all on edge. Not a good state of mind for men holding loaded crossbows.

"If you want to talk," she said, "why don't you first lower your weapons? I'd hate for any accident to happen, wouldn't you?" She flexed her arms as she spoke, ready to whip out her swords at the first sign of trouble.

The leader of the group shifted from foot to foot. "We have no wish to talk to you." He nodded to one of his comrades who lifted his head and whistled loudly through his teeth.

Wings flapped in the distance. Through the drooping ivy branches, Kara caught a glimpse of a large bird rising into the sky.

*A messenger hawk?* A chill ran down Kara's spine. The Majat used trained hawks to send messages on the march, but so did pretty much everyone else with a sophisticated long-distance messaging system. Hawks were more reliable than pigeons, which often fell victim to birds of prey, or ravens, which tended to gravitate to their colonies and had limited use for a party on the march. Hawks were also very pricey, which made them the birds of choice only for those nobles who were not only very rich but also haughty enough to show off their wealth. It was quite possible that the lord of these lands, whoever he was, fit the mark. But now, with the Majat party so close by and likely looking for her, this explanation did not seem comforting enough.

"What do you want from me?" she asked.

"Our lord's orders are to keep you here until help arrives."

*Our lord's.* She glanced at the men's livery again, hoping against reason that all this turmoil had to do with no more than her accidentally trespassing on the lands of an overly territorial Bengaw nobleman.

She tried for her best easygoing smile. "Have I done anything wrong?"

The man frowned with resolve. "Like I said. We're not here to talk to you. We have our orders."

Her smile widened. "Do your orders involve shooting me if I refuse to cooperate?" She flicked her eyes to the loaded crossbow, her hand closing over the hilt of her dagger. It wasn't her most dangerous weapon, by far, but it was the most showy one, its wide blade nearly a foot long, its hilt custom-made to fit over her knuckles with a jagged edge that sometimes came handy in a fight.

The man's jaw tightened, his wary look confirming her suspicions. He seemed to know exactly what she was capable of – a near impossibility if this was a chance meeting.

To find her so soon, Mai had to have had help. But how could he possibly know anyone on this side of the Lakes?

"If your orders involve shooting," she said, "do it now. I'm in a hurry."

The man's eyes narrowed in disbelief. "You want us to shoot you?"

"Since you have crossbows all armed and ready, I assume you're planning to use them. I'd rather get it over with, so that I can be on my way."

He licked his lips nervously, exchanging a quick glance with his comrades. Kara could see the way his knuckles went white as he tightened the grip on his weapon and hoped the safety catch was on. Of course, being killed was exactly what she came here for, but she couldn't possibly trust the job to the amateurs.

"I've no time to wait around for your lord," she said. "Frankly, I don't want to harm you over this, but I'll do it if I have to." She drew her blade, noting how the men backed off, clearly hesitating whether to stick to their orders or run for their lives.

Kara quickly reached forward and sliced off the string of the nearest crossbow, stepping aside as the bolt discharged into a tree trunk. Another man fired a half-hearted shot. She hacked down the bolt with her dagger, stepping out of the way of the flying splinters.

The men dropped their weapons and backed away. She was impressed, however, that they didn't run far or attempt to mount their horses. One of them even tried to interfere when she picked up the reins of the nearest animal. She stopped him with a short glance and jumped into the saddle.

A low-pitched whistle cut the air behind her, followed by the cracking of broken branches and pounding of the approaching hoofbeat. Kara swore under her breath and threw her captured horse into gallop across the clearing. Only the Majat used sound arrows as their signals, notched at the base to produce noises of different pitch. She was willing to bet that this one was meant to alert the Majat searching parties to her whereabouts. She should have acted faster when she had run into the Bengaw patrol, but it was too late for regrets.

She glanced around her shoulder in time to see two riders cut through the line of bushes on the far end of the clearing. More arrows whizzed behind and she heard her horse grunt as it shuddered under her, its front legs folding to the ground, sending her flying. She hit the ground rolling, whipping out her swords as she rose back to her feet.

Lance approached her at full gallop, leaping off the saddle into her path. The Jade at his back pulled his horse to a stop and raised his bow. *A Diamond and a Jade.* Kara felt an unpleasant hollowness in the pit of her stomach. This was a pair the Guild would send after a renegade Diamond, an undefeatable combination that could take down someone of her skill. Jades, known for their superior accuracy with ranged weapons, would cover the fight from a distance, giving the attacking Diamond the needed advantage to win. Clearly, Mai had anticipated resistance if he sent such a pair after her. Probably several pairs, riding in different directions. That's how they were able to get here so quickly.

The fact that Lance was the one to find her first was pure bad luck. Lance's specialty was in his brutal head-on attack, one she would have more trouble countering with her lighter build.

She considered trying to outrun them, but with the Jade already cocking another arrow onto his bow this seemed like a bad move. She didn't mind him shooting her, but she knew he wouldn't be shooting to kill, only to disable her enough to secure her capture. The last thing she needed right now was an arrow wound. She glanced with regret at the dead horse she had tried to steal, an arrow sticking out of its eye – a stark reminder of what the Jade now targeting her was capable of. The animal's needless death would undoubtedly run up Mai's debt to this local Bengaw lord, whatever the reason was for his willingness to risk his men to help the Majat.

A tug at the back of her conscience became more insistent. She suddenly realized that she had been feeling it for a while, but in the heat of events she had completely dismissed it.

Her forehead instantly covered with cold sweat. *When did I sense it first? Probably when I first drew my weapons… Dear Shal Addim. My skill. They are draining my skill as long as I'm using it. And now, if I fight with Lance I will play right into their hands.*

*Damn it, how do I keep falling for the same trap over and over?*

She dropped her swords.

"I'm not going to fight you, Aghat Lance," she said. "I *can't* fight you without opening up my skill to the enemy. Please, just let me go."

He briefly shook his head. "You know I can't."

She stepped closer and paused as he raised his sword. His warded look hit her like a lash. *He doesn't know if he can trust me. Hell, I don't know if I can trust myself, can I?*

"You know things can't possibly end well, as long as I'm around," she said. "The Kaddim are doing everything possible to use me to win this war. My mere presence on our force puts everyone in danger, starting with Mai. I'm not asking you to do anything at all, just look the other way for a second so that I can leave quietly."

His gaze wavered. "I'm sorry, Aghat. We both know this isn't my decision to make. My ranking at the Guild wouldn't mean much if I tried to take the matters into my own hands."

Kara's eyes narrowed. This was exactly what got her into trouble with the Guild before. Taking the matters into her own hands. She didn't wish this on Lance. If he helped her escape just now, Mai's wrath would know no bounds. And yet, they both knew that Mai's opinion in this matter couldn't be fully trusted. However good a commander Mai was, he was blindsighted where Kara was concerned. If the events were allowed to run their course, his feelings toward her were going to bring about the Guild's end. Yet, she knew she couldn't possibly force Lance to shoulder all this responsibility.

Rustling and cracking at the edge of the glade announced the arrival of a new pair of riders. Entranced, Kara watched Mai dismount, a Jade at his back releasing a sound arrow with a different pitch into the sky. *Calling off the search,* Kara guessed. She locked gazes with Mai as he stepped up in front of her.

They stood for a long moment looking at each other. Kara's heart raced as she read Mai's emotions, visible only to her in his outwardly impassive face. Relief, at finding her unharmed. Disbelief, at the knowledge of what she had done. But the one that stung the most was the distrust, similar to the one she saw in Lance's eyes just a short time ago. *He isn't sure he can believe me anymore. He doesn't even know if I am acting of my own free will.*

*Am I?*

She swallowed a lump rising in her throat. Up until now her way of dealing with emotional challenges had been to close up and detach herself from the situation. This didn't work at all between her and Mai. The Majat assassins were not supposed to love, if only because of this vulnerability.

The recent events raised too many questions in her mind. Was it her own idea to abandon her party and seek solitude, or did the Kaddim instill this thinking?

Was this another ploy to make sure she was forced to use her skill and they could tap into it? She saw no possibility of her plan to kill herself benefiting the Kaddim, but the way it compelled her to hide in the woods rather than just finish the job on the spot did not really stand up to scrutiny. Even less so did her sudden fear that the Keepers' cures could bring her back from the dead. *The Kaddim are able to resurrect. Have I become afraid of someone resurrecting me?*

*Dear Shal Addim.*

She lifted her chin.

"I apologize for causing all this trouble, Aghat Mai," she said formally. "I thought I was helping. I now see that I was wrong."

A tug at her mind felt like a stab of a sharp blade. Her vision blurred and she sank to the ground.

# 12
# RETURN

Voices around Kara kept getting louder, making it impossible to concentrate. They seemed to be coming from all sides, some clear, as if the speakers were nearby, others indistinct and hollow, as if echoing through deep stone hallways. She could not make out the words.

She felt as if falling, searching and not finding any solid support. The air around her became damp and chilly, then dry and dusty as she emerged into a chamber. In its vast semidarkness, she could see two men spread in a lover-like embrace on top of an elevated stone platform that emanated a strange form of power, comforting and frightening at the same time. Sickening details came into view as her vision cleared, the man below a rotting corpse, the one above him sinking his hands into the dissolving flesh. Then she saw the corpse move, eyes inside the disintegrating sockets rolling wildly, his body thrashing in agony under the other man's touch. *Pain. So much pain.* Her ears opened to hear the howling of the wind outside, and piercing screams that shook her to the core.

*Come... to me... Kara...*

*Kara!*

Sharp pain pierced her head like a needle and she cried out, trying to shield her face. Strong hands pried her arms away. She fought back with all her might, until she was pinned down and immobile. Strangely, as she struggled uselessly against the iron-hard hold, the pain in her head slowly receded, the reality around her surfacing with additional senses – a touch of cool wind on her cheek, grass stems biting into her neck. She smelled earth and ivy, leather and sweat, and horses some distance away. Then, a sharp medicinal scent hit her nostrils, snapping her back to alertness.

She opened her eyes, taking in the scene. Mai was straddling her chest in a nasty leg block, his knees pinning down her outstretched arms, his weight balancing over her fluidly to prevent any attempts to escape. Lance was crouching beside him with a small dark flask in hand. *Milk of thorn.* Her eyes teared up from the memory of the sharp scent, normally used to repel insects but very effective as a smelling salt. *Damn it, what is going on?*

She unclenched her hands, relaxing back into the grass to show her surrender. The two Diamonds exchanged quick glances, as if deciding if she was worth their trust. Then Mai released his block and rolled off, the absence of his weight making her feel light, as if flying. She flexed her muscles, wondering at the soreness she felt. How long did the fight last?

Lance rose from his crouch and stepped away, corking his flask and shoving it into a pouch at his belt. Mai sat on his heels next to her, watching. She saw his muscles flex as he peered into her face, as if bracing for another attack.

"What did I do?" she asked.

Mai frowned. "You were clawing at your head. When I tried to stop you, you…" He paused, a shadow running over his face.

"I… what?"

"You lashed out," Lance said. "You also spoke in a strange language. We weren't sure you were yourself."

*Clearly not.* She glanced at the bruises darkening on Mai's skin, at the long rip in Lance's grass-stained shirt. It was hard to imagine how she could have caused all this ruckus. Diamonds were more or less equal in strength and skill, and when it came to wrestling on the ground she had a disadvantage by being smaller and lighter than either of them. *Did the two of them have trouble holding me down?* She suppressed a shiver, taking exaggerated care to pull herself upright and remove grass stems and dirt from her own clothes.

"Do you remember what happened?" Mai asked.

She rubbed her wrists, tingling as if they had been devoid of circulation for quite some time. "Not the fight. The last thing I remember is this feeling… as if someone was stabbing my head. I also heard voices. And I saw…" She glanced around. Definitely no stone hallways here, not even a rock sticking out of the wavering grass.

"Saw what?"

"I… I think it might have been a chamber inside the Kaddim fortress. I saw a man, dying." She tried to stifle the memory. The dissolving flesh, rotting while the man was still alive. She had seen it once before. There was no mistaking it, the agony of a man bitten by the spiders. *The Kaddim brother, bitten during our recent battle? Not possible.* Yet, no matter how hard she tried, she couldn't come up with any other explanation.

Mai peered into her face. "Are you all right?"

"Fine." She flexed her muscles, massaging the life back into her sore arms. Mai's block had been vicious, his knees pressing only inches away from the spots that would have dislocated her shoulders. Clearly she had left him no choice but to subdue her with maximum force.

"Sorry," he said. "I was trying to avoid knocking you out."

"I understand." With her strength and combat skill, she could do serious damage thrashing in a semi-conscious state with no awareness of her surroundings. It was fortunate that Mai and Lance happened to be nearby. Or was it deliberate, another Kaddim ploy to trick her into using her skill? She felt nauseated at the thought.

"Do you have any idea what happened?" Mai asked.

"No." She looked up at him, her heart quivering at the mix of concern and unease in his eyes. He still didn't trust her. She wasn't sure she could live with that. "You shouldn't have come after me. You should've let me go."

"Go and do what, exactly?"

Her lips trembled. "My mere existence is putting everyone in danger. None of us knows for sure what happens every time the Kaddim tap into my skill. For all we know, their warriors can already fight like Gems. Hell, they will all fight like Diamonds if I stay alive long enough."

"*Alive?*"

"Yes."

"Is this why you ran away?"

She averted her gaze, unable to face his expression. He looked at her in hurt disbelief, as if she had just attempted to stab him.

"Think of it, Mai," she said. "You're fighting a war. If you lose, our Guild will cease to exist. Kingdoms will fall. Everyone will perish. Don't you think it's unreasonable to weigh it all against one person's life?"

Mai's eyes narrowed. "You are forgetting one important thing. This way of thinking, your belief that you pose this kind of danger, might be the Kaddim's trick too. If Magister Egey Bashi is right about your death benefiting them…"

"Do you really mean it?"

Mai's nostrils flared. "Did you forget what I told you before, how your death could potentially play right into their hands by releasing your skill to them? Of course we don't know for sure yet, but last time I checked Magister Egey Bashi was still under this impression."

"How come he never said anything to me?"

"Because I asked him not to. I know his tendency to chew things over and over again. The last thing I wanted was to subject you to these conversations. I thought me talking to you would be enough. Wasn't it?"

She sighed. "I thought you were just trying to make me feel better after what I heard at the King's council."

"Would I ever do this to you? Do I actually look this bloody stupid?"

"No. But–"

"Just think about what you just said," Mai insisted. "Does it make any sense?"

"Yes."

"Well, then maybe I'm not the one being bloody stupid right now."

She stared at him wide-eyed, realizing with chilling intensity that he was absolutely correct. He would never have lied to her just to make her feel better. Not about something as important as this. Only in a very altered state of mind could she have allowed herself to entertain this idea. Worse, she could see now that the entire plan she had concocted had so many logical flaws that even without this additional knowledge it didn't really stand up to scrutiny. It couldn't possibly have come entirely from her own head.

"Mai," she said. "You know as well as I do that this can't continue. You can't keep protecting me at all costs. I've become your handicap. With everything you're facing, you simply can't afford it."

His lips twitched. "I'll worry about that, thank you very much."

"Think about it," she insisted. "In the very least, you should sedate me, like the Magister suggested. If nothing else, it should prevent these kinds of outbursts."

"Can you try to control them?"

"I… I don't know." She looked away briefly. "Hell, half the time I'm not even sure my thoughts are all coming from my own head. Just now, I spoke a strange bloody language. I *attacked* you, for Shal Addim's sake. What would have happened if you and Lance weren't right here to subdue me?"

His eyes stirred with a gentleness that made her shiver. "I guess from now on I'll just have to make sure I am always next to you."

"What if I hurt you next time?"

"Not likely."

She heaved a deep breath. This seemed like no solution at all. With time, he was bound to realize it too. But it was also clear they wouldn't be able to decide anything now, with everyone watching. She would have to talk to him again in private to convince him. Maybe when they returned to their party Egey Bashi could help her case? He was seemingly the only one whose decisions were not dominated so heavily by emotions and feelings.

She glanced at the Majat standing around them, so still that they appeared inanimate. Her eyes briefly met Lance's, but she saw no support there. *He's loyal to Mai. They all are, no matter what.* This was definitely a good thing, from the Guild's standpoint. Yet, how could she possibly stay around, knowing that her mere existence was jeopardizing Mai's command and was likely going to bring about their defeat?

She looked further to the group of men in Bengaw livery who had originally apprehended her. They looked frightened. Yet, they stood their ground, apparently resolved to carry out their orders to the last.

"Who are they?" she asked.

"Their lord is an old acquaintance," Mai said.

She raised her eyebrows, too many questions rising in her head. One day, she hoped to learn how Mai, whose life had been spent entirely in the open, could possibly have acquired an old acquaintance on this side of the Lakes – let alone one who was apparently willing to risk lives to help Mai's cause.

"How did they find me so quickly?" she asked.

"They patrol the lake every day. I calculated your possible routes and the distance you could have traveled on foot, and relayed the information by hawks. Several patrols were involved, but these men found you first."

She only shook her head. Despite everything,

she felt so relieved to see Mai. She thought just this morning that she would never see him again. Thinking of betraying him had been unbearable. And now, she was grateful that all the important decisions could be postponed, at least for the time being.

Mai beckoned for the local men to approach. "I didn't have a chance to thank you properly. You've done an exemplary job, and I am deeply grateful for your help." He glanced at the fallen horse Kara tried to use for her escape, then signaled to one of the Jades, who counted out coins from a small bag. "I hope this gold can compensate for the loss of your mount."

The men bowed, but made no move to take the money.

"Are you Aghat Mai?" their leader asked.

"Yes."

"Lord Garet gave us special instructions. We are to aid you with everything we can, including our lives. I'm certain it wouldn't go well with him if we took money from you."

Mai smiled. "Lord Garet is most kind. But I'm sure I can persuade him to change his mind."

The men bowed. "With all due respect, I doubt it, Aghat. Lord Garet was very insistent. He also asked us to relay a message. He is on his way here, in the hope to personally bid you his greetings."

Mai briefly inclined his head. "My men are setting camp near the port. It would be an honor to welcome Lord Garet as my guest."

Kara watched, wide-eyed. Who in the world was this Lord Garet, the man that apparently commanded such an enormous influence in these parts? And how did he and Mai know each other so closely? She glanced at

Mai with question, but he merely smiled in response.

"We didn't bring a horse for you," Mai told her. "You'll have to ride with me." He mounted and reached down to help her up in front of him.

Their party kept to a slow trot over the newly formed trail that marked the Majat comings and goings. Kara kept her eyes half-closed, leaning back against Mai's chest, enjoying his closeness and the absence of pain in her head. She and Mai rode in the front, and she knew that as soon as they arrived at camp all eyes would be on both of them. She wanted to save the strength for the show.

She had no idea what was happening to her. For the moment, her Kaddim link seemed dormant, but she knew she could never trust her own judgment after the absurd decision she had made today. Something was changing inside her – the way she had passed out and gone berserk without a visible reason, the way her head throbbed every time she tried to still her mind. Worse, the frightening visions she saw simply wouldn't leave her head. Were the voices she heard in her unconscious state, the sight of the man rotting alive, truly coming from the Kaddim fortress? Were these visions related to the man who was controlling her link?

Her heart raced. She knew that with every passing moment she was becoming more and more of a tool, a weapon that could bring about the downfall of the Majat. Worse, she seemed powerless to do anything at all about it.

# 13
# SOUTHERN LORD

Kyth's knees weakened with relief as he watched the Majat ride into the camp. Kara looked calm as she sat on the horse in front of Mai, so close to him that every inch of their bodies seemed to touch, his arm clasped possessively around her waist. She seemed unharmed. Yet, Kyth noticed the disarray in her clothes, the stems of grass tangled into her hair, as if she had been rolling over the ground in a fight. Mai's clothes showed rips and stains too, as well as Lance's. Did they have to fight and subdue her? Or did they encounter something else? Kyth knew he probably would never know. At least Kara didn't act like a captive, indicating that her return to camp was unlikely to have been achieved by force. Kyth dismissed his doubts, focusing instead on his relief at seeing her, on her calmness and grace as she dismounted, on the smiles she exchanged with her fellow Majat lined up to greet them near the command tent. Mai leaned forward and said something to the Emerald guards at the entrance, then led her inside.

Kyth turned to Ellah and Alder, bustling around a simmering pot hanging over the fire. Smells of spices wafting his way reminded him of his childhood in the Forestlands. Mistress Marfa back in Swamptown Inn used to cook this mushroom soup, spiced with ginger, mint, and pine tips. Now that they found all the ingredients, abundant on this side of the lakes, he hoped they could finally get the recipe right.

He tried to concentrate on the meal, but his thoughts kept returning to Kara. Before their recent breakup, it would have been his prerogative to be the first to greet and comfort her. And now, she didn't even glance his way as she entered the Majat command tent. More, despite her outward calmness, he couldn't get rid of the feeling that something was off about her. Perhaps it was the way several Diamonds crowded behind her, as if she needed the top skilled guards to watch, rather than protect her? Or was it the way Mai's words sent one of his Emerald guards running through the camp to bring over Magister Egey Bashi? The frown on the Keeper's face as he followed the guard to the command tent made Kyth's heart race in alarm.

He glanced at Ellah who had turned away from the cooking and was also watching the scene intently. "Did Kara seem all right to you just now?"

"Outwardly, yes," Ellah said. "But I sensed a lot of uncertainty from everyone around her."

"Uncertainty about what?"

Ellah sighed. "I know it's hard not knowing, Kyth, but you must trust that they will tell you when they can."

*Like hell they will.* Kyth lifted his chin. He was a prince, and formally one of the leaders of this march, with men under his command and a crucial part to play in the upcoming battle. He could grudgingly understand

Mai's reluctance to share extra information where Kara was involved, but like it or not, Kyth cared too, and Mai knew it very well. If the Majat felt uncomfortable about it, too bad for him.

Kyth abruptly rose to his feet and strode toward the command tent.

"Where are you going?" Alder called after him, but Kyth ignored him.

Light steps rustled behind him as Ellah hurried to follow. Alder made a move to go as well, but apparently thought better of it and returned to his cooking.

Two Emeralds guarding the tent exchanged uncertain glances as Kyth and Ellah approached. Kyth looked past them and raised his head haughtily, lifting the door flap to step inside.

It took a moment for his eyes to adjust to the semidarkness and take in the scene. Kara was seated cross-legged in the center of the tent, with Egey Bashi kneeling beside her next to his medicine pouch. The rest of the Majat formed a circle around them, watching the scene intently. Their gazes instantly locked on the newcomers with a nearly palpable threat. Kyth ignored all of them as he approached Kara and lowered to the floor beside her.

She seemed calm, but Kyth could see the paleness of her drawn face that made her brown skin seem grayish. Her weariness was visible in the drooping set of her shoulders, in the way her eyes seemed unfocused as she stared into the distance. The taint of the Kaddim power was unmistakable on her. Kyth sensed it as an aftertaste, a lingering scent of burning in the air.

"Are you all right?" he asked.

Her face held a mix of dismissal and uncertainty,

covered by a mask of calmness. "Do you sense it on me?"

"Yes."

She nodded, as if Kyth had just acknowledged a well known fact. Her eyes briefly darted to Mai, tense like a tightly coiled spring as he watched the conversation. Kyth smirked inwardly. *Don't like me sitting closer to her than you? Well, now you know how I feel all the time.* He willed himself to look away, not to meet the challenge in Mai's gaze. Even with all the resentment he felt, this wasn't the time for a cock fight.

The tent flap lifted again, a beam of sunlight momentarily cutting through the gloom. A young Majat warrior slid inside and said something to Mai in a hushed voice. Mai flicked a hand sign, which sent his entire Diamond entourage out of the tent.

"We're about to have company," Mai said. He wasn't looking at anyone in particular when he said it, but Kyth felt the need to respond.

"Who?"

"A local lord."

"Is he the one you asked for help this morning?"

"Yes."

"How do you know him?"

Mai tossed his head impatiently, but his answer came out level. "An old acquaintance."

Kyth looked at him in disbelief. Mai was only six years older than Kyth, hardly old enough to have any "old" acquaintances.

"Aren't you going to tell us anything about him?" Kara asked.

Mai's impatient look made Kyth feel like an intruder. "I worked for him on my first assignment."

Kyth looked away. He hated how this simple statement seemed to clarify everything to Kara, while only raising more questions in Kyth's own mind.

"I assume this lord has a name," he said.

"Lord Garet von Eyvern."

*Von Eyvern.* The name seemed familiar, even if Kyth did wish right now that he had been more attentive in his classes on the political situation in the south. To his memory the prefix "von" came from Bengaw and meant something important among their nobility. He also remembered hearing that the Eyverns were obscenely rich and influential, which made them operate more like the allies of the Tallan Dar king than the direct subordinates they were supposed to be. He wasn't sure he was comfortable with the idea of meeting one of them out here in the near-wilderness with only a minor military force to his own name. But worse, the fact that Mai apparently had a close connection with the man, enough not only to expect personal favors but to also have the lord go to some lengths to seek an audience, made him feel even more uncomfortable. Up to now he had been trusting Mai unconditionally when it came to his personal safety. But now, for the first time in this campaign, he found himself questioning the wisdom of it.

Another Majat entered the tent, flicking silent hand signs. Mai and Kara rose to their feet in near unison.

"He's here." Mai flung his formal Guildmaster's cloak over his shoulders and strode to the tent entrance.

After a hesitation, Kyth fell into step beside him. Ellah shuffled her feet to keep closer to Kyth's shoulder.

"Mai is telling the truth," she said quietly, only for the Prince to hear. "He hasn't tried to hide anything from you. He did seem annoyed at some point, but I didn't sense any problems, not even a hesitation."

Kyth felt only partially relieved. Until recently, Ellah had a crush on Mai, which precluded her from sensing the truth where Mai was concerned. She had since overcome these feelings – or so he believed. Yet, Kyth felt he could never fully trust Ellah's gift when it came to Mai.

After the semidarkness of the tent, the sunlight outside seemed blinding. With narrowed eyes, Kara watched a large group of riders at the edge of the camp, their black cloaks adorned with silver embroideries of the crossed sabers – a lavish choice of thread that sharply contrasted the practicality of the rest of their outfits. Lord Gareth must be very rich, which made the fact that he was willing to ride an extra distance to meet with Mai even more unusual. Was he expecting a major favor in return for his help in apprehending Kara? The thought lingered at the back of her mind as she watched the lord dismount and approach Mai in long strides.

Lord Garet looked to be in his late forties, a wiry man with a long, expressive face. His piercing gray eyes sank into deeply etched lines that started underneath his bushy eyebrows and linked with other creases and clefts all the way to his mouth. They crinkled as he talked, as if harboring a smile. Watching him, the way he looked over Mai with father-like pride, forced down some of Kara's worries. He seemed to be genuinely pleased at this reunion.

"Aghat Mai!" Lord Garet extended his arms for an embrace, but the Majat of Mai's suite closed around him protectively, forcing a change to a long handshake instead.

Kara smiled at the lord's perplexed expression. Mai's guards knew their jobs. An embrace made it too easy to sneak an attack – an unallowable risk for a man as important as the Majat Guildmaster.

"It's a joy to see you, Lord Garet," Mai said. He too was smiling, piquing Kara's curiosity. Mai must have been in his teens during his assignment for this lord, a boy young enough to be his son. What kind of a bond could these two possibly develop?

Lord Garet stepped back and ran another appraising glance at Mai. "A Guildmaster, eh? I always said you were destined for greatness. And, you've grown even more attractive, if you would forgive the old man for saying it."

Mai laughed, and Kara was surprised to see his cheeks light up with a faint blush. *More attractive?* She felt more and more curious.

"Please accept my utmost gratitude, Lord Garet, for the help your men provided to me this morning," Mai said. "Their service was exemplary."

Lord Garet shook his head. "No trouble at all, Aghat Mai. I was glad to be of assistance in recovering your, um, missing companion." His sharp eyes sought out Kara, and over all this distance she imagined she saw him wink.

She kept her face impassive, stepping away deeper into the crowd of the Majat as she watched Mai introduce Lord Garet to the rest of the command group. Kyth was watching the lord with a guarded expression that made her wonder. She assumed Lord Garet was a vassal to the crown, but here in the wilderness these loyalties seemed distant compared to the day-to-day reality. Was Kyth feeling threatened by the lord? She hoped not, yet she couldn't blame the Prince for his insecurity. His main protection on this march came from the Majat, and the way he and Mai kept arguing every time she was around didn't help at all.

The procession moved toward a large area set with logs and blankets around a large campfire. She slid between Lance and Raishan, doing her best to keep a low profile.

Mai settled into his seat with the ease that made the log he was sitting on seem as relaxing as a soft armchair. Lord Garet clearly did not share the same ability to blend into any surroundings. He winced as he shifted around to find a more comfortable spot, smiling with gratitude as one of Mai's guards offered him a rolled-up blanket as an additional cushion.

"Forgive us for being unable to offer you the comforts you are accustomed to, my lord," Mai said.

Lord Garet smiled. "Think nothing of it, Aghat Mai. Sharing the simple joys of a campsite meal surely brings back memories, eh?"

Mai's smile mirrored the lord's, his eyes gleaming with merry sparkles.

"I've heard of your current campaign against the Kaddim Brotherhood, Aghat Mai," Lord Garet said.

Mai went still, a barely perceptible change that did not erase the easygoing smile from his face. Only those familiar with him could tell how surprised he was at this statement. "You have? How, if I may ask?"

"I have my sources."

Mai glanced around the assembly. "I suppose we haven't made a big secret of it. Everyone by now must have heard of our last battle. But I must say, I didn't expect the news of our march to precede us."

Lord Garet smiled. "Oh, they didn't precede you, Aghat Mai. I made inquiries only this morning, after I received your request for help."

"Still. Your sources must have been exceptionally well informed to make the connection so quickly."

"Indeed they are. But I can give you my assurance that the news will spread no further than this gathering – unless you want it to, for any reason."

"I appreciate it, Lord Garet," Mai said. "In our march, we are not exactly counting on a surprise, but I prefer to be the one calling the shots."

"Of course." Lord Garet laughed. "Some things never change, do they?"

Mail laughed too, his look stirring up with the warmth of a shared memory. Kara hoped to be able to learn the story one day.

The food arrived, travel rations of smoked meat and dry flatbread creatively mixed with fresh vegetables and herbs that must have come from the local market. The apple brew served with the meal went to the head far too quickly, but Kara gulped it down anyway. With all the excitement of today she had managed to completely neglect food. And now, she devoured her meal as she listened to the conversation.

"Apart from the pleasure of seeing you again, Aghat Mai," Lord Garet said, "my visit has another purpose. I'm here to offer you any help you need in your campaign."

A smile briefly touched the corners of Mai's mouth. "I am grateful for this, Lord Garet. But as a friend I must warn you that it's not something to say lightly.

Not to a Majat Guildmaster."

"I would never say this lightly, Aghat Mai. Especially not to you." Lord Garet pecked at a stem of basil on his plate, then put a strip of meat into his mouth and chewed thoughtfully. "I also harbor no illusions about the way my military force compares to yours. Being a realistic man, I will not insult you by offering my troops. I believe I have something better to offer."

Mai looked at him with silent question.

"Perhaps you still remember from our prior acquaintance how I came by all my wealth?"

"Yes, I do," Mai said slowly.

"The mine on my lands supplies no less than half of the kingdom's Algarian-grade ore. Chances are, some of your Guild's recent weapons are forged from the steel we produce. I know one could never have enough. So, here's my offer. For this campaign, we'll give you as much as you need."

Mai lifted his head. "When you say 'give', you mean–"

"Give freely, without expecting anything in return."

Mai hesitated. "This is a generous offer, Lord Garet. Especially after the favor you already did for me today."

Lord Garet chuckled. "What happened this morning was nothing, really. No more than a small distraction for my men from the boredom of their daily patrolling duties."

Mai held his gaze. "It was more than that, Lord Garet. Your men risked their lives. And, they also lost a horse."

Lord Garet waved his hand dismissively. "Think nothing of it, Aghat Mai. It was my pleasure to help."

"I appreciate it, Lord Garet," Mai said. "And, as a

friend, I feel obliged to tell you that your men's help today meant more to me than you could possibly imagine."

Once again, Lord Garet glanced at Kara with curiosity. This time, she didn't try to hide as she returned his gaze. She felt dumbfounded. Mai had just publicly acknowledged that her return meant more to him than free supply of the Algarian-grade weapons, a resource some kingdoms would go to war over. She noticed Raishan's smile, and Seldon's deep frown, followed by a stir among the Diamonds that died out at Mai's quick look.

Lord Garet observed the activity with amusement. "As I said, Aghat Mai, while the knowledge that my men's service to you has been satisfactory fills me with joy beyond measure, it meant nothing to me. What you are setting out to do is far greater than simple favors like this. Besides, I would be an ungrateful man if I did not acknowledge that I owe you not only all my wealth, but also my life."

"You owe me no gratitude, my lord," Mai said. "You've paid for my services in full. The Majat Guild holds no debt to your name."

The lord shifted in his seat, his face crinkling with laughter as he took a long swig of brew from his mug. "I'm sure you know, Aghat Mai, that some kinds of debt can never be repaid."

"I wouldn't say such a thing to a Majat Guildmaster, Lord Garet."

"Just like the Majat Guildmaster probably should not have said all those things just now to a wealthy lord offering his help, Aghat Mai. It is good that we are talking merely as friends, isn't it?"

Mai grinned as he glanced at Kara. She felt a warmth run down her spine as she met his gaze. *He said all this for me. He wanted me, and everyone else listening, to know how much I mean to him.* The fact that by making this confession he was also risking an offer of unimaginable wealth filled her with concern. Yet, Lord Garet's reaction, his expression as he continued to look at her thoughtfully, told her that the nobleman understood this too, and that his offer wasn't going to change because of Mai's words. They were lucky to have such an ally, and she knew that nearly everyone here – except Seldon, perhaps – trusted Mai to achieve the best in this conversation.

"Let's get down to business, Aghat Mai," Lord Garet said. "My sources informed me that while your own people are sufficiently outfitted, you are leading an allied force that may as yet grow in numbers and is significantly inferior to the Majat in weapons."

"Among other things," Mai said.

Lord Garet's brisk nod looked very businesslike. "I feel fortunate to have resources at my disposal to supply them with top grade weapons, including Prince Kythar's men and any new allies you may recruit on the way. If time permits, I will send a delivery wherever you need me to."

Mai held his gaze. "This offer is more generous than a king's, my lord."

Lord Garet's brief smile spoke of how pleased he felt. "Consider it a personal gift. You may, of course, keep the weapons after your army emerges victorious – as I expect will be the case."

"I can only wish our enemies share the same expectations, my lord," Mai said. "In fact, this type of thinking could save us all worlds of trouble."

Lord Garet chuckled as he reached into his pocket and produced a folded parchment glinting with an elegantly engraved seal.

"If you use this paper to send your message, Aghat Mai, anyone on the western side of the Forestlands, from here to Bengaw, will follow your bidding."

Mai reached over and took the parchment.

"I accept your generous offer, Lord Garet," he said, "only because of the dire need to defeat the Kaddim as soon as we possibly can. I hope, when this is all over, we can repay you."

The lord waved his hand in dismissal. "No need, Aghat Mai. I'm sure you've been hearing this a lot, but seeing you in charge of the Majat Guild for the first time in years puts my mind at ease. I cannot imagine a better man for the job."

Mai's lips twitched. "I hope I won't disappoint anybody by the end of the campaign."

He did not look at Kara this time, but his words sent her heart racing nonetheless. She was his weakness. Her predicament made him vulnerable and threatened their entire army. *Dear Shal Addim, how did I get myself into such a mess?*

"I have another piece of information to share with you," Lord Garet said. "The southeastern border of my lands neighbors the Forestlands. For days now, my men have been speaking of unrest in the area."

"Unrest?" Mai lifted his chin, his tense look making Kara wonder. Did he know something she didn't about the Forestlands? Was this rural area part of his plans?

The answer came too easily, making her skin creep. *The spiders.* She felt a surge of panic, and then hope. If their path was going to take them near the Forestlands, the local spiders would surely detect the Kaddim's magic on her, even if Alder's spiders had somehow become desensitized. They would finish the job, even if she couldn't do it herself. Won't they?

"The trees are restless. Moving, if you know what I mean." Lord Garet ran his eyes around the gathering, and Kara noticed how everyone sprang to alertness, confirming her guesses. They must have stakes on the Forestlands, part of the plans that were never shared with her before departure.

"My land's borders," Lord Garet went on, "have become much more densely overgrown in the last few days. Some of the trees look ancient, as if planted centuries ago, but we all know it not to be the case. So far they haven't crossed any boundaries, but I know for a fact that if you ride south from here for about a day, you may find yourselves in some of the thickest woods you've ever imagined. I'm not sure how avoidable it is, but I hope this information may help you choose your best route."

"Any suggestions, Lord Garet?" Mai asked.

"Depending on where you're headed."

"South." Mai threw a tense glance at Kara.

*I'm not supposed to hear any of this.* She moved to rise, but he stopped her with a short gesture.

"I assume, further south than the Forestlands," Lord Garet said.

"Yes."

"I can offer you passage through my lands. Along with my hospitality, if you're in need of it. But if my guesses about your destination are correct, this may take you too much out of your way."

Mai chuckled. "You do seem to know a lot about our plans, my lord."

"Only privately, Aghat Mai. I assure you, no enemies will learn of your plans from me."

"What about your sources?"

"They're loyal to House von Eyvern."

Mai smiled, his eyes meeting Lord Garet's with affection that spoke of the true friendship these men shared. "Good enough for me."

Lord Garet rose to his feet. "Now that it's all settled, I'm afraid I must take my leave. It has been a true pleasure, Guildmaster."

"Likewise." Mai rose too, exchanging a hearty handshake with the older man. "I hope some day I can find a way to repay your generosity."

The lord patted him on the shoulder. "You will repay it by defeating the Kaddim, Aghat Mai. If they win, I stand to lose all my wealth. I cannot possibly afford it."

"We'll do our best," Mai assured.

Kara kept her place between Lance and Raishan as she watched the lord mount his horse, with his suite gathering around him.

"I wonder what Aghat Mai's assignment for Lord Garet was like, to merit all this," Lance said quietly as he watched the guests depart.

He wasn't looking at anyone in particular as he said this. Even though the same question was probably on everyone's mind, no one should have felt obliged to answer. Yet, to Kara's surprise, Seldon cleared his throat and spoke, equally matter-of-factly.

"I'm certain, Aghat Lance, you remember Aghat Mai's signature blow, the viper's sting." He glanced at Kara. She felt an unpleasant tingle at her neck and forcibly kept herself from touching the spot. That fatal blow at the base of the throat resembled a very similar but harmless one, enabling Mai to fool the Guild into believing she was dead and averting her execution on orders of their previous Guildmaster. Like everyone in the Guild, she heard that inventing those blows made Mai instantly famous, right at the time he had received his Diamond ranking.

"It was during Lord Garet's assignment that Aghat Mai first demonstrated it in action," Seldon said. "Before that, no one believed it would actually work. Afterwards..." He spread his hands in a wordless gesture.

Many heads nodded. However, Kara still couldn't quite understand it. Such things mattered only to the Majat. It was hard to imagine how Lord Garet's friendship with Mai could have been sealed by something like this.

"I am not privy to all the details of that assignment," Seldon went on, "but as I heard it, that blow enabled Aghat Mai to dispose of the man who kept these lands in terror and had a claim on Lord Garet's entire estate, without losing any other lives. Von Eyverns do owe everything to this assignment, even if their gratitude should really be directed not at Aghat Mai personally, but at our whole Guild."

Kara understood what he meant. The Majat Guild was the one who planned the assignments and selected the best warriors to match each job. Yet, in Lord Garet's place, it was probably hard not to feel grateful personally to Mai for performing his assignment so well.

"Is it true that Aghat Mai was only eighteen at the time?" Lance asked.

"He was," Seldon said. "One of the most troublesome young trainees we ever had at the Guild. The fact not known to many was that due to the unique nature of Lord Garet's assignment, Aghat Mai was sent to fulfill it before he was officially ranked."

"*Before*?" Lance stared, his surprise reflected in every face nearby.

"Yes. Aghat Mai's youthful looks – as well as his, um, attractiveness – made him uniquely suited for the job. From what I heard, the warlord had a weakness for young boys, which proved to be the only way to gain access to his private chambers. I'm not privy to all the details, of course."

Kara looked at him thoughtfully. It now made sense why Lord Garet referred to Mai's looks when they first met. Mai was her senior by five years or so, and she still remembered him in his teens, the iconic boy all women swooned over, too slender and innocent-looking to fit the image of the ruthless killer the Majat were training him to be. She could see how encountering Mai at that time could have been deceiving to an outsider who didn't see him on the practice range every day and didn't witness the brutal strength Mai was capable of.

She wondered why Seldon felt it necessary just now to divulge the details of an assignment not normally shared among the Majat. Was he trying to paint Mai differently from the way his men saw him?

Was this part of Seldon's plan to discredit Mai's command?

She needed to have a conversation with Seldon – and soon.

# 14

# UNDER GUARD

The Diamonds dissipated after Lord Garet's departure, but Raishan stayed behind, stepping up to Kara with decisive finality. She guessed his discomfort by the way he averted his gaze, as if his presence here wasn't entirely voluntary.

"Are you tasked with guarding me again, Aghat Raishan?" she asked.

Raishan nodded. "I'm afraid so, yes. By Aghat Mai's orders it has to be a Diamond from now on, at all times. We all received a dire warning. Apparently, when they found you this morning, you put up a fight?"

She rubbed her sore arm, grateful for the long sleeves that hid the bruises. "I temporarily lost control of my actions, I'm afraid."

"Apparently it took considerable effort to apprehend you."

*Two Diamonds.* She swallowed. "When I woke up, they'd already subdued me. I don't remember any of it." *Except the smell.* She wrinkled her nose, the scent of milk of thorn lodged there seemingly permanently. The plant it came from looked so innocent. Who would know that its juice, when extracted in a correct way, would be so potent?

Raishan's lips twitched. "Let's hope nothing like this would be necessary again. My only intention is to stay out of your way as much as possible. Unless, of course, you'd rather I kept you company."

She watched Seldon's retreating back as he headed to a small campfire at the edge of the camp. He was alone, affording an excellent opportunity for a conversation.

"Your company is always welcome, Aghat Raishan," she said. "But I do have some business I'd like to see to first. Do you think you could, um, stay out of the way while Aghat Seldon and I have a word?"

Raishan lifted his eyebrows. "Are you planning to reprimand him for insubordination?"

"That too, yes. He had no business divulging excessive details about Mai's early assignments, even if Lance was the one who started the conversation."

Raishan's eyes trailed after Seldon too. "He hasn't crossed the line yet, but a couple of times he has treaded dangerously close to it. Keeping him around is putting Aghat Mai into a precarious position."

Kara shrugged. "At least, Aghat Seldon and I share this quality, if nothing else. But we can't have him do anything to jeopardize Mai's command."

"He will not."

"I certainly hope so, if only for his own sake."

"Are you planning to threaten him?"

"If I have to."

"But–"

"Look, I already have a reputation of being so unstable that I need a Diamond guard with me at all times. At the very least, this gives me an excuse."

A quick smile slid over Raishan's lips. "Very well. I'll stay beside that tree over there. I will rejoin you as soon as your conversation is over. If you need me at any point, just wave."

She smiled. "Thank you, Aghat Raishan."

Seldon sat up straight, watching her approach. He didn't seem surprised. In fact, his guarded look told her he was expecting a confrontation. Against reason, she felt relieved. No point in wasting any time on pleasantries.

"I need a word with you, Aghat Seldon," she said.

The Diamond gestured to the campfire and sat down in a smooth, fluid move, not to be expected from a man of his age. Inadvertently, Kara remembered Lord Garet wincing just recently as he settled by the fire. He was probably younger than Seldon, yet not nearly as fit. Still, even with this prowess, at his age Seldon could never possibly measure up to her if it ever came to a fight. The same thought reflected in Seldon's eyes as he watched her apprehensively.

She sat across the fire from him.

"What you said about Aghat Mai just now," she said, "was out of line. With your seniority, you should know better."

Seldon frowned. "I wasn't aware that our Guild's affairs are any of your business."

"Anything that concerns Mai is very much my business, Aghat, whether you like it or not. As to our Guild's affairs, whether or not they are my business, I know enough about them to spot a problem when I see it. I am aware that your presence here was not part of Mai's plans. Why are you really here, Aghat?"

Seldon crossed his arms on his chest, and she

imagined she saw just a touch of smugness behind his outward impassiveness. "Last time I heard, Kara, you were not supposed to be privy to any plans."

*Kara.* He didn't use her rank, which told her where he believed he stood with her. She tried to tell herself that it didn't matter, but his contempt as he looked at her reached deeper than she liked to admit, even to herself.

"You are correct," she said. "If you noticed, I haven't *asked* you anything about plans. This conversation is meant as a warning. For now."

"A warning?"

"Yes."

"Are you threatening me?"

"You have nothing to fear from me, Aghat Seldon, as long as it remains clear to me you are not Mai's enemy."

Seldon lifted his chin. "You speak of enemies, but if you noticed, I'm not the one under guard." He glanced at Raishan leaning against a tree trunk at a distance, watching them.

"Point taken," she said. "And yes, I may not be always acting as myself. I am now, however, and while this is true, I wanted to make sure to tell you one more thing. If you as much as step the wrong way, you will have me to deal with. Please bear this in mind."

She rose to her feet before he could respond, rewarded by his hunted look. He was afraid of her, that was clear. And, he was possibly up to no good. Kara regretted not having thought of bringing Ellah along, so that she could know for sure when Seldon was telling the truth.

She was turning to go when Seldon's words stopped her in her tracks.

"Aghat Kara?"

She froze, then slowly turned to face him. Questions raced through her mind. Was he referring to her by her rank as a form of peace offering? Or did he have something else in mind?

"I know Aghat Mai quite well, ever since his training days," Seldon said. "And despite everything you have been thinking about my plotting against him, I do consider him to be a capable and talented commander. As such, I'm sure you realize that if he is ever faced with a choice, he would give you up without a flinch. It's a price we all pay for being the Majat."

She forced her face into a calm mask as she met his gaze, unwilling to show how much these words affected her. Seldon was right. Mai always did the right thing, and he put his responsibility to his men above all else. If she ever turned against him, she had no doubt where his loyalties would be. It was a good thing, she told herself firmly. She wouldn't want it any other way.

Seldon nodded knowingly as he watched her expression. "Aghat Mai's relationships with women were troublesome when he was still a trainee. We all hoped he'd overcome it after he achieved his ranking. He did, for the most part. I know he has encountered a challenge in you, due mostly to the fact you share the same training. But in the end it's still the same."

"It's not," she said. "But more importantly, this is not a topic I am ever going to discuss with you again, Aghat Seldon. Just remember everything I said."

She turned and strode away.

"How did it go?" Raishan asked, stepping up to her.

She shrugged, angry at herself for feeling so

flustered. "I think he got the message. We'll see if it changes anything."

"Where to now?" Raishan asked.

She pointed to another small campfire, where Magister Egey Bashi was sitting by himself, deeply submerged in a scroll rolled out over his lap.

"Mai may not approve of the conversation I must have with the Magister," she said. "But there are things I really need to know. It's up to your conscience, Aghat Raishan, if you want to join me on this one or stay away like before."

Raishan shook his head. "My charge did not involve controlling you or restricting your actions, Aghat Kara. I'm here to keep you safe. With this in mind, I'd rather stay close to you."

She didn't say anything as she turned and led the way to the campfire.

Egey Bashi put down his scroll, watching their approach. He did not show surprise or apprehension. Rather, his expression as he looked at Kara was that of deep interest, as if he encountered a worthy object for his scholarly studies. In a way she was, Kara reflected as she followed the unspoken invitation and lowered to a log near the fire.

"I have some questions for you, Magister," she said. "Ones that will not necessarily meet with Mai's approval."

Egey Bashi folded his arms over his lap, curling up into a more comfortable position.

"I am not Aghat Mai's subordinate," he said, his eyes sliding over Raishan sitting on the other side of the fire. He did not comment on the Diamond's presence, and Kara did not blame him. Of the three people present, Raishan was the only one who stood to lose if Mai had issues with her and the Magister having this conversation. Yet, she knew that Mai would probably appreciate Raishan listening to what they had to say, rather than being excluded with no knowledge of the topics discussed.

"My link," Kara said. "You mentioned once that death can sever it. Mai told me later that you have information to the contrary, but I'm afraid I didn't take it seriously – a mistake which led to the recent ordeal. Mai said that he forbade you to speak to me about it, but I need to hear it from you, one way or the other."

Egey Bashi's eyes briefly dropped to the scroll he had set aside. "It's not that simple, Aghat, and my research is taking more time than we have, mostly due to the need to decipher some of the languages I am really not that good at. It's true that killing – either you, or the man who controls the link on the Kaddim side – would sever the bond. Yet, apparently, the killing has to be done in a proper way to work."

"Proper way?"

"I'm still researching this. From what I've learned, it's a bit of a ritual, one where the death itself needs to be drawn out into a process, rather than an act. I'm not sure how it works, not yet."

Kara could have guessed things had to be more complicated than she believed, even if her mind still refused to enfold the information. Inadvertently, the image from her recent vision floated up in her mind. *Two men spread on the stone platform.* Did she have to do this too, to embrace a man rotting alive and share his agony?

"What if it's done improperly?"

Egey Bashi sighed. "That's where it becomes complicated."

"Complicated, how?"

"A simple death, without the formalities observed, can release one's entire soul, including all the special abilities and knowledge, into the other's mind. If your Kaddim counterpart were to be killed in battle, you would acquire all his skills instantly – except that, of course, his resurrection would revert that and renew the link. But if you were the one to perish, your death would instantly empower our enemies with all your abilities. I don't know the extent of it yet, not for sure, but if it's true, this actually makes your life even more precious to us than we all knew before. We can't possibly afford to risk it at all."

Kara let out a breath, feeling as if the ground was spinning from under her feet. To think that she nearly succeeded in killing herself today, just because of not taking Mai's words seriously enough. Or was this, too, part of the Kaddim plan?

"There's more, Magister," she said. "When I decided to take the matters into my own hands and kill myself, I…" she hesitated. How could she possibly say it out loud? "I… have reasons to believe the idea did not come from my own head. The fact that Mai told me about the danger of it and I did not believe him is only one illustration of it."

Egey Bashi shifted in his seat. "If my information is correct, the Kaddim stand a lot to gain by your death, don't they?"

"They certainly do." Why wouldn't the hollow feeling in her stomach go away? "And, there's something else."

"Something else?"

"Thinking clearer now, I am aware that I could have easily slit my own throat, or stabbed myself in the heart, with everyone watching. With my training, I know of so many ways to kill a person without any possibility of a remedy that I shouldn't have even given it a second thought. Yet, I consciously discounted such a method. I felt very driven to get as far away as possible before doing it. This was what enabled Mai to capture me." This, and the fact that he had friends in unexpected places. She thought back to Lord Garet, to the way he looked at Mai like a long-lost son. Mai had a talent for leaving deep impressions in everyone. And he loved her. How could she ever think of acting behind his back?

Unbidden, Seldon's words floated up in her mind. *He would give you up without a flinch.* In a twisted way, she hoped this was true. She was becoming a burden, one that apparently wasn't even easy to get rid of. She would never allow herself to become Mai's downfall.

"What exactly were you afraid of when you decided you needed to get as far away as possible?" Egey Bashi asked.

She swallowed. "Of someone reviving me. I thought of your elixir, of how it can heal deadly wounds nearly instantly. I also thought of other Keepers' cures you may have, ones you haven't even had a chance to use on any of us. Common folks always whisper that the Keepers can bring back the dead." She paused, trying to compose herself. "I cannot be certain, Magister, but if we assume the Kaddim have been driving me at the time, I believe I must have been worried about resurrection."

In the stunned silence she saw Raishan's narrowed

eyes as he watched her, so still that he seemed inanimate like a statue. She knew how bad it sounded, even if rolling this thought over and over in her head was probably even worse. And if true, this sealed the information she already suspected but never had a chance to confirm until now. The Kaddim were in her thoughts, which meant she couldn't be trusted to make any decisions or learn any information at all.

Every time she used her skill, however briefly, the Kaddim were gaining part of it to benefit their warriors. And, there was no way to break this stalemate, unless they could get to the Kaddim before it was too late.

The enormity of the situation was just beginning to dawn on her. Regardless of his feelings for her, Mai had no choice but to rush to the Kaddim's fortress as fast as he could. But with the amount of time it was likely going to take, there was no possibility for him to arrive there faster than the Kaddim needed to steal her gift.

Mai and his Majat army were headed for slaughter. And there was no power in the world capable to avert it.

# 15
# GIRL TALK

"Any more conversations planned for today?" Raishan asked.

Kara shook her head, but before she could speak, a movement between the tents caught her eye. Lady Celana was striding toward her, calm and confident as if this busy camp was part of her father's court. She wore a loose white dress, her flaming red hair tied into a bundle at the back of her head. Ellah hurried in her wake, clearly nervous at the heads turning their way.

The two girls approached Kara and stopped in front of her.

Kara sighed. She normally did not mind Ellah's company, if only because the girl's truthsense tended to simplify all conversations, putting everything into a clear perspective. But Lady Celana was different, a born politician to whom evasions and half-truths were as natural as breathing. Kara knew Celana saw her as a rival. As the royal lady measured her with a calm, unhurried glance, Kara couldn't help wishing she was somewhere else.

She knew Kyth wasn't over her yet, no matter how

clear she tried to be about her lack of romantic feelings for him. She couldn't do much about it, but she still felt guilty. Kyth was a sensitive man with a pure heart. He deserved better than someone like Kara, whose warrior upbringing made her so different from a normal girl, even if she could look like one to an untrained eye. Inside, she was not just a ruthless killer, but one of the best at her job. Even when she had believed that she shared his feelings, she also knew she could never give him what he needed. Lady Celana, on the other hand, seemed like a perfect match for Kyth – both in her political station, as the heiress of the second oldest royal house in the kingdom, and in the way she obviously cared about the Prince.

The challenge in the royal lady's gaze made Kara feel affronted. She had her own problems to deal with. She couldn't do anything about the past, could she? She was about to say this, when Celana's words caught her by surprise.

"There's a small lake behind those bushes," Celana said. "Aghat Mai ordered it off limits for half an hour, to give us privacy. Would you like to join us for a swim?"

Kara slowly let out a sigh. A swim. It did sound good after a day of running and fighting. She was surprised, though, that Lady Celana thought of including Kara, whose fighting skill, the way she trained with the rest of the warriors, always made the ladies treat her like one of the men. A private swim, away from everyone's scrutinizing eyes, would be so nice.

She glanced at Raishan with question.

"I'm not sure Aghat Mai would approve of this," Raishan said.

Lady Celana folded her arms over her chest, an

amused smile playing on her lips. "Perhaps, Aghat Raishan, Ellah and I could take over your guarding job, just briefly?"

Raishan returned her gaze impassively. "I can name many reasons, my lady, why this couldn't possibly work. However, perhaps a solution could be found. What if I stay nearby – with my back turned – to get there instantly if something goes wrong?"

Kara hesitated. She should refuse, she knew. She shouldn't put both Raishan and the girls into this uncomfortable situation. Yet, the offer sounded so tempting. Was there really any harm in doing it quickly?

"Thank you, Aghat Raishan," she said. "I really appreciate it."

Lady Celana threw another amused glance at Raishan as he fell into stride in their wake, staying far enough behind them not to intrude on their privacy, but close enough to catch up at any sign of danger.

Feeling like a nuisance, Kara followed the girls to a secluded spot among the reeds and quickly took off her clothes. She tried to ignore the side glances her companions threw at her as she stepped into the water, quickly submerging and swimming ahead with swift strokes to clear her head.

The water felt warm and soothing, so different from early this morning when she had to spend a long time out in the open lake searching for escape. It felt so good to relax, to flip over on her back and float, taking in the surroundings as the clear, brownish water caressed and supported her tired limbs. Low sunbeams licked her dark skin with long, fiery tongues. She could hear the other two girls splashing near the shore, laughing and talking in discreetly muffled voices. Discussing her?

She didn't really care.

It may have been more polite to stay closer to them. They did invite her to share their swim, after all. Yet, she knew it was no use. These girls would never accept her as one of their own. Definitely not now, when the Kaddim's mind link made everyone shun and avoid her.

The sun rolled down toward the horizon, slowly sinking into the distance. Regretfully, Kara flipped over and slowly swam back to shore. Back in the reed thicket, she quickly rubbed herself dry, aware of the other two girls watching her intently.

"Anything wrong with me?" she asked.

Lady Celana let out a short laugh. "We were curious," she admitted. "You have an amazing muscle tone, but shape-wise you don't look that different from other young girls. How could you possibly be so strong?"

Kara's eyes widened. Such frankness caught her by surprise.

"I guess I was born this way," she said.

"Still." Celana exchanged a quick glance with Ellah, who looked uncomfortable, studying Kara with quiet challenge. "We expected that up close you would look more like... like a man." Her face darkened with a blush in the gathering dusk.

Kara laughed. "Is this why you invited me for a bath? To take a closer look at me?"

"No," Celana said. "We invited you because it was a natural thing to do. There are only three of us – I mean, girls – on this trip. It's just that I... I couldn't quite contain my curiosity." She looked down briefly, as if embarrassed, but the way her eyes returned boldly to Kara's face suggested otherwise.

Kara watched her with interest. This royal lady was probably raised with people watching reverently while she followed her every whim. Any hint of embarrassment on her part seemed like a big step.

"Personally," Lady Celana went on, "I couldn't stop wondering how you could possibly have swept the two most important men in our party so completely off their feet."

*Here we go*. Kara glanced away to hide her irritation. The last thing she needed was a confrontation with her traveling companions over men. At the same time, if this were to be hanging between them for the rest of the trip, it seemed better to have this conversation sooner rather than later.

"Did seeing me naked up close answer your question?" she asked.

For the first time in her life she saw Celana look genuinely uncomfortable. "No. Except..."

"Except what?"

"You... You are very beautiful," the royal lady said quietly.

"So are you." Kara meant it. Even without the dramatic combination of green eyes, flaming red hair, and porcelain white skin, Lady Celana would have been considered a beauty. Her air of royal confidence definitely added to the effect.

"Thank you," Lady Celana said. "I am used to hearing that, of course – but not from someone like you."

"Someone like me?" Kara felt intrigued.

"You have nothing to gain by saying that."

Kara couldn't help but smile. To hear Celana speak with such open honesty was arresting. Unexpectedly she found this conversation refreshing, like the swim in the lake itself had been.

"I suppose not," she admitted. "So you must know I'm speaking the truth, don't you?"

"*I* do," Ellah said.

"Of course you do," Kara mumbled. "You're a truthseer." *And I'd do well to remember that.* Despite the civil tone, she knew when she was being confronted.

Celana tied her wet hair into a knot at the back of her head and smoothed away the loose fiery-red strands, keeping her eyes on Kara all the time. "So, beauty is clearly not the answer."

Kara chuckled. "Did you expect me to be different from you?"

"There is a difference between us, yes – one that, as I heard, men tend to find irresistible." Lady Celana's blush deepened. "You... You are experienced."

Kara lowered the knife belt she was about to slip on and looked at the royal lady in disbelief. "You think my sexual experience helps me seduce men?"

"Doesn't it?"

Kara sighed. "I don't seduce anyone on purpose. I never think of it, in fact."

"You seem to enjoy the effect, though."

"What do you mean?"

Celana held her gaze. "Every time you are around, Prince Kythar has eyes only for you. As if the rest of us are not even there."

Kara's lips twitched into a smile. "I don't do this on purpose, if that's what you mean... I would much rather he didn't."

Lady Celana looked into her face searchingly. "Really?"

"Yes."

"You have no interest in him?"

Kara's eyes widened. Could Celana seriously think Kara was interested in Kyth?

"No," she said.

The royal lady's shoulders sagged as she exhaled. A quick triumphant smile lit up her face.

Kara hesitated. Perhaps it was the darkness, but she suddenly couldn't read Celana at all. Did the lady think she just handed Kyth to her? Was she genuinely interested? Or did she see him merely as a tool for fulfilling her political ambitions?

"I have no romantic interest in him," Kara said distinctly. "I assume this was what you were asking. However, as a close friend, I want to see him find happiness. I would feel very personal if anyone hurt him for their own gain." Lady Celana lifted her chin. "You do care about him then?" The words sounded almost like an accusation.

"Yes," Kara said. "I do. As a friend. Which means, you are free to pursue your feelings for him – but only if you mean well. He is a good man who deserves happiness, not another heartbreak."

Once again, she felt amazed how the royal lady showed no disconcert at all. She merely nodded, as if receiving a simple piece of information.

"Thank you," she said. "That's all I wanted to know." She turned and walked away toward camp, her slim, elegant shape melting into the gathering dusk.

Kara turned to follow, but Ellah stepped forward, blocking her way. Kara lifted her eyes, surprised. Being a superb warrior she wasn't used to this, especially not from someone who wasn't even pretending to be proficient with weapons.

She looked at the girl with silent question.

"I do care about Kyth too," Ellah said softly. "As a friend. I'm sure you are aware that my friendship with him goes much further back than yours, and I know him much better than you do. What Lady Celana said was true. My heart bleeds too, every time I watch him looking your way."

Kara held her gaze. "If I could just disappear from his path, I'd be glad to. But, for better or worse, we are all stuck together until we finish off the Kaddim."

Ellah's sharp-featured face looked hazy in the darkness.

"I know you speak the truth," she said. "My gift tells me this much. I know Kyth wouldn't care for you if you weren't a good person. And Mai – he would never fall in love with you if you weren't worthy."

*Mai.* Kara lifted her eyebrows. To hear Ellah speak his name so tenderly, as if talking about a very close person, made her wonder. She was used by now to the way non-Majat often omitted warrior titles because they did not fully appreciate their significance. But the way Ellah spoke just now suggested more.

How did this girl become so familiar with Mai as to speak of his love life?

"Do you really think you know everyone so well?" It was hard to keep the sarcasm out of her voice.

Ellah shrugged. "I can tell if people truly mean what they say. It's eye-opening to realize how often this turns out not to be the case. My gift has told me one thing about Lady Celana. She may be hard to read at times, but her intentions are true. She loves Kyth. And, she could truly make him happy – if he lets her."

Kara forced her thoughts back to Kyth, away from

the way Ellah mentioned Mai's name, so matter-of-factly and yet with such deep interest in his feelings. It didn't take a truthseer to realize that there was more here than met the eye – at least on Ellah's part. She ached to know more. But she would be damned if she ever let these thoughts surface. Questioning Ellah about this would suggest that she doubted Mai, and nothing could be further from the truth. She loved him and she trusted him more than she trusted herself. Nothing in the world could ever change that.

"Lady Celana has nothing to worry about on my account," she said. "If she can make Kyth happy, I would feel deeply grateful to her."

"As long as you don't stand in the way," Ellah said.

"What do you mean?"

Ellah measured her with a long stare. "You have so many ways of being alluring to a man. We all feel challenged when you are around."

Kara let out a short laugh. "Is this why you two looked at me so closely today? Why Lady Celana talked of my sexual experience? You think I use my *body* to be attractive?"

Ellah took a step back. At least she had the decency to look ashamed – unless she was putting on a very good pretense.

"Don't you?" she asked quietly.

Kara leaned closer, meeting her eyes in the semi-darkness.

"I've grown up learning to avoid men," she said. "Perhaps it's a lesson to be learned if you ever want to find a good match?"

She turned and strode away, trying to quiet her racing heart. She was surprised at herself, how in one day she found herself first doubting Mai's intentions toward her and then feeling jealous of a girl Mai couldn't possibly have anything in common with. It must be the mind link, she decided. The Kaddim were using all means to drive her mad. And she'd be damned if she let them.

When Kara emerged from the bushes, she was surprised to find Raishan gone and Mai sitting on the ground in his place, with his back to a large tree. He rose to his feet when he saw her, watching her approach. Enclosed by the dark shade of the trees that separated them from camp, his face was hard to read.

"Where's Raishan?" she asked.

"I relieved him. Think of it as a change of guard." She sensed a smile in Mai's voice, but the way he peered at her also betrayed his concern.

"I'm not sure if I should be alone with you," she said.

He stepped closer. "That's new. Why not?"

"I can't be trusted."

"With what, exactly?" He grinned. "I hope you don't mean my virtue."

She let out a short laugh, his easygoing tone putting some of her tension at rest. His virtue. She definitely could not be trusted with that, even if there was no possibility on the march to put this to the test.

"I wanted to make sure you are all right," Mai said.

She shook her head. She couldn't possibly be all right, not until the Kaddim link was removed. Mai knew it too. Yet, it was so tempting to pretend everything was normal and this was just one of their regular conversations.

"I spoke to Magister Egey Bashi," she said. "He

confirmed what you said, that my death could potentially release my power to the Kaddim... You should have told me."

"I should have, if I knew what you were going to do. For now, I'm just glad we were able to stop you from following through with your plan."

His voice held an edge that answered so well to her own feelings. If she was allowed to do what she planned, the Kaddim would have won and she and Mai would not even be talking right now. Once again, Mai's resolve and ability to take quick actions had saved her from an unimaginable disaster.

"I've lost count of how many times you saved my life," she said.

"As many as it takes," Mai said. "But, other considerations aside, I hope you realize that if the Magister's information is right, your life is easily the most precious one among our group."

She shivered. "I don't know how to deal with this. It seems that everything I do only makes things worse."

"Let me try to make it a little bit better." He reached out to her and she stepped into his embrace.

It felt so good to relax against his chest. When he was so close, when he held her like this, it was difficult to imagine anything could ever go wrong. She stifled the images that crowded in her mind, Kaddim armies fighting with the skill of a Diamond Majat, her friends and comrades falling under their blades.

He rested his cheek against her hair, drawing a long breath. The tender gesture made her stomach flutter. If only they could stay like this forever, forgetting all their problems. He owned her, body and soul, and this awareness was the most thrilling one she had in a very long time. The Kaddim could never put a claim on her as long as she was with Mai. She would hold on to this bond she had, at all cost.

A distant guard call signaled the start of the night shift. She stirred, drawing away from Mai briefly.

"Won't they miss us?" she asked quietly.

He smiled. "I told Raishan we may take a while. He promised not to let anyone pass this way."

She laughed. "I would have gone insane at least several times today, if it wasn't for Raishan."

"I hope this is one of those times." Mai drew her closer and she submerged into his caress.

# 16
# TREE ULTIMATUM

"This is where our forces separate," Mai said.

Kyth looked at the flat area of land stretching in front of them, covered by ivy and dense hazel growth. According to the Majat maps, the thicker line of trees in the distance signified the official boundary of the Forestlands, the place where he had been raised as a child, hidden to protect his magic gift from the wrath of the Church. The thought of being so close to the place he had considered his home when he grew up made his heart race. Yet, the scenery here did not look familiar at all. It was hard to imagine they were only a few days' ride away from the Forestland thickets.

He looked at Alder, sitting very still, his attention focused entirely on the trees. The spiders on his shoulder kept still, yet Kyth could detect a tension. Were they all sensing closeness to their home? Could Alder feel something nobody else could?

"Kyth." Mai's voice brought him back to his senses, to realize that everyone was looking at him expectantly.

"What?"

Mai sighed. "Last time we discussed this, you were

supposed to be the one to lead your party to Lady Ayalla. The Majat were planning to go around by the caravan roads. Are you still on board with this plan?"

"Yes." Kyth wasn't sure what brought on the question.

"Then pay attention," Mai said.

Kyth bit his lip, stifling a retort. He knew, whatever he said just now, Mai would use it as an opportunity to humiliate him. Perhaps it had to do with the way Kyth's eyes kept drifting toward Kara, sitting at the far edge of the camp, distant enough to avoid any possibility of overhearing their conversation? He couldn't blame Mai for being protective. Had Kara belonged to Kyth now, he might have done the same.

"You, Alder, and Ellah, will enter the forest and seek out Lady Ayalla," Mai said. "Then you will travel down the Groves to meet us at the Gard'hal outpost. Hopefully with reinforcements."

*The spiders.* Once again, Kyth glanced at his foster brother's shoulder. To stand a better chance with the Kaddim, they had to convince Lady Ayalla to lend them a large number of these deadly creatures. Too many to conceal easily during the travel.

"How are we going to transport them?" he asked.

Alder lifted his head. "We should leave all this up to Ayalla." It didn't escape Kyth how intimate the name sounded when Alder said it, his cheeks lighting up with a faint color. Was his foster brother looking forward to this meeting? If so, it had to be reassuring. Surely she wouldn't bring any harm to someone so close to her?

"Just don't mess up," Mai said.

Kyth did open his mouth this time to tell Mai everything he thought of this conversation, but a loud rustle at the side of the glade froze the words on his lips. He turned toward the sound, feeling a chill run down his spine.

When they had settled down in this glade only a couple of hours ago, it seemed a lot more open than now, with far fewer trees crowding along its sides. The wall of tree trunks around them stood so dense now that they blocked away most of the light. All of them couldn't possibly grown out of nowhere in the past two hours. Did he remember wrong? Was it all his imagination?

"It reminds me of the Dark Mire," Alder said.

From across the fire, Ellah nodded. Her tense set of shoulders matched well with the eerie feeling in Kyth's chest, so different from the ease of Alder's relaxed posture.

Mai glanced at the map he was holding in his hand, then ran his eyes around their group.

"I did expect the trees here to be more... normal," he admitted. "Our scouts reported nothing unusual when we chose this campsite."

Kyth looked at the forest wall around them again. In the gathering dusk, it seemed as if the trees were creeping in, smothering them in their shade. Despite all the hacking just an hour ago when they were setting up camp, it seemed as if they were seated in the middle of woods never before invaded by men. In fact, even the path they had followed here today from von Eyvern lands was no longer visible.

"Perhaps," Egey Bashi suggested, "Lady Ayalla is making a move to facilitate our meeting?"

Mai's eyes darted around the trees and Kyth saw a tense cord in his neck, the only indication that the

Majat was probably feeling as unnerved as everyone else.

"I haven't actually planned to bring our entire force into her realm," Mai said. "Perhaps we should have taken Lord Garet's warning more seriously."

Egey Bashi shrugged. "On this side of the Lakes, all bets are off, Aghat Mai. Lady Ayalla heeds no borders. She comes and goes as she pleases."

Kyth glanced at Celana seated by his side and gave her an encouraging smile. Inadvertently, his eyes slid further to Kara, curled up with her back against a tree, her knees pulled up to her chest. She looked drawn, exhausted. During the past few days she had been getting visibly worse. Kyth was dying to find out what was going on, but with the way Mai kept Kara by his side day and night it was all but impossible to steal a private conversation.

"The trees are talking," Alder suddenly said.

Mai's eyes darted toward the gathering gloom around the camp. "I am not sure I like this."

Egey Bashi sighed. "Under the circumstances, Aghat Mai, it may be a good idea to consider a change of plans. You are the formal leader of this force. Perhaps you should be the one meeting with Lady Ayalla."

Mai shook his head. "I like my meetings to happen according to my plans, Magister – not to mention, on my terms."

"So does Lady Ayalla, I would imagine. I may be wrong, of course, but it seems to me that she has already made a decision to meet you in person."

Mai didn't respond to that, but his wary look spoke of more uncertainty than Kyth had ever seen him capable of.

"In any case," Alder said, "there isn't much to be done about all this right now. No saying what could happen if we tried to get out of this thicket in the dark. I think we'd all do best to get some sleep."

Kara was having trouble falling asleep. During the past few days her headaches were getting more frequent, the incessant whispering in her ears making it hard to concentrate. The inky blackness inside the looming forest line seemed impenetrable to her tired eyes. Worse, despite being unable to see much, she kept imagining movement inside the tree shade. Branches, coiling and twining faster than the tree appendages should be able to move. Shadows crawling along the ground like the spiders that cornered her back at the King's castle in Tandar. She shivered, pulling her cloak tighter around herself.

Mai was asleep by her side, his closeness putting some of her worries at ease. Still, she wished the headache would stop and the noises in her ears would go away, for once giving her some privacy inside her own mind.

Were the Kaddim taking firmer hold of her?

Could the trees sense it?

She suddenly realized that the tree line seemed a lot closer than she remembered it to be when she lay down to sleep. She tried to reassure herself. Even if the trees here did move faster than normal at Ayalla's bidding, surely they couldn't possibly mean harm – not with the cause the Majat were fighting for. She cuddled closer to Mai. As if sensing her unease, he draped an arm around her.

The movement eased her fear. Mai was superbly

trained, just like her. If he sensed any danger he would instantly wake up. The fact that he was sleeping tightly meant that this was all a figment of her imagination driven by the Kaddim mind link. Just like they did for the past few weeks, they were messing with her head. If she managed to still her mind, the whole thing would go away.

She curled up against Mai's chest, trying her best to clear her mind to any outside thoughts.

Something leathery touched her arm.

She whipped out her dagger, hacking at the invading object, but her blade met thin air. *Dear Shal Addim, am I going mad?* She sat up, wondering how everyone around her was still fast asleep. Even the watchmen Mai had left around the smoldering campfires. This shouldn't be happening. She spun around at a rustle at her back, and froze.

A group of trees was moving toward her at high speed, their snaking roots whirling over the ground like the legs of a giant centipede. Before she could cry out, a leathery branch whipped around her mouth, another one squeezing her throat until she had no air left. More branches enclosed her, weaving a cocoon around her that rendered her immobile.

With darkening vision she saw the ground fall away, her sleeping comrades not even stirring as she was lifted above them, right out of Mai's arms. A tight cord caught her around the chest, squeezing out what breath she had left. The noise in her ears rose to a painful ringing that drowned all the other sounds.

*Am I dying?* The thought didn't seem important anymore. At least, if she was dying, it wasn't from a spider bite, which made the whole ordeal seem a lot better. She clung to this thought as her vision blackened and the world around her sank into oblivion.

"What do you mean, *gone*?" Mai demanded.

The Jade took a nervous step back. Kyth didn't envy the man his position.

"There're no tracks, Aghat Mai."

"You mean, she covered them." Mai's face was so still that even Kyth felt scared. He remembered Mai's reaction when Kara ran away from the barge. Here, in the wilderness, with no means to summon help, it seemed infinitely worse.

The Jade lifted his chin, clearly struggling to keep his composure. "I mean, Aghat Mai, there are none, at all. We have our best trackers on it. No matter how well she could cover her tracks, they would have spotted something. It looks as if someone just... lifted her off the ground and swept her away."

"Lifted her."

"Yes."

Mai heaved an exasperated sigh. "What did the other watchmen see?"

The man averted his gaze, throwing a nervous glance at the men crowding behind him. No one seemed willing to break the silence.

Mai ran a disbelieving gaze around the group.

"Do you mean to tell me that all of you just happened to fall asleep at the same time?"

More silence. Kyth saw the Jade's lowered hand tremble. Men around him shrank away from Mai's gaze.

"I think, Aghat Mai," Egey Bashi said, "there was

nothing your men could have done."

"You leave my men to me, Magister."

"I mean it, Aghat Mai. However powerful the Majat Guild is, respectfully, you are no match for Lady Ayalla."

Mai's gaze spelled challenge. "We'll see about that."

"I hope not." Egey Bashi spoke quietly, but in the smothering silence from the trees around them his words echoed clearly around the group.

"Perhaps," Kyth said, "you can lead a parley into the forest, Mai?"

Mai glanced at the dense tree line. "Do I have a bloody choice?"

Branches rustled in response. Kyth couldn't tell for sure, but to his ear the pitch sounded threatening.

"No," Alder said.

Mai spun around to face him. "No?"

"You're not to enter the forest. Not with your men."

"I'd like to see somebody bloody stop me." Mai drew his staff from the sheath at his back.

Egey Bashi slid forward and caught him by the arm. At Mai's glance he let go, slowly. "You well know the forces at Lady Ayalla's disposal can stop you easily, Aghat Mai. It's time to exercise reason."

Seldon stepped forward, his frown reflecting poorly disguised contempt. "With due respect, Aghat Mai, I must point out that you are hardly impartial in this situation. I fear that your feelings in the matter may stand in the way of resolving it."

Mai's short glance forced him to retreat. Kyth also noticed how Raishan and Lance suddenly grew taller by Mai's sides, as if offering protection.

"By all means, Aghat Seldon," Mai said, "if you can point to a solution I'm overlooking, I'll welcome it."

"Respectfully," Egey Bashi put in, "I don't think any of you can offer a solution here. At least, not the Majat-style one."

"*Respectfully*," Seldon said, "this is not a matter for an outsider, Magister."

Egey Bashi's smile showed a touch of impatience. "It seems that in this case it is, Aghat Seldon. The person taken from our party is not a Majat." He glanced at Mai. "However unofficial, our march is driven by an alliance, and as the representative of the Order of Keepers I have a say. Of course, Aghat Mai's military authority supersedes mine." He bowed to Mai.

"It's not the military authority that's an issue here," Seldon said.

Mai glanced up. "You have something else you wish to say, Aghat Seldon?"

"Yes, I do."

The Diamonds by Mai's sides crowded in closer. Kyth saw how they all kept their arms toned, as if ready to draw their weapons at any instant. Their eyes kept darting to Mai, looking lower than his face. *Waiting for a hand sign. Damn it, are they going to fight each other?* He edged away, hoping the movement did not seem obvious.

Seldon seemed the only one unabashed by the threat.

"Even a Guildmaster's authority is not absolute, Aghat Mai," he said. "I hope you still remember that your predecessor's downfall happened to involve Kara and the Kaddim. I hope I am not the only one seeing a connection here."

"Really, Aghat Seldon, this hardly seems the time to…" Egey Bashi began, but Mai's short glance stopped him.

"By all means, Magister." Mai's voice was quiet, but in the dead silence it still echoed loudly like a shout. "We must hear what Aghat Seldon has to say. What better time to get this all over with?"

The way all the Majat around Mai tensed up reminded Kyth of a battery of strung crossbows about to be released at the enemy line. He marveled at the way Seldon acted as if oblivious to the tension, even though a small bead of sweat glistening at his temple said otherwise.

"It came to my attention, Aghat Mai," Seldon said, "that after assuming your post you've failed to appoint a new Shadow Master. In fact, I heard our seniors say that you've made plans to permanently abolish the post."

Mai smiled. "I assume, Aghat Seldon, that this discussion is somehow relevant to our situation here."

"I believe so, Aghat Mai. I cannot help but think of how this action would give our Diamonds – including yourself – far less incentive to follow the Code."

Mai continued to smile, but something about his stance sent a chill down Kyth's spine. "Are you accusing me of violating the Code, Aghat Seldon?" Mai said.

Seldon shook his head, looking just a bit deflated. "By no means, Aghat Mai. My words are meant merely in caution. Your devotion to Kara could place you directly at odds with your duties to the Guild. For instance, right now you are planning a confrontation with a powerful forest being for no reason at all except to save the woman you love. Worse, it seems that no one here is even willing to offer an objection to what seems to me like an insanely dangerous plan."

Mai held his gaze. "Since we are talking so freely,

Aghat Seldon, let's compare my actions to yours, just for humor's sake. We are trapped by the trees, with a key member of our party whisked away from under our noses without even raising an alarm. That's a bloody threat to our security, among other things. Yet, you can find no better conversation topic than discussing my love life?"

"Not your love life. Your *duty*, Aghat Mai." Seldon shifted from foot to foot, his darting eyes searching for any support among the silent group.

"Speaking of duty," Mai said, "I believe in a situation like this, when you challenge my authority in the face of a deadly threat, the Code dictates for me to hack off your head, or do something equally unpleasant. However, just this once, I am giving you a chance to stand down and end this peacefully."

"How convenient," Seldon mumbled.

Kyth dropped his gaze just in time to see Mai's hand unclench, a signal that sent all the Diamonds forward, their hands unfolding with blades that pointed at Seldon, who seemed too terrified to move. Mai remained in place, his posture losing none of its graceful ease.

"We are at war, Aghat Seldon. Perhaps now is a good time for you to get this fact through your head?"

"Do you hope that if you win the war everyone at the Guild will just let you do whatever you please, for the rest of your life?"

Mai's body unfolded in a move that would have seemed leisurely if it hadn't been so fast. His staff slid into his hand, as if alive, its tip pressing against Seldon's throat. Watching wide-eyed, Kyth's saw Mai's finger resting at the spot where, as he knew, a hidden spring could release a retractable blade at a very light touch. At this angle the movement would likely sever Seldon's head.

Seldon paled but he kept Mai's gaze, calm and tranquil like the summer sky.

"If we win this war," Mai said, "I would gladly have a conversation with any of the Guild's seniors who have issues with my command style. However, given that we are currently on the march, I cannot possibly afford to tolerate any further discussions of this kind, and will stop them by any means necessary. I'm sure you understand, Aghat."

Seldon's eyes darted to the Diamonds around him, then finally dropped to the ground in a gesture of obedience.

"Please forgive me, Aghat Mai," he said. "I've spoken out of turn. You are correct of course. I will gladly accept whatever punishment you deem warranted."

Mai stood still for a moment, then withdrew his staff. All the Diamonds around him lowered their weapons.

"Consider it a warning, Aghat Seldon," Mai said. "If you act bloody stupid yet again, I won't be this forgiving next time." He turned away and walked toward the line of trees, staring into their dense thicket.

Seldon swallowed. Hs flaring nostrils, the rolling muscles in his neck and throat, showed Kyth that beneath the death fear the man had just experienced he was fuming. Kyth's own hands were shaking just from watching the encounter. Worse, he knew there was a grain of truth in Seldon's words, even if now was definitely not the time to mention it at all. Mai's and Kara's affair couldn't possibly come to any good, especially with the way it served as the focus of all Kaddim's plotting.

Or perhaps it was Kyth's own jealousy speaking?

He glanced around the group, noting how everyone was still tense and alert. Mai seemed like the only exception, his posture calm and relaxed as he strode back from the tree line. His eyes fell on Egey Bashi.

"You were saying, Magister?"

Egey Bashi let out a sigh. "Nothing important, Aghat Mai. I was merely going to suggest that we wait."

"Wait for what?"

"For Lady Ayalla to make her next move."

Mai shifted in place, the only sign that betrayed his restlessness. "Since we seem to have nothing else to do, perhaps you can fill the obvious gap in our knowledge about her powers?"

Egey Bashi nodded slowly, his eyes darting to Alder then wandering off to stare into the distance. "The question of Lady Ayalla's powers goes back centuries, Aghat Mai."

"I'm all ears, Magister."

"It started with the situation in the Forestlands."

Kyth raised his eyebrows. He had grown up in the Forestlands and always thought it to be one of the most peaceful places in the world. "There was a situation in the Forestlands, Magister?"

Egey Bashi shot him a quick glance. "I'm sure, Your Highness, that you've probably heard a thing or two about the Dark Mire."

"Yes." Kyth paused, remembering. The Mire, a deep area of the Forest to be avoided at all cost, spawned all kinds of dark and exotic creatures. The large hairy spiders Alder carried on his shoulder, ones that could dissolve a man with one quick bite, were by far not the worst. Yet, even with all these horrors, he had to admit that Ayalla herself was by far the strangest and the most frightening of all. A woman rumored to take lovers so that she could give birth to trees, one who could heal with a touch and command the landscape to shift its way... He shivered.

Egey Bashi sat still, watching his reaction. "The Dark Mire is considered to be the apex of magic, all that was left of the Old World when the Holy Wars drove the magic control laws into place. Folk tales say that Lord Shal Addim had once bound all the ungodly magical powers into a sack, but the Destroyer slit a hole in it, letting all the magic pour into this one spot at the center of the Forest. This rumor is not as far from truth as it may seem."

"What do you mean, Magister?" Mai asked.

"The Dark Mire is the place where, during the Holy Wars, all the magic users gathered together to take their last stand. Many perished in battle. To preserve themselves, all the survivors breathed out their magic essence into Ayalla – a common woman who, until that time, possessed only one gift of her own. Slow aging, also known as the Power of Immortality."

Kyth's eyes widened. "You mean, Ayalla is not only immortal but also possesses magic gifts of many?"

The Keeper hesitated. "Not directly. What she possesses is a blend – a new, unique power that is also known as the Power of Life."

*Life.* Kyth glanced at the deep tree wall around them, at the spiders shifting restlessly on Alder's shoulder. In a way all the miracles he saw Ayalla perform, the way she commanded powerful and frightening creatures, could indeed be thought of as life. Except that she also wielded death, more frightening than he could ever imagine.

"Is this is why she can give birth to trees?" Mai asked. "If this rumor is true, of course."

"It *is* true, Aghat Mai. And it makes perfect sense, actually. Trees are the essence of life. They also age slowly, just like her, even though in the end she outlives them all."

Kyth stared unseeingly into the distance. Ayalla was old, older than any living being he knew. It seemed mind-boggling to think of this kind of power, life and immortality blended together, the essence of all the magic users trapped in this realm. He felt delusional about their plan of securing her alliance. With this kind of power at her disposal, why would she possibly care about helping them in a war?

"What else can she do, Magister?" he asked.

"No one truly knows. Her powers have to do with everything living, which is why she is the only true opponent to the Kaddim."

Kyth noticed how all the Majat were listening now, as if the mention of their enemies had clicked a new awareness into place.

"How so?" Mai asked.

"The Kaddim spawn death. The ultimate manifestation of their mind power is known as the Power to Kill – essentially telling a person to die."

"But they can resurrect too."

"Resurrect, yes, but not to give a new life. The resurrected ones are technically undead, even if they may not look this way. People connect the Kaddim magic to the power of the Cursed Destroyer, which is why the Kaddim leader is rumored to be his direct reincarnation. Whether it is true, nobody knows, but one thing is certain. The Kaddim Reincarnate and

Ayalla are the exact opposites in their powers, as well as a match in their strength, or very close so. To defeat the Kaddim once and for all, Ayalla must not only lend us her spiders. She must be there herself."

Mai's eyes narrowed. "Did you know this all along, Magister?"

"I suspected it, yes."

"And you didn't think it fit to tell me?"

The Keeper held his gaze. "Would you have acted differently if I did, Aghat Mai?"

"Perhaps. But it's too late to entertain this now, is it?"

"Too late? Hardly. We are doing nothing but waiting, are we?"

Mai glanced at the wall of trees around them. "I suppose so. However, on this short notice the only change we could possibly entertain is to have me, not Kyth, discuss the alliance with her."

Egey Bashi looked at the trees too. During the last fifteen minutes or so they seemed to have crowded even closer. *Are they trying to crush us?* Kyth shifted in his seat, only partially reassured by Alder's calm face.

"It seems, Aghat Mai," the Keeper said, "that this choice has been made for you already. The fact that Lady Ayalla took Kara likely means she already has a plan and it probably involves you. Perhaps you could use this time to put yourself into the right set of mind to listen to what she has to say?"

"My set of mind is just fine, thank you, Magister."

Egey Bashi leaned back, as if trying to look at him from a greater distance. "Please forgive my doubts, Aghat."

Mai shrugged again. "You know I'll do what I have

to, Magister. As long as Kara is not harmed."

"Yes, Aghat Mai, this worries me too. But I'm sure you know that you can't stake the outcome of a war on any condition, even one as important as this."

Mai's jaw knotted, betraying his tension. Kyth was worried too, but watching Mai when he was this way seemed even more unnerving.

Were they ever going to see Kara alive?

# 17
# THE FOREST MOTHER

Kara blinked, trying to make sense of her surroundings. The greenish, suffused light reminded her of being underwater, the impression further enhanced by the way her body seemed weightless, as if floating. Yet, the air she inhaled was normal, only slightly damper than she remembered when she was falling asleep last night. Its sharp, earthly scent felt refreshing, leaving a slightly salty taste on her tongue. Even better, she could feel no headache or any invading presence in her head.

*Am I dreaming?* She didn't have time to wonder when a movement at the corner of her eye caught her attention. She tried to turn her head, but quickly realized that she was unable to move. Not only her head, but her entire body was encased in hard, leathery restraints that left her suspended face-up – in the air? In water?

The memories of what happened last night flooded into her head. They had crossed into the Forestlands. And then, she had been whisked away from camp by what looked like a giant walking tree.

Ayalla, the Forest Mother, seemed to have taken

personal interest in her. Was this because of the Kaddim magic she carried?

A hairy shape lowered into view. A large spider, hanging on a thick thread right in front of her face.

Her skin tingled. Did the creature sense the Kaddim magic on her? Was it planning to finish the job its comrades had abandoned back in Tandar?

Kara's mind raced. She tugged at her restraints, wondering at the way they did not budge at all despite all her Majat-trained strength as she threw her weight against them. Spread out and helpless, she had no choice but to watch the spider lower over her until she felt its weight and the tingle of its hairy legs on her chest.

*Make it quick,* she mouthed, certain that the creature could not possibly understand her. This wasn't her choice of way to die, but at least this would accomplish what she had set out to do last time, when Lord Garet's men acting at Mai's bidding interrupted her. Perhaps Ayalla knew a way to kill her without passing on her gift to the Kaddim? Perhaps only the spider bite, dissolving her body alive, would do the job, just like it did when it came to preventing Kaddim resurrection?

She waited for the sting, but felt no pain at all, only the patter of the spider's legs as it ran around on her chest, as if trying to find a cozy spot. She kept very still, trying not to think about what was coming. *Being dissolved alive. Right. I've had worse pain.* She knew it wasn't true, but if the spider was truly here to kill her none of this mattered. At least it wouldn't take too long. Hopefully.

Time passed, but no spider bite came. After a while Kara forced her protesting muscles to relax, trying to distance herself from the weight of the creature on her chest, shifting her attention to the surroundings. Did she hear a rustle? A crack of a dry twig? Footsteps?

Ayalla came into view unexpectedly, her pale, beautiful face, framed by a waterfall of dark golden hair, looming over Kara. A pair of indigo eyes looked down at her with quiet interest, as if she was a rare insect caught in a trap.

"Curious," Ayalla said. She spoke softly, as if to herself, but she also kept looking at a spot above Kara's head, making it seem as if there was someone standing there, listening.

Kara flexed her muscles, but the restraints – whatever they were – held tight.

"You may release her," Ayalla said.

The restraints let go. Kara relaxed her body for a fall to the hard floor, but her back sank into soft moisture instead, drenching her already damp clothes. *A puddle? A mud pit?* She rolled over, sweeping the spider off her chest in one quick move. Her hands darted to her weapons, finding none.

She crouched on one knee in an ankle-deep pond of water, looking up at Ayalla.

The Forest Woman smiled. "Going for your weapons, of course. This is the only thing you Majat ever do." Her relaxed posture suggested no immediate threats were forthcoming. Or was she so confident around Kara that she didn't see the need to keep alert?

Were Ayalla a regular woman, Kara would have no trouble overpowering her in a blink of an eye. But there was no telling what the Forest Woman was capable of. The way Ayalla was looking at her, as if Kara wasn't one of the deadliest fighters in the world but a child playing at her feet, screamed caution. Kara did not pretend to understand the powers that made Ayalla the way she was, but she knew better than to test them right now. Besides, the spider was still here, now joined by a dozen or so of its comrades, and she was well aware of the dangers to expect from those creatures at least.

Kara shivered. Last time she met Ayalla, the Forest Woman had been wearing a dress of live spiders, a crawling mass covering every inch of her body and ready to attack on command. Now, Ayalla's dress was different, a soft, shimmering mist that clung to her skin and pooled around her feet like a pile of gauze. As she moved, the mist parted briefly, revealing a glimpse of bare skin underneath.

"You don't like Majat, do you?" Kara said. She knew it was foolish to challenge Ayalla, but hours of being suspended and immobile did little to improve her already rotten mood. Besides, the sooner Ayalla killed her, the better. She saw no purpose in having a long conversation beforehand.

Ayalla shrugged, the movement baring her shoulders for a brief instant. "I don't like anyone whose lifetime occupation is to kill."

Kara nodded. In an odd way this made sense. Ayalla was a lifegiver, her magic supporting the life around her. Except she also owned the spiders, easily the deadliest creatures in existence. "Why capture me then?"

"Did you prefer I left you out there to let the Kaddim destroy your mind and use you to defeat your friends?"

Kara sat back on her heels. She didn't expect such a turn of the conversation. Ayalla always seemed so detached that it was difficult even to guess if she was following the same train of thoughts. The fact that she knew so much about Kara's predicament didn't fit into the image Kara had for her.

"What do you mean?" she asked.

Ayalla shrugged again, an impatient gesture that parted the mist around her shoulders all the way to the top of her full breasts. "No time for idle talk. The Kaddim are my enemies too. The last thing I want is for you to carry their magic straight into my realm." She turned around, the mist hastily swirling to follow her slender form. "Follow me."

She walked away, not bothering even to turn her head to make sure Kara would follow. The mist of her dress folded into an exquisite mantle, partially concealing the path behind her.

Kara glanced around. The forest clearing around her was small, mostly occupied by the shallow pond she was sitting in. She could see no sign of her weapons, or any indications of a person – or object – that had been holding her in such tight bonds until Ayalla showed up. Her skin tingled as she surveyed the smooth tree wall at her back, so dense that it left no room whatsoever for a person to squeeze through.

The path Ayalla took was the only way out. As Kara watched, it began to narrow, the trees moving in subtly, as if intending to seal her in. She hastily scrambled to her feet and rushed forward to catch up with the Forest Woman.

The path led to a bigger clearing, a small forest glade surrounded by trees on three sides and a bigger pond on the fourth. As Kara emerged from the tree shade, she also became aware of the movement, in the tall grass and along the tree trunks. A chill ran down her spine as she realized that the whole area was covered by spiders, and that what she mistook for the tree bark and glimpses of earth between the grass stems, were actually their dark, velvety bodies milling around in constant motion. She stopped dead in her tracks.

"You need not be afraid," Ayalla said from the far end of the glade. "Your Kaddim link is silent at present. However, I intend to open it now, so that the Guardians can decide how far gone you are."

*The Guardians.* Did she mean the spiders? Kara clenched her teeth. Whatever games Ayalla was trying to play with her, it hardly seemed to matter. She assumed the bite of many spiders had to be better than one, since more poison would dissolve her body much faster. At least she hoped this was the case. It was probably going to hurt more too. She swallowed, willing herself stop the treacherous tremor in the pit of her stomach.

Ayalla surveyed her calmly, as if aware of every bit of her discomfort. Kara willed herself not to give a damn. She knew when she was outpowered.

"Ready?" Ayalla asked.

"For what?"

The headache pounced unexpectedly, the intensity of it sending Kara to her knees. The forest glade in front of her eyes fell away, opening into a void. Kara felt as if falling. Her grasping hand came upon a moving object that hastily scrambled out of her reach – a spider, but this didn't seem to matter anymore.

She was standing in a stone hallway, the chill emanated by the low ceiling and roughly hewn wall mixing with the heat of the wind that swept in dry sand from the outside. *The desert. All around us.* The thought seemed foreign, as if not coming from her own head.

Hooded figures lined up by her sides, watching a man pace back and forth along the opposite wall. His hood was off, revealing a bald head, parched skin stretching over the bones of his skull. His eyes had a red tint, and in the semidarkness of the chamber they glowed like embers fresh from the fire.

Animal fear rose inside her at the sight of the pacing man.

*The Kaddim Reincarnate.*

*How do I know that?*

Her lips stretched, the voice coming from her throat alien, male.

"Her link has been temporarily blocked, Cursed Master. And now it's active again, but somebody is tampering with it."

She barely recognized the voice, altered by the echoes in her own head. *Nimos. Damn it, am I inside his head?*

The pacing man stopped, peering into her eyes.

"I sense an intrusion, Kaddim Nimos," he said. "Stop using your link. Now."

More searing pain that made her head feel as if it was exploding. A moan escaped through her clenched teeth and she felt a hand steadying her, pulling her up to her feet. She opened her eyes with a gasp, taking in the familiar glade, the glistening pond, the crawling spider bodies... Ayalla's indigo eyes peering into her face.

"It's worse than I thought," Ayalla said. "But I can see now that your mind is still intact. You are not one of them."

Kara shrank away from her, the memory of the pain

still rolling through her exhausted body. "One of them? Are you insane?"

Ayalla laughed softly. "Many think that I am. However, this is not important. I will block the Kaddim link in your head – for now. However, when you get close to the man who controls your link, my power will fail. Your allies will have to use their skills to kill him and free you, once and for all. If you manage to remain intact until then."

*Intact.* Kara slid down to sit against a tree trunk at her back, her trembling legs refusing to support her – a feeling she was not used to at all. Spiders rushed all around her, but suddenly it did not seem to matter anymore. She tried to focus on Ayalla as the Forest Woman knelt on the ground in front of her and put her palms on the sides of Kara's face. Cool mist enfolded her, streaming down in droplets of moisture that brought unexpected relief to her pain and fatigue. Her vision darkened and she drifted off into sleep.

# 18
# EMBASSY

Kyth and Alder sat by the fire in the heart of their camp when shouting from the side of the woods forced them to jump up to their feet. The foster brothers exchanged quick glances and rushed toward the noise.

Around them, Jades were drawing their crossbows and fanning out along the sides of the clearing. Mai strode through their ranks toward a spot invisible behind a small tree grove, a train of top gems forming in his wake. Kyth hurried to catch up.

The lone man waiting for them at the forest clearing ahead hardly seemed to merit such an upheaval. He wore no weapons, his worn clothes of patched brown and green blending with the colors of the forest at his back. He eyed his welcoming party with curiosity rather than fear, a touch of amusement in his gaze as he glanced at the impressive array of bows and crossbows pointing his way.

Kyth's heart leapt as he recognized the newcomer. "Garnald!" He swept past Raishan into the man's bear-like embrace.

The old Mirewalker had been around when Kyth

and Alder were growing up in the Forestlands, a man who made the Dark Mire his home, whose closeness to Ayalla spawned rumors and fear among the villagers. Kyth felt relieved that Ayalla had chosen Garnald as her messenger. This, more than anything, told him they likely had nothing to fear.

Alder and Ellah pushed past him, exchanging greetings with the older man. Out of the corner of his eye Kyth noticed weapons lowering everywhere in sight.

"I can't wait to catch up with you lads," Garnald said. "But right now I am here on official business. I believe he is the one I need to be talking to." He pointed at Mai, standing at the edge of the clearing at the head of his Gem-ranked retinue.

"Of course," Kyth muttered. "Who else?"

"I am sent by the Forest Mother," Garnald went on.

Mai stepped forward, the Majat around him receding at his brief hand sign. Kyth was amazed at how they were able to do all of it without actually moving all that much.

Garnald looked at him with interest, measuring him with an unhurried gaze. "Lady Ayalla would like to speak to you. I believe you know why."

"Actually," Mai said, "I don't – except that I assume she is holding a hostage I'd like to get back."

Garnald slowly inclined his head. "She does hold a member of your party, but not as a hostage."

"As what then?"

"This is something she will tell you herself."

Mai moved to go, but Garnald's gesture stopped him.

"She will not allow weapons, or any of your men, into her domain."

"Out of the question."

Garnald squared his jaw. "In Lady Ayalla's realm, things are done on her terms, and no other way."

Mai lifted his chin, but before he could speak Egey Bashi rushed up to his side.

"You need Lady Ayalla's alliance, Aghat Mai," he said. "Not to mention that the leverage she holds over you right now is far too great to risk over something like this. Even with your weapons, you will be helpless as a child once you enter her realm. A confrontation over it would not only jeopardize your chances, but would also put Kara in even more danger."

Mai cocked his head. "Are you expecting, Magister, that I would venture into this forest alone without any weapons?"

"Not alone," Garnald said. "You can bring Kyth and Alder with you. And the Keeper, if he agrees to join you."

"'The Keeper' would be delighted," Egey Bashi muttered, his scowl a poor replacement for a friendly smile. "The name's Egey Bashi, by the way."

Garnald's eyes flickered with a strange expression, half irony half challenge. "Yes, I remember you, Magister. I also know that your gift of slow aging stems from Lady Ayalla's own power."

Kyth frowned in disbelief. He knew that the Keeper was much older than he appeared, but hearing his age mentioned on the same scale as Ayalla's didn't make any sense at all. Magister Egey Bashi looked to be in his late forties, perhaps early fifties. Kyth always assumed that with the way people talked about him being older than he looked he might be actually closer to sixty or so, just very well preserved. Ayalla was completely different, a magical being who spoke of events centuries ago as if they were recent. Surely Egey Bashi couldn't be nearly as old as that?

"You may also bring one more person of your choice," Garnald said to Mai. "As long as it's not a Majat."

"Ellah," Mai said. "I'd like Ellah to come. Will you?" He looked at the girl.

Kyth felt resentment rise in his chest at the sight of her cheeks lighting up with a faint blush as she nodded, even before Mai could finish phrasing his request. He knew that Ellah was attracted to Mai, who seemed to have no problems with using it to his advantage. Right now, he assumed the Majat needed her truthsense, and he was unlikely to consider the girl's safety at all to get her at his side.

Kyth's heart raced. Venturing into Ayalla's realm on less than friendly terms, with Mai in a volatile mood, was dangerous, to say the least. While he supposed he and Alder definitely needed to be there, if only to do their best to keep Mai from doing something foolish, putting Ellah on the spot raised the stakes. The last thing she needed was to be asked to report if anyone told a lie and risk an outburst that could not possibly end well.

"Couldn't you at least leave Ellah out of this?" he asked.

Mai's lips twitched. "And what are you, her guardian now?"

"For lack of a better one, yes." Mai squared his jaw, but Kyth didn't budge. "What are you going to do, scold me for insubordination? Or maybe you want to threaten to hack my head off?"

Mai's face went mask-still. Kyth wondered at the

way he felt no fear, even if he knew he was probably risking his life by pursuing the argument.

Mai leaned closer, his voice terrifyingly quiet. "Stay out of my way."

Kyth lifted his chin. "Or what?"

More people crowded around them now, Ellah tugging at Kyth's sleeve, looking at him with wide, worried eyes. "Kyth! Mai is right, I can decide for myself. I *want* to go with all of you."

Kyth held Mai's gaze a moment longer, then turned to the girl. "Don't you see it? He is using you. He's putting you into danger for no good reason."

Ellah shook her head earnestly. "I'm grateful for your protection, but you are the one who is missing the point, Kyth. Mai is trying to win a war. We all are. And if my ability can be of use – even if only by putting Mai at ease in a difficult conversation he is facing – I will be glad to go. It's my decision, Kyth, not yours."

Kyth gave an exasperated sigh. Everyone was looking at him now, Mai with threat, everyone else with various degrees of surprise. He spotted Lady Celana at the back, watching him with the wonder that made his heart swell. He turned away from her before his eyes could linger any longer.

He knew that, tempers aside, Ellah was probably right. A lot in the upcoming conversation with Ayalla depended on Mai's ability not to muck up, and the man needed all the help he could get, as far as Kyth was concerned. He hesitated, watching Alder approach, his foster brother's face folded into a concerned frown.

"There's no danger for Ellah," Alder said with quiet certainty. "Ayalla would never harm her. She knows that we are friends, that Ellah has a gentle soul and a pure heart. You of all people should understand that, Kyth."

Kyth gaped at the reproach in his foster brother's voice. He could vouch for Ellah's pure heart, but he wasn't sure about her gentle soul at all. Ellah had a sharp tongue and wasn't shy to express her opinion if anyone got on the wrong side of her. More than that, he did not know anything at all about Ayalla, except the fact that she commanded armies of deadly spiders and wielded magic beyond anyone's comprehension. All this hardly made her seem any less dangerous or more trustworthy. He nodded nonetheless. Whatever he had to say didn't matter right now. Besides, Kara's life and safety likely depended on the outcome of this embassy, which made their time too precious to waste.

His gaze drifted to Mai, standing at the edge of the clearing beside Garnald. The Diamond's face held a mix of anger and concern, but underneath them Kyth sensed a more complex mix. The guarded way Mai eyed Kyth was new, as if the Prince posed a previously unforeseen danger. And there was even more. Understanding? Respect? At the moment Kyth couldn't care less. He stepped sideways, abruptly looking away.

He hoped Mai wouldn't be asked to do much talking. He doubted the Forest Mother would tolerate his cockiness or cope with his constantly shifting moods. It seemed unfair that Mai was coming at all. The Majat Guild stood for everything Ayalla resented, and Mai was the leader of their force. If he and Ayalla could not agree, she would never help them – which meant that with the current turn of events they were likely, at best, to leave the forest empty-handed and rely on their own resources to defeat the Kaddim.

Mai strapped off his numerous weapons and handed them to Raishan before stepping up to Garnald's side. Without his gear, he looked oddly vulnerable. Only by knowing him well could Kyth sense the tension building up inside, like a ball of flaming liquid ready to burst. He hoped nothing in Ayalla's realm would trigger the explosion. Mai's wrath could be terrifying, even in a one-on-one confrontation. And now, with the way his men's obedience to him bordered on downright worship, things could easily get out of hand. No way of telling what a small Majat army could do, even when faced with the ancient might of the forest.

Rustles echoed around them as they stepped into the cool tree shade. Walking in Mai's wake, Kyth did not realize at once that these sounds had nothing to do with the breeze, or the sound of their footsteps. The trees in front of them were parting way, opening a narrow path that closed behind them as soon as they passed through. When Kyth dared a glance back, he could see nothing but the dense forest thicket with no indication of the Majat camp behind.

He hoped they could leave this forest alive.

After about an hour of walking, the trees started to part wider. Kyth stretched his neck trying to see further ahead, but it seemed as if every time his eyes focused on something it shifted and became a wavering mass of branches and leaves. After a while he felt dizzy. He kept his eyes on Mai's back instead, the only solid object in his direct view. The Majat's black cloak with the gray and white embroidery of the diamond-set throwing star stood out like a beacon in the forest dimness. Up until now Kyth had always thought of black as the color that allowed one to blend in, assuming that the

Majat favored it so that they could be inconspicuous if it came to an ambush. Now he realized this was far from true, leaving him to wonder if the Majat actually chose this color for flashiness and effect.

Absorbed in these thoughts he barely caught the moment when the trees in front of them opened like doors swinging ajar, letting their group into a large glade. Suffused light filtering through the leaves overhead made the giant space look like a cathedral, its walls lined evenly with tall tree trunks, its arched ceiling woven from intertwined branches. The trees behind them closed in as soon as they stepped through, leaving them trapped in the large space with no visible exit.

Mai shifted from foot to foot restlessly, his eyes darting around the dense tree line. "What now?"

"Now, we wait." Garnald said.

"Of course," Mai muttered under his breath. "What else?"

The wait did not last long before the trees on the other side parted again. A whirl of mist wafted through, pooling over the grass to form a small cloud. It took Kyth a moment to see the tall, slender woman walking inside it. Leaf-filtered sunlight briefly outlined her shape, then receded to play on the surface of the mist that folded around her densely, cladding her like an exquisitely tailored dress.

She stopped in front of the group and ran a slow glance over everyone in turn. "I know why you are here. All of you." She paused her eyes on Alder, giving him a quick smile, then on Kyth, and finally on Magister Egey Bashi. She did not look at Mai at all. "You need my help to defeat the Kaddim."

*What about Kara?* Kyth's heart raced with worry. Given the invitation relayed by Garnald, he had expected Mai to be the target of the conversation, and Kara to be the first topic of the discussion. He supposed he should be feeling relieved that Ayalla came straight to the point of their entire campaign, even if it left too many open questions for his liking.

"We do," Egey Bashi said. "Will you help?"

She regarded him calmly, her face showing no emotion at all. "It depends."

"On what?"

"Many things. The offer I have for you is not the one you came to seek. But before I decide if it is even on the table, I must speak to your leader." She finally turned to Mai. "Isn't this what you consider yourself to be?"

Her eyes narrowed as she surveyed the Majat with a slow appraisal, as if deciding whether to kill him on the spot or give him a chance to speak. Her face contorted for a brief moment, making her look savage.

Mai seemed undisturbed as he kept her gaze. "Only when it comes to military operations."

Her lips twitched. "A better answer than I expected from you. Come."

"Where?"

"Does it matter?"

"I suppose not." Mai glanced around their group before following her.

Kyth couldn't tell for sure, but it seemed that despite his calm demeanor Mai was looking a bit deflated. And of course, separating him from the rest of the group meant that if the Majat messed up – a very likely possibility in Kyth's mind – there would be no one around at all to come to his aid. Kyth tried to tell himself that it was Mai's own grave to dig, but with Kara's well-being on the line, with their campaign at risk, he just couldn't feel convinced.

Ayalla paused again as she reached the edge of the glade. "The rest of you should make yourselves comfortable. This may take a while. And you," she turned back to Mai. "You were allowed to choose one person to accompany you. You may bring this person along."

Mai turned to Ellah. "I have no idea what I am asking you to do, or how dangerous this is. Given this uncertainty, you should feel free to stay behind." His smile was disarming, suddenly making him look very young. While this was probably pretense for Ellah's sake, Kyth couldn't help the worry steering up in his heart. He had no idea what awaited Mai, but he didn't envy the Diamond for having to walk unaided into Ayalla's lair.

Ellah showed no hesitation as she stepped forward to his side. "Of course I'll come with you. If I cannot offer any help, at least I can be there for support."

Ayalla's eyes lit up with quiet interest. "The truthseer? Are you hoping she will detect if I am telling the truth?"

Mai eyed her levelly. "This was my original reason for choosing her, yes. I can now see that I was being naïve. Am I endangering her by asking her to come?"

"What if you are?"

"I will not let Ellah follow me into danger."

Ayalla's gaze became thoughtful. "Another good answer. We may yet be able to speak to each other, Majat. And no, Ellah will not face the kind of danger you are in. In fact, whatever happens to you, I promise to return her to her friends unharmed."

She turned and stepped through the parting tree trunks onto a path ahead. Kyth marveled at the way Mai didn't falter even for an instant as he followed. His own heart raced with worry as he watched Ellah stand still for a moment and then rush after them.

He supposed that Mai's Diamond ranking had to come with this ability to make instant decisions to risk your life without even flinching. Yet, it had to be infinitely more frightening when it came to dealing with beings of Ayalla's powers, especially after her explicit threats to Mai, and no one else in the group. The way Mai still followed her without any hesitation made Kyth see him in a new light. Despite all the resentment he felt, he knew this was one of the things for which he would always admire his rival.

# 19

# NEGOTIATION

Ellah followed Mai down the narrow forest path. Without his weapons, he looked vulnerable, stirring a deep compassion in her heart. She had to remind herself that this was a ruthless warrior who commanded an invincible army and was trained to kill with no more than a casual flick of a hand. But it also occurred to her that here in Ayalla's realm Mai's power and deadly skills were all but useless. Kara was no less ruthless or capable, yet Ayalla whisked her away without even raising an alarm.

When Mai singled Ellah out as the person he wanted to bring along into Ayalla's realm, it took her by surprise. She rarely spoke to Mai at all, even if on the occasions they did he was usually friendly and courteous, at least when Kyth wasn't around. Like most, she admired Mai for many of his qualities, even aside from his dazzling looks, but she was also aware of his other, frightening side that drove his deadly Majat skill. She also saw the way he and Kyth were always at odds, and she found their constant rivalry troublesome to say the least. It was as if the two men ignited the worst in each other, an effect greatly compounded by the fact that their complementary skills forced them to stay side by side all the time.

It felt almost like a comfort that in the upcoming meeting with Ayalla she had to play only a passive role, powerless to affect things in any way. She couldn't even begin to understand the reasons that prompted Ayalla to take Mai away for a separate conversation, and she didn't want to venture any guesses into what was going to come down when they reached the place they were headed for. She knew that Mai, used to being in charge and feeling powerful in every situation, must be lost here where he had no power at all. Whatever his reasons for choosing her to accompany him, she hoped she wouldn't let him down.

Ayalla led them to a small clearing, with a small brook running on the other side, and gestured to two grass mounds fashioned like piles of soft cushions. Mai lowered onto one of them, natural as if he was sinking into a comfortable chair. Ellah followed suit, feeling far less graceful as she settled by his side.

Ayalla remained standing, looking like a teacher about to address a class.

"I am aware of your nature," she said to Mai. "You kill. This is the only thing you know how to do, especially when driven to the edge. In this place, you will control yourself at all times – or die instantly." She glanced into the shadows.

Ellah's stomach clenched as she watched a group of large spiders emerge and form a circle around Mai, thankfully staying clear of her own seat. She marveled at the way Mai didn't move a muscle. He must be scared, for surely even the Diamond Majat were not immune to fear, but he wasn't showing it in any way.

She lifted her chin. Since she was, for whatever reason, included into this meeting, she couldn't possibly sit quietly when she felt things were being unfair.

"With due respect, I don't believe you are right about Mai, Lady Ayalla," she said. "He knows a lot more than killing. He is a kind and compassionate man. In fact, even when he must kill, he always goes out of his way to spare as many lives as he possibly can. He is known for that, even among the Majat."

She was aware how both Ayalla and Mai were staring at her in surprise. In fact, she felt surprised herself at the force with which she spoke these words. She knew this to be true. But under ordinary circumstances she would never be caught saying something like that.

Ayalla raised her eyebrows. "You feel the need to speak in his defense?"

Ella kept her gaze. "I am here because Mai asked me to come along. I see my part as speaking on his behalf in matters he would not talk about. And, what I said is true. You can ask anyone."

She didn't look at Mai as she spoke, but she could tell he was still staring at her. The spiders around him started to move, as if wondering if they should target Ellah too. But she did not care.

Ayalla turned to Mai. "Did she speak the truth?"

Mai shrugged. "This is the first time anyone ever asked me to make this kind of a call on a truthseer."

Ayalla's eyes narrowed. "If you avoid my questions, it won't go well for you, Majat."

Mai went still as the spiders around him raised their legs threateningly. "Yes, Lady Ayalla. To the best of my knowledge, Ellah believes what she said. Beyond that, I cannot attest to the truth of her words. I never thought of myself as kind or compassionate. Our training greatly discourages these qualities. But it's true that I do try to spare lives whenever I can – not that it is of any relevance here."

Ayalla's lips twitched. "If you really believe so, it is fortunate that you brought your friend along."

"Yes, indeed." Mai shot Ellah a quick smile. He was holding very still, as if not to disturb the spiders. The thought that he might die in agony in front of her eyes if he made a wrong move made her feel nauseated.

"Are the spiders really necessary, Lady Ayalla?" Ellah asked.

The Forest Woman surveyed her with a thoughtful glance. "You are an impressionable young thing, far too innocent and kind to keep company with the likes of him. Have you fallen for his charms?"

Ellah's cheeks warmed up with a blush. "No. I mean, not in that way." Well, perhaps a little bit in that way, but she was damned if she was going to admit it. She hoped that one day she may earn the right to call Mai a friend. But with the way Mai looked at Kara she knew how utterly unavailable he was for any other kind of relationship.

"Very well then," Ayalla said. "On with our conversation." She turned to Mai. "My spiders can sense fear. They can also sense lies – just like your friend here. So, you must pay very close attention to what you say."

"Is Kara all right?" Mai asked.

Ayalla's eyes flared. "I will be the one asking questions."

Mai receded slightly, and once again Ellah felt a pang

of pity at how defenseless he looked. Yet, even in his trapped state he exuded a sense of power. She hoped he could pass Ayalla's test, whatever the Forest Woman had in store for him.

"I am aware," Ayalla said, "that in your war with the Kaddim my spiders have become an important tool that can help you achieve your victory."

"Yes. Even though it was never part of my plan to ask you for this in person."

"Why?"

Mai briefly glanced at the spiders. "I am aware how… incompatible we are."

"And yet, you hope for my help?"

Mai shook his head. "Not I, personally. The Kaddim threaten everyone. The only reason I'm in charge is that, like it or not, the Majat have been the only force able to resist them so far – apart from your spiders."

She held still for a moment, then slowly inclined her head. "You show no fear when you speak to me. At least, my spiders don't sense any."

"I have nothing to fear from you, Lady Ayalla," Mai said. "If you choose to kill me, I can hardly do anything about it. Being afraid won't help, would it?"

"Not many would say this when facing certain death."

"Probably not. But I don't believe I'm facing certain death either. Am I?"

"If you make a wrong move."

He smiled. "In this case I just have to make sure I don't."

She folded her arms over her chest, the movement disturbing the mists around her to briefly bare her shoulders. "So, why do you think I should help you, Majat?"

"Because I hope our goals are aligned, even if our ways may be different. This is what alliances are all about."

"Last time I heard, the Majat Guild didn't form alliances at all."

"Not the ones that are ever recorded in written history, no."

"What makes you think our goals are aligned?" Ayalla asked.

"Don't you want to see the Kaddim destroyed?"

Ayalla spread her hands. "The Kaddim cannot reach me here. As for whatever goes on outside my realm, it's none of my concern."

Mai shifted in his seat and froze as the spiders raised their legs threateningly.

"With respect, Lady Ayalla, I don't need the powers of a truthseer to tell that you are not being entirely honest right now."

Her eyes widened. "No one ever said something like this to me."

"I'm not surprised." Mai glanced at the spiders again.

She slowly relaxed her shoulders. "Why do you think so, Majat?"

He leaned back, a half-smile playing on his lips. "My name is Mai."

"Mai." To Ellah's amazement, the Forest Woman seemed to recede, as if she was considering Mai a worthy opponent.

"You are a giver of life," Mai said. "The Kaddim are threatening all life in existence. They serve the Cursed Destroyer. They stand for everything you oppose. Even if they cannot reach you in your Forest, I doubt you would wish to see them succeed."

She looked at him silently, as if making a decision.

"I don't think we are that different," Mai went on. "My training is to kill, but to achieve my Majat rank I have to be much more than a killer. By killing a few, we maintain peace in the entire realm. Without the Majat, people would die by thousands in senseless wars that never have a chance to erupt when our Guild is in control. As a result, we bring balance to the world."

Ayalla slowly let out a sigh. "That's one way to put it."

Mai's smile widened. "I can also put it in another way, my lady. You send your spiders to kill on command. I assume they are going to kill me if this conversation doesn't go your way – and my death in this case would be far worse than that from a blade. This makes the spiders your weapons, even if you use your thoughts, rather than your hands, to wield them. How does this make us any different from each other?"

Ayalla held a pause for a while longer, then sat down opposite him onto a thick grass mound that, Ellah could swear, wasn't there just moments ago. The mist of Ayalla's dress twirled around her to rearrange itself, covering her curves evenly, like real cloth.

"You've surprised me." Ayalla held a pause. "Mai." She pronounced his name slowly, as if tasting it. "I can understand now what people see in you. And yes, in a way, you are correct. We are similar, and we do have the same goal. I will help you." She briefly inclined her head, and the spiders around Mai receded, disappearing into the shadows.

Mai kept his smile, but Ellah saw a tense cord relax in his neck and felt a pang of sympathy again. In Mai's place she would have been an emotional wreck by now. Yet, he looked undisturbed as he shifted position to settle in more comfortably.

"Thank you, Lady Ayalla," Mai said. "We all greatly hoped you would say this."

Ayalla's mouth curved into a brief smile. "Saying is one thing. Doing is quite another. What kind of help did you expect from me?"

"Originally," Mai said, "we hoped you can lend us your spiders. But just yesterday, I learned more. According to Magister Egey Bashi, to destroy the Kaddim Brotherhood once and for all, you have to be there in person to defeat the Kaddim Reincarnate."

Ayalla's gaze wavered. "Once and for all. Is this what you plan?"

"It's the only permanent solution as I see it right now, yes."

"A very ambitious one."

Mai smiled. "Is it?"

She hesitated, then shook her head. "I can lend you the spiders, perhaps. They can help you win your battle. But the rest of what you're asking is impossible."

"I can never leave the forest. My power depends on the trees. The Kaddim are in a desert, where trees cannot grow. Their choice of location was not incidental. Without my trees, I am no match for their Reincarnate."

Mai held still for a moment. "Is there another way?"

"Did your Magister also tell you that my power comes from the elements?"

She nodded. "Elemental magic is ancient, and rare, after your Church went on their frenzy to eliminate all magic users. But you have someone in your midst whose elemental magic is nearly as strong as mine."

*Elemental magic.* Ellah's mouth fell open. "You can't mean... Kyth?"

"Yes, Kyth."

Ellah gaped, meeting Mai's awe-struck look. *Kyth. Nearly as powerful as Ayalla.* She was having serious trouble absorbing the information.

Ayalla glanced at Mai. "I know you and he are engaged in foolish rivalry, which should be long forgotten by now. I also know that his command of his gift is not fully developed yet."

"You know a great deal, it seems," Mai said.

"My spiders at the King's court, the ones fair Alder carries on his shoulder, serve as my eyes and ears. I am aware of all your plans. Including the one to seek help from the Olivian Queen."

Mai raised his face hopefully. "Can your knowledge of the Kaddim's whereabouts spare us this trip?"

"I *have* no knowledge of the Kaddim's whereabouts." She frowned. "Have you been listening? My powers feed off earth and water. The desert the Kaddim are hiding in feeds on fire. Fire is my enemy. It clouds my mind."

Mai's gaze became distant. "Then we will go through with the original plan."

"Yes, you must. I will open a path for you to reach Shayil Yara quickly."

"And Kyth?"

"I will keep him with me and train him in the use of his magic by the time you are done. I will also keep Alder and train him to command the spiders. When they are ready, I will open a path for them to meet with you. Your Magister, the one who knows so much, is receptive to my magic. If you bring him with you, I can use him to relay a message so that you can all meet in the right place."

Mai heaved a slow sigh. "Thank you, Lady Ayalla. This is more than I hoped for."

She shook her head. "Perhaps, but you mustn't think, even for a moment, that this would be enough. To enable Kyth to defeat their Reincarnate you have to bring him all the way into the heart of their fortress. Which means, you will still have to deal with all the Kaddim's fighters, who, as it seems, have recently gained access to your friend's Diamond skill. There is no telling how powerful they will become by the time you get there.

"Which brings me to your original question. Kara."

Mai lifted his head so fast that his shape blurred, the mix of hope and pain in his gaze making Ellah shiver.

"You love her," Ayalla said quietly.

"Yes, I do."

"Then you must hope that your love carries her through. It's the only thing that can. She has been badly damaged by the Kaddim."

Mai's gaze wavered.

"I know you hate them, if only for that," Ayalla said. "You must not let this personal hatred drive your actions."

"I won't," Mai said. "I know I can't possibly afford to."

Her gaze softened. "I have another thing I can do for you then. I will put a spell on Kara that will disable her Kaddim link. For now."

Again, Ellah's heart quivered at the hope that stirred in Mai's gaze.

"She will become herself again," Ayalla went on, "and the Kaddim won't be able to tap into her skill while my spell is in place. But once you get close to their stronghold, once she finds herself in proximity to the man who controls her link, my spell will be broken and the link will become active again."

Mai smiled. "I see a simple solution for this. We can leave Kara behind. This way, she would never have to get close to him at all."

"If only it were so easy. The man who controls the link carries a part of her soul – just as she carries a part of his. She must be near him when he dies, or she will never get her soul back. She must be touching him, sharing his agony when he heaves his last breath. If she doesn't, she will die too."

For a brief moment, Mai went very still. Then he nodded.

"I guess," he said, "this lays out our plan of action, doesn't it?"

"You must be careful," Ayalla said. "I know now that you are very strong, but the challenges you are facing are formidable. Your love is a burden when you also have to carry the weight of the world on your shoulders. Don't let it destroy you."

Mai lifted his eyebrows. "What do you mean?"

"Once you reach the Kaddim, Kara will turn against you. When this happens, what are you going to do?"

Mai's jaw tightened. "Is this a certainty?"

Ayalla sighed. "Yes."

"But–"

"I know what you are thinking. She is a fighter and she has resisted them well so far. But the Kaddim are stronger than anything you faced before. You must be prepared."

"I am. Or so I believe."

"Your beliefs have nothing to do with it. Not in this case. And, you didn't answer my question. What will you do once she falls under the Kaddim's control?"

Mai shook his head. "This is not a question I can answer, Lady Ayalla. I hold a responsibility to my men. I will never let them down, no matter what. But once that is fulfilled, the rest is up to me, isn't it?"

She hesitated. "I hope you can handle what's coming. In the very least, my spell will allow you and Kara a break for the time being. And, it would enable her to fully participate in your negotiations at the Olivian court. Trust me, you would need a strong woman down there to champion your cause."

"Yes, so I heard."

Ayalla laughed. "I am beginning to like you, Mai. I never expected I would. In fact, if your heart was not given already, I could have considered you for a consort – which is not what I would ever expect from a man of your occupation."

Mai stiffened. "I assume I should thank you, Lady Ayalla." He glanced around and Ellah saw his cheeks light up with a faint touch of color.

Ayalla reached forward and patted his arm. "My consorts normally don't have a lot of time to assume anything, not when they are in my presence. I keep them otherwise occupied. But since you are not suitable for the role anyway, it doesn't really matter, does it?" She rose to her feet in a fluid move that briefly parted the mist around her. Ellah felt both awed and embarrassed at once. She had never seen women this beautiful all the way down, or as unabashed about showing their nakedness. Perhaps Ayalla did all this on purpose?

She saw Mai gaping too as Ayalla laughed and beckoned. "Come. I will take you to your loved one."

## 20
# THE SPELL

When Kara opened her eyes, she could not see anything at all. It took a moment to focus her eyes on the swirls of white mist in front of her eyes, cold and moist, as if she was being enfolded by a cloud.

She tried to move, finding no restraints this time, nothing that would hold her in place at all. By the feel of it, she was lying down on a thick carpet of grass, the mist around her so thick that she couldn't even see the ground. Or was there something wrong with her vision? Panicked, she brought her hand up to her eyes, relieved to see her fingers moving in front of her face. The rest of the hand wasn't visible at all. This mist must be magical, akin to the one she saw Lady Ayalla wearing as a dress just a short while ago.

Her head was still throbbing, the memory of the Kaddim vision she saw when Ayalla opened her link clinging to her mind with nauseating clarity. The inside of the Kaddim fortress, as real as if she was standing there in person. A foreign, male voice coming out of her own throat. *Nimos*. Egey Bashi had guessed right, back at the King's council. Nimos had to be the one controlling her link.

The realization made her skin tingle.

The mist started to dissipate as she rose to her feet, finally affording her a view of her surroundings. The glade was smaller than the one before, covered with soft, silky grass. The brook running at the side opened into a wider pond, a smooth bed of rock along the bottom making it look like a very large bath. The water breathed warmth, beckoning. She felt so tempted to dive in.

Just when she was beginning to seriously contemplate the possibility, she heard the approaching sounds. Rustling and voices, the trees parting at the far end of the glade to let in two people.

*Mai.* Kara's heart leapt as he rushed toward her, sweeping her into an embrace. She clung to him, instantly drunk with his scent and with the reassurance of his solid warmth. She hadn't known until now if she was ever going to see him again, a feeling that was becoming too frequent of late and far too unsettling to deal with.

After a while he set her down, holding her close as he turned to Ayalla. Kara felt curious at the expression of motherly indulgence on the Forest Woman's face. She never expected Mai and Ayalla could possibly get along – yet they did, if appearances were any indication.

"I liked your man," Ayalla said in response to her questioning gaze. "Mai. He surprised me. You are very lucky to have his love."

"I know." Kara felt puzzled. Should she be worried about Ayalla liking Mai? Should she feel glad? At least for the moment this seemed like a better option, so she decided to stay with it, dismissing all else.

"How is your headache?" Ayalla asked.

"About the same, thanks." Kara's lips twitched. She was used to pain, inevitable for someone with her training, but the way this pain never let go made her feel exhausted. She supposed this was partially responsible for how weak and shaky she felt.

"And the mind link?"

"Still there, I believe."

"I'm about to block it."

"*Block* it?"

"Hold still." Ayalla grasped Kara's arm and pulled up her sleeve to expose her forearm. Kara gasped.

In all the excitement of the past days, she never had a chance to examine her arm closely. Last time she looked, the mark had been a light shadow, like a healing bruise. This time the spot seemed much darker. Worse, it was shaping into the unmistakable resemblance of the Kaddim brand mark – a downturned triangle with elongated corners, like a crude depiction of a goat head.

Ayalla frowned. "It's deepening. I'm amazed you haven't turned yet."

*Turned?* Kara bit her lip, thinking it best not to ask.

Ayalla held out her hand. A sharp object resting over the tip of her forefinger drew Kara's gaze. It looked like a very thick thorn, about half an inch long with a sharp tip and a broad oval base the size of a thumbnail. Nested over Ayalla finger, it looked like the tip of a huge scorpion's stinger poised to strike.

"This will hurt," Ayalla said. "A lot. You must do your best to keep still."

Kara nodded.

In a deft movement, the Forest Woman drew the thorn all the way into the dark spot on Kara's forearm.

The pain was exquisite, instantly erupting from the entry point, shooting through her body in sharp spikes. She was grateful for the warning that enabled her to brace herself and control her reaction. Still, it took all she had to remain motionless, to bite back a cry. She felt Mai's hand tighten on her other arm, to support or restrain her, she wasn't sure. Through their touch he was bound to know how much it hurt, and she was grateful that he didn't try to say anything at all.

She felt dazed as she rode through it, the sharp stabs penetrating her head, shocking away the dull headache she had gotten used to lately. In an odd way, the sensation felt like cleansing, the agony washing through to leave nothing behind.

She wasn't sure how long it lasted, but when the pain finally receded she felt light, as if filled with air. She moved her limbs experimentally, finding herself in full control of her movements, her head swimming with the liberating absence of any pulling sensations or lingering presence at the back of her mind. She hadn't felt this good in a very long while.

"Now," Ayalla said. "Take off your clothes and get into the water."

Kara obeyed without hesitation. If she had felt the water in the pond beckon her earlier, by now the pull seemed nearly irresistible. She moaned as she submerged into its warmth, caressing like a lover's arms. The water tingled, making her feel lightheaded, drunk.

Ayalla looked at her with satisfaction, then turned to Mai.

"She will need time to adjust," she said. "Stay with her. Help her through the transformation. Take as long as you need. You will not be disturbed, not until dark. When you are ready to leave, tell the trees and they will lead you to your camp."

*Tell the trees.* In Kara's new state of mind, the instruction seemed natural, as if there was nothing to it. She briefly wondered if Ayalla's spell had also infused her with the forest magic, if the transformation Ayalla was talking about involved changing Kara into a forest being the trees listened to. She was vaguely aware that she should feel frightened by the thought, but, strangely, it didn't bother her at all.

She watched Ayalla exit the glade, the trees closing behind her to leave no trace of any path. *You will not be disturbed.* The knowledge felt comforting, and arousing as she fell into a new reality where everything was allowed.

She turned to Mai, standing beside the water, watching her.

"Get in," she said, surprised at the need she felt, surely incompatible with the danger they were in, with the way they both barely escaped death to be together right now. A distant part of her mind knew they should be dressing up and walking back to camp. A more immediate, carnal one, couldn't wait to get him naked next to her. She knew a lot of Ayalla's power came from raw sexuality, the way she took men whenever she pleased, the way she used their seed to gain even more power. Was this power now part of her too, planted into her by Ayalla to block the Kaddim magic? With the need she felt, she didn't really care.

She saw Mai hesitate briefly as he likely considered and dismissed the same questions, then obeyed her command, taking off his clothes and sliding into the water next to her. She trembled with need as she drew on top of him, arching to take him in as deep as she could. Her body shook as she rode him in a mad, accelerating rhythm, building up her pleasure so fast that it threatened to burst her from the inside, then releasing it all at once in a sweet, unbearable agony that clenched her insides like a very long freefall. She spasmed again as his release inside her sent her into a new spiral and then, when she felt she could not take another moment of it, into a blackout that robbed her of every bit of strength, every moment of tension she felt ever since the Kaddim link inside her got activated.

The warm water lapped around them as she lay splayed over his chest, the movement of his caressing hands over her back the only sensation that linked her to the outside world. She did not know how long it lasted, and she did not care. She never wanted it to stop.

When she finally found the strength to raise her head, he was looking at her, a grin playing on his lips.

"I could get used to you being like this," he said.

She raised her eyebrows, feigning surprise. "Like what?"

He laughed, closing his arms around her.

She leaned back into his chest, his closeness stirring her desire anew. *Take as long as you need,* Ayalla had said. She was surprised to realize that despite the fear of the forest she felt only this morning, despite how frightening Ayalla and her magic seemed, despite the way she had felt so spent only recently, she needed more.

She shifted over him, turning his face toward her, leaning over him to meet his lips. Her stomach quivered with the rising excitement as he responded, his tongue claiming her mouth, his hands caressing her in long, powerful strokes. When he flipped her in the water and entered her again, she shook with the intensity of the pleasure that instantly drove away all other thoughts. She arched into him once again as he built up the rhythm, making every nerve in her body sing in response. It didn't matter anymore if this carnal need stemmed from Ayalla's power inside her, or the desires she had been suppressing for so long. Right now she didn't care.

Just a short while ago she was preparing to die, unable to find any way out of the Kaddim trap. And now, Ayalla's magic granted her this short rest, where she could pretend that everything was normal and nothing in their lives had ever gone amiss. She intended to spend every bit of her strength riding with this feeling, fully giving herself to it.

They stayed in the water nearly until dusk, enjoying each other again and again, unable to leave each other's arms. She knew they had to stop before it got dark, but when they finally emerged and dressed up, she felt regret that they could not stay longer, with no one else but the trees to see and hear them. They held each other for one last kiss before turning their backs to the glade and stepping toward the dense line of trees in front of them.

*When you are ready to leave, tell the trees.* But how did one talk to trees, exactly?

"We, um, we'd like to return to our camp. Please," she added, aware that even with the beings she used to think of as inanimate it probably didn't hurt to be polite.

For a moment, everything was silent. Then the trees rustled and fell away, a path opening in front of them much faster than seemed possible. She grasped Mai's hand and set her foot on it.

Kara looked at her mark as they walked, bringing it closer to her face to see in the gathering dusk. The thorn, level with the skin around it, looked like an odd oval-shaped birthmark, smooth and wood-hard to the touch. Despite its size and the vicious strength with which Ayalla had driven it in, she felt no pain at all.

"You have to tell me everything that happened at Ayalla's," she said.

Mai reached over to put an arm around her as they walked. His hand squeezed her shoulder briefly, an emotional gesture that sent a surge of warmth down her spine. "I will. Along with all our plans that involve you."

She heaved a slow breath of the damp cooling air, infused with the smells of earth, trees, and grass. Her heart swelled with happiness. As long as they were together, she wasn't afraid of anything at all.

Tomorrow she would be able to finally take full part in his campaign. She hoped this would make a difference to their chances against the Kaddim.

# 21
# PROMISE

Kyth couldn't get over his disbelief. He knew Ayalla had no reasons to lie to him about his gift, but everything he learned in the past few hours simply refused to settle in. His power, strong enough to take down the Kaddim Reincarnate? It seemed even more impossible than the idea that he and Alder would be spending the next couple of weeks with Ayalla, who seemed confident enough that this short amount of time would be sufficient for him to master his ability enough to face the reincarnation of the Cursed Destroyer himself, on top of protecting their entire army against the Kaddim magic.

He was only marginally less surprised to find out that Mai did not end up messing up his part and somehow managed to charm his way into Ayalla's trust. And of course, knowing that Kara was all right, and, for the moment, free of the Kaddim link, made everything else seem worth it. Watching her and Mai emerge from the forest at dusk looking exhausted but happy in the way he hadn't seen them in a very long time brought so much relief that he forgot even to feel jealous.

He lifted his head when he saw Lady Celana walking toward him. As she approached, he rose to his feet, offering his hand to help her down by the campfire. She accepted it gracefully, settling on the outstretched cloak beside him.

The royal lady was dressed for the march, her dark pants suit plain and practical, her hair tied into a smooth knot at the back of her head. Not for the first time Kyth marveled how well she fit into their camping life, while also maintaining the same refinement she did at court. It was as if she had a unique ability to wear her surroundings like a garment, bringing them with her wherever she went. To his surprise, he found himself thinking that in her own unique way this quality made an odd parallel to Ayalla. If Lady Celana always wore an invisible mantle of her royal upbringing around her, Ayalla wore a piece of her forest, albeit in a much more literal sense.

"I hope you don't mind me joining you, Prince Kythar," Lady Celana said.

"I am delighted, my lady." The polite phrase came out automatically, but as soon as it left his lips, Kyth realized he meant it. Lady Celana always made him feel good, not only because of the way she tended to lighten up the conversation, but also because of the way she made his self-esteem soar just by looking at him with shy admiration, as if she genuinely cared. He was going to miss her when she departed with the Majat, leaving him behind at Ayalla's place.

"I, um, was hoping to trouble Your Highness with a request." Lady Celana's uncomfortable look piqued his interest. What could she possibly ask him for that she would also find so embarrassing?

"Anything I can do, my lady," he said earnestly.

Her cheeks lit up with a faint blush. "I would like to ask your permission to stay with you and Alder at Lady Ayalla's. If this is agreeable to you, of course."

Kyth's eyes widened. "You'd like to stay with us? Why?"

Her blush deepened as she continued to hold his gaze. "Consider this a personal request, my lord. I'd like to, if only because there seems to be no good reason for me to travel to Shayil Yara."

Kyth shook his head. "You will be a lot safer with the Majat."

She smiled. "I doubt it, Your Highness. But more than that, I feel that…" She paused.

"Feel what?"

Her blush rolled down her neck. He had never seen her look so flustered.

"I must confess, Your Highness, that when I asked to join this campaign against the Kaddim, one of my main reasons to do it was the fact that it would enable me to stay by your side. This is the place I'd like to keep – if you let me, with full understanding that I never intend to impose on your privacy or make you feel uncomfortable."

Kyth heaved a breath. He knew she seemed to like him for some reason, but he always believed this was mostly due to the fact that he was the only young man here who shared her high station and thus seemed like worthy company – not that she ever showed inclination to pull ranks with the others. He had originally been opposed to the idea of her joining their party, but had to give in to his father's insistence, likely driven by the idea that Lady Celana may help him forget his heartbreak and secure an eligible match for marriage. With all these political considerations, he had never given enough thought to the possibility that Celana genuinely cared about him. And now, the way she was looking at him, the way she stated her preference to stay by his side, made him wonder.

He knew her reserve. It never seemed easy for her to communicate her feelings – especially with the way he tended to brush her off every time Kara was in sight. Watching her chest heave as she sat in front of him, blushing to the roots of her hair, made him feel guilty.

He reached over and took her hand.

"My friends call me Kyth," he said.

Her eyelids fluttered as she raised her eyes to him. She looked so vulnerable that his heart quivered.

"I would be honored if you could address me this way, my lady."

She smiled. "Kyth."

The way she pronounced it, as if caressing each sound with her tongue, made Kyth blush too. It felt so captivating to see her look at him like this. Unexpectedly, he found himself wondering what her skin would feel like under his fingers, what it would be like to run his hand through her hair. He stopped himself. Lady Celana was a friend, no more. He was trying to make her feel better, but he shouldn't be acting as if he could ever promise her anything else.

"Perhaps it would be easier if you could call me by my name too?" she asked.

"Celana." He felt oddly intimate as he said it, as the use of their names instead of the formal address broke a boundary between them. He laughed "This would take some getting used to, won't it?"

She lifted her eyes to him. "Yes, it would. And… I am honored to call you my friend. You can't possibly know how much it means to me."

Her voice sank to a near whisper, her eyes wide as she looked into his face. Warmth pulsed off her skin as her blush rolled down deeper, all the way into the low cut of her shirt. Kyth hastily averted his gaze before it ventured anywhere improper.

He covered her hand he still held, cupping it between his, feeling so helpless under her disarming gaze. She was beautiful, and smart, and the admiration with which she always looked at him made his heart soar. Was he going to let his heartbreak, the way he just couldn't stop thinking about Kara, ruin all this?

"I haven't been very good to you, have I?" he said quietly.

She smiled, her hand inside his hold briefly squeezing his. "You have a deep heart wound. The fact that you are capable of such loyalty to someone who no longer shares your feelings just proves in yet another way how great a man you are… Kyth. And, the last thing I want is for you to feel any guilt. I am not asking you for anything more than just allowing me to be by your side. As a friend."

"This couldn't possibly be enough."

She swallowed. "I haven't made it a secret of how much I admire you. I cannot help hoping for more between us, but I know this is not something you or I can possibly control. I'll take what you can give – with no regrets or false expectations, I promise you."

A lump rose in his throat as he looked at her. He felt ashamed for not being able to answer her feelings any better than this. He had no right to keep her by his side.

But if she wanted to stay, he also had no right at all to turn her away. Not with the way she had opened her heart to him just now.

He lowered his eyes to her hand he was still holding, aware how warm and soft it was, how it quivered in his hold. Carefully, he brought her hand to his lips and kissed it.

"I am not worthy of you," he said.

She smiled. "Isn't it for me to decide?"

"I suppose it is." Kyth hesitated. "If you truly feel you know me enough."

"I do." Her smile widened. "I think I am a better judge of character than you give me credit for."

He met her gaze. "I find your company very pleasant. And refreshing. I find myself missing you when you are not around. One day, I may be capable of more. But I know that here and now this cannot possibly mean much."

She reached over and lightly touched his cheek. "It does, actually. And, that one day that may yet come – it's worth waiting for, even if in the end it never happens this way."

His gaze wavered. "I find it perplexing that you would be interested in me at all."

She laughed. "I know you do. If you forgive me for saying so, this makes you even more alluring."

*Alluring.* This simple word made his head spin. Suddenly, the sight of Kara and Mai, sitting together on the other side of the camp like a pair of love birds, no longer disturbed him so much. He shifted so that he could turn his back to them, facing Celana more directly than before. What would it feel like, to sit this close to her, feeling their entire bodies touch? The thought sent a new wave of blush into his face.

"I wouldn't want to lead you on or create any false pretenses," he said.

"I don't think you need to worry about that," she said. "So far you have been nothing but honest about your lack of interest in me – as a woman, I mean."

*Honest.* He wasn't so sure this was true, not anymore. Was he feeling this pull for a while? Was he purposely trying to push her away and immerse into his heartbreak instead? "I have?"

"Yes. But I am only saying this to dissolve your fear of leading me on. Not to make you feel guilty in any way."

"If I made you feel this way, why do you want to stay with me then?"

She looked up at him. "I said I have no false expectations, Kyth. But I do have hope – when and if you are ready for it, of course. Even if this possibility turns out to be ungrounded, I would never forgive myself if I did not explore it to the end."

*Hope.* He kept her gaze as they sat leaning toward each other, so close that he could feel the heat of her blush, the smell of her skin, fragrant like fresh lake wind. How was it possible that he never realized her skin smelled so good? Or was it just because he never got close enough to notice?

Her look, shy and direct at the same time, made his heart race. He suddenly realized that if she did continue traveling with the Majat while he stayed at Ayalla's, he would miss her terribly – not only her cool wit and entertaining stories, but also the way she made his skin tingle and his toes curl when she looked at him like this.

"I don't want to lead you on or make any false promises," he said quietly. "But I feel very tempted to take advantage of you right now."

She leaned closer, until he could feel her breath on his cheek.

"Please do," she whispered.

He cupped her chin, drawing her into a kiss.

She tasted fresh and sweet, like a sip of the Lakeland cider that instantly went to his head. He could sense her uncertainty, as if she was unsure what to do, and her eagerness as she opened up to him, beckoning him to explore. She kissed like the virgin she probably was, yet also like a woman in love, willing to give him everything he would take from her. He took it slowly, first touching only her face, cupping it to stroke her skin and hair, giving her time to ease into his embrace. Her lips opened slowly, hesitant when he first ventured in, then growing bolder as she responded to his caress. Slowly, she relaxed into his hold.

Her body told him so much more about her than words possibly could, her trust as she opened up to him so overwhelming that he felt his head spin. The way she melted into his embrace made him feel as if she always belonged there, urging him to do anything he will, uncertain yet so responsive to his hands.

He gave her all the time she needed, holding back at each step until he felt she was ready for more, finding the places that made her shiver, the ones that made her moan and turn deeper into his kiss. He never thought of himself as a skilled lover, but with her, he felt like one. Perhaps it was because his experience at lovemaking was far more extensive than her non-existent one. Or maybe there was just such a thing as being compatible, fitting together so naturally that everything came easily, without any effort at all.

He knew that in this public setting, with the way he was giving her no promises to hold him to, he couldn't possibly take this very far. But the way she yielded to his hands told him what they could do if they ever took their relationship to that level. This promise made his head spin as he finally eased away from her, afraid to let this last any longer for fear of losing control. He knew he had no right to her. Not this way. Not just yet.

She was gasping as she drew away, the daze in her eyes telling him so much more than words. He slowly returned to his senses, realizing that the sky now looked much darker than it did when she first approached his campfire. He knew someone could have seen them, and probably had, by the way their side of the camp suddenly seemed emptier than before. He took a breath of air, feeling lightheaded as he met her smile.

"Please forgive me," he said. "I didn't mean to..."

Her look stopped him.

"I liked it," she said. "Very much. And if I may guess what you were going to say, you were probably planning to tell me that despite what happened, you cannot promise me anything and wouldn't want to give me false hope."

"I..." He took a breath. He *did* want to say just that, but as he looked into her eyes, he suddenly realized that the hope she talked about was not an impossibility at all. She was so different from Kara, in every imaginable way. And now, more than ever before, it seemed like a good thing.

She shook her head. "You don't have to say anything, Kyth. I understand. As I said, I am willing to wait, and

I will not push you in any way. But…" She hesitated.

"But what?"

Her eyelids fluttered. "You still did not tell me if you will let me stay with you at Lady Ayalla's."

He smiled, feeling ashamed. "Yes, of course I will – if this is truly what you want."

"It is." She raised her eyes to him. "Thank you. And…" Her voice dropped to a near-whisper. "If you ever want to take advantage of me again, you have my permission to do it any time."

# 22
# A PILE OF ROCKS

Kyth stood next to Garnald, Alder, and Celana, waiting his turn to say goodbye to the departing group. He gave a brief hug to Kara, marveling at the way she seemed so radiant and carefree, now that her curse had been temporarily lifted. Mai stepped up to Kyth in her wake, and the Prince's heart quivered at the happiness he saw in the Diamond's eyes. No matter what else, Mai did love Kara deeply, and this knowledge, now that it had fully sunk in, made it so much easier to let go.

The two young men exchanged a long handshake.

"Sorry for everything I've put you through lately," Mai said once Kara was out of earshot.

Kyth raised his eyebrows. "You are *apologizing* to me?"

"Did it sound like a bloody insult?"

Kyth stared at him for a moment, then relaxed his shoulders, flexing his hand in Mai's iron-hard grasp.

"It didn't," he said. "And you don't have to apologize. Not for anything that happened lately, anyway. I understand. For whatever it's worth, I am glad that you and Kara are happy together."

Mai's eyes briefly drifted away and Kyth shivered at the glimpse of uncertainty and pain he saw in the Majat's face. He also saw the knotted jaw, signaling that this was not the topic they were ever going to discuss in any detail. He could relate to both feelings very well. The war was only beginning, and Kara's well-being depended on whether they would be able to achieve victory – a burden that lay directly on Mai's shoulders, in addition to everything else. Besides, Kyth's recent relationship with Kara made him probably the last man in the world Mai would ever want to confide these feelings to.

"Just remember," Mai said. "Your ability, the things that Ayalla said you can do, are the key to our victory. My men and I are tools, no more. It's all about you, Kyth. Make it count."

He turned and walked away before giving Kyth a chance to respond, leaving the Prince gaping. Did Mai just say he was considering Kyth to be the main person in this campaign? Did he characterize himself, and all the Majat under his command, as *tools*, with no more than a secondary role?

Did he really mean it all?

For the first time since Kyth knew Mai, he found himself worrying. Was Mai having self-doubts? Or, did he truly think this way all along? He'd probably never know for certain. For the moment it didn't seem to matter, anyway. Mai was right. Kyth's ability to learn from Ayalla did hold a key part in their plans. He needed to do his best if he hoped for their venture to succeed.

He came back to his senses as he realized that Ellah was standing in front of him, her surprised expression suggesting that she had probably been there for quite some time, without any reaction on his part. She frowned, turning to glance at Mai's retreating back.

"What's the matter, Kyth?" she asked. "Did Mai say something nasty to you again?"

Kyth slowly let out a breath. "Not exactly."

She stepped closer, drawing him into a brief embrace. "Don't pay attention to what he says. He's a good man. He just doesn't know how to handle you, that's all. But he'll get over it, I'm sure."

Kyth nodded. Ellah was right, of course. Jealousy was a poor accompaniment to any relationship, especially given their history. Spending some time apart would do them all good, Kyth knew, even though he couldn't help feeling sorry for seeing Kara go. He turned to Celana, trying to draw strength from her presence, from her resolve to stay by his side. At least someone here cared. He found himself surprisingly comforted by the thought.

His thoughts wandered back to Mai's words just now. The more he thought about them the more he realized the kind of responsibility that lay on his shoulders. Was he ever going to be able to live up to it and do his part as well as everyone needed him to?

"Are you going to be all right?" he asked.

Ellah nodded. "Mai needs me. Just like in Tallan Dar, at the Olivian court, everyone's always lying as a matter of daily life. It's part of politics as I came to understand it. And, it's critical to know when it happens if we ever want to succeed."

Kyth felt unsettled about letting Ellah go. He, Alder, and Ellah grew up together and hadn't separated for long in many years. She and Alder used to be sweethearts, until Ayalla came along. And now, the way Ellah looked at Mai when she thought no one was watching, made him feel concerned. Yet, he also knew she was perfectly capable, even though he was used to thinking of her as a little sister in need of his protection. Besides, Magister Egey Bashi was going with her too, and Kyth trusted the Keeper probably more than anyone else he knew.

"Take care of yourself," he said, squeezing her in a long embrace.

"You don't need to worry about me, Kyth. Just relax and enjoy this opportunity as much as you can." Ellah's eyes briefly lingered on Celana, leaving Kyth wondering which opportunity she meant. He almost decided to ask the question when Egey Bashi stepped up to them.

"It's time." The Keeper turned to Kyth and briefly patted him on the shoulder. "Good luck."

"Thanks, Magister." *I'll need every bit of it.* "You too."

The Keeper smiled as he departed, with Ellah in his wake.

Kyth was still feeling surreal as he watched the Majat party mount their horses and melt away into the thick forest growth. Then he turned and followed Garnald through another forest path, with Celana and Alder by his side.

Behind him, the Kingsguard of his suite were settling into the remainder of their old camp, determined to stay in wait until Kyth was ready to leave and they could accompany him. Their captain had made a request to keep some men at Kyth's side, but Ayalla would not let them into her realm. For the next couple of weeks Kyth, Alder, and Celana were going to be entirely on their own.

•••

Garnald led them into a small glade, next to a narrow brook that widened downstream behind the bushes to provide a perfect secluded place for a bath. Four small tents were set around a stone-paved pit, ideally suited for a campfire. It looked perfect, as if someone had taken time to create a special piece of landscape that could fit all of the traveler's needs. Very likely this was indeed the case, Kyth reflected. Ayalla could command landscapes to change around here. Creating a perfect glade and a brook seemed easy, compared to some other things he had seen. *Am I going to be able to do such things too when I complete my training with her?* He dismissed the thought, too wild and far-fetched to dwell on.

Garnald led the way into the center of the camp and threw down his pack near one of the tents.

"Take your pick," he said. "They're all identical, as far as I know."

Kyth and Alder turned to Celana, who smiled and pointed to one of the tents closest to the brook and the bushes on the far end. "I'll use this one, if you don't mind."

They brought forward her packs to set them by the tent's door.

They were still busy settling in when a rustle at the side of the glade announced Ayalla's arrival. Her eyes lingered on Alder, then drifted thoughtfully over the rest of the group, before fixing on Kyth.

"Come," she said. "It's time to begin your training."

Kyth didn't expect it to start so soon, but he supposed there was no reason to waste time. They had so little of it. He tried to stifle his worries as he followed Ayalla down a narrow side path that stayed open all the way through – perhaps to prepare for the fact that they were going to travel it every day?

The path led into another opening, one of the many around here which, he believed, popped up and disappeared almost instantly at Ayalla's command. This one, like many others, had a brook running through and a large pile of rocks rising in its center. Ayalla gestured toward it and walked on to stop by its side.

"Now," she said. "Show me what you've learned so far."

"I..." Kyth paused. Inadvertently, his conversation with Egey Bashi back on the barge came up in his mind. His training so far had been all about weapons. But now, standing opposite to Ayalla who resented everything weapon-like, it seemed like a bad idea to even bring this up.

"Go on," she said. "You must've learned *something*, if they all place such heavy hopes on you."

"I'm afraid my training up to now has been all wrong," Kyth said. "At least from your perspective, if I understand it correctly."

"What makes you say that?"

"I've been trained by the Majat, mostly. I know how you feel about them."

She raised her eyebrows. "The Majat? I didn't know they were the experts in elemental magic."

Kyth sighed. "They're not. It's just that, through a combination of circumstances, I came to think of my power as a weapon. It's what they are best at, as you well know. They've been training me to focus, so that I can wield it correctly."

He looked at her, expecting resentment and mockery, but she merely nodded. "It's one way to look at it, yes. There's truth in the fact that your power has a lot to do with focus, something the Majat know so well. Why don't you show me what they taught you?"

He drew his sword, searching for the powers around him that he could use. There wasn't much to work with in this secluded forest glade, but the light breeze descending from the tree crowns, mixing with the twirl of the water in the brook, seemed sufficient at least to sharpen his movements as he circled around the glade. In the absence of a real opponent, he focused on an imaginary one, like he often did when practicing alone, thrusting and parrying with the dexterity he was never capable of if he wasn't using his magic.

Ayalla made no move to interrupt or comment, only watched him with a thoughtful expression. After a while, he stopped on his own and lowered his sword, wiping the sweat off his forehead.

"Not as bad as I thought," she said. "Your natural talent is impressive. But you can never expand yourself fully this way. Surely you feel this, don't you?"

"Yes, I do." Kyth was surprised to realize that he meant it. Using his power felt good, yet he could indeed sense his limits with it. Now, under Ayalla's watchful gaze, he realized that these limits did not necessarily mean he had reached the limits of his ability. He could do more, he was certain of it. Except that he didn't know at all how to go about it.

"Let me show you," Ayalla said. "Come here."

She picked up a small rock from the pile in the center of the glade and held it in her outstretched hand.

"This rock," she said, "is made up of the element earth. The element's power holds it together, makes it strong. Without it, the rock would turn into dust." She frowned as she looked into her palm.

A brief sensation of pressure pounced onto Kyth's ears. The rock shifted in Ayalla's hand, hazy as if its boundaries suddenly became blurry, less defined. A brief sigh-like sound echoed in the air, faint like an exhaled breath.

Kyth wasn't quite sure what happened next. The rock just… disappeared, as if it was never there. A pile of fine dust settled into Ayalla's palm in its place.

Ayalla smiled at his awed expression. "This is but a simple example. I extended my power to the bonds that held this rock in place. And then, I dissolved them all at once. You can do the same. Try." She picked up another small rock and handed it to Kyth.

*Try.* Kyth swallowed as he took the rock and placed it onto his palm. It looked so solid and hard. Its rough edges grazed his skin and he clenched it briefly, trying to feel it out. *Elemental earth, holding it together. Can I ever see it this way?*

"You're looking at the surface," Ayalla said. "Try to look inside it instead."

"*Inside* it?" Kyth stared. Some rocks were opaque, or nearly transparent, making it easy to see at least some way inside. This rock was nothing like that, all solid and gray, impenetrable to the eye.

"Close your eyes," Ayalla said.

Kyth did.

"Imagine you are still looking at the rock."

This was easy, after how hard Kyth had been staring at it just now. He could probably recreate every bump, every rough edge in his mind's eye.

"Good. Now, try to see what's under its surface."

Kyth tried. It seemed easier without actually looking at the rock to imagine it losing substance to appear semi-transparent. He took it further, gradually stripping away all the grayness until the rock in his imagination looked clear, like an exquisite crystal. It helped to feel its reassuring roughness in his hand, to flesh out all the crests and edges that prickled his skin as he traced his fingers over them, imagining them at the same time.

"Do you see the power holding it together?"

*The shine.* With surprise, Kyth realized that the crystal he imagined in his mind was not only transparent, but glowing, as if bathed in sunlight. He wasn't sure where this glow was coming from.

"It's glowing," he said.

"Yes. That's one way to look at it. Do you see the bonds between the elements of the rock?"

*The bonds.* He kept his eyes closed as he peered, imagining tiny threads that extended like a meshwork through the substance of the stone. "I... I think so, yes."

"Try to imagine these bonds are made of air, not stone," Ayalla said. "Let them blow away."

*Air, not stone.* Suddenly it all made sense. The glow, the tiny threads, they *had* to be there for the stone to remain in its form. And at the same time, they didn't have to be there at all. The threads could shift out of the stone easily, blend with the air instead of the earth. And once shifted, Kyth could make them all blow away, couldn't he?

He tried to recall the sigh-like sound he heard when Ayalla dissipated her rock a short while ago. *Poof.* Was *this* how it went...?

"Open your eyes," Ayalla commanded.

Kyth obeyed. His eyes widened as he stared at a small pile of dust in his hand.

"I... Did I do that?" he asked weakly.

She smiled. "Yes, you did."

"But how?"

"You tell me. What did you do?"

Kyth stared at the dust in his hand again. No matter how hard he looked, it still didn't make any sense at all.

"I imagined the rock being transparent," he said. "And then, I started seeing a glow holding it together. Like sunlight, made of tiny threads. When you mentioned I should let it become part of the air and blow away... it just did."

She nodded. "You created an image in your mind that helped you to wield your power. Just like you did before, when you imagined a sword. Your image is different this time, but the purpose is the same."

"Is this how it works, then?" Kyth asked. "Thinking of my power as a glow of tiny threads?"

"No."

"No?" He felt lost again. He just thought he was getting a grasp of it.

Ayalla smiled. "Images are what help you cope with your abilities. Many magic users do that, or so I heard. What you need to understand now is that these are only images, not the real thing. You can use these images to help yourself, but you should not let them obscure the truth."

"I... I don't think I understand."

She shook her head. "You will. But for now, I'll leave you to practice. See this pile of rocks?"

"Yes."

"By the end of today, you must turn them all into dust. Use any images you want to do it."

Kyth looked at the pile, rising about waist-high from the thick grass. *Dear Shal Addim, there must be hundreds of rocks here. "Each* rock?"

Ayalla shrugged. "Once you get good at it, you can do several at a time. In fact, you have it within you to dissipate the entire pile on the spot."

Kyth swallowed. He knew he had to master his magic, one way or the other. He supposed sitting here staring at the rocks until he turned blue in the face could be one way to do it.

"Why is this important?" he asked. "Blowing up rocks?"

"Apart from teaching you to control your power, you mean?"

Kyth hesitated. It *was* important to learn to control his power, and he was grateful for a different image to work with, compared to his usual sword, but everything he had been doing up to now under the Majat's tutelage – focusing the powers of the elements to aid in swordplay, to defend his allies against the Kaddim – seemed useful, at least. But blowing up rocks?

Ayalla stepped closer. "Everything you learn about your ability is critical. No matter how useless it may seem to you at each particular moment. When you are ready, I will tell you the purpose, and what you must do to achieve your army's victory. For now, you must trust me, that's all. Do you?"

"Yes," he said.

She held his gaze. "This seems halfhearted, but it will do. For now. When you're done with these rocks, a path will open to take you back to your camp. I will see you tomorrow."

She turned and walked away.

Kyth sighed. He still had a lot of questions, but they didn't seem to matter for the moment. Ayalla was powerful and wise, even if a bit odd at times. Besides, following her guidance seemed like his best hope if he ever wanted to defeat the Kaddim, even if practicing turning rocks into dust seemed like a roundabout way to achieve it. Still, he should at least entertain the possibility that this was important.

He picked up the nearest rock from the pile. It seemed too large, bigger than the one last time, but he had no reason to be picky, given his task to dissipate all of them.

He closed his eyes, trying to imagine the same rock turning transparent. The feeling came easier this time when he knew what to look for. He briefly peeked at the rock's true shape, trying to make sure he recreated all the crevices and clefts correctly in his mind's eye, but this threw him off, making it much harder to imagine the rock being transparent when he could actually see its solid gray surface. He closed his eyes and tried again, this time clenching his hand to feel around the stone instead of looking at it.

Once he felt he could see all the way through the stone, he tried to call in the glow. He imagined the transparent crystal in his mind's eye bathed in sunlight, then drew it out, watching the light retained in the crystal's clear depths like a meshwork of tiny threads. The sensation was enjoyable once he got the hang of it. He felt almost sorry as he sucked in a breath, forcing the glow out of the stone all at once, feeling the dry dust trickle through his outstretched fingers. *Dear Shal Addim, I actually did it.*

He opened his eyes and turned back to the pile of rocks. It looked so large. If he took this much time with each of the stones, he could never be done in one day.

Yet, he now noticed that some of the stones composing it were bigger than others, increasing in size toward the inside of the pile. Did Ayalla place them this way on purpose, so that he would practice on the smaller ones and then progress to the larger size? Peering closer, he realized that the ones in the middle seemed much bigger than something he would ever be able to pick up. His heart raced with worry. Would he be able to dissipate a stone without holding it in his hands first? Could he do it with his eyes open and not be distracted by the stone's true appearance? He guessed toward the end of this day he would be able to find out all these things, to test his ability to dissipate rocks in every possible way. This was the whole purpose of the exercise, wasn't it?

If he wanted to get out of this glade before he starved to death, he'd better get started.

He took a deep breath and stepped toward the rock pile.

# 23
# CONFRONTATION

Kara sensed the change of scenery even before the glimpses of empty space through the trees ahead announced that they were approaching the forest hedge. After two weeks of nonstop travel through the dense forest thickets the feeling seemed surreal. By the time they rode out of the tree shade, she felt lightheaded, the pull of the wind on her face so strong that for a moment it seemed as if it was going to carry her away.

She was aware that Ayalla's way of travel, in a straight line through rapidly parting trees, saved them at least a fortnight, sparing the need to go around and find roads passable for a large group on horseback. The trees not only guided their way, but also seemingly ensured that every campsite had adequate water supply, as well as food reserves in the form of berries, mushrooms, and game, to supplement their food rations. Overall, the trip seemed relaxing, with no dangers to worry about and very little to do except spend day after day in the saddle.

Being part of the command group made a big difference too. She felt painfully aware of the distrust in

Seldon's eyes as he followed her around, but she knew this likely had nothing to do with the Kaddim. The rest of her comrades accepted her back into their ranks with the eagerness that made her feel warm inside. During the time they had been forced to shun her because of her mind link, she came to fear that she would never be able to fit in again. It felt so reassuring to know that she had been so utterly wrong in that regard.

She turned her face into the fresh wave of wind as she rode out of the tree shade, then stopped as the sound of heightened voices up ahead.

She spun around, her heart racing as she took in the scene. Mai and Seldon sat in their saddles facing each other, their flaring nostrils betraying anger. The rest of their group gathered at a distance, clearly reluctant to interfere.

Kara kicked her horse to throw it into gallop, leveling up with Raishan and Egey Bashi at the edge of the front row of spectators.

"What is going on?" she asked.

Raishan glanced away, visibly irritated.

"A difference of opinion, no more," Egey Bashi said soothingly.

Kara kept her eyes on Raishan, who turned back to her reluctantly.

"I don't normally feel this way," Raishan said, "but I almost wish Aghat Mai would have carried out his threat last time they argued."

Kara frowned. She wasn't sure what Raishan was referring to, but Egey Bashi's uneasy look spoke without words. "What threat?"

Raishan glanced away again.

"Aghat Mai indicated he could take Aghat Seldon's

head off for insubordinate behavior," Egey Bashi said.

"His *head*?"

"Perhaps," Raishan said mildly, "Aghat Mai should have threatened another body part instead? I couldn't help feeling, in the case of Aghat Seldon it just might have been more effective."

Kara's eyes widened, but before she could respond to this statement, Mai's raised voice drew her attention. As she spun around to look at the argument, she saw Mai's staff swing in an arch that made the air around him whistle. The tip of the weapon came to a perfect standstill to rest against Seldon's windpipe.

Mai's Emerald guards drew their weapons with breathtaking synchrony, kicking their horses toward the arguing pair. Kara urged her mount into a gallop, covering the short distance just ahead of them to throw herself between the two Diamonds. She saw Mai's face contort, his eyes flashing murder in the split instant before he registered her identity.

"Mai! What the hell are you doing?" Kara demanded.

His gaze hardened. "Stay out of this."

"So that you can, what, cut his head off?"

"If warranted."

Kara turned to Seldon, mesmerized by the mix of anger and fear in the older Diamond's gaze.

"What did you bloody do, Aghat Seldon?" she snapped.

Seldon pursed his lips. "I merely pointed out certain flaws in Aghat Mai's chosen course of action – not that it's any business for an outsider like you."

Kara quickly glanced at the Majat, all keeping their distance around them. "You should thank your stars that I'm an outsider, Aghat Seldon. I'm the only one here who can interfere on your behalf without formally challenging Aghat Mai's command."

"Don't," Mai said.

"Why?" She turned to him again, searching past his anger for any signs of reason in his eyes.

Mai's hand clenched around his staff, his finger dangerously close to the trigger mechanism that released his retractable blades. Kara edged her horse just a bit forward, to be sure he didn't have a clear shot.

"Why don't we all dismount?" she said. "And resolve this without weapons involved."

Mai shrugged. "There's nothing to bloody resolve."

"Isn't there anything Aghat Seldon could do to redeem himself?"

"Keep away from me, for one."

"But–" Seldon began.

Kara stopped him with a short glance. "I'm sure this could be done. Anything else?"

"Don't act like a bloody idiot all the time."

Seldon lifted his chin. "Really, Aghat Mai, I–"

Kara shot up her hand in a warning gesture. "As soon as we camp, we can hold a hearing and determine your punishment, Aghat Seldon. Until then, I strongly suggest you do as Aghat Mai says."

"But–"

She grasped the collar of his shirt and leaned over in the saddle to bring her face closer to him.

"Listen to what you're bloody told," she said, "and you may yet stay alive."

Seldon watched her for a moment with poorly controlled anger, then receded into his saddle. Kara let out a small sigh as she turned to Mai. "Would that be all right?"

Mai appeared to hesitate.

"You can still kill him if you deem it warranted," she said soothingly. "Just give this decision another few hours, all right?"

Mai didn't respond as he flicked his weapon into its sheath and rode away toward the group of Diamonds watching them from a safe distance.

Kara turned her horse around to Seldon, who was sitting very straight, his face set into a stone-hard expression.

"What the hell did you do, Aghat Seldon?" she asked.

The older Diamond shrugged. "Only my duty."

"Meaning what?"

Seldon heaved a sigh. Kara could swear his hand was trembling, but he steadied it when he saw her gaze flick that way. "Aghat Mai seems to forget he is not the highest authority in the world. All his actions are weighted by the Guild at all times, and if he continues like this they may yet serve as his downfall."

His cold glance sent a chill down Kara's spine. She knew he was speaking the truth, and Mai was well aware of it, even if he never factored this into his daily operations. Seldon's bad report about him could promote an unpleasant inquiry that would cost Mai his command – or worse. This knowledge was the source of her own fears, even if lately these fears were greatly overshadowed by the more immediate Kaddim threat. Yet, what new could have possibly happened now to promote this kind of an outburst?

"Care to explain that, Aghat Seldon?" she asked.

"No, actually."

"Even with the knowledge that I have just, very

likely, saved your life?"

"I'm not so certain he would have carried through his threat."

"Do you enjoy playing with fire?"

Seldon shrugged. "What else was I supposed to do? Aghat Mai had purchased thoroughbred lizardbeasts for our entire party!"

Kara frowned. "That's reasonable, isn't it? We can't possibly ride horses through the desert. Lizardbeasts are the only possible means of transportation, once we reach Shayil Yara."

"Yes, but do you know how much they cost?"

"Would you rather have us walk, Aghat?"

"I'd rather have a discussion about this first. We could have had mixed breeds, for one."

"It would have cost us speed."

Seldon shook his head. "You young people just don't appreciate how hard-earned our Guild's wealth is."

"However hard-earned, it would mean nothing if we lose this war."

Seldon's nostrils flared again. "You're just like him, a child who has stuck a hand into a bag of gold. Don't pretend you know how our Guild operates."

"I don't pretend anything, Aghat Seldon. I just suggested that Aghat Mai may have had his reasons. In any case, it's his decision isn't it?"

"Yes, it is. And that's the whole problem here."

Kara sighed. She was beginning to see the reasons for Mai's behavior just now. On top of everything he had to deal with, Seldon's constant insubordination must have been taxing. While she was glad she interfered when she did and prevented the impending violence, she was hoping Seldon could rein in his temper for the duration of the journey. Of course, it was probably too much to hope for.

"Aghat Mai was right," she said. "You are acting like a bloody idiot. Next time you get into trouble, don't count on my interference." She kicked her horse and leveled up with the command group.

The road from the forest outskirts descended in a very shallow incline down to the distant line of the deserts. Built for caravans, it enabled six riders to ride abreast, pulling their party into compact formation. Kara kept her place between Lance and Raishan, glad for once to be able to ride in the lead and be the first to take in the scenery. She dreaded the conversation that awaited them all at their next campsite, but there was no way around it. For now, at least, all she could do was enjoy the view.

The sea of roofs and tents stretching out of sight made her eyes narrow in disbelief. She always considered caravan outposts to be no more than small settlements, housing just enough people to supply travelers on their road. The place up ahead rivaled the trade city of Jaimir in its size and grandeur. She supposed in an odd way this discrepancy actually made perfect sense. Like any other outpost, Gard'hal was indeed built to supply travelers; it was just that the amount of travelers it saw on a daily basis far exceeded any normal scale. The kingdom of Shayil Yara supplied many things to the northern lands, all of them brought by caravans across the deserts. Every one of these caravans had to stop here on their way north or south.

In Gard'hal, a word loosely translated from the local nomadic language as "desert spring", the majority of the Majat were expected to stay in wait until their embassy to Queen Rajmella's court supplied them with the information about the location of the Kaddim Fortress. Mai was leaving Raishan in charge, taking the rest of the Diamonds along. This included Seldon, but now Kara wasn't sure that was a good idea anymore. Hell, she wasn't even sure where she and Mai stood after she had confronted him so openly. But she didn't regret her decision. Mai generally had a very cool head, but if he lost his temper in a major way he could easily do something he'd regret for the rest of his life. She didn't want to stand aside and let this happen, not when she was the only person in their party who could interfere without putting her life and rank in jeopardy.

A group of men greeted them on the Gard'hal outskirts, leading them to a large area set with enough tents to accommodate their entire group. Up until now Kara kept thinking of their traveling party as very large, even after the Kingsguards stayed behind with Kyth. Now she realized that by local standards a group of three hundred was hardly enough to surprise anyone at all. Many caravans were larger than that. Perhaps this was one of the reasons Mai chose this place for his base, enabling the Majat to remain as inconspicuous as possible.

Mai made no further mention of the conflict with Seldon, even if the way he avoided the older Diamond was very noticeable. He avoided Kara too, and she felt a pang of pain every time he steered clear of her when overseeing the preparations. She kept trailing him while staying out of sight, looking for an opportunity to speak to him alone. It took a while, before she saw him enter a centrally set tent he had designated for command.

Kara approached it and exchanged meaningful glances with the Emeralds on guard, then slid inside.

She stopped near the entrance, waiting for her eyes to adjust to the semidarkness after the sunlight outside, blazing bright even at this late afternoon hour. Mai had his back to the door and he showed no awareness of her as he spoke in turn to several of his men and dismissed them one by one. Only when the last of them left the tent did he turn around slowly to face her.

She kept still for a moment, trying to access his reaction, but saw no indication where she stood with him. The pause stretched, until it became too long for her comfort. She heaved a breath, holding her head higher as she approached him and stopped right in front of him.

"I came to apologize," she said. "I don't regret interfering, but I am aware that I've caused problems by doing it. I'm sorry for that."

He didn't respond, watching her. A shadow fell on his face and even now, fully adapted to the dim light, she couldn't read his expression at all.

"You can still punish him as you see fit," she went on after a moment. "Feel free to punish me too. I would gladly accept any penance for challenging you openly in front of your men. I just... I didn't want you to do anything you'd regret."

His lips twitched. "Did you think I needed your help to keep in control?"

"No."

"Why step in, then?"

She sighed. "Seldon is one of our Guild's seniors. It makes him... different from a regular insubordinate warrior."

"No, it doesn't."

"He believes it does."

Mai heaved a sigh, then turned away abruptly. She waited out another pause, her heart quivering as no response came. She had never seen Mai this way.

"What did Seldon say to you?" she asked.

Mai shrugged, looking at her with hesitation, as if deciding if he should speak. She waited, afraid to move, shivering at the detached expression in his face.

"He said he won't stand for my decisions," Mai said at length. "He said he'll inform the Guild of my incompetence. But the way I reacted had nothing to do with these words, actually. I had far more trouble with his attitude, which could easily cost us our victory when the time comes. One way or another, I must bring him to heel."

"And you felt threatening his life was the best way to go about it?"

Mai shook his head. "I wasn't threatening, not for the purpose of controlling him, at least. I just... I came very close to a decision that I could not possibly win this war with him around."

"You could've sent him back to the Guild."

Mai tossed his head. "He's here by a decree from the Guild's seniors. This means, it's not up to me to exclude him from our party. His death is the only way."

"Would you have done it if I hadn't interfered?"

Mai hesitated. "I don't know."

She dared a step closer, but his guarded look warned her from approaching all the way.

"For whatever it's worth," she said, "I don't regret what I did."

He peered into her face. "Do you think you know better?"

"I know how much you hate killing."

Mai turned away abruptly, pacing back and forth along the tent. It took him a while to speak again. "This campaign has been bloody hard even without Seldon. Dealing with him on top of all else..." His voice trailed off into silence.

*It's all my fault. I'm the one who is putting Mai under an unbearable stress on top of the burden he's already carrying.* Kara knew she would never say this, not now when Mai was already on the brink of losing control. She wanted to step into his arms, to comfort him, but it wasn't time for that. She forcibly kept her place.

"I'd like to help," she said.

Mai stopped his pacing. "You have already. And, you're right. I didn't really want Seldon's blood on my hands. For a moment there I just felt I had no other choice."

She stepped closer. "So, you aren't mad at me?"

He looked surprised. "Mad at you?"

"For being insubordinate."

"You're not formally under my command, are you?"

She smiled. "I guess there are still some advantages to my position."

"Some?"

"Many. A lot. Just the fact that I'm allowed to kick some sense into you if you behave like a bastard is worth all else."

Mai raised his eyebrows. "Did I really behave like a bastard?"

She laughed. "No. You would have noticed if I felt I had to kick some sense into you, I promise."

Mai grinned. "Do you really think you can?"

"Care to find out, Guildmaster?"

Mai threw a restrained glance at the tent entrance. "I'd love to. But I don't think my guards would possibly approve."

"Well, then, I'll settle for the next best thing." She reached for him, their embrace fierce, near-violent in its passion. It lasted only moments, but when Kara finally found the strength to draw away from him she felt as if she had just stepped into a better world.

"I must go," she whispered. "Before we're brutally interrupted."

Mai's dazed look lingered on her, slowly shifting back to his usual calmness.

"I'll deal with Seldon," he said. "No weapons this time, I promise."

"Is he still coming with us to Shayil Yaran court?"

Mai's nod looked reluctant. "I have no bloody choice. If I leave him here with Raishan, he will continue poisoning everyone's minds the entire time. At least by keeping him nearby I can have some control of the situation."

She smiled. "Well, if you do behave like a bastard when you talk to Seldon just now, make sure to call me back in afterwards to deal with you."

"Promise."

She briefly pulled him into another kiss, then turned and walked out of the tent.

In this campaign, Mai was carrying the weight of the world on his shoulders. She bitterly wished that he didn't have to handle everything else on top of that, from Seldon's pettiness to her own problem, when each step toward their enemies' secret fortress made her more and more vulnerable to the Kaddim's magic. Ayalla's spell was great as a temporary relief, but she knew when they got closer to the enemy stronghold it would stop being effective and all bets would be off.

Whatever the cost, Kara needed to make the most of the time she had.

## 24
# DESERT GEAR

Mai had chosen a minimal party to travel to the Olivian capital – five Diamonds, six Jades, and six of his personal Emerald guards in addition to Egey Bashi and Ellah, whose truthsense was essential in the upcoming negotiations. They spent the night at the Gard'hal outpost's camp with the rest of the Majat, setting out early next morning to continue on to Tahr Abad.

Kara had just finished packing up her gear when she heard a commotion at the entrance to the camp. She hurried toward the noise.

A group of men were rushing around a large cart, pulling off packs of what looked like tightly bundled cloth. Further on, two herders were observing the activity, each holding a large metal ring with a dozen leading ropes strung through. Lizardbeasts. Kara looked on, thinking of yesterday's conversation.

They didn't look impressive enough to cost this much gold, even if their sleek, muscular lines told Kara that as far as breeding went these beasts were the best. Despite Seldon's rebellion, Kara fully approved of Mai's choice. In the fight they were facing they needed every bit of advantage. They couldn't possibly risk losing a battle because of inferiority of their mounts. The Majat never operated this way, the fact that made her strongly question Seldon's judgment in calling Mai on this decision. Or was the older Diamond scrapping for every opportunity to challenge Mai's authority?

True to their name, the beasts indeed resembled large lizards, four legged and flat footed, with tails sweeping the ground behind them and chair-like saddles strapped at the bases of their long necks. Their yellow eyes surveyed the activity calmly, scaly skins glistening in the sunlight. Their sheen, ranging from green and purple to charcoal-gray, was somewhat silky, but not, Kara supposed, to someone who had issues with the whole idea of a lizard-like mount.

Most of the departing party gathered nearby, but there was one person Kara prominently did not see.

"Where's Ellah?" she asked a Jade passing nearby.

The man hesitated. "I think I saw her at the back of the camp a short time ago. Not sure why. She should be getting ready to leave, shouldn't she?"

Kara nodded. "I'll see to it." She turned around and strode to the back of the tent rows.

Ellah was sitting by the wall, staring into the distance. She looked pale, her arms clasped tightly across her stomach as if the girl was fighting a serious bout of nausea.

"Are you all right?" Kara asked.

Ellah raised her face, her lips twitching as if she was having trouble controlling them.

"I'm fine," she said after a pause.

"I don't think so. Care to tell me what's the matter?"

Ellah turned away abruptly. After a long pause, Kara

sighed and lowered down to the ground next to her.

The silence seemed to stretch forever, but Kara knew better than to start the conversation. From her experience with trainees at the Guild, as well as her long-term familiarity with Ellah, she knew that whatever troubled the girl could not possibly be dragged out by force. Ellah had to venture the information forth on her own, however long it took.

"I can't do it," Ellah said eventually.

"Can't do what?"

Ellah's lips curved down with disgust. "I... I *hate* lizardbeasts. To think of touching one, let alone riding them..." Her voice trailed into silence.

"Why?"

"They... They have scales all over. Like snakes!"

"They're nothing like snakes, actually. Their scales are smooth, silky."

"*Silky*." Ellah spat out the word, as if it had a bad taste.

Kara let out a sigh. "You know that in this kingdom you can't travel anywhere by horse."

"I don't have to travel, actually." Ellah swallowed. "You'd do just fine without me. I can stay here. Or, go back to the Forestlands. Grandma always told me I would come to trouble if I ever allow anyone to talk me into traveling too far away from my village."

"You know we need you, right? Without your truthsense..."

Ellah pursed her lips. "You'll do fine without me. They'll listen to you at the Queen's court. You look like you were born here, don't you see it?"

Kara held a pause. She did look Olivian, but if anything, it made her mission as a negotiator at the

Queen's court harder, not easier. With her looks, everyone would assume she was closely familiar with every local custom. If she messed up the talking, it would seem much worse to the locals than if she was an obvious foreigner. Without the feedback Ellah's gift of truthsense could provide, she would feel like a fish out of the water.

"Does preventing the end of the world as we know it mean less to you than a trivial thing like riding a lizardbeast for a while?" she asked.

Ellah shook her head. "It's easy for you to say. You were probably never afraid of anything in your entire life."

Kara smiled. "Do you really think so?"

Ellah lifted her chin, a challenge in her gaze. "What were you ever afraid of, then?"

"Men."

"What?" Ellah's eyes widened.

"Look," Kara said hurriedly. "It's not really important. The point is, all of us have some fears. All of us have to make sacrifices to overcome them and go on with our lives."

"*Men*?"

Kara glanced away. She supposed now that she started this conversation there was no way back. Yet, even after all this time, she found the subject too difficult to talk about. She paused, trying to find the right words.

"When we train, the Majat Guild encourages us to take lovers, so that we could explore our bodies in every way we can. To most, especially the male trainees, it comes easily. By their ranking age, in early twenties, they explore all they want and get over it." She paused.

"They learn to channel it all into fighting. We all do."

"What about you?" Ellah asked slowly.

Kara took a deep breath, unwelcome memories flowing over her.

"I was showing so much promise that the possibility of my Gem ranking was brought up earlier than it normally is. I was fifteen when my trainers first started asking me to explore my sexual side. Sixteen, when they started really pushing me into it..." Her voice trailed away.

Ellah watched her wide-eyed. "I admit, this seems a bit young. But... you knew you were going to do it eventually, anyway. Why did it frighten you so much?"

Kara looked away. "I was one of the few women on the training grounds. Probably the only one most men found attractive. I could see them all looking at me this way since I was twelve. Worse, those not bound by the code of our Guild pretty much assumed I would jump at the possibility. Let's just say, something like this tends to leave a mark."

"But... you did do it in the end, right?"

"Yes. When I was nearly eighteen. By that time, my trainers were about to give up. In fact, they'd come very close to reaching a decision not to train me for a Gem rank at all."

"Just because of this?"

Kara shrugged. She might never know for sure how close it came for her. It felt so good, in retrospect, to put it all behind her.

"It takes a lot of resources from the Guild to train a Gem," she said. "Especially in the last years of training. They didn't want to invest into anyone with problems, no matter how much promise I showed."

Ellah's eyes hovered over her thoughtfully. "I heard they now consider you one of their best warriors ever."

"Exactly."

"So, how did you do it?" Ellah asked after a pause.

Kara leaned back, forcing her mind back into calmness. "Simple, actually. One day, I just asked myself: does my fear of men mean so much to me that I am willing to renounce my lifetime dream because of it?"

"And?"

"Once I realized this was my only choice, my fear of men seemed meaningless in comparison to everything else at stake. Putting it behind me took no effort at all."

"Really?"

"Yes."

Ellah watched her a moment longer with a mesmerized expression. Then she rose and made her way to the front of the camp.

When Kara followed her, the sight that opened in front of her made her mouth fall open. The merchants had unraveled their bundles of cloth, laying out sets of clothing.

"What's this?" she demanded.

"Desert gear." Lance stepped up to her, holding out a headdress fashioned somewhat similarly to the ones the merchants wore. It looked a bit like a helmet made of cloth, with long flaps of fabric extending over the shoulders and back and another one hanging at the side of the face to fit over as a mask, if needed.

"Are we all going to wear them?" The thought trailed off as she realized that the man standing near the lizardbeasts was not a herder as she originally believed.

"*Mai?*"

He grinned and held his arms out to his sides, giving her a full view.

She had never seen him in anything else but his elegant Majat blacks – except, of course, for the times when he wore nothing at all. And now, her mind simply refused to accept the way he looked in the new clothes, no less stunning than he always did, but completely unrecognizable. The yellow-white fabric, draping around loosely to soften the lines of his muscular body, brought out color in his pale skin, making him look darker than he did when accented with the black – and far less threatening, even if every bit as handsome. His eyes shone like pale blue jewels in his laughing face. Seeing him this way made her gape, the blend of the familiar and the foreign in a way that made her see him in a completely new light.

Of course, Mai was always known for his ability to blend in into any surrounding. She had just never seen such a radical change occur so effortlessly before.

"You and Ellah can change in that tent over there," Mai said. "Hurry up."

## 25

# THE POWER OF LIFE

"You've been doing well," Ayalla said.

Kyth raised his head, surprised at the relief he felt at this brief praise. He was exhausted, hauling rocks all day, learning to dissipate them with and without touching them first, and to put them together at Ayalla's command. Unlike her rocks, he was never able to recreate the original shape exactly, but on the grand scale of things it didn't seem to matter. If she was happy with his progress, he was going to take it, no questions asked.

"And now," Ayalla went on, "I will tell you why we have been spending so much time on rocks. You wanted to know this, didn't you?"

Kyth merely nodded. He had felt curious about it at some point. But now, after days and days of this endless practice, he felt so tired it didn't matter anymore. He had accepted the fact that he was here to do Ayalla's bidding for as long as she deemed necessary – and not just him. Every night after she returned him back to their camp, she left again with Alder, who kept her company at night and returned in the morning looking no less exhausted than Kyth, even if much happier. The Forest Woman seemed to have infinite energy and no need to sleep at all, which made Kyth feel even more surreal about the fact that she was apparently still intending to train him to use a power similar to her own. He hoped she didn't expect him to develop the same kind of stamina – not in this short time at least.

"Now, listen closely," Ayalla said. "Inside the Kaddim's fortress there is a special chamber, the one that feeds their Reincarnate's power. Many who speak about it believe it leads directly to the underworld. But very few of those know that it's not the chamber but a stone inside it that links the Reincarnate to the Cursed Destroyer. It looks like a platform, an elevated rectangular slab in the middle of the room."

Kyth froze. He knew about the chamber. Once, after Kara's escape and re-capture, he'd overheard her talking about her vision of the stone slab. His skin prickled at Ayalla's words, the realization of what he was learning cutting through the haze in his tired mind, snapping him back to attention.

"This stone," Ayalla went on, "is infused with the Destroyer's magic. So much so, in fact, that very few realize a very simple fact. No matter how much magic it holds, it's still a stone, made of the element earth. As such, it is held together by similar types of bonds that hold together the rocks you have been practicing on. And now, with your training, you have the ability to turn it into dust once you get close enough to have it in your direct view. If you do, it will sever the Reincarnate's link to his source of power. It will make him vulnerable."

Kyth gaped, absorbing her every word. Everything

she taught him up to now suddenly made sense. He shivered at this realization, for the first time filled with hope that this plan of training him in the use of his magic could actually work.

"Is this the way to defeat him?" he asked.

"It's the first step, yes."

"The *first* step?" Kyth's heart sank again, tiredness settling in anew. What she said just now seemed hard enough to accomplish. The chamber she spoke about had to be at the very heart of the fortress, in the place protected by the entire Kaddim's defense force. Worse, by the time Kyth and the Majat arrived there, the Kaddim would likely be aware of the menace. Was destroying the stone not enough...?

Ayalla laughed. "Don't look so forlorn. You didn't think it was going to be this easy, did you?"

"Actually I did, for a moment."

"There is a bright side," Ayalla said. "Through the stone, the Reincarnate's power will be feeding all his warriors, especially the Kaddim leaders who call themselves Brothers. After you dissolve it, their link with each other will weaken. They will no longer be able to feed off him at all. This will make them all the more vulnerable, giving your Majat friends more of a chance. It will also give you your opportunity to end it all."

Kyth pulled himself upright. In all his prior Majat training he had learned too well that he couldn't allow himself to feel exhausted or to assume he could relax before time. Mai and his trainers had beaten this attitude out of him once and for all, often in quite the literal sense. Ayalla was no different. Of course here, in her realm, he didn't need to be afraid of bruises and scratches earned in weapon practice, but these bouts of tiredness he felt after each training session seemed bad enough, even if they always passed after a good night's sleep.

"My power is not normally meant to kill," Ayalla said. "But since it feeds off the elements, it could be used this way. The human body is made of elements too, just like everything else around us."

Kyth's eyes widened. "You want me to dissipate his body, as if it was a rock?"

Her lips twitched. "Close, but not exactly. To kill a living being, you need to call upon another element – fire. The bonds that hold a human body are made of water. Fire can aid you in dissipating them."

"Fire?"

"Yes. The process is much the same, actually. You must see the watery bonds holding his body together. Then you must call upon the fire to dissipate them, make them boil. It should be easy in the middle of a desert filled with fire and wind."

Kyth nodded slowly. As with everything he learned here, it made sense. He knew exactly what he had to do. Except that practicing it seemed impossible. Unthinkable. He couldn't possibly suck the life out of another living being simply for the sake of perfecting his skill. Yet, could he do something like this, even to his arch enemy in the middle of a battle, without ever trying it on someone else first?

Ayalla seemed to read his thoughts.

"You hesitate, and rightfully so. And no, I will not ask you to kill anyone to practice this. I will, however expect you to learn to dissipate water. Starting with this pond."

Kyth looked. The pond was small and shallow, feeding off the brook running into the glade. Yet, it held so much water – much greater in size, it seemed, than any of the rocks he had worked with before.

"How do I do it?" he asked.

"It's much like the rocks, only when you blend with water you must go deeper. Submerge into it."

"Submerge?"

"Yes."

"How about when it comes to the Reincarnate?"

"The same. You must submerge into him. There are different ways to do it, but given the constraints of a battle that will be going on around you, I recommend a kiss. A deep one, like a lover's. He will know what you are doing, so you will have to force him into it."

*Force him into a kiss.* The idea of kissing a man, forcing him into it, seemed disgusting. The thought that he had to do it to their worst enemy, one also filled with the bitter stink of Kaddim power made him want to throw up. Yet, Ayalla's expectant gaze, the way she looked at him without even a hint of a smile, made him realize that she meant everything she said.

He swallowed. "I… I'll try."

"Yes, you will. We'll start practicing with water tomorrow. In the meantime, I will also start teaching you and Alder to control the spiders. But all of this must wait until you rest. Let's walk back to your camp."

Kyth didn't question this as he rose to his feet and followed her.

The sky was still bright as they emerged into their campsite, but the tall trees around the glade made it seem dark, the glowing campfire in its center beckoning

with light and warmth. Kyth trudged toward it and
lowered down next to Celana, who smiled and edged
sideways on the log she was using as a seat to give him
room.

As if on cue, Alder rose from his seat on the other
side and stepped toward Ayalla. She drew him into a
deep kiss that made Kyth look away in embarrassment.
Then she turned and walked away, Alder following her
like a sleepwalker.

Kyth sat for a while, aware of Celana's blush and
of the way Garnald looked at them nonchalantly, as
if everything happening here was normal and natural.

Kyth raised his eyes to the old Mirewalker with
wonder. He knew that to achieve this title, to become
Ayalla's errand man, Garnald had to have been her
lover too, at least at some point. From the lack of
jealousy or restlessness as Garnald watched Alder's
nightly forays, Kyth had to assume that this love
affair was in the past. It made him worry. What would
happen to Alder when he got older or Ayalla outlived
her fancy for him? Would he become heartbroken? Or
would he turn into one of Ayalla's errand men, bound
to her without seemingly getting much in return, like
Garnald?

He wanted for Alder to be able to find happiness and
lead a normal life. Being Ayalla's lover, growing old in
the forest to come and go at her beck and call, didn't
fit the bill, however much Alder seemed to be enjoying
his time here at the moment.

"Does Ayalla ever let her men go?" Kyth asked.

Garnald briefly glanced down the path Ayalla and
Alder had disappeared a short time ago. "Yes, she does.
Frequently, in fact."

*Frequently.* Somehow, the information brought no reassurance at all.

"What happens to them then?"

Garnald shrugged. "Nothing bad, if that's what you're thinking. It feels somewhat like a spell being lifted. The men remember the pleasure of being with her, as well as all the lovemaking skills they learned, but they are no longer consumed with obsession over her. They can return to normal life, as if nothing happened. It feels quite good, actually."

He leaned forward and filled his mug from the kettle hanging over the fire, taking a long sip. Kyth also poured two mugs, handing one to Celana, and drinking from his own. The tea felt fragrant, so good after the exhausting day.

"Was it the same with you, Garnald?" he asked.

The Mirewalker chuckled. "At some point, yes. But since I had no other family, no woman who waited for me at home, my relationship with Ayalla continued longer than normal, on and off. In fact, I got so used to this life that I can imagine no other way, really."

*Does she still sleep with you?* Kyth knew he would never dare to ask. Yet, he felt glad at seeing the contentment in the older man's face. Garnald seemed genuinely happy with his life. That was all that mattered, wasn't it?

"What about Alder?" he said.

Garnald raised his eyebrows. "What about him?"

"Do you think some day she will let him go too?"

"Probably," Garnald said. "At some point, he will most certainly run out of stamina. Men do, as they age, and I've never yet seen her drive anyone that hard."

Kyth blushed, stealing a quick glance at Celana. She

asked to be here, of course, but he knew this kind of talk wasn't appropriate for the ears of a young girl. He supposed talking was better that watching the foreplay as Ayalla took Alder away every evening, but he still felt guilty for pressing the subject in Celana's presence. Only his concern for Alder drove him to continue the conversation.

"Alder is different," Garnald said thoughtfully. "She likes him a lot, almost like a lover, not merely someone to sate her urges."

Kyth's heart sank. "Do you mean, because of this she may keep him by her side?"

Garnald shook his head. "On the contrary. My guess is, she may release him earlier than usual. Perhaps when this war is over?"

Kyth let his tired eyes wander, looking into the greenish depths of the darkening forest. When they were growing up, Alder had his sights set on Ellah and she seemed to be agreeable with the idea. This was of course before Ayalla took him as a lover. If she ever lifted her spell off him, was it too late for this relationship to take off again?

*When this war is over.* To an extent it was up to Kyth to see to it. Yet, the knowledge didn't seem to settle in his head. He was so used to thinking of himself in a supportive role, a shield that could protect the formidable Majat force. He never thought of becoming a central player in this battle. Was he truly capable of living up to the hopes everyone was placing into him?

Was this war ever going to end, to allow them all a chance for happiness?

# 26
# SANDSTORM

"Is this bloody weather ever going to improve?" Mai asked.

They were sitting in a shelter, a plain stone building with a flat roof, its gaping windows doing only a little to protect them from the raging sandstorm outside. Kara felt only partially comforted by the knowledge that the people who built this place, more than a century ago, felt it important enough to bring large blocks of hewn rocks for reinforcement, making it withstand even the very strong blasts of wind. According to the locals they met a day earlier, this storm was minor compared to the others to be expected this time of the year.

Egey Bashi pulled the flap of his mask tighter, covering his face against the flying sand. "You have to stop thinking like a Majat Guildmaster, Aghat Mai."

Mai's lips twitched. "You can't be serious, Magister."

"Perhaps not entirely. But even the Majat Guild can't defeat the weather."

Mai grumbled something indistinct as he receded deeper into the corner.

"There's a well in a sheltered area outside," Lance

said. "And an outhouse. Given that the storm is showing no sign of stopping, I believe we should settle here for the night."

Mai glanced at the window. "At this rate, we'll surely be buried by morning."

"I remember," Egey Bashi said, "that these shelters are supposed to have storm shutters one could fit into place if the storm rages a while. Let's dig near that wall."

Digging through the sand revealed a trapdoor leading to a shallow cellar, too small to accommodate any people but large enough to store a stack of flat boards, along with ropes and metal straps. They also found a shovel and a broom, a pile of firewood and a flint, a supply they decided to leave alone for now.

It took some time to figure out how to fit the shutters into the brackets near each window, finally blocking out the worst of the sand. The air was still full of it, creaking on the teeth and parching the tongue, but at least it didn't hit the face anymore.

They took turns with the shovel and broom to sweep out the thick layer of sand, revealing a smoothly polished floor, comfortable enough to spread their bedrolls.

"Why don't they leave the shutters on all the time?" Ellah wondered.

Mai examined the nearest one. "I can only guess if they do, the wind would destroy them too fast. For those who know where to look this seems like a better system."

"Especially since most travelers normally take shelter here *before* the storm," Egey Bashi pointed out.

Mai shrugged. It was his idea to continue traveling despite the weather warnings, driven partly by the hurry they were in, and partly by the knowledge that no matter what they would be likely to reach this shelter on time. Deep inside, Kara suspected that Mai was simply having trouble letting go of his own sense of weather, which of course did nothing useful here, where all the signs seemed to be opposite to what they were used to. How could one in their right mind suspect that a storm like this would follow the clear sunny sky they enjoyed only a few hours ago on their last stop?

Just as they were about to settle in, the doors swung open again, letting in a group of five people. They removed their masks, revealing a handsome middle-aged Olivian woman and four men that bustled around her, shaking off the sand and spreading out cushions for her to sit on. She accepted it casually, as if used to enjoying excessive comforts even on a march.

Her curious eyes moved around the group, singling out Kara. Her smile held strange recognition, as if identifying her as her only equal in their group. With unease, Kara remembered the Olivian matriarchal society and the way that her looks made everyone believe she was a native. It was perhaps to the best that they met the woman here. The earlier she settled into this role, the better.

"On your way to Tahr Abad?" the woman asked, addressing only Kara as if the rest of her companions were not here at all. Did she think they were all servants?

"Yes," Kara said.

"You live there?"

Kara glanced around. "My companions and I have business there."

"Your companions." The woman's eyes lit up with

new interest. "Your family must be very rich."

Kara felt a blush rise into her cheeks as she belatedly remembered the double meaning of the word "companion" in these parts. Rich Olivian women kept male harems. With her Olivian looks and a large retinue of young men someone might assume she was one of those women too, but she didn't expect to have to deal with this before they reached the Queen's court.

"We do things differently in the north," she said.

"I must definitely travel to the north myself." The woman clicked her tongue appreciatively, her eyes lingering on Mai.

Now that one of the men had a chance to wipe her face clean of the sand, Kara realized that the woman wasn't as old as she originally thought. She looked to be in her mid- to late thirties, and still very good looking. Her meaningful glances made Kara feel less and less comfortable, even more so when she saw Egey Bashi snigger and cover his face with a flap of his head gear to hide his grin.

She had to remind herself that each of her companions was a deadly warrior quite able of defending his honor – assuming that they were even interested in defending it against this kind of attention. The Majat ranking did not forbid casual affairs. And now, the men's smiles as they caught the woman's eyes made her wonder.

"I am Meera," the woman said. "A merchant in the lower city."

"A merchant? What are your wares?" Kara asked, more out of politeness than of real interest.

"Garments. Some of the finest. Even the royal family buys from us." Meera's eyes drifted to Mai again. "Perhaps, when you reach the city, you and your, um, companions would like to visit my shop?"

Kara nodded stiffly. She wasn't normally a jealous type, and she was long used to the reaction Mai stirred in pretty much every woman who came near him, but she wasn't accustomed to anyone undressing him with their eyes so openly without being in the least bashful about it. Were things going to be this way at the Queen's court?

"Perhaps," Meera went on, "when you visit, we could also consider an exchange?"

"An exchange?" Kara's eyes widened.

Meera laughed. "Come now, don't look so terrified. You don't keep all these gorgeous men exclusively for yourself, do you?"

"I, um…" Kara paused, seeing Egey Bashi in the corner doubled up, shaking with silent laughter. She swore to herself to have a conversation with the Magister as soon as she could.

"I have spent most of my life in the north," she said. "I am not familiar with this custom."

"It's lucky that you met me, then, isn't it?" Meera winked to her conspiratorially. "With how handsome your men are, you will get offers everywhere you go, I'm sure."

"Offers?"

"Come now." Meera smiled. "However many men you have, you surely want a variety from time to time. If you send some of your men to entertain me, I can send you some of mine – for a night, or longer, if they strike your fancy."

Kara gaped. She knew she shouldn't be looking so appalled at the idea, but she just couldn't help it.

"Don't worry," Meera said "These ones that travel

with me are not my best. I have more at home to pick from. Just got a new boy from down south – he is more your age, and he does wonders with his tongue."

"Thank you." Kara brought a flap of her head dress to her own face to hide a twitch in her lips. Thinking this through in any detail made her feel nauseated. Yet, things could probably only get worse from now on, so she'd better get used to having these conversations without flinching. "It's very kind of you, Meera. I will consider it."

Meera smiled. "Good. My house is a large white one, right by the port. Ask anyone."

The storm died out some time during the night, enabling them to leave just before dawn. Kara was glad that they were able to leave quietly enough not to wake Meera and her men who were still sleeping in the opposite corner of the room.

When they saddled up and set on the road, she maneuvered her lizardbeast to ride next to Egey Bashi.

"You could have warned me, Magister," she said.

Egey Bashi grinned. "I thought I did. They view men differently in Shayil Yara. This is why you need to lead the negotiations when we reach the Queen, remember?"

"That is not what I meant."

Egey Bashi turned to watch the road ahead. His face looked calm, but the crinkling lines around his eyes and in the corners of his mouth told her he was trying his best to suppress laughter. She wanted to feel angry, but deep inside this reaction calmed her down. Magister Egey Bashi was a wise and experienced man. He wouldn't be laughing if the situation was dangerous in any way.

"Seriously, though," she said. "Exchange? Offers? Is this how it's going to be?"

"Much worse, actually."

"*Worse*?"

"The women of power at the Queen's court are used to always getting what they want."

Kara's eyes widened. "Mai is the Majat Guildmaster. The women of power should know the meaning of this title."

"They do. Yet, they are only human. You know well what kind of reaction Aghat Mai stirs in women everywhere he goes. Olivian noblewomen are much less inhibited in showing it."

"Still. Do they expect him to... to entertain them?"

"They will probably respect his title – even though I wouldn't be surprised if they proposition him at some point or another. If it's any comfort, these relationships are always expected to be consensual, so you really don't need to worry so much."

Kara averted her gaze. She knew she should be used to women ogling Mai by now, but the idea that he would be propositioned by women used to getting what they want and not in the least bit shy about it still did not sit well with her.

"What about the other men in our party?" she asked.

Egey Bashi's grin widened. "The Queen and her key advisors would understand these men are not your consorts. But the rest of the courtiers would surely have problem grasping this idea. You should probably be prepared for offers of exchange."

"Bloody great." Kara turned away abruptly. She did feel angry now, even if mostly at herself. Why did she of all people have to be the one to end up in this position?

"Come now, Aghat." Egey Bashi spoke soothingly, but she could see that he was still holding back laughter. "Your conversation with Meera wasn't all that bad, was it?"

"It bloody was. How am I supposed to handle these kinds of offers?"

"Why don't you let the men worry about it?"

"The men?"

Egey Bashi sniggered. "See? You are already thinking like a Shayil Yaran, assuming that men in your party cannot take care of themselves. You should give them more credit."

She nodded. Put this way, it did seem ridiculous that she should hold herself responsible for the men's well-being. All Majat trainees learned early on how to handle the opposite sex. She was probably the only one among them who had serious problems with it. Was this why she had such issues with this aspect of Olivian customs?

"I hope they can handle it," she said.

"Back in the shelter," Egey Bashi said, "I was observing the scene closely. I don't think any of them minded Meera's attention. I would venture to guess the men probably found it flattering. I'd say you should relax and focus on your negotiations with the Queen, Aghat. Let the rest of it sort out on its own."

"If you want me to stay out of this, I should probably do my best to make it very clear that these are not my men."

"Not a good idea."

"Why?"

"If you do, this could become distracting. Everyone would believe these men are available for the taking."

"*Taking?*"

Egey Bashi laughed. "Why do you think they always employ female negotiators here?"

"Didn't you tell me this was because they don't take men as seriously?"

"Exactly. This goes for more than business talk. An unattached man is sort of like a stray child. Even if they know he comes from a different culture, their instincts tell them otherwise. Many feel more or less obliged to pick him up and bring him home. The Queen is not like this, of course, but even for her, the distraction could become too great for comfort, not to mention the effect it would have on the women at her court. This is why male-only parties are often turned away without even gaining audience."

"It seems they are making things far too complicated."

"Or simple, if you will. In the end, this is no more than a cultural difference."

Kara fixed her eyes on the road. She never thought she would be able to serve as a protector for a group of their top warriors. It seemed even more strange that this protection in their case was based entirely on gender.

"Just remember," Egey Bashi said. "When you do get offers of exchange, as I am sure you will, no one would expect you to make a decision on the spot. You should feel free to take your time. More than that, no one would be offended if you refused to share – even though if you do it repeatedly, they may find it strange."

Kara continued to look ahead. She was aware of the way Egey Bashi was studying her face, but she didn't want to acknowledge it.

"There's more to it, isn't there?" he said.

Kara squared her jaw. "I saw Meera's men look at me, especially after she proposed the exchange."

"And?"

"At the Olivian court, am I expected to receive... offers from their men?"

"You are a very attractive woman. You also look exactly like one of their own. I'd say they'll try, yes. Do you have a problem with it?"

"Yes."

"Why?"

She glanced at him briefly, noticing the way his gaze softened as he watched her.

"I find these kinds of relationships very odd," she said.

"At the times of the Old Empire," Egey Bashi said, "the emperor and the nobles used to maintain harems of females."

"Yes, I heard."

"These women were kept far stricter than the Shayil Yaran women keep their men. They were expected to spend their lives in seclusion, hidden from other men's eyes. This kind of an arrangement, however imperfect, worked for centuries. Of course, men are different in that regard."

"Different? How?"

"If you keep a bunch of men in seclusion competing for affections of one woman, they would all kill each other before long. You need to give them something else to do. To make it work seamlessly, you should also keep their options open to other women. The noblewomen here show off their men and share them freely. Those who assume you are one of them would expect you to do the same."

"So, how do I deal with this exactly?"

"By coming to terms with it. You don't have to agree to anything, but if you show the kind of discomfort you are showing now, it would affect your negotiations too."

"Would it?"

"The Queen is a talented politician, or so I heard. If she sees how flustered you are at the men's attention, she would make sure you are surrounded by them any time you are having an important talk. A distracted opponent is much easier to manipulate."

Kara nodded. This situation stirred up the worst memories about her training, overcoming her fear of men in order to get her Diamond ranking. She had done it once. Now, with so much depending on her, she had to find that strength again. She had no other choice.

# 27
# ALJAHARA

"The desert gear was bad enough," Ellah said. "Are we now expected to wear *this*?"

Kara gave the clothing laid out over the bed a long, hard stare. *Damn it, they couldn't possibly be serious about it.* "They have different customs here."

"Yes, but..."

"I think we must, if we want the Queen to give our request her full consideration."

"You don't really mean it, do you?"

Kara swallowed. This would indeed have looked like a bad joke if she hadn't spotted similarly dressed women in the inn's common room early this morning. The inn was one of those on the Majat Guild's payroll, but it also accepted regular customers and was apparently popular with the upper classes.

"You can probably get away with wearing your regular dress," she told Ellah. "You look like a foreigner anyway."

Ellah looked relieved as she edged away, wrapping her cloak around herself in a forceful gesture, as if to prevent anyone from ripping it off.

Kara sighed as she stepped decisively toward the bed. She had already changed from her usual clothing once, and the change served her well on their trip through the desert. She supposed she should view it as normal that she must now wear this outfit, even if she couldn't help feeling bitter that as the negotiator she was the only one in their party obliged to dress according to local customs. The innkeeper did try to offer court clothing to the entire party, but Mai had pointed out to her, politely but firmly, that in this official embassy he and his men should retain their normal appearance. Kara couldn't help wondering how much of his firmness was due to the fashion of the local garb.

She did her best to distance herself from the process as she donned the wide silky pants with an ornate belt that settled low over the hips, and a gold-embroidered sleeveless blouse that looked more like a scarf wrapped around her upper torso, seemingly designed entirely for the purpose of outlining her breasts. The clothes left her stomach bare, low enough to see her belly button.

The light silver sandals that came with the outfit fastened in numerous straps, offering far less support than her usual boots. Feeling defiant, she clipped on her knife belt and strapped on her sheathed blades across her back.

Her resolve weakened when she saw Ellah gaping. The girl's widened eyes drifted down to Kara's bare stomach before returning to her face.

There was no mirror in the room, far less luxurious than the one Kara had been originally offered to share with all the men, but she hadn't minded that much until now, when she realized that she would be expected to wear this garb to the inn's common room without having any prior reference point.

"What?" she demanded.

"You look… amazing," Ellah said.

*Amazing.* Kara forced herself not to dwell on it, taking care to adjust her sword sheath to lie more naturally against her back. The deep violet silk, by the innkeeper's admission specially selected to complement her eye color, was actually comfortable enough not to suppress any movements if it came to fighting, but she definitely wasn't used to showing so much skin.

She paused for a moment to compose herself, before opening the door and stepping into the hallway outside.

Her arrival in the inn's common room was met with dead silence. She tried to distance herself from the way everyone was staring at her as she made her way up to Mai and Egey Bashi.

"Are you sure this is really necessary?" she asked.

Mai closed his mouth slowly, his stunned expression so unlike his unusual calm composure. Even Egey Bashi seemed momentarily distracted, his wistful look making her feel angry. If the men in her own party, ones she trusted, were staring at her this way, what could she possibly expect at the Olivian court, where everyone, apparently, had only one thing on their mind?

"Rules or not," she said, "I'm going to bloody change back into my own gear. Wait here."

She turned to go, but before anyone could respond, the innkeeper hurried toward her. The elderly woman was beaming, her large lamp-like earrings clinking in rhythm with her steps.

"My lady Kara! You look so wonderful! So much like…" The woman paused, stepping backward and around to look at Kara from different sides. Her expression turned wistful, her eyes darting to a lit alcove on the wall.

Behind her a group of servants was staring too, talking to each other in hushed whispers.

"What is it?" Kara demanded.

The innkeeper looked at the alcove again. Kara strode forward to have a good view, Mai and Egey Bashi in her wake.

The painting hanging in the niche was clad in a heavy ornate frame, surrounded by glowing lanterns to illuminate it so that it stood out in the room's dim lighting. It depicted a woman in flowing red silks, adorned with heavy golden jewelry.

Kara's mouth fell open as she saw the woman's face.

She never spent much time looking in the mirror, and of course mirrors were very different from paint when it came to portraying reality, but even she could spot her undeniable likeness to the woman in the portrait. Her own new clothes were of a different color, and without the special sheen that must have come from the exceptional quality of the fabric. She also wore no gold, covered instead by numerous straps from her sheaths and weapon belts. But there was also something incredibly similar, not only in the woman's features, but also in her posture, the way she tilted her head and lifted her eyebrow, as if listening to a conversation beside her.

Kara spun around to face the innkeeper.

"Who is this?" she demanded.

The older woman took time to answer, looking at Kara distractedly. "Queen Jameera. She ruled about twenty years ago."

Kara looked back to the portrait, trying to shake off the eerie feeling, as if she was looking at a painted depiction of her own face. "What happened to her?"

"She died in childbirth, to everyone's sadness. She was a great queen. People of Shayil Yara still mourn her. Her Majesty Queen Rajmella is her younger sister."

Kara nodded. The explanation seemed normal, right up to the fact that for some inexplicable reason this dead queen looked so much like her. She glanced at Mai and Egey Bashi, their distracted expressions telling her more than words.

"This seems like yet another reason to change back into my gear," she said. "I wouldn't want to offend the Queen by showing up at court looking like her long-dead relative."

The innkeeper shook her head earnestly. "Oh, no. On the contrary, the Queen will be so pleased that you took the effort to abide by our customs. This portrait – it's unofficial, painted in the Queen Jameera's younger years, before she assumed the throne. Some of these paintings still circulate through the city, but they would only have the official ones up at the palace, painted when the Queen was in her prime. I am certain no one would even spot the likeness. Besides, Queen Jameera favored garnet and red. Purple was not her style."

Kara exchanged a questioning look with Mai and Egey Bashi. If she looked the part, if she did everything right, their chances of getting out of here as soon as possible were higher than if she took any other course of action. Which meant she had to show up at the palace dressed properly for the audience and behaving according to local customs. Besides, she couldn't help her looks, could she? Most likely the portrait here just happened to appear more similar to her than any others.

"If you show up at court wearing your gear instead of the local clothing," Mai said, "we might have a harder time getting what we want."

"I agree," Egey Bashi put in. "Besides, a likeness to a random portrait of a popular sovereign is hardly damning, is it? Given that you couldn't possibly have any relationship to Queen Jameera, no one would probably give it a second thought. I'd say we go and get this over with."

Kara glanced down at her bare stomach. With all this strangeness, she temporarily forgot even to feel embarrassed, but now the thought that she was about to march through the city dressed like this hit her anew. She glanced at Mai, hoping she didn't look as trapped as she felt, knowing he understood exactly what was going through her head.

"It looks natural on you," Mai said. "If I haven't been used to you dressed differently I wouldn't even give this a second thought."

She nodded. He was right. For someone who didn't know her, she would look exactly like other Olivian ladies, which was what she wanted. Besides, the fascination she saw in Mai's gaze when she first stepped into the room could be worth going into this little bit of trouble. If she kept by his side, if she let everyone know very clearly that she wasn't available, things could hopefully go smoothly at court. If she did want to get this negotiation over with, she would do best to play along.

•••

The palace was only a short walk away, but Kara's showy sandals with thin soles and ornate silvery straps did not provide enough support for her feet. She was finding it difficult to maintain her warrior's stride, even if she was never going to show it. Keeping her chin high and her shoulders square, she walked in the lead with the confident look of one who owned the place. She hoped it looked convincing.

The way people in the streets followed them seemed curious at first, but after a while it started to unnerve her. She supposed her suite of fair-skinned northern men should stir a reaction, but she never expected it would draw such a crowd. She couldn't understand this at all. As far as she could tell, she looked exactly the same as the noble Olivian ladies, perhaps dressed a bit more elaborately for the audience with the Queen. People here should be accustomed to a woman and her harem walking through. Did they sense something different about her?

Her resemblance to the portrait back at the inn could be the only other explanation. Yet this, too, seemed superficial. Everyone knew this Queen Jameera – or whatever was her name – was long dead. Surely they wouldn't possibly fret over a stranger bearing a fleeting likeness to her?

By the time they reached the palace, the crowd at their backs grew so large that it flooded the entire plaza. Their excited chatter gradually turned into a chant. Kara strained her ears but couldn't understand the words.

"What are they saying?" she asked Egey Bashi walking just behind her.

Egey Bashi hesitated. "I am not sure. It sounds like 'Aljahara', I believe."

"Some word in a local language?"

"They use mostly common speech here in Tahr Abad. The only prevalent local dialect is that of the Cha'idi nomads, but this doesn't sound like it."

"Perhaps a name?"

Egey Bashi glanced around at the people crowded behind to watch them ascend the palace steps. "Damned if I know. The way they look at you does seem curious. I'll see into it as soon as I can, and perhaps find out the meaning of their chant if the circumstances allow."

Kara shut her mind to the crowd's noises as she approached the guards stationed at the large palace gate. Trying to look as haughty as she could, she handed them the Queen's invitation letter she had received through the innkeeper early this morning.

The guard on the left read it, then lowered the parchment and looked over her entire party with a suspicious eye. "The Majat Guildmaster, eh?"

"Aghat Mai," Kara pointed with her upturned palm, following the Olivian custom.

"And the rest of the men?"

"The Majat of Aghat Mai's suite. And Magister Egey Bashi from the order of Keepers, with his apprentice, Ellah." They all agreed that hiding Ellah's gift of truthsense was the best strategy that could give Kara the maximum advantage during the negotiations. She glanced at the girl's hand, folded over her white robe with one outturned finger. Kara hardly needed this indication that the guard was being truthful – especially since he was the one asking the questions right now – but she felt reassured anyway. Ellah was paying attention. If she heard a lie, she would hold out two fingers to signal it without alerting anyone else.

The guard shuffled his feet in place, as if hesitating. Kara waited, looking at his golden shoulder plate shaped like a lion head, holding his crimson cloak in place. The man was from the Golden Lions battalion of the Queen's elite guards. She knew them to be formidable warriors, even if they couldn't quite compare to the Majat.

"Queen Rajmella has ordered accommodations to be prepared for you at the palace," the guard said. "You all must leave your weapons there before you are allowed into her presence."

Kara looked at Mai, his quick shrug of acceptance giving her a cue. She supposed it was all right to stay at the palace, even if it did change some of their original plans. She also saw no threat in the idea of leaving their weapons behind in their living quarters, as long as they could also leave someone to guard them. It made sense that the Queen would not want to let a small army of Majat's top Gems come into her presence fully armed. And, given their combat skill, having no weapons hardly put them into any extra danger. If a fight erupted, capturing the guards' weapons to defend themselves should not be difficult at all.

"We thank the Queen for her hospitality," she said.

The large suite of rooms opened to a private courtyard, dominated by a large pond inlaid with blue marble and gold mosaic. It seemed even more luxurious than the royal suite Mai had been previously offered at King Evan's court. The only step back in comfort lay in the fact that in these chambers there were no beds. Instead, each room contained low and wide cots covered with soft rugs and piled up invitingly with pillows, each of the cots large enough to sleep ten. Kara didn't want to venture any guesses into what these cots were normally used for. They would just have to think of this as camping, and space as evenly throughout the rooms as they possibly could.

Walking through the suite, Kara felt instantly reassured. The size and luxury of it befitted the Majat Guildmaster's station, showing that the Queen acknowledged the embassy and was prepared to follow the protocol. In fact, even the invitation to stay in the palace went along with the rules. Mai's station required an in-palace apartment rather than a room at an inn.

The servants helped them settle in, serving small basins to each of them to wash their hands and faces, followed by light refreshments – mint tea and tarts, filled with sliced almonds and rose petal jam. Another group of servants came in as they were strapping off weapons, bringing in the gear and packs the Majat had left at the inn this morning. Clearly, the Queen took her offer of hospitality seriously enough to make sure her guests settled in fully, even if Kara couldn't help wishing that this could be a very short stay. She did not relish the impending prospect of walking into a room full of people dressed the way she was, let alone without even wearing any weapons.

They were just getting ready when a commotion at the door to their suite announced the arrival of a tall, majestic woman, dressed in flowing green silks that left her stomach bare and her full breasts bulging out of the tightly fitted blouse. She looked to be in her forties, and not in the least abashed by the effect.

"Aghat Mai." She folded her palms together in a respectful Olivian greeting. "Lady Kara. I am Hamala, the grand vizier of Shayil Yara. Queen Rajmella sent me to greet you personally and to escort you into her presence."

Kara mirrored the greeting gesture, looking at the woman with curiosity. Hamala's keen eyes seemed to miss nothing as they glanced around their entire group with a quick appraisal, briefly pausing on Ellah, who stood next to Magister Egey Bashi wrapped in her white Keepers' cloak.

"Please follow me," Hamala said.

Kara's eyes inadvertently drifted to the four men that came with Hamala and now kept close on Kara's heels, edging out the Majat walking in her wake. They were all young and muscular, dressed in soft silky pants and ornate vests that ended above their waists and gaped open as they walked, seemingly designed specifically to emphasize their chest muscles rather than to cover them up. The way they looked at Kara made the effect seem even worse, their eyes sliding over her bare stomach with the intensity that made her skin creep.

Hamala grinned as she noticed Kara's blush. "Don't mind my consorts, my lady. Rumors of your arrival reached all through the palace. They're curious, that's all."

Kara grasped the opportunity to change the subject. "I was surprised our arrival caused such a stir, my lady. The crowds…"

Hamala frowned, and Kara had an eerie feeling she had touched on a forbidden topic. "The crowds are bored, that's all. They would jump on any excuse to cause a ruckus near the palace."

"They chanted a strange word," Kara said. "Al–"

Hamala raised her hand in a halting gesture. "Forgive me for offering unbidden advice, Lady Kara, but during your stay in the palace it couldn't possibly bode well with the Queen if you take the habit of repeating the nonsense you heard in the marketplace. These folk chants are of no significance, believe me."

Kara kept her gaze. The incident at the plaza suddenly seemed far more important. She lowered her eyes to catch sight of Egey Bashi's white robe, glad that he was walking close enough behind her to catch the exchange.

"Thank you for your advice, Lady Hamala," she said. "I need every bit of it. My northern upbringing is definitely a handicap when it comes to the Olivian customs."

Hamala smiled. "Any time, my lady. Actually, knowledge of your northern upbringing was another reason why I felt it useful to bring some of my consorts along."

"Another reason?"

Hamala's smile widened as she glanced around their entourage. "I know of your northern customs enough to understand that these gorgeous men that came with you are probably not yours to share. Some of the ladies at court may not understand it, though. I thought, by seeing my men, you would know what kind of a reaction to expect. I purposely brought the less inhibited ones. I wouldn't want you to feel too overwhelmed all at once when you step into the throne room."

*Too overwhelmed.* Kara looked at the Olivian men again. With the way their eyes devoured her as they crowded far too close for her comfort, she doubted they even saw her face, or would recognize her again if she came wearing different clothes. She felt almost relieved at the sight of the double doors ahead, swinging ajar to greet them. Stepping through those doors would mean that this uncomfortable walk would come to an end. Yet, if Lady Hamala's words were true, what awaited her inside was probably worse.

## 28
# QUEEN RAJMELLA

The throne room looked vast, yet it also created an impression of being far more intimate than the formal audience halls Kara was used to. Perhaps this was due to the room's low ceiling, painted in warm terracotta tones that brought to mind sun-baked clay and warm wind. Or the way the windows along its sides opened into the greenery of the garden beyond, alive with bird songs and splashing of the numerous fountains. For a brief moment, the waiting crowd of Olivian courtiers made Kara feel as if she was returning home, greeted by her eagerly waiting relatives after a long absence.

A wave of gazes hit her like a storm as she walked steadily toward the throne, with Mai by her side and Egey Bashi one step behind. It occurred to her belatedly that they should perhaps have requested a more personal audience. On the other hand, it probably wouldn't have mattered in the end. After the request had been sent, the Queen was the one calling all the shots.

She stopped ten paces away from the throne and folded into a respectful bow, then straightened and looked up at the Queen.

Queen Rajmella looked much younger than Kara imagined – perhaps not that surprisingly, since her eldest daughter, raised at the court in Tallan Dar, was only five. She seemed to be no more than ten years Kara's senior, and very beautiful, her dark skin accented by hair of such a rich golden color that even her jewelry seemed pale by comparison. She wore a lot of it, starting with an elaborate head piece that wove into her hair, to a set of massive golden bracelets that snaked all the way down her left arm, covering it from shoulder to wrist. The bracelets of station, worn in place of the crowns favored by the northern kings.

The Queen's violet eyes stayed on Kara as she leaned over and whispered something to a handsome young man standing next to the throne. The man looked to be about Kara's age, and was probably the only one in the room whose eyes didn't venture anywhere lower than her face. There was no lust in his gaze, just a quiet curiosity that made Kara feel instantly alert. She glanced at the woman sitting on the Queen's other side, a bit younger than the monarch, bearing an unmistakable likeness to her. Princess Nelimah, Rajmella's younger sister, Kara guessed. But who was the young man? A consort? Not likely. He looked far too haughty for the role.

"Aghat Mai," Queen Rajmella said. "It is our honor to receive the Majat Guildmaster as our guest. I must admit, however, that I was surprised to see someone of your young age at this post. What happened to Aghat Oden Lan?"

Mai's lips creased into a brief smile that didn't quite touch the rest of his face. "He has been deposed, Your Majesty."

"Deposed?"

"Yes."

"Why?"

"Due to an internal Guild matter, Your Majesty."

The Queen looked at Mai with curiosity, then leaned over and whispered something to her sister, who giggled and blushed, looking away.

"You are very spirited, Aghat Mai," she said. "Not to mention handsome. Looking at you, I cannot help but find it a shame that northern men hold themselves so unavailable to women. Especially the Majat. Such a fine display of men you brought with you, and none of them open for an exchange. Isn't it so, Lady Kara?"

Her direct look made Kara instantly uncomfortable. Or was it all because of the young man by the Queen's side, whose eyes hadn't left her face during the entire exchange?

"Northern customs are indeed different, Your Majesty," Kara said. "In the north, Aghat Mai would have been speaking to you directly, without the need for my interference."

"Directly." The Queen looked at Mai thoughtfully, then ran her eyes over the Majat of his suite. "I do like my men to be direct with me in my bedchamber, but there is no place for this kind of demeanor in my audience hall. Besides, your company is so delightful, Lady Kara. Wouldn't it have been a shame to miss it?"

"You are too kind, Your Majesty." Kara kept her eyes on the young man as she spoke, unable to escape the feeling she was being tested. She wished she understood the game, or at least had been given some clue on who this man could possibly be.

"Not at all," the Queen said. "I mean it. Perhaps, after

our talk about Aghat Mai's business is over, we could have a chance to get more personally acquainted?"

Once again, Kara saw a short glance that passed between the Queen and the young man by her side. She stifled a pang of concern as she forced her face into a smile. "It would be an honor, Your Majesty."

The Queen nodded, and Kara imagined she saw the older woman's shoulders relax, as if Kara's agreement to get acquainted, whatever it meant, had resolved an important question in the Queen's mind. "Very well. And now, pray tell me what kind of a business has prompted the Majat Guildmaster himself to venture this far south?"

"Aghat Mai and his men are in pursuit of a very dangerous enemy," Kara said. "We have information that they are hiding out in the deserts along your Bengaw border. The land of the Cha'idi nomads."

The Queen frowned. "Does your information suggest that the Cha'idi are allied with this enemy you speak of?"

Kara shook her head. "We possess no such information, Your Majesty. In fact, our hope is that the Cha'idi would help us find the enemy's secret stronghold. All we need is for Your Majesty to sanction this – as well as to allow Aghat Mai's army to pass freely through your lands."

The Queen raised her eyebrows. "His army?" She glanced over Mai's suite again. They wore no distinctive signs, not even their weapons. Kara hoped the Queen wouldn't be able to guess that the men in this room, a dozen of their Guild's best, were equivalent to a small army all on their own. With the numbers waiting for them back at Gard'hal outpost, they could easily wipe out the entire kingdom of Shayil Yara – not that she would ever feel necessary to bring up the possibility.

"Aghat Mai's men are waiting at the edge of your lands," she said. "In the hope that your support would enable them to proceed."

The Queen smiled. "I feel flattered that the Majat would ask for my support. Normally, they have been dealing only with Tallan Dar. We were beginning to wonder if this selectivity may have been due to the fact that they find us inferior." She looked at Mai as she spoke, her gaze spelling challenge.

He calmly returned her gaze. "The Majat deal with everyone equally, Your Majesty."

The Queen's full lips twitched. "Hardly true, Aghat Mai. You know well that your Pentade duty to the king is no more than a form of tribute the Majat Guild receives from Tallan Dar, both in the gold your Guild is paid for these services – a rather high price for the ceremonial job the Pentade is expected to do – as well as in the way it gives your top men the right to be present at all official functions alongside the king. No dealing in Tallan Dar ever happen without the Majat's knowledge, or so we heard."

Mai smiled. "I suppose it could be viewed this way. However, we did prove, on occasions, that our help could be invaluable when it comes to the King's protection."

Rajmella measured him with a dry gaze. "I heard of those, as you put it, occasions, Aghat Mai. Including the most recent one, where my daughter's life was nearly jeopardized."

Mai bowed slightly. "If you are this well informed, Your Majesty, you will also know that Lady Kara here is the one who saved your daughter's life."

"Yes, I am, Aghat Mai, and I am very grateful to her for this. I also know that you were the one who threw your life on the line to save them both in the end. Please believe me that this gratitude I feel toward you both does factor into my decisions, especially when you tend to so charmingly breach the protocol all the time by speaking directly to me." She leaned toward her sister again, and again Princess Nelimah blushed and giggled at the Queen's words.

"Please forgive me, Your Majesty," Mai said.

He looked easy and relaxed, but Kara noticed the way he kept his arms by his sides, ready to act in a blink of an eye. His men echoed his stance. Her skin prickled. One wrong move, and this whole room would erupt in chaos. She hurriedly turned back to the Queen.

"The enemies who threatened your daughter," she said, "are the same ones we are pursuing right now. Your help would ensure that they never bother anyone again."

The Queen looked at her, as if hesitating, then briefly inclined her head.

"I will consider Aghat Mai's request," she said. "I will give you my answer tomorrow. In the meantime, I hope you will all enjoy our hospitality."

Kara bowed, feeling only partially reassured. The way the Queen looked at Mai, the way the conversation tended to skid off into edgy topics, seemed to be a recipe for trouble. Worse, the young man by the Queen's throne kept looking at her with calm evaluation, as if eyeing a thoroughbred horse he was considering buying. Despite the lack of open lust, Kara was beginning to wonder about his intentions toward her. Princess Nelimah did not help much either as she ran her eyes over the Majat with an appraising look of her own, then leaned over and whispered in the Queen's ear.

"Before you go," the Queen said. "My sister wants to know if any of your men would be open to an exchange. She is prepared to send you an equal number of her own consorts."

Kara opened her mouth wordlessly. She had been preparing for this, and she had practiced a number of suitable answers that would keep them all in the clear, but she never imagined for the request to be coming from the Queen on behalf of a member of the royal family.

"Our northern customs–" she began, but the Queen waved her hand to interrupt.

"I am aware of your northern customs, Lady Kara. However, I believe, you are also well informed about our customs here. My sister especially fancies the tall blond one over there." She pointed at Lance, standing beside Mai. "Of course, if this particular one is not available, she would be glad to consider others."

Kara glanced around helplessly, somewhat relieved to see Lance grinning as he bent over to Mai and exchanged a few whispered words. The two men seemed unabashed, but she couldn't fully share their calm reaction. In fact, she was beginning to panic. An exchange the Queen proposed was supposed to be done by consent – and discreetly, without putting anyone on the spot. Of course, this probably didn't apply when it came to the royal family. And now, she had no idea how to deal with it.

Lance and Mai exchanged more quiet phrases. From

the few words she caught, Kara could tell they were using the Majat language, but she wasn't standing close enough to understand what they were talking about. She was still wondering when Lance stepped forward past Mai and bowed to the Queen.

"I would be honored to entertain Princess Nelimah," he said.

Kara's mouth fell open as she stared, at a loss for words. The whole situation simply refused to fit into her head. She had to assume Lance understood exactly what he was agreeing to. She also assumed by his calm look, as well as by Mai's spreading grin, that he didn't mind. She looked at Princess Nelimah who rose from her seat excitedly, whispering into Queen's ear as she kept her eyes on her prize.

The Princess looked to be no older than twenty-five, and beautiful enough to turn heads. Did her looks factor into the easiness with which Lance agreed? Kara felt her cheeks warm up at the mere thought, her blush deepening as she noticed Queen Rajmella's eyes fixed on her.

"Excellent," the Queen said. "Princess Nelimah is willing to send you one of her favorite consorts in return."

Kara took a much-needed breath. "I thank Her Royal Highness, but this won't be necessary."

The Queen nodded. "I thought so. Besides, since you have so graciously accepted my hospitality this evening, I hope to be able to engage you otherwise. My own consorts would be more than happy to entertain both of us. And of course, I also invited Prince Jamal." She pointed to the young man standing by her chair.

*Prince Jamal*. Kara didn't remember learning this

name when she was studying up on the Shayil Yaran royal family. She also didn't quite recall accepting this sort of hospitality from the Queen, but it didn't seem to be a good moment to bring this up. She forced herself to relax, reminding herself that with her combat skill she couldn't possibly be afraid of anything awaiting her in the Queen's chambers, even if she had to go there alone and unarmed. Perhaps, if she played along, she could even use this chance to gain enough trust to facilitate a favorable outcome to the negotiations?

"Thank you, Your Majesty," she said.

"Good. I will send someone to pick you up from your chambers, Lady Kara. I look forward to it."

Just then, Kara became aware of the excited chatter behind her. Court ladies were giggling and pointing, some stepping toward the Majat, mixing into their group.

"It seems that everyone's taken Princess Nelimah's experience to heart," Egey Bashi said quietly. "I think we're about to get more offers."

Kara glanced at Mai only partially reassured by his smile.

"You should relax," Mai said. "I see no harm in it."

"*No harm*?" Her eyes widened. The way the court ladies devoured the men with their eyes seemed unnerving. Were the Majat men really prepared to do what these women wanted? She blushed, hastily looking away from the mingling crowd, where the noble ladies were ogling the men like goods on display.

"They can handle it," Mai said.

*I hope they can.* "But…"

Mai laughed. "You look far too terrified. They're all grown men. Don't worry about them."

Kara let out a sigh. She supposed he was right. She should stop putting herself in their place. Besides, she herself was already committed to a visit this evening that she might find potentially challenging in more ways than one. She glanced at Prince Jamal. Why was he looking at her like this? Did he hope his status as a prince meant she would grant him some special favors?

"What do you know about Prince Jamal?" she asked on the way out of the throne room.

"He's the Queen's nephew," Egey Bashi said. "The son of Queen Jameera, whose portrait we saw this morning at the inn."

Kara's heart raced. Was this why Jamal was looking at her this way? Did she remind him of his dead mother? Kara let out a breath. This was highly unlikely, given that he couldn't possibly have remembered what his mother looked like. Besides, very few painters could actually portray a person well enough to achieve extensive resemblance to the original. That portrait at the inn must have been a coincidence, that's all.

"They say Jameera died giving birth to him," Egey Bashi went on, "but from the way the chronicles are written, I'd say there was definitely foul play."

Kara frowned, turning to look at the Keeper. "Foul play? Was Rajmella behind it?"

Egey Bashi shook his head. "Unlikely. Rajmella was eleven at the time. Her grand aunt ruled as regent until she came of age. To the best of my knowledge the plot was conceived by an outsider, a woman of power who paid in full for her crimes. People here don't like to talk about it much."

Kara wished she would have had a chance to learn more about the royal family, especially given the fact that she was about to get so closely acquainted with them.

The group of the Majat around them pretty much dissipated by the time they left the throne room and made way back to their chambers. Seldon was the only one left, walking with his head high and an air of defiance around him. Kara wondered if he was the only one who didn't receive any propositions, or if the women who approached him didn't strike his fancy. Whatever his reasons, she didn't feel comfortable venturing any further thoughts into this.

The four Emerald Guards left behind in their chambers greeted them in stunned silence. Mai threw a few words over his shoulder in a brief explanation as he led Kara into the inner room of their suite and closed the door behind them.

"We have nearly no men left," she said.

Mai laughed. "Let them all have some fun."

*Fun.* "Are you sure they would see it this way?"

"Have you seen these ladies?" Mai continued laughing at her frozen expression. "I'd say our men will all have the time of their lives tonight."

"But…what if something happens here in their absence?"

Mai shrugged. "We have you, me, Seldon, and four Emeralds. I don't believe we should worry about our safety tonight. On the contrary, if anything were to happen, I see it as a tactical advantage to have a top Gem stationed near pretty much every powerful woman in this palace. Don't you?"

*A tactical advantage.* It was good that Mai was able to keep a cool head in a situation where she got too easily flustered.

"You and Seldon are the only ones they didn't pick," she said. "No offense."

He laughed. "Seldon got propositioned all right. He just chose not to do it. As for me, I don't think anyone dared. It hardly befits my station, does it?"

"I suppose not."

He grinned. "Besides, they probably noticed the way I looked at you. Even these ladies can recognize a hopeless situation."

Her stomach fluttered. She and Mai hadn't had privacy for a very long time, not since that time back in Ayalla's realm. It seemed cruel that she had to abandon an opportunity to spend time with him so that she could go to the Queen's chambers, where she knew she would be made uncomfortable in so many ways.

Mai seemed to have read her thoughts.

"In my estimation," he said, "you have about an hour before the Queen sends for you. I asked Lenart to make sure no one disturbs us until then."

Her eyes widened. "You did?"

"Yes."

"Then," she said, "we'd better make good use of the time."

She felt lightheaded as he scooped her into his arms and carried her to the bed.

It seemed far too soon when she heard distant banging on the outer doors, followed by footsteps and voices, and finally, a tentative knock on the door of their own chamber. She stirred, not ready to move just yet, immersed in the movements of Mai's hands over her bare skin that left trails of goosebumps in their wake until she was tingling all over.

"Aghat Mai?" the Emerald Guard called from the outside. "The Queen's messengers are here for Kara."

"She'll be out in a minute, Jahib." Mai shifted Kara in his arms, holding her close so that she could rest her head on his shoulder.

"Are you ready?" he asked quietly. "Or did I exhaust you too much?"

She nuzzled him. "You always do."

He grinned. "I try to. Especially now, when you are about to face the temptations of the Queen's consorts."

She shuddered at the reminder, lifting away from him. *The Queen's consorts.* What was she getting herself into?

Mai sat up and looked at her thoughtfully. "You don't look like you are ready to move just yet. How about I dress you up?"

"You?"

"You think I don't know how to do it?"

She smiled. "Let's see it then."

Deep inside, she felt grateful for his help. She was feeling so spent, not only from their lovemaking just now, but from the whole day that preceded it. She wanted nothing more than to curl up by his side and sleep, not dress up and depart alone for an encounter she really didn't look forward to.

Mai picked her up and carried her to the next room, where the servants had prepared a bath for the evening. He got into the water with her as he washed her clean, then lifted her out and rubbed her with a towel. She could feel the energy he put into his movements, massaging her back to life, his closeness filling her with a surreal sense of happiness she did not experience in a very long while.

His hands moved deftly as he dressed her up in a new silky outfit the servants had left out for the occasion, even more luxurious than the previous one, then brushed out her hair until it shone.

"You make a wonderful lady's maid," she said.

Mai grinned. "Thank you, my lady. I pride myself on having many different talents."

"I could get used to this."

His grin widened. "I hope you will. If it was up to me, I'd never let you dress by yourself – perhaps, never dress at all?"

She pulled him close for a brief kiss, then stepped toward the door and flung it open.

## 29
# PRINCE JAMAL

The two men waiting for Kara in the outer chamber made her pause in the doorway in a sudden uprush of panic. They both looked more muscular than many of the other men she saw here, their silky vests so scant that they seemed nearly non-existent. Their dark purple eyes devoured her with the expressions that made her instantly hot with embarrassment. She felt grateful when Mai stepped up behind her, his brief look forcing the men to recede. "My lady Kara," one of the newcomers said, bowing. "I am Valmir, Queen Rajmella's First Consort. This is Dahim." He indicated his companion.

Kara looked at the man with curiosity. The title of the First Consort meant that he was not only the Queen's favorite, but likely the father of her First Daughter Aljbeda, raised in Tallan Dar. This made this man as important as men could possibly be at this court.

"I am honored that you personally came to pick me up, Valmir," she said. "Please forgive the wait." She glanced at Mai, hoping her blush wasn't too obvious.

Valmir smiled. "The honor is all mine, my lady. The

Queen is very interested in getting to know you better. Are you ready?"

She stepped forward, but Mai placed a hand on her shoulder, halting her. The men stiffened, their eyebrows flying up in surprise.

"Valmir? Dahim?" Mai's tone forced them to pull to attention. "Bring her back safe. I am holding you two personally responsible."

The two men exchanged uneasy glances as they bowed and escorted Kara out of the chamber. Kara smiled at Mai as she followed them. They both knew she didn't need any physical protection. But Mai's warning, and the way he manhandled her briefly to show the kind of relationship they had, would likely make these men, and others in the Queen's quarters once made aware of it, think twice before trying anything improper.

She soon lost count of the winding hallways and corridors. This palace seemed to have no stairs at all, only rooms and passages, with plenty of niches and alcoves holding ornate benches and divans. The whole environment, in fact, seemed as suggestive as the glances the men threw at her, echoing those she had encountered in abundance back in the throne room.

The Queen's chambers looked even more luxuriously suggestive. The large area Kara was shown into had a complex shape, set with semi-private areas along the sides – used, she assumed, to entertain small groups without providing any real seclusion. Kara followed her guides to one such area at the back, separated from the rest by a fountain that trickled down the wall into a deep stone basin large enough to fit ten.

Rajmella reclined next to it on a low divan, a well-

muscled man leaning over her from behind to massage
her shoulders. When the Queen saw Kara she smiled
and waved, gesturing to another divan beside her. Kara
took the invitation, trying not to act too openly curious
as she glanced around the room. She stiffened briefly as
another man appeared at her back, running his fingers
down her neck so deftly that her body reacted to the
touch even before she could give it any conscious
thought. She met the Queen's eyes, but saw nothing
threatening in the woman's encouraging smile. After a
brief hesitation, she relaxed into the massage, ready to
protest the moment the man's hands ventured to any
place she didn't feel comfortable with. She wasn't sure
how far Olivian hospitality went, but she was fairly
certain about her limits in that regard, even at the risk
of appearing impolite.

"I am happy your Majat companions proved to be
so agreeable," the Queen said. "Their compliance with
our customs surely came as a relief."

"Relief, Your Majesty?" Kara frowned.

The Queen laughed. "We heard rumors that the
Majat are required to give up their manhood in order to
receive their high ranking. However, my sister assures
me this isn't the case. In fact, when I stopped by her
chambers just now, I found her quite preoccupied."

*Preoccupied.* Kara knew she should probably be glad
that Lance was pleasing the Queen's sister so well, but
the mere idea of what was going on over there made
her cheeks burn. She always thought of her fellow
warriors as brothers, with the added awkwardness
of having to deal with the gender differences when
it came to sharing training quarters and camping
together on the long marches. Thinking of any of them

as sexually able men felt like a taboo. Now that she was faced with this kind of a situation, she couldn't stop feeling embarrassed.

"I am very glad things are working out so well, Your Majesty," she said.

The Queen smiled again, shifting on her couch to give the man massaging her shoulders access to her lower regions. Kara remained firmly in place to prevent a similar change in her own massage. The Queen watched her growing discomfort with barely disguised amusement.

"You certainly *look* the part of an Olivian noblewoman," she said. "But you don't act like one at all. You're far too shy. If you are to succeed in your career as a negotiator, you definitely need to work on that."

Kara hated the way these words made her blush deepen. "I'm only here this one time, Your Majesty. I don't expect to do this again." *Not if I can help it.*

The Queen shook her head. "That would be a shame, Lady Kara. You are beautiful and well-spoken. Perhaps, if you do not wish to be a negotiator, you would consider a position at my court? I can give you an easy job to start with. A chancellor, perhaps. How about it?"

Kara's eyes widened. She certainly didn't expect an offer like this.

"I am very honored, Your Majesty," she said truthfully. "But I must return to the north as soon as this assignment is over."

The Queen nodded knowingly. "The Majat Guildmaster is a very handsome man. If not for his station, our ladies would probably have ripped him apart. Don't think I didn't notice the way you look at him. Does he feel the same way about you?"

Kara's blush rolled down her neck. She didn't realize she was being so transparent.

The Queen laughed. "Now that I know his manhood is likely just as intact as that of his subordinates, I can only congratulate you on your choice, my dear. I know that the Majat Guildmaster enjoys more freedom in this regard than any other man commanding this kind of power. At least, his choice of women is not constrained by considerations of rank and birth."

*It is, just not the way it works with others.* Kara kept her silence. Discussing her relationship with Mai in this chamber couldn't possibly lead to anything good.

"One aspect of the negotiation process that you grasped especially well," the Queen went on after a pause, "is the art of being secretive. In my observation, the things we don't say are sometimes far more important than those we do."

Kara frowned. Did she imagine an implied threat in the Queen's words, or was this just a friendly comment? She bitterly wished she had brought Ellah with her, but she knew it would have been not only impolite, but also likely useless. Ellah was even more shy than Kara when it came to men. The sight of all the well-muscled bodies as the consorts gathered around their divans was beginning to feel oppressive. She could only hope they were drawn closer by the conversation, and not by an upcoming activity she couldn't possibly consent to.

A movement in the back rows caught her eye, a chill running down her spine as she recognized the newcomer. *Prince Jamal.*

He strode toward them with an easy grace that inadvertently made her wonder about his skill with weapons. His quality of movement lacked the refinement of a top-ranked Majat, but it definitely drew enough attention to make her feel instantly alert. She kept relaxed not to show the reaction to her masseuse, who could likely sense her moods through touch by a slightest shift in her muscles.

As if to confirm these suspicions she noticed the sharp glance the Queen cast past her shoulder to where she was sure the man's face currently was. Kara frowned. Had the man been placed by her side to detect her mood changes and signal them to the Queen? She forced her muscles to stay relaxed, making sure not to give him anything to report.

Prince Jamal knelt by the Queen's side and whispered something into her ear. She patted his bare shoulder before turning back to her guest.

"Please forgive me, Lady Kara," the Queen said. "I have been impolite just now. I also believe that back in the throne room I failed to introduce Prince Jamal properly. He is my nephew, the son of my dear older sister, who, alas, departed this world far too young, without leaving an heir."

Once again Kara noted the Queen's glance past her face, as if she had expected the man massaging her to detect a reaction to these words. She also realized that as the Queen spoke just now he had kept his hands flat and relaxed over her shoulders, in a position ideally suited to sense the slightest twitch of muscles. She kept still, returning the Queen's smile.

"It's a pleasure to meet you, Prince Jamal," she said.

The Prince briefly bowed his head, then sat on the floor between her and the Queen. Some of the other men crowded around her too, their meaningful glances suggesting the activities were about to change.

Kara sat up straight. "I'm afraid I must take my leave, Your Majesty."

The Queen smiled. "So early, my lady? My men were just about to serve refreshments." She signaled into the depth of the room and a younger man hurried forward with a covered tray.

The masseuse resumed his circular movements over the back of Kara's shoulders, parting her hair to touch the sensitive spot at the nape of her neck. Kara stiffened, refusing to give in to the pleasure. She briefly noted Jamal's stare, as if the Prince was interested in joining the exercise, and edged away. Being entertained by the Queen's nephew definitely wasn't part of the plan, if only because saying no to anything he had in mind would likely be viewed as an insult. Consensual or not, members of the royal family were clearly used to getting what they wanted. The way Lance's services were requested told her this much.

Absorbed in these thoughts, she didn't pay much attention to the man with the tray, who knelt in front of her and placed it on a small table in front of her, as if the covered dish was intended only for her. As he lifted the lid, the masseuse at her back pushed her down toward the table with unexpected force.

Her body reacted instantly with all her trained reflexes, twisting out of his hold and flipping away from the table faster than thought, but even as she landed on the floor and rolled over to avoid the men trying to grab her, she knew it was already too late. She recognized the smell, thick and smoky, lingering in her nostrils long after the brief exposure. This sleeping powder was one of the nastiest substances around, banned from most places she knew precisely because of its potency. Inhaling a full breath of it knocked a person out instantly. Even the half-breath she took was enough to make her limbs heavy and her reflexes far too slow to defeat a roomful of muscular men.

She kicked the divan into the way of her advancing attackers and rolled over, trying to stand up. She made it as far as kneeling when something heavy pounced onto her shoulders, iron-hard arms grasping her, pinning her to the ground. Her blurring eyes recognized Jamal, moving so fast that in her dazed state she couldn't anticipate him at all. Where the hell did he learn to fight like this? She sensed more than saw his fingers descending onto the pressure points that could render her immobile, and summoned all her skill to shift out of the way and kick him under the ribs, using the brief moment as he tried to recompose to throw him off.

She did make it up to her feet this time, and halfway to the door, before she faced him again, popping into her way as if out of thin air. She frowned, cursing her poisoned limbs for not being able to move any faster. Jamal's reflexes were definitely far superior to anything she had ever expected to encounter outside of the Majat Guild. She didn't know how this was possible, but there was no time to wonder as he advanced on her. She stumbled over his leg, which grew in her way as if sprouting out of the floor. He grasped her across her chest and threw her over his hip, the fall knocking the wind out of her. Before she could catch her breath, he landed on top of her, pinning her down. More weight piled on her legs and arms, then the brief wisp of the smoky smell enfolded her, making her feel as if she was falling into a dark, bottomless void.

# 30
# HOPE

Kyth was sitting in his tent, getting ready for sleep, when shifting shadows by the entrance signaled the movement outside. Kyth lifted his head. Alder? Unlikely. His foster brother still spent his nights with Ayalla, arriving in the morning, dazed and distracted, to catch up on sleep when Kyth departed for his lessons. He felt worried how long Alder's stamina would hold up. It was a marvel how Ayalla always arrived at their lessons fresh and unperturbed, as if spending all nights in a healthy beauty sleep. Perhaps that was how she viewed their nightly activities? Kyth could only wonder.

He peered at the door curtain, wondering if he should go outside and take a look, but quickly decided against it. Here, in Ayalla's realm, even wild animals never bothered them at all. The movement was probably wind, or trees shifting around at Ayalla's bidding.

He was settling down on his bedroll when the door curtain wavered and moved aside. Kyth sat up straight, surprised to see Celana step through the doorway.

"You had a lantern on, so I knew you were not asleep," she said. "I hope I haven't disturbed you."

"Not at all." Kyth tried to rise up to his feet to greet her, but in the cramped space of the tent standing straight wasn't possible at all. She smiled at his efforts, then lowered to the floor and crept inside.

Her long silky dress looked so light, more like a night shift than an outer garment. Her loose hair falling down her shoulders framed her slim body like flames, its fiery-red tongues licking the skin of her bare arms.

"I couldn't sleep," she said. "It's overwhelming to think that we are departing in a few days."

Kyth felt overwhelmed too. Under Ayalla's tutelage, his power had grown so much that at times he was finding it hard to contain. His previous experiences at handling his magic seemed feeble, a pale shadow of everything he was truly capable of. Still, even with this power at his command, the task he was facing seemed enormous. He hoped he was up to it.

"Do you feel you'll be ready by then?" Celana said.

He shrugged. "I don't know. Ayalla believes so. But whether I can actually do what she expects of me..." He spread his hands.

She smiled. "Only one way to find out."

"Yes."

She edged forward and lay down by his side, leaning on one elbow. He lowered too, so that their faces were level. This position seemed natural, the most comfortable one in the low tent. But it also made him aware that she was now sharing his bedroll, a thought that made his cheeks warm.

She blushed too, but her eyes gleamed with mischief. "If you forgive me saying this, I find you so adorable when you blush like this."

His blush deepened. "Adorable?"

"Yes. It's as if you worry about my virtue even more than I do."

*Her virtue.* He swallowed. The thought *did* worry him, especially when they lay so close to each other. "As your traveling companion, I feel it is my duty to protect you."

She grinned. "It's very sweet of you, if somewhat old-fashioned. I hope, though, you don't doubt at all that I have no need of your protection. I can protect myself just fine."

He nodded. Celana was an adept archer. She was also far more fit than could be guessed by her slender build and delicate upbringing. He knew she could defend herself in a tight spot. Yet, he just couldn't stop feeling responsible.

"Besides," she said, "I hardly need any protection from you."

His blush was instantly back as he peered into her face. "Perhaps you are giving me too much credit? I've already taken advantage of you, once."

Her eyelids trembled. "Yes, you did. And I gave you my permission to do it again, remember?"

He opened his mouth to turn this into a joke, but her expression stopped him, a mix of shyness and expectation in her gaze freezing him to the spot.

"I… I want you to," she said quietly.

"Is this why you came to my tent?"

"Yes."

He peered closer, feeling the heat rise into his face.

It came to his mind that during their entire stay at Ayalla's he hadn't thought of Kara even once – not romantically, at least. At the same time, the kiss he and Celana had shared back at the Majat camp before their parties separated came to his mind often, even if with his intense training schedule he never had a chance to pursue this train of thought very far. He missed her scent, the feeling of her smooth skin under his hands, the boldness with which she had given herself to him, inexperienced but eager. He kept telling himself he had no right to her, not with the way he had given his heart to another. But now that they were so close, lying together in a tent, he found himself wondering if he was taking his restraint around her a bit too far. He didn't want to lead her on or give her false hopes. But it was different if the hopes felt real, wasn't it?

Their faces were so close that he didn't even need to reach forward to cup her cheek. She briefly closed her eyes as she turned her face into his caress. He brushed her lips, tentative at first, until she responded, opening her mouth to invite him inside.

His hand slid into her hair, then down her back as he pulled her into an embrace. Her scent enfolded him, a fresh Lakeland wind that carried his mind out of bounds, beyond the smothering walls of the forest around them.

Her dress was thin and silky, and as he ran his hands over it he detected no garments underneath. The thought of her naked body so close, separated from him by no more than a thin layer of cloth, made him sweat. *Her virtue.* No matter how eager she seemed, he couldn't allow his desire to overcome his senses and take this encounter too far. He had to stop himself before it was too late.

He gasped as he drew away from her, holding her at arm's length as he tried to quiet his racing heart.

"We shouldn't," he said.

She peered into his eyes. "Why?"

"You… You are a virgin, aren't you?"

"Yes." She looked at him curiously, as if puzzled.

He kept her gaze, caught in a conflict he didn't know how to deal with. His body urged him on, wanting nothing but to ravage her and claim every bit of her. His mind pulled him back, telling him this wasn't the right way.

"If I went on right now," he said, "I would be taking advantage of you in more ways than I believe I should."

"Didn't I already give you permission to do it?"

He heaved a breath. "With your inexperience, you don't even know what you are asking me to do."

Her lips curved into a quick grin. "However naïve you consider me to be, I think I have an idea."

He looked down at her helplessly, summoning all his strength to will his body into stillness. "It could hurt. I heard it does, the first time."

"Are you suggesting I remain a virgin for the rest of my life for fear of a brief pain?"

He shook his head. Put like this, it did seem ridiculous.

"What if I get you with child?" he asked.

She laughed. "Haven't you ever heard of warding spells?"

"No." He frowned. Looking at her, he was beginning to feel as if he was the naïve one.

"In wealthy families, every girl receives one at birth, to be removed by a priest on her wedding day. This was introduced as part of the Church's breeding law, after the Holy Wars."

*Breeding law.* The law imposed strict rules on everyone, giving the Church power to approve marriages and prevent the birth of illegitimate children with magic. Of course, it made sense that wealthy families found a way around it to allow their girls more freedom. Kyth's own inborn magic led his father to hide him among commoners when he was growing up, which was likely why he had no idea at all about such things as warding spells.

"We are headed to a war," Celana said. "No one knows if you or I will even survive. Before the worst happens, I want to make sure that I have a chance, at least once, to be with the man I love."

Kyth went very still, looking at her. She wasn't smiling, not even blushing as she looked at him with a mix of openness and vulnerability that sent his heart racing. *Love. She can't possibly mean it, can she?*

"I am not asking you for anything more," she said. "Not until you are ready. Not ever, if this is not meant to be. Just for this." She glanced down her outstretched body, then back up to his face. "Assuming, of course, that you find me desirable enough to consider it."

Kyth felt his head spin as he leaned forward and kissed her again. This time he let his hands go all the way down, caressing her, lifting her dress, pulling it off to expose her naked beauty. He stripped off his clothes too, so that he could feel her with every bit of his skin as he stretched beside her, submerged in her silky smoothness and warmth.

She was so responsive, each of her shivers echoing through him too, each of her movements forcing down another restraint in his mind. He held back, taking it as slowly as she needed, giving her time to adjust, waiting for her body to signal him each time she was ready for more.

His fingers stroked her stomach, then slid between her legs to trace the sensitive skin on the inside of her thighs, tentative as he sensed her hesitation. She briefly clenched her knees, then relaxed and let them fall open, letting him inside. Her wetness beckoned as he stroked her there, lightly at first, then more steadily as she turned into his touch, pressing into his hand to show him that she wanted more. She trembled as he built up the tension, her moans echoing through him with an arousal so intense that he could barely contain it. When she gasped and fell back, convulsing, he felt her release echo through him too, as if he was a part of her.

He hesitated, still unsure if he should go any further despite his raging need, but she gave him no time to think. Clinging to him, she shifted in his embrace, pulling him over her parting legs until he was poised for entry. Her hips turned up into his thrust, a movement that took him by surprise, forcing him to push deeper inside her than he intended to go.

He froze as he felt her stiffen, cursing himself for not being able to exercise more control. He had planned to take it much slower, if at all. And now that he was inside her, holding back seemed even more impossible than before, even if he knew this was what he must do. He felt so conflicted again, his body screaming for him to go on, his mind telling him to wait until another time. He clung to the reasonable part, stifling his need, holding still with every last bit of resolve. He had just taken her virginity, he was sure of it. He should leave her alone and give her time to cope with this change before he took it any further.

Just as he thought he had gotten a grip on himself, she shifted under him again, her legs wrapping around him to push him deeper inside her. His body reacted before he meant it to, his next thrust followed by another, and another, answered by her moans urging him on. As he picked up speed, her head rolled back, her inner muscles clenching around him in a building release that forced away the last bits of restraint. He spiraled out of control, only vaguely aware of her gasps, of her fingers raking his chest. Her body erupted in convulsions that took him too, shaking him all the way to the core and into oblivion.

He held her close as they rode through the aftershocks, finally finding the strength to ease out of her and lie down by her side. The lantern had gone out and he couldn't see her face, but he could sense her smile against his neck as she curled into his hold. He wanted to ask her if she was all right, if he had caused her pain, but he knew this was a wrong time to say anything at all. She kissed him lightly, nuzzling him as he wrapped his arms around her and pulled her close.

He hoped that, barring the pain he was sure she felt at that first moment of entry, he had made her first time with a man as enjoyable as she hoped it to be. But even that didn't seem to matter right now. If there would be a next time, and ones to follow, he would make sure that every single time he would learn more and more about her, finding new ways to make her feel as special as she deserved to be. He took so much enjoyment from seeing her pleasure. Next to her, his own pleasure, however exquisite it was, didn't even matter that much.

He knew if they were destined to die in their war with the Kaddim, he would die with no regrets. Just a short while ago, he wasn't sure he could ever love again. And now, for the first time, he found a very real hope.

# 31
# A COUP

"It's taking too bloody long," Mai said.

Ellah leaned back into her chair, watching him tiredly. Mai had been restless the whole evening. For the past hour he had been up from his seat, pacing their common room despite Egey Bashi's attempts to distract him with a conversation. It was indeed getting late, even though Ellah was sure the Queen's invitation did not specify the time of Kara's return. For all she knew, Kara may be expected to share someone's bed, an obvious thought that none in their party dared venture into the conversation. Mai seemed near enough to the edge without discussing that possibility.

"Why don't we all have some sleep, Aghat Mai?" Egey Bashi said soothingly. "I'm sure, with her combat skill, Kara couldn't possibly be in any danger."

Mai looked at him for a moment, as if considering the suggestion, then resumed his pacing.

"I assume, Aghat Mai," Seldon said, "you are not similarly concerned about Aghat Lance, or any of our other men, not showing up by now?"

Mai paused again. Ellah flinched at his expression.

It felt as if the weight everyone had been waiting for dropped, leaving only a brief pause before an explosion.

"Are you trying to make a bloody point, Aghat Seldon?" Mai said.

Seldon's guarded look told Ellah that he was fully aware of the reaction he was causing, even though he clearly wasn't going to back down. His jaw knotted with resolve as he spoke.

"I *am* making a point, Aghat Mai. Kara is a grownup, and given her rank and her exceptional skill, she is more than capable of taking care of herself – just like our men, who willingly ventured out for the evening. You shouldn't exhaust yourself with worry about her well-being. The best we can all do right now is get some sleep, so that we are all ready for the negotiations tomorrow."

Mai froze, his face briefly contorting into a mask that made him nearly unrecognizable. Ellah braced for the fight she was sure was about to erupt, but, to her surprise, Mai merely turned around and left the room.

After a long moment they all heard a distant thud of a door slamming in the depth of the suite, followed by a silence that hung heavily in the air.

"Perhaps I should go talk to him?" Egey Bashi offered, without much enthusiasm.

Seldon shook his head. "Aghat Mai is a reasonable man. Just give him some time to cool off."

"But what if he is right and we do have reasons for concern, Aghat?"

Seldon smirked. "Kara is probably enjoying a version of every woman's paradise right now. Do you really want to pull her out of it?"

*Every woman's paradise.* Ellah looked at him

thoughtfully. Clearly, Seldon knew very little about women. Perhaps that was not too surprising, given his advanced Majat rank that probably afforded him very little opportunity to interact with women at all.

Ellah thought back to the conversation she had with Kara at Gard'hal outpost, and Kara's surprising confession about her fear of men. From her own experience, Ellah knew that fears like this never disappeared without a trace. While Kara had clearly found her balance with men – and was enjoying a very close relationship with one – Ellah was sure Kara would be terrified at facing all those scantily clad consorts, apparently with only one thing on their mind, throwing themselves at her, as she was sure they would try to do in the Queen's quarters.

Ellah still remembered Kara's expression when she first encountered this kind of attention from Hamala's consorts on their way to the throne room. Besides, Kara was deeply devoted to Mai. Ellah was certain Kara was anxious to return to him as soon as possible. She had been gone more than four hours. Perhaps Mai was right and it was indeed time to worry?

She rose to her feet. "I think I'll, um, go and talk to Mai myself."

Egey Bashi regarded her for a moment. "Are you sure?"

"Yes." She understood the Magister's hesitation. None of them knew what Mai was capable of in his current volatile mood. Yet, she was sure that even on the brink of losing control Mai would never harm someone like her, a person with no weapon training at all. Well, at least reasonably sure. In any case, this was what friends were for, wasn't it?

It looked as if Egey Bashi was about to say something else by the way he raised his head, but he receded back into his seat under her questioning gaze. "Make sure to stay out of his weapons' range – if you can help it, of course."

Ellah nodded. "I'll do my best, Magister."

Egey Bashi rose too. "Good luck. As for myself, I feel this may be a good time to pay a visit to the palace library. Nothing like the late hours of the night to search around for hidden volumes and scrolls, is it?"

Ellah straightened out her dress as she stepped to the door, hearing the echo of the Magister's steps down the hallway. She knew visiting the library was a good idea, yet his departure left her alone in the company of the Majat, with Mai being the only person she felt even remotely familiar with. She hurried to the door, but Seldon's words stopped her.

"You really think you can calm him down?"

She turned and looked at him. "Why do you ask?"

"Because I noticed the way you look at him. You like him, don't you?"

Ellah heaved a long breath. "Is everything always so… so perverted in your world, Aghat Seldon?"

"Perverted?" He seemed genuinely surprised.

"Yes," Ellah said. "It seems that your opinion of people is dictated entirely by what you believe you know about the urges of their bodies. I hate to break it to you, especially given the difference in our ages, but people are really far more complicated than this."

She didn't wait for him to respond as she left the room, but she could feel the silence behind her, palpable like a thick pile of sand.

When she knocked on Mai's door she didn't hear

any answer. After a long pause she dared to push it tentatively. The door swung inward, letting her inside.

Mai was sitting on the low bed in the corner, staring into space. Her heart quivered as she saw his sagging shoulders, the way his face looked pale and drawn, exhausted. She tried to tread lightly as she crossed the room and sat on the bed by his side.

"I think you may be right," she said.

He lifted his head, looking at her as if she had spoken a foreign language. "*Right*?"

"Yes. I know that Kara is hating every minute of her stay in the Queen's chambers. And knowing that, it does seem strange that she has been gone so long."

His lips twitched. "How could you possibly know that?"

She frowned. "You are not doubting her loyalty to you, are you? Not over some men who think that oiling their skin and showing off their chest muscles makes them look irresistible?"

He shrugged and turned away.

Ellah felt an urge to grab him by the shoulders and shake him, but with everything she knew about his skill and his temper she really didn't think it was a good idea.

"Kara is uncomfortable around men," she said. "She told me herself once. She hides it well, but surely, you of all people should know this about her. Don't you?"

He hesitated, his eyes for the first time in this conversation acquiring just a touch of reason.

"I know that she really resents the way all the consorts here have been eyeing her since we arrived," Ellah went on. "So, while she may indeed be staying in the Queen's chambers by choice right now, I think with how long it has been, with everything both you and I know about her, it wouldn't hurt to check, would it?"

"Check?"

Ellah felt a pang of pity when she saw the way he looked up at her, hesitant and hopeful like a child.

"You do still remember that I can detect whether people are telling the truth, do you?" she asked.

Mai raised his eyebrows. "Is this a trick question?"

"No. It's just that with the way you looked at me right now, I wasn't sure your mind is truly in this conversation."

He leaned back. "Point taken. And yes, I do remember. So what?"

"Let's go to the Queen's chambers," Ellah said, "and ask about Kara."

"At this hour of the night?"

Ellah sighed. "Look. You made no secret of the way you feel about her, or the kind of relationship you have. If you disturb anyone, they would just assume you are being possessive and jealous, right?"

"Right." His side glance held only partial embarrassment about it.

"You don't mind, do you?" she asked.

He lifted his gaze to her. "No. That's what I am, isn't it?"

She shook her head. "Not exactly. You're being protective. And, for all we know, you might have a very good reason for it."

Mai looked at her thoughtfully. Ellah was relieved to see reason back in his eyes, but she also ached at the vulnerability she saw. Losing Kara would break his heart. If nothing else, this knowledge alone was worth doing everything possible to make sure she was safe.

•••

The royal guards stationed outside their suite sprang to attention as they saw Ellah and Mai emerge from their quarters. Their demeanor suggested that they had originally planned to go for their weapons, but paused at the sight of Mai's determined look.

"Anything we can help you with, Aghat Mai?" one of the guards asked.

Mai lifted his chin. "I wish to go to the Queen's quarters."

The guard frowned. "At this late hour?"

Something in his tone of voice stirred Ellah to attention. It wasn't exactly a lie, especially because the guard's words weren't even a statement, but her truthsense told her this guard knew more than he wanted them to believe, and that Mai's wish to find the Queen's quarters had alarmed him. She held out two fingers to indicate a lie.

Mai's hand unfolded with a dagger that seemed to have instantly sprouted off his wrist. Ellah blinked, watching the razor-sharp blade press against the guard's throat, forcing the man into stillness. She edged away. With the amount of time she spent with the Majat she should be used to these kinds of displays by now, but Mai just had a way to take her by surprise every time.

The other guard glanced at Ellah, but before he could move, two Emeralds stepped up to his sides. He froze, his darting eyes taking in the scene in the obvious realization that he and his comrade were badly outnumbered. He turned to Mai, his face folding into a semblance of a friendly smile.

"Are you worried about your woman?"

Mai's eyes flared. "Don't push it."

The guard swallowed nervously. "She is fine, I am

sure. The Queen's consorts are, um, very experienced at entertainment, if you know what I mean." He winked. "Why don't you go back to your quarters and wait until morning?"

Mai's eyes flicked to Ellah's hand, still holding out two fingers. She saw a brief acknowledgement in his gaze as he reached forward in a gesture that would have seemed lazy and drawn if it wasn't so fast. His fingers briefly connected with the guard's neck. Ellah watched, wide-eyed, as the large man folded down to the floor, slowly and gently, as if curling up to sleep. She glanced at Mai, still holding the other guard at blade point without as much as a glance at his fallen opponent.

"Now," Mai said. "Let me repeat my original request. I wish to go to the Queen's quarters."

The guard led them through a network of winding passages, some broad and well lit, some narrow and dark. It felt fortunate that at this hour of the night the palace stood empty. Ellah had no doubt that Mai, and his two Emerald guards that kept up their determined stride behind him, were easily up to the challenge of handling anyone in their way, but she was glad that for the moment it didn't seem necessary. As she focused on keeping up, she briefly wondered if the royal guard was intentionally trying to lead them in circles, but the colors in her mind told her the man was at his wits' end with fear, too scared to entertain any possibility of a deliberate plotting. She felt relieved. Mai seemed far enough on edge to break the guard's neck at the merest of provocations. While she knew that Mai normally didn't kill unless he really had to, she didn't want to test his resolve right now.

When they finally arrived at an ornate set of double doors, Ellah felt winded. The Majat didn't show any signs of tiredness, but the guard Mai was still holding at a blade point was panting too, from fear or exhaustion, she couldn't tell. Either way, she didn't envy his place right now.

After a lengthy knocking, a sleepy-looking young man swung the door open. Seeing Mai, he moved to slam it shut, but Mai stepped into the door frame with the speed that made Ellah blink. His free hand flicked to the neck of the guard he was holding in a brief gesture that sent the man tumbling backward, collapsing like a large sack. The Queen's consort watched the scene with widening eyes.

"Where's Kara?" Mai asked.

The man's face lost some of its distracted expression as he looked up at Mai again, and turned into a sneer. Ellah braced herself, preparing for the worst.

"She's sleeping," the young man said.

To her surprise, Ellah detected no lie in this statement. She saw Mai's eyes briefly flick to the one finger she was holding out.

Mai receded a bit, sheathing his knife. "Is she all right?"

The man's grin widened. "She's fine. Just exhausted, after our men showed her a really good time. I'd say you shouldn't be expecting her back any time soon."

A complex set of colors flickered up in Ellah's mind. The man wasn't exactly lying, but his words certainly carried a double meaning. Worse, she detected pride in his voice at his own skill of skirting the truth.

She held two fingers up, to make sure Mai could see them well, but she didn't need to bother. Mai's face froze, the dagger instantly back in his hand as he lay the blade across the consort's neck, pressing him against the door frame. He heaved a long breath, leaving Ellah to wonder how close he actually came to slitting the man's throat.

"I want to see her," Mai said, his voice terrifyingly quiet. "Now."

The consort's eyes darted around, trying and failing to find any possibility of escape.

Mai held his dagger in place as he kicked the door open, revealing a large room dominated by a pond at the far end. Ellah edged inside after him, glancing around. The room *did* look as if it recently housed a very large orgy, with overturned divans and pillows scattered among the serving trays and half-emptied goblets. She frowned. Was it truly an orgy that caused such ruckus? Or was it a fight?

"Where is she?" Mai asked.

The man's voice came out broken, so different from the way he sounded just recently. "Not here."

Mai pressed his blade tighter against the man's skin, drawing blood. "I'm only going to ask you one last time."

The man gasped. "I... I don't know where she is. The Queen and Prince Jamal, they... they took her somewhere."

Mai turned around to look at Ellah, holding out one finger. He glanced past her to his Emerald guards. Following his silent signal the men darted into the doorway leading from the large room presumably to the sleeping quarters.

"The consorts are all sleeping," Mai's captive said. "Your men are going to wake them up."

"Bloody shame."

The consort kept very still against Mai's pressing blade.

Voices and screams carried in from the inner chamber, followed by half-naked men stumbling in through the doorway. Ellah counted more than two dozen, all of them tanned, muscular, and young. Some wore no more than a loin cloth. She hastily looked away.

"No sign of her, Aghat Mai," one of the Emeralds said.

Mai's captive raised his head. "I told you. She's not here. The Queen ordered us all to stay quiet when they left with Kara."

"Where did they take her?" Mai demanded.

The consort shivered. "Not sure. The Queen spoke about the secret dungeon..." He swallowed, words pouring out of him in a nervous clutter. "Lady Kara fought like a lion. Even half-drugged, Prince Jamal had to use all the help of his men to apprehend her." The phrase ended in a yelp as Mai pressed his blade tighter against the man's throat.

*Prince Jamal.* The reverence with which the consort mentioned his name didn't escape Ellah. Apparently they all held his fighting skill in high regard, the fact she assumed Mai was now keeping in mind.

"What do they want with her?" Mai kept his eyes on Ellah when he asked the question. The consort may have guessed the game, because he looked at Ellah too, with a plea in his eyes.

"I... I don't really know. They spoke of Aljahara, I heard them."

*Aljahara.* That word again, the one the crowd had

chanted as it followed them to the palace. Ellah kept one finger out, for Mai to see.

"What does it mean?" Mai asked.

The consort raised his eyebrows. "Don't you know any of our history?"

Mai's eyes flared. "Do I look like a bloody scholar?"

The consort whimpered as he pressed tighter against the wall. "It's a legend. Of a rightful queen. Someone who would have ruled if Queen Jameera hadn't died in childbirth nineteen years ago."

"A legend." Mai's face contorted again and Ellah saw his hand holding the dagger clench briefly, as if he was finding trouble controlling it. She took a step back, praising her stars that she wasn't the one he was holding at a dagger point right now.

"Can you please let me go?" the consort asked. "I really don't know anything else."

"You will take us to the dungeon."

"I... I don't know the way ... Only the Queen and her few trusted advisors know where it is."

Mai's gaze slid over Ellah, holding out one finger, onward to one of his Emerald Guards. He flicked a quick hand sign. The man picked up one of the groveling consorts, holding him at knife point as he dragged him through the doorway. Ellah heard their muffled arguing as they sped away.

Mai exchanged a few words with the other Emerald in a strange language – the Majat dialect, Ellah assumed. She watched the Emerald grab another consort off the floor and rush outside.

"Now." Mai turned to the rest of the men. "Go back to sleep. If anyone here runs off to raise an alarm, we'll skin him alive and hang him by his toes in the palace gateway. I trust, with this knowledge, you can all enjoy a good rest until morning." He turned to his captive. "Lead the way. We're going back to our quarters."

The consort stumbled forward. Mai signaled for Ellah to follow. Only now did she realize why each Emerald captured a consort. They all needed guides to navigate the meshwork of palace passages.

Her stomach clenched with worry. She had no idea why the Queen had turned on Kara after acting so friendly in the throne room, but she hoped Mai would be able to rescue her before it was too late.

# 32

# THE SECRET DUNGEON

As they approached their quarters, Ellah heard a strange sound coming from inside. She could have sworn it sounded like a woman's scream, muffled by the distance and the thickness of the doors in between. She glanced at Mai, reassured by his lack of reaction. She must have imagined it. No way Mai would have remained so calm at the mere possibility of it.

By the time they reached the doors, she thoroughly convinced herself it was all in her head. Just then another, louder scream cut through the stillness. This time there was no mistake. Worse, the sound was definitely coming from the inside of the Majat quarters. Ellah stiffened, glancing from Mai to the calm face of the Emerald guard standing by the door.

Mai still seemed unperturbed as he dragged his captive consort inside, pressing the dagger to his neck tighter as the man tried to twist his head in search of the source of the screaming. Ellah followed them, ignoring the sudden weakness in her knees, trying to convince herself that whatever waited for them inside couldn't possibly be that bad. These thoughts disappeared instantly as she stepped into the common room's doorway.

A dozen scantily clad women huddled on the floor at the center of the room. Armed Majat formed a ring around them. It took Ellah a moment to put the two together, realizing that the Majat were mostly the ones who had been picked out from the throne room to entertain the court ladies, and the women were the ladies themselves, the noblewomen and officials of Shayil Yara. They all looked flustered and very underdressed, as if dragged out of their beds and rushed away without a chance to even grab a suitable garment to cover themselves.

Ellah's eyes trailed to Lance. The Diamond's own clothes looked less neat than usual, as if donned in a hurry. The sight of the beautiful dark-skinned blonde shriveling at his feet sent her heart racing. *Princess Nelimah. Dear Shal Addim.* Ellah edged away, hoping that in the turmoil her shock wouldn't be too noticeable.

Mai didn't break his stride as he threw his captive consort into the group of women. Some of them screamed and leaned away, others held out their hands to steady the young man. Mai didn't even glance at them as he swept past, headed toward Lance.

Belatedly, Ellah thought back to how Mai had sent away his Emerald guards from the Queen's quarters, giving them orders in the Majat dialect. Her thoughts unraveled slowly, like poorly oiled gears, as she worked out the entire gambit, a devious plan that must have been obvious to Mai and his men right from the start. She had been so naïve thinking that the Majat went with the noble ladies solely for entertainment. The fact that this also enabled them to take hostages any time they pleased hadn't even crossed her mind. And now, she was having serious trouble coming to terms with the idea.

She wondered how the Majat were able to bring their ladies here so quickly, ahead of her and Mai. She guessed they all had to run with all their might to get here on time.

Mai and Lance exchanged a few brisk phrases, then turned to Princess Nelimah, who shrank away, sobbing and pulling the light fabric of her night shift tightly around herself. A chill ran down Ellah's spine. With the stakes they were facing, she was certain Mai was not going to show any mercy if the Princess didn't cooperate.

She was debating with herself whether she should speak up and risk drawing Mai's wrath onto herself, when a light rustle behind her announced the arrival of Egey Bashi. The Keeper stopped beside her, his jaw falling open at the sight. Mai spun around, his face relaxing as he recognized the newcomer.

"I found out something important, Aghat Mai," Egey Bashi said. His voice was composed, but the way he kept his eyes on the women told Ellah how shocked he was. Still, she knew that even Egey Bashi wouldn't be able to convince the Majat to change their tactics. They were witnessing Mai's ruthless side, the one he normally hid so well under his dazzling façade.

Mai's eyes briefly flickered to the scene. "More important than this, Magister?"

"No, but potentially relevant to this situation. I think I know why they took Kara. It has to do with Aljahara, the word we heard on the streets this morning."

Mai stiffened, his hand pointing to the consort he had dragged in earlier, now huddled between two women in the center of the room. "Our new friend, Lamar, just told me of this legend."

Egey Bashi shook his head. "Not a legend, Aghat."

Mai raised his eyebrows.

"Well, it *is* a legend, according to the official chronicles," Egey Bashi went on hurriedly. "Fortunately, my experience with libraries taught me where to look for unofficial ones."

Mai shifted his grip on the dagger. "Forgive me, Magister, but unless this is important, I have other things I need to do at the moment."

"It *is* important, Aghat Mai. Please listen."

Mai lowered his dagger. "Very well. But make it quick. We don't have much time."

The Keeper stepped forward. "When Queen Jameera, Rajmella's older sister, died nineteen years ago, official chronicles recorded it as death in childbirth as she brought Prince Jamal into this world."

Lamar leaned forward earnestly. "It was. My father was one of Queen Jameera's personal guards. He felt shattered when it happened. She was the greatest Queen – and still so young when she died."

Egey Bashi nodded. "True, this was a tragedy, even if perhaps a preventable one. Officially, Queen Jameera's life did indeed end with the birth of her son. Unofficially, however, I was able to learn not only that her death was far from accidental, but that she also bore a daughter on that day. The Queen lived long enough to name her. Aljahara. If this daughter still lived, she would have been the rightful heir to the throne."

Lamar shook his head, flinching and receding under Mai's gaze. "It's a legend, no more. There *was* no Aljahara."

Egey Bashi turned back to Mai. "Well, my source says otherwise. The Queen's death was part of a coup, aimed to destroy the entire royal line. Fortunately, the plot was discovered in time to save the rest of the royal family. The perpetrators were executed, and Rajmella, the Queen's next of kin, was placed on the throne at the age of eleven. However, before all that, the conspirators were able to smuggle a newborn girl out of the palace. According to the chronicle, this girl was sent to the Majat Guild, and her past has been erased from Shayil Yara's official documents, leaving only the legend of Aljahara."

A silence filled the room as everyone, Majat and Shayil Yaran alike, stared at the Magister wide-eyed. Then Mai spoke.

"The Majat Guild?"

"Yes."

"Nineteen years ago?"

"To the day."

"Impossible."

Egey Bashi shook his head. "It all fits, especially given her remarkable likeness to the portrait we saw at the inn this morning. None of us took it seriously enough, but the crowds in the streets must have seen it too. Not to mention members of the royal family, who must have been stricken by the resemblance as soon as she entered the throne room."

Mai's face froze into a mask as he stared at the Magister. Ellah gaped, her mind having serious trouble keeping up with the information. *Kara? The lost heir to the Shayil Yaran throne?*

*Is this what the turmoil is all about?*

Mai spun around and grabbed Nelimah by the arm,

dragging her to his feet. The Princess screamed, but Mai's short glance forced her into silence.

"Lead us to the Queen's secret dungeon," Mai said. "Now."

Nelimah sobbed and shook her head, but the sight of a dagger pointing her way pulled her to attention. She stumbled as Mai dragged her out, signaling Ellah, Egey Bashi, and about half of his men to follow.

The Princess proved to be a poor runner. Her feet, clad into ornate but highly impractical slippers, skidded and slipped on the marble floors as she led them down the endless hallways to an older part of the castle. Mai was getting visibly frustrated as he jerked her up every time. Ellah felt tempted to interfere, but thought better of it. With the stakes they were facing, she was certain Mai was farther over the edge than she had ever seen him before.

Eventually, Mai dropped Nelimah's arm and barked a short order to Lance, who stepped forward and picked the Princess up. Ellah was surprised at the way the Princess curled into the Diamond's arms contentedly, as if he was her savior, not her abductor who had betrayed her trust when she had least expected it.

Nelimah pointed the way into a long dark hallway, down a narrow staircase, through a vaulted torchlit passage that smothered all sounds as they rushed along it. The massive door at the end of it stood closed. Mai halted in front, bending down to examine the lock, then gestured for Lance to set Nelimah down to the floor.

The Princess edged away, whimpering.

"Ask them to open the door and let you in," Mai said quietly. "Act casual."

Her lips trembled. She glanced at Lance. The Diamond quickly inclined his head, his hand on her shoulder urging her closer to the door.

Ellah watched the scene in disbelief. The way Nelimah's cheeks lit up with color as she pressed into his touching palm seemed so inappropriate for the situation. Ellah didn't want to venture her thoughts any further into what might have gone between the two of them to ensure the Princess's cooperation, but the results were obvious, even if somewhat disturbing.

Guided by Lance's encouraging smile, Nelimah used the massive iron ring as a knocker, then leaned closer, listening to the sounds inside. The Majat lined the walls on both sides of the door, ready to rush into the room as soon as the door opened.

Nelimah frowned as no response came. She glanced around helplessly, then blushed again as she looked at Lance, standing visibly taller under the Diamond's expectant gaze.

"Rajmella!" Nelimah called out. "It's me, Nelimah! Open the door, please!"

Seconds passed, the Majat standing still and tense, like tightly strung weapons. Ellah watched Mai's face set into a mask that made him look deceptively calm. Her stomach clenched at the thought of what he would do if they found that any harm had come to Kara. She had never seen this ruthless side of him laid out so openly in plain view. All she could do was pray that things on the other side of the door would not turn out too ugly to watch.

After a long moment, she heard the jingling of keys and the click of the turning lock. Her heart raced. She clasped her hand over her mouth not to let out a sound as the door swung open to reveal Valmir, the Queen's First Consort.

Ellah barely had a chance to blink as the Diamond nearest to the door clasped an arm around him, pressing a dagger to his neck. The other Majat rushed past them into the room. At Mai's signal, one of the Emeralds grabbed Nelimah, also holding her at blade point.

Ellah peered into the chamber.

At first glance, the vaulted space reminded her of an alchemist's lab, with rows of glass flasks and retorts lining the benches along the walls. Beyond them, metal racks held an array of hooks, tweezers, and blades, some of them very unpleasant-looking. Ellah's eyes wandered to the large table in the center and the body laid on it. *Kara.* Her stomach turned, nausea rising to her throat.

Torches set around the table poured their reddish light over her, as if illuminating a stage. Kara lay on her stomach, her head twisted to the side facing away from the door, her shape so still that she didn't seem animate at all. Ellah refused to follow the thought any further. Her eyes glossed over the tightly fastened shackles, securing not only Kara's wrists and ankles, but also the top of her arms and legs, the ripped clothes, the hair, pulled back at the nape of her neck as if someone had been preparing to cut off her head. *Dear Shal Addim.*

Prince Jamal stood over Kara, holding a scimitar to the base of her neck. Queen Rajmella, behind him, pressed against the wall next to Hamala the Grand Vizier and several consorts. Ellah thought she recognized Dahim, one of the two men who led Kara away earlier tonight, but she wasn't sure.

Jamal's stance screamed caution, his grace and ease

with the blade telling of his weapon skill. The Majat froze, clearly aware of the menace.

Jamal smirked, his dark purple eyes fixed on Mai. "Call off your men. Or, she dies."

*Dies.* Against reason, Ellah felt a surge of relief. The threat meant that Kara was definitely alive. She saw a tense cord in Mai's neck relax, likely reflecting the same thought.

Princess Nelimah whimpered loudly. The Queen took a step toward her, but the Emerald holding the Princess pressed in his dagger, halting her in place. The Princess screamed as the dagger pierced the skin, drawing blood, and Ellah saw Rajmella blanch and briefly close her eyes. Illogically, this brief gesture brought reassurance. The Queen was not the monster Ellah imagined her to be when she first saw the scene. Perhaps, if everyone just calmed down a bit, a solution could be found.

"Jamal," Mai said. "If you bloody touch her, I'll cut you to pieces. Slowly. Now, step away and hand me the key to those shackles."

Jamal's eyes briefly darted to the Queen.

"I said, now." Mai signaled with his hand, and the Emerald holding the Princess slid the dagger tip deeper into her skin, evoking a new gush of blood and another piercing cry. "If you hesitate again, she loses an ear. We'll get creative from there."

Nelimah wailed, tears streaming down her beautiful face.

"For Shal Addim's sake, Jamal!" Rajmella pleaded. "Stand down, before they harm Nelimah!"

Jamal hesitated, then stepped away and lowered his scimitar.

Mai moved in the same instant, his hand fanning out with throwing daggers. He sent them flying all at once, pinning Jamal to the wall at multiple points.

Ellah clasped her hand to her mouth just as the screams erupted around the room. Rajmella pressed to the wall, her breath coming out in shallow gasps. Nelimah dissolved into a fit of sobs, sagging in her captor's hands. It took Ellah a moment to realize that the daggers pierced only the clothes, holding Jamal in place without harming him. Well, that wasn't entirely true. A streak of blood oozed from the Prince's shoulder where one of the daggers must have grazed the skin. She was certain the damage, and its extent, were intentional on Mai's side, calculated precisely to drive the message home without causing any actual harm.

She drew in a much-needed breath.

"Listen carefully, Jamal," Mai said. "If you as much as move, the next set of daggers goes in an inch inward. I promise, it will hurt." He turned to the Queen. "The key to the shackles. Now."

Rajmella's hands shook as she pulled a thin chain off her neck. Mai ripped it out of her hand before she could move any further and slid to the table, clicking numerous locks.

Ellah's heart quivered when she saw Kara's body hang limply as he flipped her over. *Dear Shal Addim. Please don't let her be dead. Please.* She forced Jamal's words into memory as she watched Kara's head roll sideways, revealing her motionless face. *She is alive. Please, she must be!*

Egey Bashi pushed past Ellah toward the table. As he fumbled with his pouches and bustled around Kara, Ellah kept her eyes on Mai, the sight of his frozen look bringing tears to her eyes.

Finally, Egey Bashi raised his head, fixing Jamal with a heavy stare. "What did you do to her?"

Jamal swallowed, glancing at Mai with a mix of fear and challenge, as if daring the Majat to deny him permission to speak. He stood very still, the daggers protruding from the wall all around him. Now that she had a chance to calm down, Ellah counted six, all spaced evenly, one right at the groin. She winced.

"Sleeping powder," Jamal said.

Egey Bashi's shoulders sagged slightly, the first indication that the situation might not be as bad as it looked. "How much?"

Jamal glanced at the Queen this time, then to Hamala, who responded with a shrug. "I don't know. She just kept fighting us. I didn't know she was so strong."

Mai's face contorted into a grimace, but Egey Bashi placed a hand on his arm, forcing him to calm down. The fact that it worked made Ellah shiver, a clear indication of Mai's turmoiled feelings. At a normal time anyone touching Mai in this state of mind was liable to lose a hand.

"Do you have the antidote?" Egey Bashi demanded.

"The antidote?" Jamal looked lost.

"Devil's root."

Hamala caught the Queen's prompting gaze and rushed to a table at the far side of the room. She searched among the retorts and flasks, finally producing a tightly corked one, filled with a sticky black liquid.

Egey Bashi frowned as he popped the cork and measured out a few drops, mixing them with some other potions in his numerous pouches. He rolled Kara's head to face up and forced a few droplets between her lips.

The moments ticked, the silence descending onto the room like a heavy blanket. Ellah couldn't bear to look at Kara at all. She watched Mai instead, the way the tense cord knotted in his neck again, as if he was bracing for action. She knew if the cure didn't work, the Majat would likely drown this palace in blood, but even that didn't seem as important right now. *Please. Just let her wake up, please.*

Egey Bashi's frown deepened. He patted Kara's cheeks gently, then forced another drop of his medicine between her lips. Mai looked on, his empty eyes making him nearly unrecognizable.

Just then, Kara's eyes snapped open. She glanced at Egey Bashi, then rolled over, doubling up in an uncontrollable fit of choking.

Egey Bashi pulled her upright, holding her against his shoulder, patting her back in a gesture that reminded Ellah of young mothers caring for their newborns – except that she could also see the force the Keeper was applying, as if trying to knock all the air out of Kara's lungs. Mai stood just short of touching them, watching the scene wide eyed.

After a moment, Egey Bashi pulled Kara away from him, holding her at arm's length. She gasped a few times, finally forcing her breath under control. Egey Bashi nodded to Mai, who continued standing in front of her with a frozen look, as if too exhausted to move.

Kara heaved a slow, tentative breath, as if she wasn't sure it would actually work. Her eyes slowly acquired focus as they darted to Jamal, still pinned to the wall by the daggers, then to Mai, as if trying to work out a complicated puzzle. Relief surfaced through her daze as Mai stepped toward her. He pulled her into his arms and she relaxed against him, hiding her face on his chest.

He shivered as he held her gently, and for a brief moment it looked to Ellah as if he was about to collapse. Then, a barely perceptible movement rippled through his body, his composure clicking back into place. He stood taller than before as he ran his eyes around the room, pausing in turn on each of their captives. Ellah couldn't read his expression at all.

She wanted to feel relieved, but she knew the worst was probably not over yet. Even though Kara's kidnapping ended well, there was no telling what Mai was going to do when pushed this far.

"Round them all up," Mai ordered, nodding toward the Olivians. "Bring them to our quarters."

He didn't wait to see his men follow his orders as he picked up Kara and carried her out of the cell.

## 33

# THE QUEEN OF SHAYIL YARA

Kara must have spent at least an hour in the cooling bath, but no matter how hard she scrubbed, she just couldn't stop feeling dirty. The memory of all the hands holding her down, of all the sweaty, muscular men that ended up piling on top to subdue her, wouldn't leave her mind. They could have done anything to her when she was unconscious. No matter how many times she told herself that this was over, that whatever they did to her wasn't under her control, she was having trouble coming to terms with the idea.

She started when she saw Mai standing in the doorway, so still that he appeared inanimate. The fact that she hadn't noticed him coming in was just another indication of how flustered she was. Or was it the damage she had suffered during her ordeal?

"How long have you been standing there?" she asked.

He shrugged as he approached her. "Long enough to tell that if you continue scrubbing like this, you're bound to remove skin. Besides, the water must be cold by now." He picked up a towel and held it out for her.

She sighed and climbed out of the bath, stepping into it.

"Don't look at me like this," she said.

"Like what?"

She swallowed. *Like I'm a desirable woman.* She knew she was never going to say this to him. She loved it when he looked at her this way. Whatever happened to her when she was unconscious, she shouldn't let it affect her life.

He frowned as he peered into her face. "What's troubling you so much?"

Her gaze wavered. "I... I don't know. They overpowered me. All of these men in the room jumped me at once. With the way they normally act toward women, I... They made me feel so dirty. When I passed out, they could have..." Her voice trailed into silence. She knew it was stupid to think this way. If the Queen took the trouble to bring her to a dungeon and shackle her, it was highly unlikely that she would have also allowed her consorts to take the time to rape her. But even if they did rape her, it shouldn't really matter. With her combat training, she should know better than to dwell on such insignificant things.

Mai's eyes stirred with deep emotion as he continued to look at her. She knew that he understood her, and that he was never going to press the subject, and she was so grateful for it.

"I believe," he said, "that during the past hour we were able to gather all the details on what exactly has been done to you. I hope I can put your mind at ease at least in this regard. They've done nothing improper – not in that sense."

She nodded gratefully. That made her feel a whole

lot better. Yet, the way Mai continued to look at her, kept troubling her. She suddenly realized that what bothered her about this look had nothing to do with the attraction she knew he felt for her. He was looking at her as if she was a stranger, as if he was seeing her for the very first time.

"Was there anything else you found out?" she asked.

Mai hesitated. "Magister Egey Bashi would like to see you."

She frowned. It was so unlike Mai to skirt a direct question. Her worry was instantly back, a hollow feeling in the pit of her stomach that made her feel even more unsettled than before. She glanced at her body, wrapped in a bath sheet. "Can I get dressed first?"

Mai handed her a cloak. "It can't wait much longer. Cover up while I call him in."

She tied the bath sheet securely around herself and draped the cloak over it until it covered her from head to toe. She supposed she did take far too long washing. And now she was about to learn something she was sure she didn't want to know. Judging by Mai's expression, her ordeal was far from over. Her heart raced as she watched Egey Bashi enter the room.

He stopped in front of her, and she imagined his shoulders briefly sag in relief at the evidence that she was all right. His next gesture surprised her, though. Instead of addressing her as she expected, he stepped around her and reached forward to touch her neck. She shied away and spun around to face him before she could think, his blank stare telling her she probably moved faster than he expected.

"What are you doing, Magister?" she demanded.

Egey Bashi exchanged a brief glance with Mai. "I

need to look at the back of your neck. Briefly. I won't hurt you."

The back of her neck. She was beginning to remember now that this part of her body seemed to draw a lot of attention during her recent ordeal, starting with the man massaging her shoulders in the Queen's quarters, and ending with Hamala's attempt to put some liquid on it, the one that ended with shackling her to the table and giving her the last dose of the sleeping powder.

She forced the memory away, holding still as she felt the Magister's calloused fingers part her hair at the back, followed by a long pause as both men apparently examined whatever they saw.

"I always thought it was a birth mark," Mai said.

She heard Egey Bashi's sigh. "It is, in a way, Aghat. They tattoo it in right after birth, to identify members of the royal family."

*Royal family?* Kara spun around. "Who the hell are you talking about, Magister?"

Egey Bashi's face darkened. "You, I'm afraid."

"You must be joking."

"On some level, I wish I was, Aghat. Even though I cannot help feeling that this turn of events would take us a long way in achieving our goal here."

"What in the world do you mean?"

"If you assume the Shayil Yaran throne, there will be no question anymore about gaining the Queen's unconditional support in our war."

"*Assume the Shayil Yaran throne?*"

"Yes."

She stared at him in disbelief. "This is, by far, the most insane thing I've ever heard, Magister. One would think it wasn't me, but you who had been recently knocked out. Unless of course I am delirious and you didn't say anything at all just now." She wished it was the case as she watched Egey Bashi exchange another glance with Mai. The sight of their forlorn expressions made her feel nauseated. She swallowed forcibly, ignoring the lightheaded feeling, as if she was about to faint. *I'm still recovering. And, he couldn't possibly have meant what he just said. There's no way.* She refused to give in to this nonsense.

"I'm afraid you heard me right, Aghat," Egey Bashi said quietly.

Her lips twitched. "Let me make sure I understand this correctly, Magister. You found some bloody spot at the back of my neck and now you are suggesting that I… I…" She paused. She simply couldn't make herself pronounce it out loud.

Egey Bashi shook his head. "Not just 'some bloody spot', Aghat. It has a perfect crescent shape. You may have noticed one like this on the back of Queen Rajmella's neck too, except that she normally highlights it with a golden dye."

Kara paused. She did notice a very small golden crescent in the nape of the Queen's neck, visible because of the way Rajmella wore her hair piled up on the top of her head. It looked unusual, but she took it for some form of a decoration.

She glanced at Mai. "Is this true?"

"Yes."

She trembled, clenching her teeth to suppress a sudden surge of weakness. "Very well, Magister. However preposterous it sounds, the fact that I may belong to the Shayil Yara's royal family doesn't mean I can just waltz in and assume the throne."

The Keeper frowned. "I'm afraid it does. You are not just any family member. You are Aljahara, the lost heir. Your claim to the throne supersedes that of Rajmella."

Kara's eyes widened as she met the Keeper's gaze, the truth of what he was saying finally settling in. *Aljahara, the lost heir. Bloody hell.*

She knew she should be thinking about their campaign, about destroying the Kaddim. She should be glad that this turn of events was giving her an opportunity to be in charge and ensure that the Majat got the support they needed within Shayil Yara's borders. Instead, only one thought dominated her head. If she was truly Shayil Yaran royalty, there was no way she and Mai could ever be together. He couldn't possibly have anything to do with a woman whose allegiance and bloodlines threatened the highly protected political neutrality of the Majat Guild.

Mai's expression told her he was thinking exactly the same thing.

She met his gaze. "What do you want me to do?"

He shrugged. "By now, they all know who you are. I see no choice but to take advantage of this situation and secure Shayil Yaran forces to our side."

She took a deep breath, then nodded.

"I will get Queen Rajmella here," Egey Bashi said. "I think we all need to have a nice, quiet talk."

The Queen carried her head high, but Kara could tell by the tense set of her shoulders that her defiance was only skin deep. When she stopped in front of Kara, her narrowed eyes held so much fear that Kara almost felt sorry for her. She had to remind herself that this was the woman who ordered her abduction, even if she was also the first family member she had ever encountered.

"Rajmella," she said. "What the hell were you thinking, when you ordered your men to detain me?"

Rajmella lifted her chin. "What the hell was I supposed to think, when you entered my palace at the head of the crowds chanting your name, with a small Majat army at your back? Did you actually believe I was going to fall for your crazy stories about some phantom enemy hiding at the north of my lands?"

Kara's eyes widened. "Did you believe I came to usurp your throne?"

"What else was I supposed to believe? The tales you told me to gain your way in? And yes, 'usurp' was the word on my mind, at least until Hamala had a chance to examine your tattoo and see that it's genuine. That's when your Majat friends showed up."

Kara continued to stare, feeling as if she was trapped in a very bad dream.

"So, what was your plan, once you found out?"

"We weren't sure. Killing a usurper is one thing. Killing my own niece and the rightful heir to the throne..." Rajmella spread her hands in a wordless gesture.

Kara's skin prickled. *The rightful heir to the throne.* It was just starting to sink in, like poison, seeping in slowly and spreading all the way through her suddenly heavy limbs.

"I choose to believe you were planning to spare my life," she said. "For now. I hope for your sake you never lead me to think otherwise."

Rajmella peered into her face. "You look surprised. And shocked."

"I am, actually."

"Why?"

Kara shrugged. "I had no bloody idea about any of this. Not until right now. I was telling you the truth from the start. The enemy I spoke of is very real, and is the only reason for our visit here. I couldn't even tell what the crowds were chanting, or why. I came here only as a negotiator for the Majat Guildmaster."

Rajmella laughed. "Yes, that was one of the most ridiculous things you said. Everyone knows the Majat Guildmaster is an old man. If you wanted one of your companions to pose as one, you should have chosen the older man that came with you. He is the only one who looks the part, even if only remotely."

*Seldon.* Kara looked at her serenely. "Come now, Rajmella. You cannot possibly be this stupid."

The Queen lifted her head sharply, as if she had been slapped. Kara knew she probably wasn't used to anyone addressing her this way, but right now she didn't give a damn.

"Aghat Mai *is* the Guildmaster," she said. "If you took this fact, and everything else we said to you, at face value, we wouldn't be trapped in this situation right now. You would still have your throne."

Rajmellashook her head. "If I took anything at face value, my rule as a Queen would be extremely short-lived."

"Shorter than now?"

Rajmella spread her hands again. "You are the rightful heir. Now that you are here, the game has changed. No matter what you originally intended, or what I believed at the start, you cannot change your birthright."

*My birthright.* Up until now, Kara never realized

she had one. And now that she discovered it, she was finding it too hard to deal with the burden that came with it.

Rajmella looked at Mai thoughtfully. "The real Guildmaster, eh?"

"Yes," Kara said. "Not that it really matters right now."

Rajmella continued to stare, a slow appraisal in her gaze. "He does have the commanding presence, I must admit. And his men do seem to listen to him unconditionally, from what I had a chance to see. Was sending them to entertain my women part of your plan all along?"

Kara sighed. "I thought it was all your idea. I tried to refuse, remember?"

Rajmella's gaze wavered. "Yes, that was my mistake, I admit."

"A mistake?"

Rajmella glanced away briefly. "I thought these men were your attack force, not that I believed even for a moment that they were really top Majat Gems. No one could possibly afford to hire this many. But since you seemed to place such faith in them, it seemed like a good plan not only to scatter them, but also to tame them, bond them to our women. Men tend to think differently right after they've enjoyed good sex. I hoped it would sway their loyalties, at least somewhat."

Kara frowned in disbelief. "You didn't consider the opposite possibility, that you were placing a top-ranked assassin next to each of the important ladies at your court?"

"I didn't imagine the men could possibly turn on the women they'd just been intimate with. Not so easily."

"No one said it was easy," Mai said.

Rajmella looked at him with curiosity. "Yet, you had no doubt they would, did you? Thinking back to the way they talked to you before accepting the ladies' invitations, you encouraged them, didn't you?"

He shrugged. "I told them they could, if they wanted to. And yes, I had no doubt they would follow orders."

"I guess I just learned something new about the Majat." Rajmella hesitated. "One thing still puzzles me, though, about all these ladies you are now holding captive out in your common room. They have all been treated brutally – dragged out of their beds, kept at swordpoint, fearing for their lives. My sister Nelimah, so impressionable and delicate that I tend to think twice even when I frown at her, has been deliberately sliced with a dagger and threatened with mutilation, for Shal Addim's sake. Yet the only thing they all seem to be able to talk about right now, Nelimah included, is the sexual prowess of your men. In fact, spending the past hour in their company has been... educational, if I try to put it politely. It's as if they have all been bewitched."

Mai grinned. "I am glad my men left an impression."

Rajmella's expression turned wistful. "If I live through this, I will definitely pay a visit to your Guild one day. I must admit, I had a completely wrong idea about your warriors before."

Kara didn't like the way she eyed Mai, with a mix of longing and lust that reminded her of the mood that dominated her earlier visit to the Queen's chambers. It was a relief to think that at least one privilege of her royal status lay in the fact that no one could ever again try to force their attention on her. Given the local customs, she was likely going to go down in history as the Untouchable Queen.

She met Mai's gaze, seeing the encouragement in his eyes that she knew was meant only for her. This new turn of events had just shattered all hopes for happiness she ever had. But these thoughts had to wait. They still had a deadly enemy to defeat, and it was now up to her to take the next step.

"I believe," she said to Rajmella, "you must surrender your bracelets of station to me."

Rajmella slid them off her arm, leaving behind a fading snake-like imprint. Kara looked at them curiously, two long winding contraptions crafted of solid gold, connected by a chain that draped over the elbow, and another one to fasten them up at the shoulder. Once donned, they lay over her arm heavily, like armor. Fighting with these on would be a chore, even though if push came to shove they would likely be useful as protection against a sword slice.

"I will get dressed now," she said. "And then we will go out to your ladies together and announce the news."

Rajmella looked at her solemnly.

"I must admit," she said. "From what I remember of your mother, you are the spitting image of her – not just the looks, but the small things, like gestures and expressions. You definitely have her regal bearing. Older people remember her well – perhaps this was how the crowds have recognized you so easily. We all still miss her very much. She was a great Queen. I hope you can be one too."

*A great Queen.* Kara glanced at Mai again. At the moment, she didn't feel like a great Queen at all, only like a very exhausted woman who could barely stand up on her feet. But even in her tired stupor, the enormity of what was going on had finally dawned on her. She had found a family, and not just any family, but one of the most ancient and noble ones in the entire land. She was among the people who had known her mother, and felt that she could potentially, one day, achieve the same greatness. She hoped to be able to live up to the responsibility.

# 34
# GOLDEN LIONS

The crowd's roar floated up in waves, booming against the stone walls of the palace at her back. Kara distanced herself from it as she looked over the plaza below. Five hundred soldiers stood in perfect rows, so still that the only movement she could detect was the golden gleam of their lion-shaped shoulder plates and the shifting of their crimson cloaks in the light breeze.

*Aljahara, Aljahara, Aljahara…*

She shifted her gaze to Prince Jamal standing in front of her. He wore the same uniform as his soldiers, but the golden lion over his left shoulder also bore a crown. His face was set into a still mask, his narrowed eyes watching her with apprehension.

*My twin brother.*

In another life, they could have been close. They could have learned to walk and talk together, grown up playing games. It made sense that he, her flesh and blood, shared her physical prowess, prompting his nation to hold him as a great warrior and put him in charge of their elite troops. Like everyone else here, he was now hers to command. But would he ever become her ally?

ANNA KASHINA
367

"Prince Jamal," she said. "I hear you have been doing an admirable job as a commander of the royal Golden Lion battalion."

He briefly inclined his head. "Thank you, my Queen."

The resentment in his voice sent her heart racing. Was he prepared to accept her, or was he an enemy in disguise? Would his attitude force her to do something terrible to her very closest kin? She knew Mai wouldn't hesitate in making the call in this kind of a situation. She longed for his advice, but with the way he was standing, three steps behind, she couldn't even see his face. Worse, even if everyone here told her Jamal was trouble and needed to be removed, she knew, deep in her heart, that she would not consider it until she had exhausted every other option. She wasn't about to lose her brother just after she found him.

"We march in three days," she said. "The Golden Lions will use this time to train with the Majat warriors."

Jamal bowed his head again, the resentment in his face so poorly hidden that even the soldiers on the plaza must be catching it by now, even though they were standing too far to hear any words. His jaw tightened as he spoke. "The Golden Lions don't need this training, Your Majesty."

She raised her eyebrows. "What makes you say so?"

"No foreign warriors have anything they could possibly teach my men."

*My men.* She lifted her chin. "They are my men too."

"Yes, Your Majesty." His gaze became wooden.

She shifted from foot to foot, regarding him thoughtfully. Even without extensive command experience she could see that Jamal was going to be a problem. If Mai was in charge he would have probably removed him on the spot, replacing him with a more compliant battalion leader. Yet, a stubborn side she didn't know she had was driving her on. Could she overcome this challenge in a different way?

"Since we haven't had an opportunity to get to know each other, Prince Jamal," she said, "I'd like to give you permission, for now, to speak freely, so that we can resolve our differences – if indeed we have any."

Jamal's jaw knotted again, but she did catch surprise in his eyes before he forced his gaze into blankness. "To what end, Your Majesty? If you want to relieve me of command, you hardly need my words to give you the excuse."

She smiled. "You are correct. I need no excuse to relieve you of command, or throw you in a dungeon if I please. I am also aware of how you seem to be driving our conversation toward this kind of an outcome. I'd like to avoid it, if we possibly can."

"Why?"

"I see you as a talented commander who inspires trust and devotion in his men. Can't we build on this to achieve a workable relationship?"

Jamal squared his shoulders. "If you leave me in charge, you will be forcing me to lead my men into a war we were not planning to fight."

"Your planning has nothing to do with it, Prince. The enemy we are after is fighting to restore the Old Empire. If the Majat can't stop them, their next step would be to obliterate everyone standing in their way, starting with the closest lands. Shayil Yara. Do you really want to see this happen when we can preempt such an outcome?"

His eyes narrowed. "And I suppose we have only

your word to prove it, Your Majesty."

"Yes."

"Not good enough."

She sighed. "I'm curious, Jamal. If I take your bait just now and throw you in a dungeon, what could you possibly gain from it? Your men will march into this battle anyway."

"Reluctantly."

She glanced at the troops, at the people lining the far end of the plaza chanting her name. She had a good feeling they would follow her willingly if it came to that, even if Jamal's imprisonment would certainly shake things up.

"Are you trying to become a martyr to your men?" she asked. "To prove a point to them by forcing a punishment upon yourself?"

He kept his silence, but his uncertain look told her that her words had hit the mark.

"I will not play this game with you," she said. "Not only because you are my closest family, even if you may not feel this way, but also because I know you are a good man, loyal to your country."

His lips twitched. "What could you possibly know about that?"

"Do you believe I'm wrong about you?"

He receded a bit. "I don't judge my qualities the same way, Your Majesty. I've been a good commander to the Golden Lions, yes. But up until now, our Queen has never doubted my ability to train my men."

She smiled. "I am not doubting it either, Jamal. The Golden Lions have a unique opportunity to train with the Majat's top warriors, whose skill is far superior to anything you've ever seen. Any good commander would beg for a chance like that – not try to push it away when it's offered freely."

The smile playing on Jamal's lips taunted her with a challenge. "Far superior?"

"Yes."

"How do you know, sister?"

*Sister.* Against reason, the word filled her with warmth. She never had any kin, never thought it was even possible for her. And now, despite all the defiance Jamal was showing her, despite the fact that he had recently participated in her abduction, she couldn't help feeling a bond with him. The feeling took her by surprise as she looked into his face, recognizing some of the features she had grown used to seeing during her very rare glances into a mirror – the line of the eyebrows, the high cheekbones, the pale golden hair lying against his neck in a smooth wave. His face looked manly where hers was feminine, but now that her lineage was uncovered, it seemed strange to her that no one had spotted the resemblance as soon as she entered the palace. Or maybe they did?

"Tell you what," she said. "If you can defeat me in a one-on-one fight, we'll do things your way. If I win, you will submit to my command, no questions asked."

He frowned, measuring her with his gaze. She could see his hesitation. He knew she was good, from the way he had trouble overpowering her even with the sleeping powder. But he couldn't possibly know exactly how good she was. Her Majat ranking was no longer an open topic of discussion, not with the way she had been cast out of the Guild and maintained her outsider status in order to be close to Mai.

"Very well," Jamal said.

She met his eyes, her nerves alit with the same excitement she saw in his gaze. If they would have had an opportunity to play together as children, it could have been exactly like this. *A game.* In another life, it could have been the most natural thing – to have a wrestling match with her twin brother so that they could determine who was the best at it.

"Bring us a pair of training swords," she said over her shoulder, not addressing anyone in particular but knowing that there would be several guards there who would know what to do.

"What type, Your Majesty?" a tall guard woman next to her asked.

She held Jamal's gaze. "Scimitars."

He raised his eyebrows, even as the sound of running feet told her that a messenger had been dispatched to fulfill her order. "Scimitars?"

"Isn't this your weapon of choice, brother?"

He crossed his arms over his chest. "You think you can beat me with a scimitar?'

She didn't respond as she took off her royal cloak and handed it to another guard standing behind her. The swords arrived, finer-looking than any weapons she normally used in practice. She tested the balance, then the edge to make sure it was sufficiently blunted, watching him do the same.

"I don't want to hurt you, my Queen," he said.

"If I were you, Prince, I would be worrying about other things right now."

Jamal didn't respond. He looked confident, but Kara could also sense the caution behind it as he raised his sword and moved into position.

Her queen's outfit wasn't ideal for fighting, her

bracelets of station weighting down her left arm, her sandals too thin to maintain proper footing. Yet, as he picked up speed, she forgot all about it, absorbed in the fun of matching his moves, leaving him openings for sneaky attacks she could counter with her own. The plaza around them became a blur, the only focus her opponent's face, so familiar and close now that she was recognizing more and more of their common features. *My brother, my flesh and blood.* During this fight she felt she was learning to understand him like no other.

His blade was flying in perfect patterns Kara recognized from her early training, his reflexes far superior to those of a regular warrior. If he, like Kara, had been sold into the Majat Guild as a child, he would have been her fellow in rank by now. But without that proper training, he was no match for her at all. Even in her awkward outfit, weakened from her recent ordeal, she would have no trouble overpowering him at all.

The chant of the crowd rose to a deafening roar as the Golden Lions joined too, clanging their swords on their shoulder plates. *Aljahara, Aljahara, Aljahara...*

Kara was sure by now that she had gotten the message across. It was time to end the show.

She held Jamal's gaze as she snaked her blade forward around his, hitting it sideways and up, close to the hilt, so that it flew out of his hand in a perfect arc, clearly visible throughout the plaza. It landed straight down, sticking between the floorboards at his feet, wavering from the impact.

Jamal stepped back, looking at her in disbelief. "You're good. Far better than I thought."

She smiled. "So are you. But you and your men can become even better, if properly trained. All you need to do is follow orders, Prince."

"If you say so." He bowed his head. "As a man of my word, I am upholding my part of the bargain. I surrender to your command, my Queen."

This time, she sensed no defiance in his stance. His awed expression made her feel so relieved. Perhaps, in time, they would be able to catch up on some of the things they'd missed, even learn to love each other, like family?

She turned to the roaring plaza and raised her hand to signal silence, bringing the tempest to a standstill.

"We face a formidable enemy," she said, putting force into her voice so that it carried easily through the large space. "I know the Golden Lions to be our best, and I expect you all to do your best, for your country and your Queen!"

"For our country and our Queen!" The cry swept the plaza, louder than before. It seemed as if the walls at her back trembled with the impact as the wave of sound hit it and rolled back, over the heads of the crowd.

She waited for the roar to quiet down, then turned to Mai, standing behind her. His smile filled her with warmth, making her feel more proud of herself than she had in a very long time.

Mai was the best commander she had ever known. Even aside from her feelings for him, his approval meant the world.

"Aghat Mai," she said formally. "The people of Shayil Yara are honored and grateful for the help you and your warriors have offered in training our troops and allowing us to march into battle by your side. We are aware of the Majat Guild's political neutrality and understand that this is by no means an alliance, and that our current dealings will have no long term effect on our queendom's relations with your Guild. For now, however, we rest in confidence that the presence of the Majat warriors by our side will ensure the complete destruction of the Kaddim."

Mai inclined his head as the wail in the plaza rose again and continued for a very long time. She held his gaze, reflecting on how her position as a queen, while elevating her rank, had also made her inferior to him in status in the way she had never been before. As a fellow Diamond, and later as the woman he was intending to marry, she had always been his equal. And now, each of their interactions had to be preceded with so many formalities and protocol that she felt lost.

The only thing she wanted right now was to step into his arms and bury her face in his chest. She wasn't sure if she would ever be able to do this again.

## 35
# THE DESERT WANDERERS

Raishan watched her with a straight face, but Kara could guess the play of emotions in the way his eyebrow rose briefly at the sight of her royal regalia and the Golden Lion guards forming a semicircle behind her. The muscles around his eyes crinkled with a hidden smile that never made it to his lips. She answered him in kind, smiling with eyes only.

As a friend, she would have hugged him right now to greet him after a long absence. All she was allowed to do as the Queen was give him a brief nod.

"It's good to see you again, Aghat Raishan."

"Your Majesty." He bowed to her exactly to the extent warranted, folding his palms according to Shayil Yaran customs. The Diamonds received perfect training in etiquette. Even under these extraordinary circumstances, he would have made their tutors proud just now.

Her heart ached as she looked at him. Would she ever again be able to openly call him a friend? Would she ever again sit side by side with her fellow Diamonds, polishing weapons and exchanging fireside tales? She knew she shouldn't be thinking about this now, but the sight of Raishan brought back all the uncertainty and frustration of the past few days, when she had finally realized the extent of the restrictions imposed onto her by her new role.

She sighed. Now that they had reunited with the Majat forces, she had far more immediate concerns, like securing the allegiance of the Cha'idi leaders, and the fact that once they reached the Kaddim fortress her mind link would become active again and the nightmare that had been haunting her before their meeting with Ayalla would return in full force. For the moment, though, she was glad to put these thoughts aside to enjoy something she had taken for granted before – standing next to a fellow Diamond without a dozen guards in between.

"The leaders of the Cha'idi nomads are waiting for you in the tent over there, Your Majesty," Raishan said.

She glanced at the group waiting near the tent entrance, wrapped head to toe in their loose sand-colored robes that made it impossible even to guess their gender, let alone distinguish any other features. Jamal stood beside them, looking determined but unconcerned. She heaved a breath of the dry desert air, tinged with the smells of smoke and stew from the cooking fires. For once, she felt grateful that Jamal was going into that tent by her side. While their bonding so far was not going as well as she hoped, as a member of the royal family and the commander of their troops he should have a much better idea what to expect. His calm look was reassuring, even if the way he narrowed his eyes when he looked her way echoed with an unpleasant hollowness in her chest. Why did her family relations have to be so complicated?

"Any word from Kyth?" she asked.

Raishan's gaze wavered. "I, um, apologize for this, Your Majesty, but at Aghat Mai's request I am not free to divulge any details to you, besides assuring you that Prince Kythar is on his way."

She nodded. Mai's orders made perfect sense. According to the information relayed by Egey Bashi, once she approached the Kaddim fortress she was likely going to forget everything she was and rush over to their side. No one knew for certain how long she had before this was going to happen, or whether anyone would even get any warning before she turned. She knew that Mai was going to do everything in his power to prevent the worst by keeping her under guard, possibly immobilized, but with her combat skill there could be no guarantees. The last thing they all wanted was for her to learn any details about their plans that went beyond the absolutely essential ones.

Her gaze trailed to a distant activity in the camp, centered around the crates that had arrived by a special delivery at their last stop. Top grade weapons, compliments of Lord Garet von Eyvern. An extra favor Mai had been able to obtain due entirely to his personal connections.

Her eyes tingled with rising tears. When they had met with Lord Garet, she still had hope. And now, she couldn't even speak to Mai without a dozen witnesses waiting to twist her every word. She didn't even have any time to compose herself before walking into a tent where one of the most important issues about their campaign had to be decided in a private conversation, with no one friendly enough to help her along. Jamal would be there, of course, but the way he was looking at her lately, with a mix of suspicion and challenge, left no hope that he would make any effort on her behalf.

She bowed her head in a brief goodbye, then turned abruptly and walked away toward the tent before Raishan could catch the emotion in her face.

The Cha'idi leaders looked nearly indistinguishable from each other, their tightly wrapped headgear leaving open only the eyes, purple like the stormy desert sky. As Kara and Jamal walked into the tent, they rose, eyeing them for a long moment. Then, as if on command, they bared their faces and sank to their knees.

Kara felt a surge of relief as she watched this display of loyalty. Up until now she hadn't been sure what to expect. She kept her face straight as she surveyed her visitors.

It should have come as no surprise that the person in the front was a woman, middle-aged, with parched skin and a commanding presence. The two men behind her were also in their middle years, each sporting an impressive set of old scars on their faces and necks. All of them looked at Kara with awed curiosity that made her feel far too exposed.

"Queen Aljahara," the woman said, her deep guttural voice reverberating clearly through the small space of the tent. "We were so overjoyed to learn of your return. You look just like your mother, if you forgive an old woman for saying so."

Kara's eyes widened. "You knew my mother?"

The woman smiled. "She and I played as children when we grew up. Our whole nation mourned when we heard of her death. It is our privilege to serve you, Your Majesty."

"Thank you…" Kara hesitated, realizing she had not been told the woman's name.

The woman bowed again. "Please forgive my manners, my Queen. I am Ulhari, the Cha'idi farseer. These are my warrior elders, Khurram and Farikh."

*Farseer.* Kara had prior dealings with the Cha'ori nomads that dominated the north, the distant cousins of the Cha'idi nation, ruled by women foretellers who could predict the future. She assumed a farseer was a title similar to that. In her position she should be far more knowledgeable about the Cha'idi customs, but all she could do right now was learn on the fly.

"I am honored to meet you, Ulhari," she said. "I understand you know my brother, Prince Jamal, the commander of the Golden Lions battalion."

Ulhari bowed her head. "We had dealings with Prince Jamal before. A pleasure to see you again, Your Highness."

Jamal kept his face impassive as he bowed in acknowledgement, but Kara saw the warmth in his eyes as they rested on the older woman. Her heart panged with longing. She wished she could see the same warmth in his gaze as he looked at her. She dismissed the thought, useless like many of the others that dominated her head lately. Being a queen meant coming to terms with her loneliness, making it a part of her daily life. She wondered how others could possibly cope with these kinds of roles.

"Rise," she said. "We have much to talk about." She gestured to the seating pillows arranged around a small camping stove, redundant in the high heat of the desert afternoon, but so welcome at night when the temperatures dropped to near freezing.

The Cha'idi rose to their feet and waited for Kara and Jamal to take their seats before settling on the other side of the stove. They kept their backs straight, the knees of their crossed legs lying flat on the floor in positions that would have seemed uncomfortable to anyone raised indoors. Curious, Kara tried to imitate it, finding it surprisingly easy once she settled into it. She smiled, catching Ulhari's approving gaze.

"You're a natural," the old woman said. "Just like your mother."

*Like my mother.* Kara forcibly kept herself from looking at Jamal. Ulhari was speaking about his mother too, someone who would have been so dear to both of them if life hadn't scattered them all around in such unpredictable ways.

"I envy you for knowing her, Ulhari," she said. "One day, when this war is over, I hope you can tell me more about what she was like."

Ulhari smiled. "I can tell you right now that you would have made her proud, Aljahara. You and Jamal, even though I can tell you both have a long way to go in getting to know each other."

This time Kara did glance at Jamal, quivering as she saw his eyes fixed on her in a slow appraisal, as if deciding if she was worthy. During the march, she was able to earn his grudging respect. But she knew they did indeed have a long way to go toward any warmer feelings.

"You speak of a war," Ulhari said. "Tell us more."

Kara nodded. "The enemy we are facing is far superior to anyone Shayil Yara has seen before. Your help would be invaluable, if you can lend it to us."

Ulhari's face darkened. "Yes, the Dark Order. We

knew they were trouble, ever since the times they started bending our people to their will to claim the lands around their stronghold."

"Bending people to their will?" Kara didn't feel surprised. The Kaddim's mind magic made it easy for them to force people to do what they wanted. "What did they do to your people, Ulhari?"

"Nothing permanent, fortunately," Ulhari said. "I must assume they didn't want to make us their mortal enemies. Over time, we have achieved a shaky balance, of sorts."

"A balance?"

Ulhari shifted in her seat. "The valley where their fortress stands is called Im'ahir. The Valley of Whispers. Anyone who ventures into it starts hearing noises, voices in their head. It feels like a madness, which lifts only after they find a way out, with no memories of what they saw inside. By now, we've all learned well which area to avoid."

*The Valley of Whispers.* A shiver ran down Kara's spine. The voices Ulhari described seemed so similar to the way she knew Kaddim's magic to work, clouding one's mind, making one unfocused and weak, unable to do even the simplest things. *Like a madness.* She hoped Kyth's magic, and Mai's fighting force, were prepared to deal with that.

"All we need is for the Cha'idi to show us the way," she said.

"And then?"

"Our allied army is making plans to defeat them." *Plans I'm not privy to.* She knew she shouldn't venture into any details about the Kaddim link, but suddenly the thought of having this conversation without divulging any further details seemed odd. Ulhari's intent gaze told her the Cha'idi woman also realized something was amiss, but she had no idea how to remedy the situation.

"Did your army find a way to resist the Dark Order's magic?" Ulhari asked.

"Yes. We have a man joining us shortly who can protect everyone."

"*One* man?"

"A very powerful one." Kara hoped it was true, after Kyth had completed Ayalla's training. In any case, even if she had any doubts, she shouldn't be showing them to the Cha'idi leader – not in a conversation that could end in a rejection far too easily, ruining all their plans.

"I was hoping," Kara said, "that the Cha'idi can work directly with the Majat. Their leader, Aghat Mai, has my full confidence."

Jamal glanced away abruptly. Kara saw the Cha'idi's eyes fixed on him.

She sighed. It was time to deal with the situation.

"Perhaps you'd like to add something, Prince Jamal?" she asked.

Jamal pursed his lips, looking at her apprehensively. "Would you like me to, my Queen?"

"Not really."

"Why ask me then?"

She smiled. "Because I value your opinion, brother. This is why you are here. Besides, I would much rather discuss what you have to say out in the open, not as rumors later on. You seem to be brimming with a desire to speak. I wouldn't want to keep you from it."

He leaned away from her. "Very well, sister. Before you throw our Cha'idi allies into this trusting relationship with the Majat, perhaps you should let them know about your own personal bonds to them?"

Kara turned back to Ulhari. "Of course. I've been raised at the Majat Guild. But, I expect you've heard about it, haven't you?"

Ulhari looked back to Jamal who sat up taller, keeping his eyes on Kara.

"Have you also heard about her... personal relationship with the Majat Guildmaster who is leading their forces?" he said.

Ulhari raised her eyebrows. "Personal relationship? What exactly do you mean?"

"They've been intimate – or so I understand."

The older woman frowned. "I thought the Majat men were celibate."

"Apparently not." Jamal kept his chin up, but he did look somewhat deflated.

Ulhari turned to Kara. "You've been intimate with the Majat Guildmaster?"

"Yes." Try as she might, Kara couldn't help the blush that rose into her cheeks.

"Did you enjoy it?"

"I did." Kara felt hot now, despite the cool evening wind wafting through the tent.

Ulhari leaned forward and patted her arm. "Good for you. Things like this make me wish I was younger, still able to chase after men I took fancy to."

Kara could have wondered at this statement, but everything she had learned in Shayil Yara made it seem natural by now. In this kingdom, men's and women's roles were reversed compared to what she was used to. Chasing men in Ulhari's case made perfect sense.

She glanced at Jamal, noting how the Prince receded

into his seat. She knew it probably wasn't going to be his last attempt to discredit her, nor their last conversation on the topic. She would just have to deal with it day to day, just like she dealt with everything else.

"Still," Ulhari said. "I believe Prince Jamal may have a valid point. However good a lover the Majat Guildmaster is, he also has a reputation for being ruthless and dominant. Are you absolutely sure you can trust him?"

Kara sighed again. Despite everything else, she felt touched by the concern. This woman had played with her mother when they were children. This made her almost like family, if only Kara had any experience dealing with family members.

"You remember how you spoke about my mother?" she asked.

"Yes."

"You feel you knew her, because you and she grew up together, right?"

"Right." Ulhari was looking at her with interest.

"I was raised in the Majat Fortress," Kara said. "Aghat Mai and I grew up together, even if he and I didn't exactly play as children." *He is also my soul mate*. She forced down the useless thought she'd best forget. "Believe me when I tell you that my trust in him has nothing to do with our... relationship. I trust him implicitly, probably more than anyone else in the world."

Ulhari nodded slowly. "The way you speak about him does make him seem special."

"I'm sure you will enjoy meeting him." *If he chooses to show his enjoyable side*. Kara dismissed this thought too. She knew Mai would do everything necessary to ensure Ulhari's trust.

"I'm certainly intrigued," Ulhari said.

Kara swallowed. "Before I invite him here, however, there is one more thing I must tell you, I'm afraid. It's about our enemies, the Kaddim. I've encountered them before. During our last battle, they've planted their magic inside me. It has been temporarily silenced by a very powerful spell, but once we reach the fortress, their closeness may have unpredictable effects on me. I may become... incapacitated." *Or murderous and violent.* She glanced at Jamal. As a man close to her and more or less in charge of her security, her link had been explained to him in detail. She knew he was still having trouble accepting it.

"When it comes to this campaign," she said, "I need you to trust Aghat Mai's judgment over mine, Ulhari. At all times."

Ulhari kept her gaze. "This is a very big statement to make, my Queen."

"Believe me, I know how it looks. I don't say it lightly. And now that you know the extent of it, you can perhaps hold your judgment until you and Aghat Mai have a chance to talk?"

# 36
# BATTLE PLAN

Kyth dismounted and led his lizardbeast toward the group of tents set out among the sands. The familiar sight of the Majat camp made his arrival feel like a homecoming, entering an oasis of the known among the hostile desert sands. He exchanged a glance with Alder and Celana walking by his side. The lady's brief smile sent a surge of warmth down his spine, bringing disbelief in its wake. How could he possibly be so lucky?

His eyes narrowed as he saw two men standing beside the nearest tent, waiting for their arrival. Mai and Egey Bashi – unescorted and unguarded, as far as Kyth could tell. His heart raced with worry. What were they doing out here, all by themselves? Where was Kara, and the Majat guards that normally followed Mai everywhere he went?

He sped down the sloping dune and stopped in front of Mai, meeting his blue-gray gaze.

"Welcome back," Mai said.

Kyth bowed, the official greeting coming naturally despite the informal setting. He couldn't help wondering at the lack of usual resentment he felt in Mai's presence. Was this a change in his own perception, due to his closeness with Celana that made him feel he and Mai were no longer rivals? Or was it coming from Mai's side? Kyth could swear that the Diamond seemed more detached than usual, as if his thoughts were otherwise preoccupied. He frowned, trying and failing to catch any signs of an answer in Mai's impenetrable face.

On their last stop Kyth had received Egey Bashi's message, relayed by a hawk, briefly describing the events at the Shayil Yaran court and the way Kara had become Queen. The coincidence, as well as the implications, seemed enormous. On the outside, this solved all their immediate political problems, putting the entire military force of Shayil Yara at their disposal. On a deeper level, however, Kyth knew enough to understand that the change of Shayil Yaran rule also shattered all possible hopes for Kara and Mai to pursue their marriage plans, and likely made it impossible for them to ever be together. Kyth was sure both of them were feeling devastated right now, even if these considerations couldn't possibly be the most immediate priority on their list.

His heart quivered. Was this why Kara wasn't here to meet him, why Mai seemed so absentminded, as if lacking some of his usual fire? Kyth never thought he'd miss their constant arguments, but he suddenly felt anxious for Mai to bait him, or at least say something edgy like he always did when Kyth was around.

"How was your training, Prince Kythar?" Egey Bashi asked, his voice cutting into the heavy pause that was beginning to feel too long. His eyes briefly drifted to Celana, standing so close to Kyth that their arms brushed each other as they moved. Kyth glanced at her too, suddenly guilty that he could be feeling so happy right now. He had to remind himself of the times when Kara and Mai couldn't stay away from each other and he had been forced to watch. Did they feel guilty about it when it happened? Well, Kara did, perhaps, but did Mai?

"Lady Ayalla believes my training is complete," Kyth said.

"Is it?" Mai asked.

Here it was. The challenge, instantly bringing back a mix of relief and the usual irritation Kyth tended to feel in Mai's presence. He smiled. The feeling seemed so welcome after the devastation he had just glimpsed. Of all things, he had never imagined he would miss his headbutting sessions with Mai.

He extended his hand palm-down over the sand, bringing up a small whirlwind, lifting it off the ground so that it swept the edge of Mai's cloak and threw a handful of sand over his boots. He turned his palm up, watching the whirlwind climb on to it, coiling down like a snake, dying down as the sand it raised in its wake showered back to the ground.

Kyth knew that this little demonstration couldn't possibly explain anything at all about the power he gained, but it was likely going to ward off any further questions in regard to his magic ability.

"I think it is," he said.

Mai didn't respond, but the way his eyes lingered on the flat patch of sand at their feet told Kyth he was impressed.

"I have something to discuss with all of you." Egey Bashi's glance included not only Kyth and Mai, but also Alder and Celana, bringing a momentary sense of relief. Kyth did want both of his companions to be a part of the planning.

"I ordered the command tent off limits," Mai said. "My Emeralds are guarding it. We can talk in there."

Kyth cast his eyes around the camp again, noticing something new he didn't spot before. People walking around or standing guard by some of the tents were wearing sand-colored desert robes. Peering closer, Kyth realized more. Some of these people looked natural, but others did not, as if the robes were only a last-minute addition to their wardrobe. Once or twice, Kyth imagined he caught a glint of golden plate from underneath them.

Mai followed his gaze. "The Cha'idi desert garments. We asked the Golden Lions, Shayil Yara's elite battalion, to wear them too, to cover their usual crimson and gold. They didn't take well to these orders. Nor do they seem able to wear them gracefully enough."

*Shayil Yara's elite battalion. The Queen's personal guards.* Kyth ached to ask more, but Mai's detached gaze warned him off.

The command tent was cooler than seemed possible with the heat outside. As Kyth settled onto the seating pillows near a small empty stove, he noticed the tent flaps skillfully raised to let the breeze waft through. He wished he had learned this trick yesterday, when they started their ride through the desert from Gard'hal Outpost to meet with the Majat and had to wait for nightfall before venturing into their oven-hot tents.

"This conversation is a secret from nearly everyone in our camp," Egey Bashi said. "After we finalize the plans, Aghat Mai will divulge the necessary details to his men to enable the attack. But I cannot stress enough that under no circumstances should Kara, or anyone close to her, learn any of this. Is this clear?"

*Kara.* Kyth realized he couldn't possibly continue his conversation without knowing more.

"What's Kara's situation?" He purposely avoided looking at Mai as he said this, but he still noticed the way the Diamond shifted in his seat, as if Kyth kicked him in a sore spot.

"Her link is still dormant," Egey Bashi said. "And, from what I can tell, she is coping admirably with her new duties. She has singlehandedly ensured that both the Cha'idi and the Shayil Yaran elite troops follow Aghat Mai pretty much unconditionally..."

He let the end of the phrase trail, as if he hadn't finished the thought. Kyth didn't want to venture any further. He had no doubt Kara would cope admirably with her new role, but he couldn't even guess the price she and Mai were paying for it.

"Have you learned anything else, Magister?" Kyth asked.

"Yes. During my last days in the Shayil Yaran royal library, I found the information I hoped for about the Kaddim link. I believe I know the worst we could expect, if the Kaddim plans in regard to Kara are allowed to succeed."

Kyth raised his eyebrows in a silent question, noting how everyone else in the group also sat up to attention – in the case of Mai, without moving at all.

"They can use the link in several ways," Egey Bashi said. "First – as we thought they would, originally – they can channel Kara's gift evenly to all Kaddim warriors. I've been able to learn, however, that with Lady Ayalla's interference they wouldn't have had enough time to do it, even if this had been their original plan."

"Are you absolutely certain, Magister?" Mai said.

"Have you noticed any change in her fighting ability?"

"I'm not sure. She has been suppressing it for so long..." Mai fell silent, as if recalling.

"If you need to think this hard, it means there was no drastic change, I assume."

"No, not a drastic one."

Egey Bashi nodded. "I thought so. If they managed to draw her power away, she would have been weaker by now."

"Isn't that good news?" Mai asked.

"Sadly, no, Aghat. My research revealed another possible way of using the Kaddim mind link, one that I would have favored in their place." Egey Bashi glanced around the group, his eyes singling out Lady Celana. "You and I once discussed how the Kaddim are ruled by the Cursed Dozen, with the Reincarnate at the head. Remember, my lady?"

"Yes," she said, her face reflecting the puzzlement of the rest of the group.

"One of their special abilities is to link their minds, so that they can all act like one, fully sharing each other's powers and thoughts. The Reincarnate's presence cements and amplifies this connection, and ensures that no outside magic or force can possibly break it."

Kyth shivered. He had seen it once, when five Kaddim leaders acted like one to throw daggers and mortally wound Kara. If twelve of them together could do it any better, if their Reincarnate could amplify and cement this, it would indeed be terrifying to face. But how did this apply to the situation they faced?

"You do remember that they recently lost one of their Dozen to a spider bite," Egey Bashi said. "My guess is, they will put Kara in his place, and blend with her during the fight to share her skill."

Mai looked up sharply. "What do you mean, put Kara in his place? She's no bloody Kaddim."

"Once she feels the draw of the link again, her mind will be altered. She will be feeling like one of them. My guess is, they are grooming her to become a new Kaddim Brother – or Sister, if you will."

Mai clenched his teeth. "Are you telling me we are about to face another family reunion?"

"Yes. And if this happens, I believe your attack force will be in trouble, Aghat Mai. You have only six Diamonds. They would have twelve, all fighting with Kara's skill, and with the unison that defeats anything the Majat could even imagine."

Mai held a pause, his stunned look sending a shiver down Kyth's spine. This sounded like really bad news.

"I'm guessing that the outcome of this war will not be decided on the main battlefield, Aghat Mai," Egey Bashi said. "Their leaders will stay behind, in the heart of their fortress, blending their magic and using it to empower their warriors. To win, you must take out this command group. With Kara in their midst, this would likely prove impossible."

"Then," Mai said slowly, "we should make sure she never leaves our camp, should we?"

"I shouldn't be the one to tell you how hard it could be, Aghat. You can't guard her day and night without jeopardizing your own strength. Remember also that she cannot be killed, or they will inherit her skill, along with her knowledge. Very likely they are already thinking of her as one of their own, even if she may not feel it yet."

Mai sat very still, his dazed look making it seem as if he had just been hit on the head.

"What options do we have, Magister?" he asked.

"I see only one, Aghat Mai. You and your men must get Prince Kythar into the heart of the Kaddim fortress as soon as possible, and at all cost. Killing the Reincarnate will destroy the link and make them vulnerable again. If you can achieve that, Lady Ayalla's spiders can finish the job." He turned to Alder. "You did bring the spiders, did you?"

Alder pointed to a large sack he had been carrying over his shoulder.

"They're dormant," he said. "Sleeping, until they sense the action. Ayalla suggested every top Majat warrior should carry some on their clothes, so that they can get as close to the enemy as possible. She said, once there, they'll know what to do."

"Show me," Mai said.

Alder reached over and carefully lifted the flap of the sack.

Curled up, with legs folded underneath their bellies, the spiders looked like small furry balls, innocent and cute if one didn't look too closely. Mai stiffened visibly as he peered into their dark mass, as if expecting to see something else deeper inside.

"Well then," Mai said after a pause. "We have our plans laid out for us. All we need to do is get close to their damned fortress."

## 37

# TEMPTATION

Kara woke up with a strange echo in her head. The wind howling outside lashed out at the tent's cover, streams of flying sand hitting it and trickling down the walls like tiny running feet. *Spiders?* She sat up and took a deep breath, settling into reality.

Her small, solitary tent looked just as empty as it did when she went to sleep, not a creature moving among the ornate rugs and pillows that seemed so excessive for an army on the march. She could see shadows moving outside the door, where her guards were stationed day and night – for protection, as well as to report on any unusual activity within. She heaved another deep breath, trying to quiet her racing heart. *Dear Shal Addim, it must be after midnight.* Mai had ordered an early start, which meant she'd do her best to catch more sleep.

She stiffened when the sand patting against the tent wall outside changed tone. The new sound resembled the echo of heavy footsteps, pounding through a deep stone hall. After a while she also started hearing voices, slowly becoming clearer and more recognizable.

*She is here, Reincarnate.*

*Are you certain she's ready, Kaddim Nimos?*

A sharp pain in her arm caused her to gasp. She reached over and pulled her golden bracelets of station off her forearm. Her eyes widened.

The thorn Ayalla had plunged into her arm was glowing red-hot, the pain radiating from it so sharp that she reacted before she could think, clawing at it until she was able to pull it out and throw it away. Its glow faded as it rolled to a standstill at the edge of the tent. Kara forced down her shiver as she continued to stare. Then, she brought her arm to her eyes.

The moon was shining in through the tent flaps and seams, throwing silvery patches onto the floor. Kara brought her arm into one of them, staring. It took her a moment to come to terms with what she was seeing, to convince herself it was true.

She had expected a burning wound, gaping in the place where the thorn had been. Instead, a black spot marred her arm, level with the surrounding skin with no signs of a wound of any kind. It resembled a downturned triangle, with the sharp end pointing down at her hand. *The Kaddim brand mark.*

Her stomach clenched as she stared at it, willing for it to disappear.

*We're waiting, Kara.*

The voice reverberated in her ears as clearly as if the speaker was standing right behind her shoulder. She spun around, looking into the empty air. No sign of an intruder, not even a shadow against the bright light outside.

Air wafted over her neck, like a sweep of a hand near her skin, just out of touch.

*Get ready, Kara.*

She froze, the sound of the strange voice fading away, replaced with the dry rustle of sand outside. Footsteps, approaching. *Are they real this time? Or is it all inside my head?*

"My Queen?" The voice at the tent entrance seemed much more solid than the ones she heard just now. She thought she recognized it. El Rashid, one of her Golden Lion guards.

She took a breath. "What is it?"

"There are people out here to see you, Your Majesty."

*People.* Her heart skipped a beat. It was the middle of the night. Everyone should be fast asleep, except for the guards.

For one illogical moment she wondered if the Kaddim had arrived to collect her, if they had somehow managed to put everyone here under their magic spell so that they could whisk her away. But she knew both Kyth and Mai were immune to the Kaddim mind control, and Kyth also had the ability to sense their magic if it was used nearby. Could the Kaddim have somehow disabled them both?

Her mouth felt dry as she jumped up to her feet, glancing over her outfit to make sure she was decent enough to face anyone outside. She strode to the tend flap and threw it open.

Kyth stood beside the doorway, with Egey Bashi, Mai, and several guards crowding behind. The bright desert moon threw sharp shadows over the Prince's drawn face.

It was the first time she saw him up close since his return from Ayalla's, and she could see how he had grown, both in power and in stature, as if his experience in the forest had completed his age-coming and turned him into a man. He frowned as he peered at her, his concerned look sending her heart racing again. She wondered at the way his closeness made her feel unsettled, as if the changes going on inside her turned her into an adversary. *The Kaddim magic. Is he sensing it on me?*

She couldn't think of anything to say as she stood there, feeling like a thief caught in the act.

Mai reached past the Prince and grasped her arm, pulling up her sleeve as he turned it toward the light. She heard a sharp intake of breath as they all stared at the black triangle branded into her skin.

"When did this happen?" Mai asked.

She swallowed. "Just now. The pain woke me up."

"Where's the thorn?"

She glanced over to the edge of the tent. One of the Emeralds rushed in and picked it up, showing it to Kyth and Mai.

"I sense no magic on it," Kyth said. "It must have lost its power."

Mai's look turned glassy as he nodded, his brief glance at Kara freezing her to the spot. *He's suspecting something. I mustn't let him see what's happening to me.*

"Did you feel anything else?" Egey Bashi asked.

Kara hesitated. "A voice. I heard someone whispering over my shoulder."

"An intruder?"

She shook her head. "No. Just the voice."

"What did it say?"

*Get ready, Kara.* "I... I didn't hear it clearly enough to distinguish the words." She was surprised at the ease with which the lie came out of her mouth. Looking at their concerned faces, she also wondered at the sense of detachment she felt. *Dear Shal Addim, am I becoming a Kaddim?* She focused on Mai, trying to ground herself in the warmth she always felt in his presence, in the fact that she was seeing him again, so close, after such a long time. The concern in his gaze made her shiver, yet, even looking into his eyes she still felt detached – as if she wasn't fully here anymore. *Mai. Have they found a way to come between us?*

*Do I even know who I am anymore?*

"Are you sure you didn't make out any words at all?" Kyth's narrowed eyes told her he was suspecting more than any of the others, but she knew she could fool him too, with the way he always cared for her, all but blind to her numerous faults.

She briefly glanced down and batted her eyes at him, knowing that the gesture made her look vulnerable and alluring, rewarded to see his gaze soften in response. "I... I tried. At some point it seemed that they said something about being close, I think. But I really couldn't understand anything else."

This lie seemed safe. They all knew they were getting very close to the Kaddim fortress. According to the Cha'idi, their current campsite stood right at the boundary none of their people dared to cross. As far as she heard, their scouts yesterday had spotted a stone wall up ahead, just before the high winds had forced them to abandon the search. *Get ready, Kara.* She was ready. Before long, she was going to reunite with her brothers.

"I... I don't feel so well," she said. "I need to sleep."

Kyth and Mai exchanged a quick glance.

"Triple the guards," Mai said to the men watching from the doorway. "I want them stationed all around the tent. If anything in here bloody moves, report to me immediately."

Kara bowed her head in acknowledgement. She avoided looking at Kyth at all as she stepped back into the tent and closed the flap behind her.

"This is the place," Mai said.

Kyth narrowed his eyes, looking at the desert ahead. In the stillness that came in the wake of last night's wind, the sands lay flat like water, the jagged peaks of rocks like reefs rising in between. They grew taller as they ran into the distance, blending with the horizon.

"Where exactly?" he asked.

"Behind those rocks over there. They've made good use of the landscape to make sure the stronghold is all but invisible, even from this close."

"Right." Kyth glanced at the rest of his party, the Diamonds crowded around Mai like a human shield, the equally huddled group of the Cha'idi beside them, with Ulhari in their midst.

"Did you find out how many there are?" he asked.

Mai's gaze wavered. "This is a strange thing, actually. All of our information says there's no steady source of water nearby, only a small spring within the fortress walls that can service no more than a hundred. Yet, my scouts report seeing many more, close to a thousand."

Kyth's eyes widened. "How is that possible?"

Mai locked eyes with Egey Bashi standing on Kyth's other side.

"I offered an explanation Aghat Mai is finding implausible," the Keeper said.

"What explanation, Magister?"

"If these warriors inside the fortress are undead,

they wouldn't need any water – or food for that matter. In fact, they would make perfect defenders for a desert fortress."

"Undead?"

"You do know, Prince Kythar, that the Kaddim are capable of resurrection."

"Yes."

"Their resurrection, done properly, would create a man indistinguishable from the original. However, a quick version would create only an animated corpse, held together by the Destroyer's magic. This magic could be channeled through the Kaddim Reincarnate nearly effortlessly, creating a fearless and obedient army that costs almost nothing to keep."

Kyth slowly let out a sigh. *An undead army. Just what we bloody need.*

"Can the Majat deal with them?" he asked.

Mai looked at him levelly. "The Magister assured us these undead warriors would still be vulnerable to our weapons. We just need to make sure we finish the job this time."

Kyth lowered his head. For once, he felt glad that his part in the battle wouldn't take him anywhere near those undead, even if the thing he had to do was probably even worse.

"What about Kara?" he asked.

Mai glanced back toward their camp, the small tent in its midst surrounded by so many guards that even a wisp of sand trying to finding its way in would probably be stopped and inspected.

"Is there anything else we can do for her?" Kyth asked.

Mai shrugged. He still didn't say anything at all.

"At some point," Egey Bashi said, "this kind of guarding will drain your resources, Aghat Mai."

"Is there another option, Magister?"

"Drug her, like I suggested before. I have a substance that could send her to sleep, and another one that would revive her with no harmful consequences when the time comes."

Mai hesitated. "I'd rather ask her first, if we're to consider something like that."

"You know she may not be acting like herself anymore, Aghat. Whatever she says, we can't possibly trust it."

"Are you suggesting we force her, Magister?"

Kyth shivered as he saw Mai's determined face. He had made a mistake last night, rushing to Mai when he sensed the Kaddim magic without bringing Ellah along. Had Ellah been there when they confronted Kara in her tent, they would have known for sure if she was hiding something.

He never thought he would see the day he wished that Mai was allowed to share Kara's tent and her bedroll, an intimate closeness that might have slowed her transformation and kept her loyalties closer to the Majat. He even had a conversation about this with Raishan, the only Diamond he fully trusted, but none of them could see any way to pursue this possibility. And now, without Mai by her side, Kara had no support at all. More, none of them had any way of knowing what was going on with her.

"Let's go talk to her," he said.

Mai paused. Kyth was sure he understood the reason for the reluctance in the Diamond's gaze. If Kara's Kaddim magic had become too strong, it might

be necessary to subdue her with force. Kyth knew Mai
wouldn't hesitate to do it, but he was sure none of
them cherished the idea.

"All right," Mai said.

*I can't wait to see you,* Nimos whispered into her ear.
*Can't wait for you to take Brother Xados's place in our midst.*

"Me too." Kara sat up straight, staring unseeingly
at the tent wall. It was amazing how, this close to the
Kaddim fortress, she was finding a way to be in two
places at once. In a short while she would be able to
escape the guards Mai had placed around her tent and
cover the remaining distance to her waiting brothers.
Her skill could make the Kaddim invincible, win the
war for them. She couldn't wait to fully extend her
link, to experience the unity with eleven others,
sharing their thoughts and skills.

She forced her face into a calm expression as she
heard a commotion outside. Probably Kyth and Mai,
who just couldn't find it in themselves to leave her
alone. She turned, waiting for them to come in.

Mai crossed the small space of the tent and stopped
beside her. "Are you all right?"

"Yes." Looking into his face stirred an emotion, a
longing of a different kind. She dismissed it. This was
her lust speaking, the fact that they used to share a
bed. Her body still wanted him, but the Kaddim had
no use for bodily needs, or giving in to simple animal
pleasures.

Mai leaned closer, peering into her face. He looked
concerned. And, he still wanted her, plain and clear.
Too bad for him.

"We, um, we thought now that we're so close to the

Kaddim fortress and Ayalla's spell is no longer effective, we should consider other options to make sure you're safe until the time comes."

"Other options?" She feigned interest,· glancing around the group. *Safe.* Mai had no idea what he was talking about. She was about to become one of the twelve Kaddim leaders. There was no way Mai and his allies could prevent the inevitable – unless they actually decided to target her with a spider right now. She put on her vulnerable look as she kept Mai's gaze, to make sure he didn't entertain the possibility.

"Magister Egey Bashi has a potion that could put you to sleep," Mai said. "We can use another one to revive you when it's time."

*A potion.* She hesitated. What would the Kara he loved say? "Yes, of course." *Right?* She noticed his frown, wondering if she had done it wrong.

*You must kill him. He stands in our way.* As the voice echoed in her ear, she saw Kyth glance at her sharply, even though she was reasonably sure he couldn't possibly have heard it. She focused her eyes on Mai.

*Ask him to hold you. Use your dagger. If you do it right, he wouldn't even feel a thing.*

"No." She started as she realized she had said it out loud. The dual conversation was driving her mad. Nimos was asking her to kill Mai. It made sense. So many troubles would be spared if Mai was dead. The Majat army would lose its edge without him as a leader. Yet, as Mai leaned even closer toward her, the animal part of her stirred to life. She longed to feel his arms around her again, to revel in his love. She couldn't possibly kill him.

*He holds his men far above you. If he was in your place, if he had to kill you to win this war, he wouldn't hesitate.*

Kara swallowed, looking into Mai's concerned face. He was speaking to her. Behind him, Kyth and Magister Egey Bashi raised their voices too, but she just couldn't focus on the words.

*Do it. Act vulnerable. Get him to hold you.*

She drew a sharp breath, her lips quivering as she held Mai's gaze. She didn't have to pretend much. She did long for him, after all this time of not being allowed near him at all. And she felt so vulnerable right now, her sanity hanging by a very thin thread.

"Mai," she said quietly. "Can you sit with me? Just for a moment, please."

He obeyed without hesitation, kneeling on the floor by her side. She leaned toward him, relaxing into his arms, inhaling his natural scent that always made her head spin. *Fresh water and pine.* Alien smells her body once enjoyed. She shifted, molding into his embrace, the hardness of his sculpted muscles fitting the curves of her body so well. They were meant for each other. In another life, they could have been so close.

*Good work. Now, draw your dagger.*

She did, taking care not to disturb her position so that he wouldn't guess the movement at all. She sensed no tension from Mai, no awareness of what she was about to do. This trust in itself was so enormous for an assassin of his training.

*Do it, now.*

She clenched her dagger.

*I said, now.*

Her hand twitched, as if about to move on its own accord. She willed it into stillness.

*What are you doing, Kara?*

*I...* She paused. She wanted so much to please Nimos, to prove herself to the Kaddim, but the thought of sliding a dagger between Mai's ribs, feeling his body go limp in her arms, seemed unbearable. She just couldn't do it.

"Mai!" Kyth screamed, rushing forward to break them up. "Get away from her!"

Her head felt as if pierced by a thousand needles, the pain sending her crouching to the floor. Mai and Kyth were arguing above her, their voices hollow and indistinct, as if they weren't standing right next to her. Then the Majat closed in around Mai, drawing him away. She rolled into a ball against the disabling pain, but someone pulled her shoulder to flip her over. Strong hands pried her arm away from her chest, so that everyone could now see the dagger she was clenching.

The tent broke into chaos, but all she could see was Mai's face, staring at her in disbelief, as if she had actually stabbed him.

She rose to her knees, shaking off the grasping hands.

"Get the hell out of here," she snarled. "All of you. Now!"

# 38

# BREAKOUT

In the end, they had to force the potion into her mouth, two Diamonds holding her down, others decisively planted between her and Mai. Kyth stared down at her, dumbfounded. He couldn't believe what had just happened, even though he witnessed it with his own eyes. Kara, turning on Mai, trying to stab him with a concealed dagger. The truth of it simply didn't fit into his head.

When Kara's eyes finally closed and her limbs relaxed, Mai ordered her release, but all the Diamonds in his force stood around her for a while, tense as if bracing for a new attack. When she didn't show any signs of life, besides the shallow breathing that Egey Bashi assured them was normal, they eventually started filing out of the tent one by one. Mai remained, standing still like a statue.

"Mai," Kyth said quietly. "We must go. I don't think there's anything else we can do for her right now."

"She will be asleep for at least four hours," Egey Bashi added. "This leaves us enough time to plan the attack. We'll give her a new dose before she fully awakens, so that we can avoid another ordeal."

Mai glanced around dazedly, as if he had just woken up.

"You are right," he said. "There is nothing we can do, except get the bloody bastard who did this to her."

Kyth sighed. He thought Mai had passed the swearing stage a while ago, when Kara's Golden Lion guards started calling for help. The fact that he was swearing again hopefully meant Mai was coming back to his usual self, even if Kyth couldn't escape the feeling that it would take time to see the return of the efficient and brilliant commander they needed for the next stage of the march. To win the upcoming battle, Mai had to be at his best, and being nearly stabbed by the woman he loved and then having to oversee her ordeal certainly didn't help.

"She will be all right." He wished he could believe it. Ayalla had mentioned the possibility that if Kara was too far gone by the time they destroyed the Kaddim – given that they managed to do that at all – the spiders were going to kill her too, a scenario he was never going to bring up to anyone else. They were going to be on time, he told himself firmly. After Mai recovered from the shock, he was going to lead a campaign just as successfully as he always did, obliterating the Kaddim's cult once and for all.

He waited out the pause as Mai stood looking at Kara, then exchanged a quick glance with Egey Bashi and left the tent.

Kara waited for her tormentors' footsteps to die down in the sand outside, then rolled her head to the side in a natural gesture designed to trick anyone who could be watching her right now into thinking she was still unconscious. She opened her mouth to let the sticky liquid she held inside trickle down to the ground. It left an unpleasant taste behind, and a light drowsiness she was sure would soon pass. She couldn't afford to waste any time feeling drowsy. She had four hours to act, if Egey Bashi was right – not nearly enough to do everything she wanted, but perhaps enough to accomplish one important thing.

*What should I do?* she asked Nimos in her mind.

The response came with a delay, echoing voices telling her he was consulting with someone. *Too late to try to kill him now.*

*I can do some other damage here,* she offered.

More echoing voices, speaking the language that was becoming familiar to her, if not quite enough to understand it when spoken rapidly in hushed tones. *No. We need you. Kill whoever stands in your way and get here as fast as you can.*

*Kill whoever stands in your way.* She could certainly do that, but if her charge also included escaping the camp and getting to the Kaddim stronghold as soon as she could, it needed to be planned more carefully. She was certain the guards outside her tent would likely be in her way, but was killing them a good idea?

She strained her ears, listening. The Majat could stand very still, but their bodies tended to break the flow of wind and sand, creating quiet spots against the walls of the tent. She could sense none of them. By the feel of it, her only guards right now were the two Golden Lions normally stationed at the entrance to her tent at all times as the Queen's honorary guard. She had no doubt she could slit their throats quietly enough not to draw attention, but she couldn't know who else may be watching from a distance. In a busy camp like theirs, two corpses sagging by a tent entrance would surely draw attention.

She felt around for her weapons, cursing silently when she found none. Of course they would have taken her weapons. She was a danger, wasn't she? Lucky that both Mai and Kyth trusted Egey Bashi's remedies so much, assuming that forcing a potion into her mouth would send her into a four-hour sleep.

She searched around for anything to be used as a weapon and found nothing of help. She cursed again. The Majat could be so damned efficient when they wanted to. All she needed right now was a blade that could help her rip open the back of the tent and slip out.

She slid toward the opening, finding a gap at the side of the tent flap below the knee level, where she knew they would unlikely to notice anyone watching even if they stared directly at the tent right now. The two guards stationed there looked unfamiliar, probably the relief ones that took the place of her regular guards, now that she was believed to be peacefully sleeping inside.

She looked at the direction of the Majat command tent, partially hidden behind the others. Two Emeralds stood at the door, but as far as she could tell they weren't even looking her way.

*How far is it to the stronghold?* she asked Nimos.

*About an hour on foot. Once you are out, I'll send riders to get you.*

*All right.*

*Try not to alert them to your escape.*

*Got it.* Stealthily, she rose behind the tent flap, extending a hand through the opening to grasp the guard's dagger and pull it out of its sheath. It slid out without resistance. She clenched it tightly, snapping her hand away into the safety of the tent. Her heart raced as she remembered the other time she had been clenching a dagger just like this. She had come so close to killing Mai. A distant, dormant part of her shivered with dread at the mere thought of this possibility. For a moment she stood still, wondering what the hell she was doing right now. Then the whispering in her head became louder, overwhelming the rest.

She wrapped herself in a sand-colored cloak and slit the back of the tent, moving quietly like a shadow as she slipped out into the desert.

The Golden Lion guard cowered under Mai's gaze, looking small and weak despite his huge size. For a very brief moment Kyth feared that Mai was actually going to harm the man.

For once, Kyth could relate well to this kind of anger. How hard could it have been for the Golden Lion battalion, presumably the best of the best among Shayil Yara's elite troops, to prevent a deeply drugged person from escaping a closely guarded tent? He knew it was useless to ask. He glanced at the man's empty scabbard hanging on his belt. Kara's stealth had to be amazing if she was able to snatch the dagger off his belt without alerting him at all – not that Kyth ever had any doubt about her skill.

A Majat warrior rushed into the tent and stopped a few paces inside, instantly tamed by the look on Mai's face.

"Report," Mai barked.

The man stiffened with effort. "We found traces of the potion soaked into the floor rug, Aghat Mai. She must have spit it out after we left."

"Impossible." Mai turned to Egey Bashi standing nearby. "I thought you said your potion bloody works, Magister."

The Keeper shrugged. "She may have only pretended to take it. If she managed to keep it in her mouth without swallowing..."

"With Raishan and Lance holding her down? I don't think so."

"She shares their training, Aghat Mai. And she is not herself right now."

Kyth saw a brief shadow of pain run over Mai's face. The Diamond turned away, firing off rapid hand signs. The tent erupted in activity.

"Aghat Seldon!" Mai stood taller as he watched the older Diamond step in front of him. "I'm placing you in charge of the attack."

"Me?" Seldon's face shifted through the whole spectrum of surprise and disbelief in one split instant.

"You will lead our forces to storm their walls. Bring everyone."

"But..."

"I assume you have the command experience to do it, Aghat. Do you?"

Seldon hesitated for an instant, then briefly bowed his head, pressing his fist to his chest in a Majat salute.

"Good." Mai turned to Kyth. "You're with me."

A chill ran down Kyth's spine. He recognized Mai's detached look, a hint of fatal determination behind his usual brisk efficiency. This was it, the mission they had all been preparing for. Except that now, because of Kara's escape, they had to do it on the enemy's terms.

"What's your plan?" he asked.

Mai looked at him calmly. "My scouts found a weak spot at the back of their fortress, one we could penetrate using a small force of top Gems. Seldon will lead our army to distract them at the front while we take out their leaders and stop the war. Simple."

"Right." Kyth turned away, for fear Mai would catch his expression. This was a suicide mission, which depended solely on Kyth's ability to destroy the source of the Kaddim's magic. He hoped all his training with Ayalla was enough. It had to be, or everyone he cared for would die.

"Good plan, Aghat Mai," Egey Bashi said. "Except that you don't have enough top Gems to take out their leaders. Not now that they have Kara on their side."

"Do you have any other suggestion, Magister?"

The Keeper eyed him in silence.

"I thought not." Mai turned to Seldon. "Engage them, Aghat, but do your best not to lay down too many lives. Your only job is to divert their full attention to the fortress's defenses."

"Yes, Aghat Mai." Seldon briefly bowed his head, but Kyth saw the wonder in the older man's eyes, an expression that also reflected in Egey Bashi's face. This was Mai's special strength, to remain calm and efficient even under enormous pressure, to care about lives and keep up the morale where another commander might have thrown his troops to slaughter. As the Diamond swept through the room giving orders Kyth saw faces light up at the sight of him, men pulling up to attention, beaming with energy and fervor.

"Listen, everyone." Mai's voice echoed clearly through every corner of the large space. "Aghat Seldon will lead you into battle. Do us all proud." He signaled to Kyth and slid out of the tent, forcing the Prince into a run to keep up.

The next hour was a blur. As he was fitting up his gear, Kyth tried to recall every detail of what Ayalla had taught him back in the forest. He thought he had been confident about his magic ability, but now it was about to be put to the test against an ultimate enemy, a magic power that was opposite to his in every way. Was he truly up to it? He did his best to force away doubt, to keep calm and detached as he watched the Majat checking and securing their numerous weapons, Alder rushing around to place spiders onto the shoulder of each man from their elite attack force. Kyth received his share, feeling them tickle under his shirt as they settled near the collar to remain out of sight while having easy access to the outside. He calmed his senses, distancing himself from the dread these creatures caused in him, establishing a link with them like Ayalla taught him to. His magic flowed out to contact every other spider in range, so that he could release them all on command or hold them back if needed.

Mai was taking six Diamonds, six Rubies, six Emeralds, and eight Jades – a small group that included all the top warriors on their force and covered a range of skills, including bows and crossbows, the specialty of the Jades, and synchronous fighting the Emeralds were so good at. Together with Kyth and Mai, their numbers added to twenty-eight, a mobile but capable force, the best they could put forward for the task. Still, given their knowledge that in addition to the regular warriors they would be facing twelve Kaddim Brothers that included Kara, all sharing her Diamond skill and acting in perfect unison, this didn't seem reassuring.

Looking at their force, setting out to fight such an unequal battle, Kyth realized sharply that many of them would likely be killed in the attack, and there was nothing he could possibly do about it. He was aware that they knew it too, and were still joining the mission without any hesitation. His job was not to let them all die in vain. The responsibility felt too enormous to dwell on.

Mai handed out sand-colored cloaks that covered their black outfits, blending them with the desert landscape. He also gave each of them a black mask that covered their faces and necks, leaving open only the slits for the eyes. As they all dressed up, Kyth realized that these outfits gave them at least a marginal element of surprise, the identical-looking top Gems fighting in near-unison making it more difficult for the enemy to figure out which ones of them to target first. Of course, fighting against Kara, who knew everyone so well, would eventually negate this advantage but at least at the start it would make their force look stronger than it actually was.

There was no time for goodbyes. Kyth briefly squeezed Egey Bashi's hand, then waved to Celana and Ellah standing on the crest of a sand dune a short distance away. The Majat were already in the saddles and he hurried to mount his lizardbeast and ride off.

"Remember," Mai said to Kyth, pulling up his lizardbeast to ride astride. "It's all about you this time. All of us will be fighting to protect you, so that you can get to their Reincarnate. You must focus only on this goal. Don't even look at what we're doing."

Kyth understood the part Mai wasn't saying. All the Majat were going to throw down their lives for the sole purpose of getting him across the room through the enemy line. If he let this sway him, he was going to fail too, and the war would be lost. He couldn't afford that.

Yet, could he keep focused while watching all these men dying to protect him?

"The Kaddim will probably do their best to target you first," he said.

Mai didn't respond at once, his narrowed eyes through the slits of the mask studying the path between the boulders ahead.

"I'm not important," he said. "You're the only one who matters, Kyth. You alone will win or lose this war."

Kyth glanced at Mai's calm profile, his relaxed posture in the saddle as he swayed with his lizardbeast's rhythmic stride. The thought of Mai dying in this battle simply didn't fit into his mind. For as long as Kyth had known Mai, despite the resentment he felt as a rival, he was always looking up to this man, so glamorous, a brilliant commander, perfect at everything he did. He didn't think he could possibly live with the knowledge that Mai had been killed protecting him.

"I won't let them kill you," he said. "Not if I can do anything about it."

Mai glanced at him sharply. "That kind of thinking could easily ruin all our plans. If you as much as flinch when you see any of us dying around you, you won't stand a chance. You must pretend that we are not there at all. Focus on what's important."

Kyth swallowed. "I understand."

Mai hesitated. "If you do get a chance to save one

person, save Kara. When Nimos dies, she must be touching him to become free of the link, no matter if she wants to or not. Promise me you will make it happen, if you possibly can."

"I promise." Kyth felt glad for the mask that hid the tears standing in his eyes.

"One more thing," Mai said. "I don't know if you still love her, but if you do, and if you choose to pursue this feeling after I'm dead, you have my blessing."

Kyth stared, then hastily looked away to prevent any possibility of Mai catching his expression. He did still love Kara. His love for her would never go away. Moreover, he couldn't help realizing that being the Queen of Shayil Yara made her a highly desirable bride for him, eliminating the political barrier that stood between them before. Yet, Kyth also had feelings for Celana now, an innocent, intelligent girl who had given herself to him so bravely and unconditionally. While this dilemma definitely needed to wait until after the battle, what Mai had just said to him made his breath catch in his throat.

"You are not going to die," he said. "None of us are. We are going to bloody win, and whatever your Guild says about it, you and Kara will find a way to be together."

Mai didn't say anything as he turned his face to the road ahead.

# 39
# THE CURSED DOZEN

The Reincarnate's eyes glowed like two red-hot coals on his pale face. Kara knew his touch was going to hurt her, but she didn't stop or even slow her approach. Her pain was not important compared to the eternity that awaited her in the cradle of her Brotherhood.

She shivered as Nimos's hand fell on her shoulder from behind, urging her on.

"Don't fear him," he whispered into her ear. "It will only hurt briefly. And then, you will be truly one of us."

*One of us.* A part of her mind told her that this was a bad thing, that she must resist it with all she had. But this faint thought didn't seem nearly as convincing as the reality, her new brothers surrounding her in a ring, waiting to become one with her. She took one last step and raised her face to welcome the Reincarnate's touch.

A bony hand cupped her chin, turning her face up, and she resisted the urge to flinch, the pain at the border of bearable. His caress felt like flame licking her skin, leaving burning traces behind. She was certain she would be scorched and crippled.

His face approached, his kiss like a sharp blade plunged between her eyebrows, piercing her head with a pain she never felt before. A scream froze on her lips as the burning-hot fingers held them shut, the Reincarnate's other hand caressing her with the tenderness of a lover, his touch shooting through her every nerve.

Voices flooded into her head, whispering, arguing and screaming all at once. She stumbled away and covered her ears, but that only made it worse. It was then that she realized the voices were coming from within.

"There," Nimos said. "We are all one mind now. We can share thoughts and actions. We can all share your gift. Try."

She concentrated. It felt as if her body had suddenly multiplied, her mind expanding to enfold the entire room. She sent a movement to its outer part and saw a man over there raise his hand so fast that it blurred. She sent him a command and he drew his sword, cutting the air until his blade became invisible from the speed of the movement.

She smiled. After such a long time of not being able to use her skill, this felt liberating, her power multiplied and shared by eleven different men. She tried to move them all and they did, in synchrony that made the Majat synchronous training seem like a joke.

"Who is in control?" she asked, no longer sure if she had pronounced the words out loud. It didn't seem to matter at all.

"We all are," Nimos said. "This is what true unity feels like."

She understood now. The feeling was so enjoyable she never wanted to let go. Her pain receded, no more than a memory as she spun across the room, reveling in her new freedom. In this state, everything was allowed. She could do anything at all.

"The Cursed Dozen is back together," Nimos said. "And we are ready to face our enemy."

Kara wanted to ask the question, but with their unity of minds it didn't seem necessary. She knew which enemy they meant. The Majat army, coming to obliterate them. Mai.

The thought brought a strange tingling sensation. She wasn't sure she wanted to kill Mai, but she knew that to win this war for the Kaddim she had to. One life dear to her was a small sacrifice to make for the greater good.

She knew for certain that had Mai been in her place, he would have done the same.

The roar of the starting battle rose over the sands. Here at the back of the stronghold it seemed like a distant echo, but Kyth knew out there the armies were clashing weapons, killing and dying. Without the Diamonds, the tip of their force, the Majat were not nearly as powerful, even with the superior weapons sent from Bengaw, even with all the Shayil Yaran reinforcements they were able to collect. He could only hope that Seldon was capable enough a commander to at least provide the diversion they needed.

It seemed to be working, at least for now. The back of the fortress adjacent to the small rocky ridge seemed empty, a vulnerable spot in the stronghold's wall. As the Majat slid over the sands to the base of the wall, lower in this place than anywhere else, they looked like silent shadows, their cloaks blending with the sands, their steps so smooth that they appeared to be gliding without actually touching the ground. Kyth did his best to match them.

Grappler hooks flew up, two masked and cloaked figures climbing at a speed that made it seem as if someone was pulling them onto the wall from above. Kyth thought one of them was Raishan, but there was no way to tell, with everyone masked and dressed so identically he kept wondering how they all recognized each other. Mai's staff made the only distinction point. All others carried swords, perhaps slightly different from each other, but for someone of Kyth's limited knowledge impossible to tell apart.

"They will recognize you by the staff," he said to Mai quietly as they waited.

Mai kept looking upward, as if avoiding Kyth's gaze. "With the fight we're facing, it would be unlikely to make a difference. It's important, however, that each of us fights with our best weapon, if we want to have even a remote chance of holding them off long enough."

*Holding them off long enough.* Kyth wished Mai would talk of victory, the way he always did when he was within earshot of his troops. He supposed it was a useful trait to be able to correctly estimate their chances, but he couldn't help wishing Mai was at least a little bit more optimistic right now.

"By the way," Mai said. "They will start blasting off their magic at our troops out there any time – if they haven't already."

"They haven't." Kyth kept his senses open, seeking out the smothering waves of Kaddim's mind magic he had learned to counter even at this distance. It seemed strange that no magic of any kind was being projected over the forces storming the stronghold from the front. Had the Kaddim given up already? Or were they anticipating Kyth's arrival, saving their strength to destroy him. Kyth shivered. With Kara in their midst, this was the most likely explanation, but he knew it was useless to think about it at all.

He cast his net wider, searching until he sensed another kind of magic in the distance, more subtle and confined, coming from the depth of the fortress.

"I believe I know where they are," he said.

Mai glanced up again. Kyth couldn't see anything over the looming wall, but the Diamond must have gotten a sign. His hand flicked up, relaying a signal to the waiting men. More grappling hooks flew up in unison, creating a path onto the wall. A Ruby nearest Kyth handed him the edge of a rope, then lowered his black mask back into place.

"You'll have no trouble climbing this, will you?" Mai said.

Kyth sighed. Last time they stormed a fortress together, Mai nearly left him behind, assuming the Prince could use a grappler hook as well as any of his men. Kyth had been training since then, and while he still wasn't confident he could throw it as well as the rest, he found no difficulty climbing a rope over a rough stone wall that provided plenty of footholds.

He didn't feel the need to reply as he grasped the rope and hauled himself up, less speedy and graceful than anyone else around him, but nearly as efficient.

The path led them along the wall, down a steep flight of stairways, into a winding passage that descended deeper into the fortress, the coolness of its stone walls scaring away the remains of the desert heat. There was not a soul in sight, but as they moved on, Kyth finally felt a blanket of force projected toward the troops fighting outside of the fortress and sent out a wisp of power to counter it. He was amazed at how easy it felt to quench the Kaddim magic that had seemed such a challenge before. But he knew all this was but a fraction of what awaited them ahead.

The corridor they were following became wider, looping around toward the large double doors at the end.

"They're in there," Kyth said.

"Are you sure they're all inside?" Mai asked quietly.

"Yes. And they're waiting for us."

"How close do you need to get to the Reincarnate to do your thing?"

"I need to be touching him." Kyth glanced away. The Kaddim must know it too, and they would probably throw everything they had at preventing him from getting within touching distance of their leader. Even if they failed, forcing a man with the Reincarnate's enormous power into an intimately close contact seemed impossible. For the first time since leaving Ayalla's place where he learned what he needed to do, Kyth started considering if he had been insane to agree to participate in this kind of a plan.

The power he was sensing from within the chamber ahead seemed strong enough to blast out the doors. As he waited for the Majat to take positions, he briefly wondered how one man like him, not even a good fighter, could possibly be enough to counter this kind of a force. He bit back the thought. *Focus on what's important,* Mai had said. Right now, it seemed like the best advice.

Mai was firing out hand signs, men fanning out around him. The Jades had readied their bows, taking cover behind the wall protrusions that would keep them out of the immediate range if they were met by bowmen inside the room, while also giving them clear shots at the defenders. The rest of the Majat lined up along the walls, ready to rush into the room as soon as the way was clear.

"Just remember," Mai said quietly. "Don't try to fight any of them, no matter how tempted you feel. Stay behind us."

Kyth swallowed. "I will."

"Get ready, then."

Kyth summoned his force, extending a shield of protection against mind magic over their entire waiting group.

Mai raised his hand to give the signal when the doors flew apart on their own, as if pushed by a force blast from the inside. The Kaddim were accepting the challenge.

The Jades released their arrows in waves, met by a crackling sound from the inside as the defenders cut them down. The rest of the Majat disengaged from the walls, pouring inside like a noiseless flood, and Kyth rushed forward inside their ring, keeping close behind Mai.

It took all his concentration to maintain his protective shield at the sight that opened in front of him. Several dozen fighters moved with a speed and precision that seemed impossible, darting around in a deadly dance. Kyth thought he had seen the best before, but stepping into this battle made him realize he hadn't seen anything at all.

The Kaddim were dressed in white – a strange choice of color that contrasted their usual black-hooded robes. Kyth quickly realized the reason for this choice, undoubtedly dictated by the inside knowledge of the Majat style. In the room's vast space, it made the attackers and defenders sharply distinct from each other, making it easy for the fighters tell friend from foe. The Kaddim were clearly intending to press their advantage in skill and put each of the Majat warriors into the spotlight.

The Kaddim defenders were numerous, but the Cursed Dozen stood out from the rest, twelve pale ghosts, terrifying in their skill and unity and in the way they reacted so instantly to each other while being on the opposite sides of the room. As the first wave of the Majat rushed in, six of them dropped to the floor all at once, sliding underneath the attackers' arms like streaks of white wind, landing behind. If Mai hadn't spaced his men in two rows, this one move would have taken the enemies straight into the heart of the formation, leaving Kyth, in the center, defenseless against them. Even now, as the fight erupted, each of the Majat fighters was surrounded, the black and white flashing leaving any observer instantly disoriented. As Kyth paused for a very brief moment, two black-clad Majat fighters fell beside him, others stepping in to take their place.

Kyth shook off the stupor and rushed forward to where Mai's staff darted between his attackers like a streak of black light. He distanced himself from the fight, his eyes drawn to the square stone slab in its center, and the hooded figure by its side, in a space all the Kaddim fighters left clear, as if avoiding an invisible shield.

The Reincarnate stood in statue-like stillness, his outstretched palms pointing to the ground. *Drawing on the Destroyer's magic.* Kyth clenched his teeth. This was his target, and nothing else mattered until he took it down.

The spiders on his shoulder stirred to life, darting off his shoulder into the midst of the fighters. He heard a scream, and one of the white-robed figures fell back, taking down a Majat with him. He could see more furry shapes scurrying over the floor, but now that the enemies were alerted, it would take much more effort for the spiders to get through. He quivered as he realized how much scarcer the defenders around him were. He was running out of time.

In the heat of the melee he couldn't possibly hope to touch the stone slab, but he could clearly see its smooth surface, hewn into a perfect rectangle. He extended his senses, reaching inside the stone, through the humming force of the Destroyer's magic that infused it. Calling back his training with Ayalla, he imagined the meshwork of tiny lines holding together the elements of the stone. Without these lines, the stone would lose its shape, reduce to a pile of dust that could be blown away by a merest breath of air…

He distanced himself from the clashing and screams around him, so close that he could probably expect a hit of a blade any moment now. Calling forth the shiny lines holding the shape together, he blended them with the air, lifted them, ordered them to dissipate.

A hissing sound, like a sharply indrawn breath, wafted

through the chamber. The weapon clashing became uneven and he heard another scream beside him.

He opened his eyes.

The stone slab was no longer there. A rectangle of dust lay in its place, so fine that the sweeps of the fighter's blades disturbed and unsettled it. The Reincarnate stood in front of it, staring at it wide-eyed as it slowly lost shape, blowing around the chamber. The flow of magic ceased, the oppressive mind power no longer rolling through the room.

*One task down.* Kyth clenched his teeth as he glanced around the room. The rows of fighters seemed thinner on both sides, the floor strewn with bodies, gleaming with streaks of blood. The Majat ring around him had reduced to six men, fighting with the determined efficiency of the doomed.

Kyth gaped. He had expected the destruction of the stone to weaken the Kaddim, to disturb their unity and skill. The only effect he could sense right now was that they had stopped any attempts to use their mind magic to suppress anyone in this room, or outside their fortress. They were lending their entire skill to their fighting link, and Kyth could do nothing about it. He had to take down the Reincarnate.

Another Majat staggered and collapsed, the three Kaddim around him regrouping to circle around the man fighting at the front. *Mai.* Kyth recognized the staff.

His heart fell when he saw Kara leading the attack, the two Kaddim at her sides crowding on Mai, leaving him very little room to defend against her. His staff flew in perfect patterns, at least for the time being holding his own against the impossible odds, but there was no way he was going to be able to hold off for long.

Kyth clenched his blade. He knew it was stupid to try to rush them and be killed. Yet, he could also see how this focused attack on Mai was changing the layout of the battle, the remaining Majat rushing to Mai's aid, the Kaddim moving to intercept them. More arrows flew from the Jades lodged outside the doors in the hallway, only to be cut down by the defenders' swords.

One of the three Kaddim around Mai crowded on him, so close that their arms nearly touched. Kyth concentrated, choosing a perfect moment to send a spider toward them. Preoccupied with the battle, the Kaddim reacted too late. A shrill cry echoed through the chamber and the white-robed man collapsed. Kyth shifted his attention at once, targeting the attacker on Mai's other side. His screams reverberated through the chamber as two spiders latched onto his neck.

Mai's body unfolded like a whip, his staff descending in a perfect arch to hit the man in the chest. Kyth could tell that it was only a light wound, but it gave him a chance to call more spiders. And then, it was Mai and Kara, fighting one on one.

They were so perfectly matched that for a moment it was easy to forget that this was a fight to the death, and that right now Kara was an enemy, driven by an alien mind. They anticipated each other like no other, her swords flying around his staff, each blow met with a perfect counterpart. Yet, it was clear that Mai was already too exhausted. He staggered, falling back under the force of Kara's blows. She pressed on, kicking his staff away, crowding on him until he had nowhere to go. Her blade descended straight down, into the spot between his collarbones.

Time slowed as Kyth watched Mai's body fold backward, skidding to the floor at his feet. For a brief moment, it seemed like a nightmare that couldn't possibly be true. Then the reality caught up, reverberating in Kyth's gut with a feeling of hopelessness worse than anything he ever felt before. His eyes locked on Kara, her face just as calm as she stepped over Mai's body and raised her blades again, advancing on to him. *Too far gone.* He wanted to scream, to shake her back to her senses, but he knew that he had to run with all his might, for letting her reach him would mean certain death, would negate everything Mai sacrificed himself for.

Two Majat stepped into her path and the fighting resumed. Kyth snapped back to alertness. The whole fight just now took only a few seconds, yet he couldn't possibly spare even this much. Mai was dead. After the few remaining Majat fell, no one was going to protect him and enable him to complete the task. It was now or never.

He gathered all his force as he rushed at the hooded figure standing still in the center of the room.

The Reincarnate darted backward as he saw the menace, surprisingly quick yet not nearly fast enough for the enraged Kyth, rushing at him head-on. His coal-red eyes glowed as he watched Kyth's approach. Even without the stone, the power he emanated seemed enormous, making the air around him seem thick like a cocoon. Kyth reached through it and clasped the Reincarnate's face, drawing toward him, covering his lips in a kiss.

The Reincarnate's skin was burning hot, the taste of his magic gagging, like the reek of death itself.

Kyth forced away all these sensations as he gathered the entire power boiling within him, drawing on the elements, searching for the bonds that held the man's body together, calling forth the fire. Power crackled around them like a gathering storm as they stood there, locked in a lovers' embrace. *Fire. You're going to burn, bastard.* Kyth clasped on tighter, pulling the bony man into him, wondering if the power that raged within him was going to consume them both, now that they were so close they felt like one. He didn't care. He committed all of himself to this bond, not holding back anything at all.

His vision filled with two glowing red eyes, bulging and twisting out of their sockets. Steam rose off the Reincarnate's skin, burning his face and hands. He distanced himself from the pain, focusing on holding his power steady, drawing on the fabric of the world, disintegrating the body in his grasp through agony that seemed to last a lifetime.

A silent shudder shook the walls of the stronghold, and Kyth sensed it extend out, spreading over the sands and rocks of the desert like a tidal wave. Steam enfolded him, hotter than the pits of hell. He heard the Reincarnate's screams, and his own, briefly wondering if he had gone too far, if the power of the elements he had called on was going to obliterate his own body too, and all life around them.

His fingers clasping the Reincarnate's face fell through it, grasping the empty robe. He collapsed with it, his mind going dark.

40

# AFTERMATH

*Kara. I must save Kara.*

Kyth lifted his head. He had no idea how much time had passed. Weapon clanging in the room had ceased, the only sounds around him moans and gasps of the wounded and dying. *Is it over?* The thought seemed strangely detached, distant compared to the exhaustion he felt. Every muscle in his body screamed in protest as he gathered all his strength and pulled himself upright.

The room was in chaos, the floor strewn with bodies amidst the settling dust dissipating from the place where the stone slab used to be. Only three figures were still standing. Two black-clad Majat, looking grim and exhausted, as if barely able to maintain a grip on their weapons. And, opposite them, a white-robed figure. *Kara.*

A chill ran down Kyth's spine.

At first he had mistaken the black circle around her feet for a heap of black cloth. Then he realized these were spiders, crowded around her to form a dense ring. The nearest ones were raising up, poised to leap, yet something seemed to hold them back.

Kyth scrambled up to his feet.

"Kara!"

She turned, the expression in her widened eyes terrified, lost.

*Is she still one of them?* Kyth looked at the spiders again. If they were sure she was a Kaddim, they would have jumped her already during the time Kyth was unconscious and could not control them at all. The fact that they hesitated told him that there was still hope left, that she still had time. *The link. We must break the link.*

"Find Nimos!" he shouted. "You must be touching him when he dies!"

She looked down at the spider wall around her.

Kyth lowered his head, sending them a silent signal. The ring parted instantly, letting her through. He rushed after her, searching for the white-robed bodies scattered over the floor. Some of them were motionless, others writhing in death agony, deformed beyond recognition by the work of the spider poison. *Dear Shal Addim, please don't let Nimos be dead already.* But even if he was still alive, could they find him in time? Could they still recognize him?

He turned to the Majat. "Get all the Kaddim together, dead and dying. Pile them up. Quick!"

They obeyed, the Jades from the doorway joining them too, drawn by the urgency in his voice. Kyth staggered in exhaustion as he dragged the half-dissolved human flesh into one big pile, like a funeral pyre consumed by poison instead of a flame. Screams and moans echoed in the air. Kyth distanced himself from it.

"Found him," Kara said. "I think."

She was kneeling beside one of the bodies, the man's bony hands, still intact, reaching up to her. Kyth shivered. The disfigured face was impossible to recognize, except for the distinct eye shape. Black on black, without any whites, like the eyes of an owl. *Nimos. Thank Shal Addim.*

The dying man clasped Kara's wrists. She screamed as he made contact. Kyth rushed to her side, watching her fall forward, twisting and screaming, the black triangle of the Kaddim mark on her arm smoldering into her flesh. She writhed on the floor in a death embrace, Nimos's arms locked onto hers, as if intending to take her with him. *Can he?* Kyth knew that whatever happened, there was nothing he could possibly do except wait. He knelt beside her, wishing he could relieve her agony, feeling utterly powerless to do anything at all.

It seemed to take forever before the grasping hands of her enemy fell away, the black eyes rolling still, then imploding and dissolving like the rest of the flesh. As Kara collapsed beside him, the chamber receded into absolute stillness.

Kyth leaned over her, stroking the sweaty hair away from her face, grasping her hand, marred by a fresh burn spreading from the place where the Kaddim mark on her arm had been. Her skin blistered away, as if she had been holding her arm in the fire all this time. It must have hurt terribly, yet Kyth knew that the burning itself must have felt like nothing compared to the rest of her pain.

The surviving Majat gathered around them – four men, all that was left of the entire elite force of top Gems that had penetrated the Kaddim fortress under Mai's command.

Kyth looked at all the bodies scattered around the room. There was no way they could leave all the Majat here, but with so few of them left, all exhausted from the battle, they couldn't possibly do anything to retrieve them. Could they count on a rescue? Belatedly, Kyth thought of the battle that for all he knew might still be going on outside. Did Ayalla ever tell him what would happen to the Kaddim defenders after the Reincarnate was destroyed? Would they lose some of their power? Would the spiders Alder had out there be able to finish the job? He extended his senses to the outside of the fortress, but couldn't detect what was going on. Just in case, he relayed the signal through the spiders to the ones Alder still carried on his shoulder. *Come and get us. We need help.*

He started as Kara's hand closed around his with unexpected force. Her eyes fluttered open, focusing on him. She looked so drawn, exhausted, her hollow face pale gray. Yet, as he leaned closer, he detected no Kaddim magic from her.

He smiled, but she didn't give him any time to speak. Her violet eyes shone with urgency as she used him for support to pull herself upright.

"Mai," she said.

Kyth paused. Did she remember anything that happened? Did she recall striking Mai down? His eyes trailed to the slim, black-clad shape sprawled on the floor a few paces away, so limp it was hard to imagine that this body had once been capable of so much power. He fixed his gaze on it, afraid to turn back to Kara and see the expression on her face.

Kara clambered up to her feet and rushed to Mai's side, kneeling beside him and pulling off his mask.

Kyth swallowed the rising tears. Underneath the mask, Mai's face looked so calm, his blue-gray eyes staring unseeingly into the ceiling, his arms thrown out to the sides as if in his death he was striving to embrace the world. The hole at the base of his throat gaped like an ugly dark void, splotches of blood around it marring Mai's flawless white skin. Kyth clasped a hand to his mouth, trying to stifle his trembling lips. A grown man like him was not supposed to cry, but he couldn't possibly control it.

He was surprised at the way Kara showed no such reaction at all. She leaned down to peer into Mai's face, her expression focused and intent, as if the sight of his death didn't affect her in the least. *Has she gone mad? Did the Kaddim link damage her mind?* Kyth felt too exhausted to wonder. He knew that no matter how hard it seemed right now, it was his job to try and comfort her, ease her grief that he knew must be choking her now.

Just as he was about to step toward her, Kara raised her hands, her fingers hitting several spots at the top of Mai's chest. His body shuddered, his head rolling to the side to face the far wall.

Kyth stared. Kara was clearly mad. He should stop her, before she defaced Mai's body. He opened his mouth to protest, but her urgent look stopped him.

"Do you have any of the Keepers' elixir with you, Kyth?"

*The Keepers' elixir.* Kyth's eyes widened. She was speaking of a magical cure the Keepers possessed, a liquid that could heal deadly wounds in a manner of minutes. Did she mean...?

He opened and closed his mouth several times, struggling to find his voice. "Did you... Did you hit him with a harmless blow?"

Kara shook her head. "Not so harmless, as you can see. With his fighting skill, it was bloody hard to hit him right."

"Then he... he's not dead?"

She clenched her teeth. "Not if I can help it. The elixir! Do you have any?"

"No. But help is on the way. They should be here any minute." *I hope.*

She grasped a knife off Mai's belt and cut off a strip of her shirt, pressing it to his wound.

"Normally," she said, "I should've been able to revive him by now. I'm afraid my blade did too much damage. I don't want to try anything else until his wound is healed – if we can do it quickly enough."

Kyth struggled through the stupor that enfolded him. He felt so worn out that every movement felt like a chore.

"The spiders," he said. "They can help to keep him stable until help arrives."

"The spiders?" She frowned, her eyes darting to the furry creatures milling nearby. Kyth couldn't blame her for being afraid, after seeing the havoc they had caused in the enemies' ranks. Just a few weeks ago they scared him witless too, before he had embraced Ayalla's magic and learned to see them in a good light.

He gave the silent command, sending the spiders running, piling onto Mai's chest to cover the gaping wound. He lent them more of his magic, to make sure they were able to sustain the life force within, to keep it from seeping away. It wasn't the same healing as Ayalla was capable of, but for the moment it had to do.

Kara stared at them for a second, then rose to her

feet, turning to the other Majat, watching the scene warily.

"Take off everyone's masks," she ordered. "Quick!"

After a brief hesitation the men rushed into action, seeking out the black-clad bodies, pulling off masks. Kyth shivered, watching the faces of his fallen defenders coming out into view. Raishan, his eyes closed, his leaden-pale face caked with a crust of drying blood. Lance, his half-opened lips still holding the cocky grin that Kyth had always found so annoying. He stood, dumbfounded, watching Kara rush around them, his mind catching up too slowly as he realized what she was doing.

"Are you trying to revive all of them?" he asked.

She didn't even look at him as she nodded. "As many as I can. And by the way, if you're not too exhausted, you can feel free to help."

Kyth rushed to her side. He wasn't sure what he was supposed to do, so he focused on seeking out bodies, pulling masks off. The first man he touched actually stirred and opened his eyes. A Ruby, the one who had helped Kyth to scale the wall. He reached to feel the pulse, finding it steady.

"How did you do it?" he asked Kara.

She frowned, kneeling at the side of an unconscious man to hit some pressure points on his neck. "The Kaddim link. They used it to share my skill. But I realized fairly quickly that it actually worked both ways. They could control me, but I could control them too – to an extent."

*To an extent.* Kyth stared. "*Control* them?"

"Yes. I had to make it look believable that I was on their side, or they would've killed me on the spot and captured all my ability at once. The best I could do was turn their blows into non-fatal ones. It worked better for some than it did for others." Her eyes trailed to Mai, her expression telling Kyth more than words.

A faint echo carried through the passage behind them, footsteps rattling down the stone hallway. Kyth's heart raced with hope. Were they being rescued – or did the Kaddim survivors find them at last?

He had no time to wonder, because just then he sensed a tremor, the stones of the fortress around them shuddering, as if no longer certain of the forces that held them together. Kyth froze.

"I think this place is going to collapse," he said. "We must get out of here as soon as we can."

Kara glanced around. Kyth didn't need to see her frown to guess her thoughts. Only seven of them were standing, with over twenty on the ground. With the distance he knew they needed to cover to clear the fortress there was no way they were all going to make it out alive.

"I will hold it together," he said. "Let's hope I can give them enough time to rescue us."

He extended his magic, reaching all the way through the stones down to the far corners of the ancient structure. It felt just like Ayalla trained him, putting the dissipating stones back together. The task was vast, but the fact that he didn't actually need to reassemble anything, just to reinforce the existing bonds feeding on the power of the air made it seem more manageable. He was surprised he could even use his magic after being so exhausted, but once he settled into the feeling, it didn't take as much effort as he thought.

Afterwards, Kyth had been told that it took less than

fifteen minutes for the search party to reach them after he sent the signal to Adler. To him it felt like hours, the strain wearing him down until it became nearly impossible to bear. By the time he saw Seldon and Egey Bashi rushing into the chamber with Alder close behind, he could barely keep up straight. He leaned back against the wall, certain he would never be able to move again.

Seldon merged into the situation naturally, firing out orders to send men rushing, picking up the wounded, carrying them out of the chamber. Alder ran toward Kyth and knelt by his side.

"Get everyone out," Kyth said weakly. "The fortress is about to collapse. I'm holding it together."

Alder nodded briskly, then rushed away to speak to Seldon, who redoubled his efforts, men moving like a blur around him. Kyth watched them with half-vision, inwardly saying his goodbyes, certain he would never see them again. Then his foster brother appeared again, reaching over to pull him upright.

Kyth struggled to keep his balance, extending the last of his strength to the stones of the fortress.

"I... I can't, Alder. Can't move. Leave me."

"The hell I will." Alder picked him up, holding Kyth up to his massive chest, easily as if he was a child. As they rushed out of the chamber, Kyth heard a screech of the moving stones behind them. Then he passed out in his foster brother's arms.

# 41

# HEALING

The beams of the setting desert sun felt pleasantly warm after the death chill of the stone fortress. Kyth gave himself a moment to revel in their heat. Then, the memory of recent events forced his eyes open. He sat up and met Alder's concerned gaze.

"Where's everyone?" he asked weakly.

Alder pointed. "Over there. Magister Egey Bashi and Ellah are healing them, with Kara's help."

*Healing them.* Kyth steadied himself. His body felt sore, so weak that he nearly keeled over trying to pull himself to his feet. He was surprised he was still able to stand upright. Even without any physical wounds, the battle with the Kaddim left him so exhausted that he doubted he would ever feel right again.

He glanced at the Kaddim fortress looming just a short distance away. Surprisingly, it was still standing, but some of the outer buildings showed cracks and gaps as they were starting to collapse. It was only a matter of time, but fortunately, by Kyth's estimation, their current location, atop a rocky plateau at least half a mile away from the fortress, should be a safe place to be at when the whole structure went down. For all Kyth knew, it was going to sink into a giant hellhole that would swallow everything in that place. He couldn't care less, as long as he was certain everyone in their party was safe.

"What happened when you attacked the fortress from the front?" he asked.

Alder shrugged. "It wasn't much of a battle, really. I heard Aghat Seldon say that the Kaddim warriors probably believed it to be as much of a diversion as we did. Everyone knew the real battle was happening inside the fortress."

"Were there many casualties?"

"Some. But not nearly as many as I expected. Seldon had the Majat spearhead the attack, which really did make all the difference."

Kyth nodded. Despite lacking their top fighters, the Majat force Mai brought was enormous by any normal standards. Even the trained Kaddim warriors couldn't possibly withstand them for long.

"How did it end?" he asked.

"At some point," Alder said, "they all just fell down and... dissipated. Not sure how. Only the robes were left behind. Everyone felt so freaked out, even if the Majat didn't really show it."

Kyth nodded again. This was likely the moment when he killed the Reincarnate, whose magic had been holding those undead warriors together.

"When they fought," he said, "did you notice they were undead?"

"No." Alder looked puzzled. "We were all warned, of course, but I thought Egey Bashi had made a mistake. I would never have suspected these warriors were different from any of us, not until they actually dissipated."

Kyth sighed. It felt so good that the war was over, even though he knew it would take him a while to fully realize it.

The Majat stationed around the healing area parted as they saw Kyth and Alder approach. Kyth stepped inside their circle and looked around with widening eyes.

Most of the wounded men were sitting up, some looking dazed and weak, but very much alive. Ellah and Celana were rushing among them, along with the Majat volunteers who helped to cut bandages, distribute drinking water, and treat light wounds. Celana smiled when she saw Kyth and ran toward him, throwing her arms around his neck. Kyth held her, feeling lightheaded as he looked into her eyes.

"What you've done was enormous," she said. "You've won the war."

Kyth glanced around the area again. "I didn't do it alone."

She reached up and kissed him. "You know what I mean. You are a hero who will go down in chronicles and be worshipped for centuries to come."

He laughed and kissed her too, inhaling her fresh scent. "I hope not."

She brushed her cheek over his, an intimate gesture of affection that made his toes curl with pleasure. "I must go. Ellah and Magister Egey Bashi need my help."

"Of course. I'll go see Mai."

She frowned and briefly glanced away.

Kyth's eyes narrowed. "He is all right, isn't he?"

Her gaze wavered. "The Diamonds suffered the

most. As I understand, not only because the Kaddim had focused all their effort on targeting them first, but because with their skill it was very hard for Kara to direct blows against them that would not harm them too much."

Kyth thought back to the occasion when Mai had to do the same thing to Kara to save her life. That time it worked well, though. Wasn't it going to be the same now?

"We spent a lot of time treating their wounds," Celana said. "Thanks to Magister Egey Bashi's magical remedies, most of them are out of danger and will recover well. But Aghat Mai..." She averted her eyes.

Kyth's skin prickled as he followed her gaze to the huddled group of people at the back of the healing area, eerily quiet amidst the general bustle.

"I have to go there now," he said.

She nodded and stepped away.

Mai lay flat on his back, as still as he had been back in the Kaddim's chamber. His hollow cheeks and creamy white skin made him look nearly transparent, ghostly. His eyes were pressed shut, on their own or through the healers' effort, Kyth wasn't sure. It seemed only partially comforting that the wound at his throat had now closed, leaving only a very small scar behind.

Kyth stood still for a moment, watching Egey Bashi's grim look as the Keeper put a small bottle carefully into a special pocket of his medicine bag. The healing elixir. Kyth tried to convince himself that the sight of this bottle should make him feel reassured. This elixir worked only on living flesh. If the Keeper had used it on Mai and the wound had closed, Mai should be all right, shouldn't he? He clung to the thought, refusing to acknowledge the way everyone here sat so eerily silent, as if attending a wake.

When Kyth stepped forward and knelt at Mai's side, Kara, raised her face to him. Her frozen expression made his heart skip a beat.

It took her a moment to recompose before she spoke. "It isn't working."

Kyth swallowed to steady his voice. "It will. Just give him time."

She shook her head. "It was supposed to work. I *learned* this blow, Mai taught me himself. He also showed me the pinch on the pressure points used to revive the victim afterwards. I tried it, but…"

Kyth touched Mai's wrist, finding the weak, uneven pulse that seemed as if it was about to fade. Mai's skin felt very cold. He rubbed it tentatively, wondering if any of the magic he learned could possibly help Mai to warm up. His mind grasped to the tiniest shreds of logic, trying and failing to find a way out. *The blow. The revival pinch.* He had seen it done before, when Mai had revived Kara after making their Guild believe she was dead. Back then, Raishan tried to do it too, and failed. Could it be that if someone else, not Kara, tried it now, it would work?

It didn't seem likely, but they couldn't just give up, could they?

"This blow," he said. "There must be someone else among the Majat who learned it too."

"Yes, all Diamonds learn it at some point. I already asked all of them. None of them are strong enough to try it yet, but they all confirmed I did it right. Nobody knows what else to do."

"How about Seldon?"

"Seldon?"

"He's a Diamond, isn't he?"

She hesitated. "Yes, but he retired, years ago. His skill is not what it used to be."

"Still, I assume he learned the blow, did he?"

Her gaze wavered. "He might have, even though I'm not sure he was still active when the blow was invented. I don't think that..."

"Is there any harm in asking?"

"I suppose not."

Kyth rose to his feet. "Wait here. I'll bring him."

It seemed as if she was about to protest, but she bit back her comment, her helpless look echoing with a hollowness in his chest. He didn't feel strong enough to handle this now, but he couldn't possibly let her down.

Kyth found Seldon on the other side of the camp, giving orders. Men obeyed him left and right, including the Cha'idi and the Golden Lion warriors rushing around together with the Majat, loading the seriously wounded onto stretchers to carry them back to camp. When Kyth approached, Seldon stopped his activity, watching him with a mix of apprehension and curiosity. Kyth was surprised when Seldon briefly inclined his head, pressing his fist to his chest in a Majat salute.

"Your Royal Highness. Allow me to congratulate you on a brilliant victory."

"Thank you, Aghat Seldon," Kyth said. "We all played our parts. Including yours, which gave us a chance to defeat their leaders. Well done."

Seldon's smile in response seemed even more unexpected. Up until now, Kyth never thought he would be in a position to praise a Diamond for a well fought battle – or to see his praise appreciated.

"I came to ask you for help, Aghat Seldon," he said. "Can you please come with me?"

Seldon nodded, then turned away briefly to give some quick orders that sent his subordinates into a new flurry of activity. He didn't ask any questions as he followed Kyth, demonstrating beyond words how deep a trust Kyth had earned by playing his part in the battle. Well, if this kind of a trust could help save a friend's life, it was definitely worth it.

He led Seldon to the place where Kara still sat, holding Mai's hand. Wordlessly, Seldon knelt by her side. Kyth could tell by the way his lips pressed together briefly as he looked down at the outstretched body that Mai's condition affected him deeply.

"I'm not sure I can do anything," Seldon said.

Kyth glanced at Kara, but she didn't even look up, or show any other reaction to these words. Still, Kyth simply refused to give up.

"I understand," he said, "that Kara tried to spare Mai's life by hitting him with a special blow that is supposed to be non-fatal. She's having trouble reviving him. I know you learned this blow too, Aghat Seldon. Perhaps you could help?"

Seldon frowned as he leaned closer and examined the small scar at the base of Mai's neck. Then he turned to Kara. "Was it Viper's Kiss you used?"

It took Kara a moment to answer, as if she was having trouble composing herself.

"I tried," she said. "But he was defending against three of us at the time. With the kind of fight he put up, there was no way in hell I could do it right."

Seldon looked calm and absorbed, as if they were discussing a scholarly matter. "Show me exactly at which angle the blade went in, and how deep."

Again, she paused briefly before taking out a saber and demonstrating. Kyth's heart quivered as he watched her detached expression.

Seldon observed Kara's movements carefully, then took the blade and measured the distance with his palms, swinging it over Mai several times, as if about to hit him again. Kyth resisted the urge to look away as they wielded such a sharp blade so close to a sick man. At some point he felt like interfering, but Kara's calm look reassured him.

Finally Seldon put the blade down and did more measurements on Mai's chest.

"I was around when Aghat Mai invented that blow," he said. "Before formalizing it, our Guildmaster assigned me to work through it with him to figure out all the possible pitfalls. It is not commonly known that we found a number of scenarios which could make this blow just as fatal as any other. You've come close to one of them, I'm afraid."

"How close?" A strain in Kara's voice showed Kyth she was on the verge of a breakdown. He didn't blame her. With everything she had gone through, anyone else would have collapsed a long time ago.

"Very close," Seldon said. "However, before giving up, I can think of one or two things we could try." He grasped the collar of Mai's shirt and ripped it open, exposing his chest. His hands flew so fast that Kyth couldn't follow them at all, hitting several points with the force that seemed strong enough to break ribs.

Mai gasped and opened his eyes.

Kara clasped both hands over her mouth, as if stifling a sob. Kyth felt a lump rise in his throat.

A smile creased Seldon's lips. Then he raised his hand and hit again, forcing Mai to double over, choking.

"Bloody hell, Aghat Seldon," Mai rasped. "What do you think you're doing?"

Seldon sat back on his heels, his smile spreading into a wide, relieved grin. Kara's hands, still covering her mouth, trembled and Kyth saw tears standing in her eyes.

Mai moved with visible difficulty as he turned his head. His eyes widened as he focused on Kyth, then on Kara, his gaze stirring with such relief that Kyth felt the tingle of rising tears again.

Kara picked up Mai's hand, pressing it to her cheek as she briefly closed her eyes.

Mai watched her, gentle as if she was the one that needed care. He moved his head with difficulty and winced, relaxing back into his bedroll. His eyes fixed on Kyth. "The Kaddim?"

"We won," Kyth said. "And most of your men are alive. Kara saved them all."

Mai briefly closed his eyes. He still looked very pale. His shaky hand reached up to stroke Kara's hair. She leaned into his palm, and Kyth saw a tear roll down her face.

"Don't try to move just yet," Seldon warned. "You need time, Aghat Mai. This Viper's Kiss was too damned close."

Mai's lips twitched. "Do I look like I'm going anywhere?"

"I'll fetch Magister Egey Bashi." Seldon rose and strode off.

Mai's eyes trailed after him, then turned to Kyth. "You'll have to tell me what happened."

"I will, when you're better." Kyth stood up. "For now, I think I'll, um, leave the two of you alone."

Mai opened his mouth to respond, but just then, a roll of thunder from down the valley forced Kyth to spin around.

The Kaddim fortress was collapsing, its walls and towers folding onto each other like an elaborate house of cards. Stones boomed as they clashed and rained to the ground, sifting, dissolving into dust, raising clouds of sand in their wake. A curtain of dust rose into the air, thickening until it hid everything from sight.

The Kaddim magic, gone. The Kaddim cult falling back into the underworld that had spawned it.

It took a while for the sounds to cease, for gusts of wind to blow the sand around, shifting it among the rising dunes. When it settled, nothing in the desert reminded them of the fortress that stood there, just a short while ago.

Mai lifted up on his elbow, watching, with Kara supporting him.

"I'll be damned," he said.

Kyth smiled. It felt good to hear Mai's swearing, to know that things were going to return to normal again. He turned and strode away.

Ellah, Alder, and Celana were sitting together at the edge of the camp, watching him approach. Kyth felt exhausted but so relieved as he lowered to the ground by their side. After a moment, Celana huddled closer and leaned her head on his shoulder. He put an arm around her, feeling happy and carefree like he hadn't been in a very long time.

# 42
# AMENDS

Kara couldn't bring herself to let go of Mai's hand. She simply couldn't find enough strength to break the connection, to stop feeling the warmth of his fingers as they closed over hers carefully, as if handling a precious and fragile piece. Numb, she watched Egey Bashi feel Mai's pulse, then rub some ointment into his temples and measure out drops of different potions into a drinking cup. Mai had to sit up to take the medicine, and she could see how much difficulty it caused him to move. *I did this. I nearly killed him.*

The numbness remained as Egey Bashi looked over her own forearm, still harboring a bad burn where the Kaddim mark had been. It hurt, the ointments he rubbed into her skin bringing only partial relief, but for once she welcomed the pain, a feeling that grounded her in reality, slowly settling in the awareness that the war was truly over.

The emotions that overwhelmed her were too enormous for her mind to enfold, far too much to deal with in such a short amount of time. Relief came first among them, and she did her best to cling to it, reminding herself again and again that her Kaddim link was truly gone, that Mai was alive and expected to make a full recovery, that despite the way the Kaddim had twisted her mind she managed to avoid killing any of her comrades. She forced away the memories of what it felt like, a unity of mind with eleven men she loathed, the fear that every time she managed to twist their movements as they went for the kill they were going to discover what she was doing and ruin all her plans.

When, at the onset of the battle, she had made her first attempts to resist and control them, the pain that came with each of those blows had been disabling. Yet, she still had to keep fighting to maintain the pretense, to make sure the Kaddim didn't spin out of her control. She tried to tell herself that the emptiness she was feeling now was the result of the trauma, that it was going to pass, but deep inside, she couldn't bring herself to believe it. Mai nearly died just now, all because of her. And now that the fight was over, their time together was going to come to an end. To marry the heir to the Shayil Yaran throne he'd first need to renounce his Majat ties, an action that would also bring about his own death warrant. She couldn't possibly allow this to happen. The best she could do was let him go as soon as possible. Except that she simply couldn't do it, not at all. As a warrior, she wasn't supposed to hesitate when doing the right thing. The difficulty she was having right now was yet another indication that she was simply too damaged to ever be herself.

After a while she realized that everyone else was gone, and that Mai had been watching her for quite some time. A smile was playing on his lips, but she also saw the concern behind it. He could understand her like no other. How was she ever going to explain any of her feelings to him?

He pulled himself upright to sit next to her, blood draining from his face from the effort. He should be resting now, but as she opened her mouth to tell him that, his look stopped her.

"Tell me what's on your mind," he said.

She knew how impossible it was to dodge the question. Mai could see into her soul. It was useless to lie to him, or try any pretense.

"It was too close," she said

He patted her arm and she leaned against his shoulder, briefly closing her eyes as she reveled in his closeness. She knew he was weaker than her right now, that she shouldn't be seeking comfort from him, but she just couldn't resist burying her face in his chest, inhaling his scent. Just a short while ago she thought she would never be able to do this again. Was there any harm in pretending, even for a moment, that this was how things were going to be from now on?

"I nearly killed you," she said. "I nearly killed everyone."

He shook his head. "Not you. The Kaddim. And now they're all dead."

"Thanks to you and Kyth."

"Thanks to Kyth. All I did, along with the others, was buy him the time."

*By throwing yourself on my sword.* The image of their last fight just wouldn't leave her mind, the knowledge that she had no choice but to strike Mai down and make everyone believe he was dead, the awareness that with his fighting skill she would never be able to do it right.

"Incidentally," Mai said, "it's over, if you haven't noticed. The Kaddim cult is gone. And, thanks to you, we're all alive to see it. So, you should really take at least a brief moment to congratulate yourself. Without you guiding the Kaddim's hands, the fight would have gone very differently."

*Congratulate yourself.* Of course he would be thinking this way. He couldn't possibly know what it felt like, having her mind and body dominated, twisted into destroying everything she loved. To go on with her life, she had to deal with this memory, overcome it, but for now she felt content just sitting next to him. *Alive.* They were both alive, her Kaddim link was gone, the war was over. Why couldn't she just focus on that?

She shifted in his embrace, so that she could see his face as he sat there, staring at the place where the Kaddim fortress had been. *Gone, as if it's never been here at all. Dear Shal Addim.*

She sensed Mai sit up straight and lifted her head to see Raishan and Lance walking toward them.

They both looked unscathed, moving with their usual grace and ease, as if they hadn't faced death just a few hours ago. Watching their smiles as they approached and lowered to the ground by their side, she thought back to the way she had twisted the blows when the Kaddim they had been fighting tried to strike them down. It had been easy to make the blow to the head Lance received look convincing – and she was sure it still hurt, despite all the treatments. It had been more tricky with Raishan, tilting the blade poised to pierce his heart into slicing the flesh over the ribs instead, targeting the pressure point that sent him to the floor in a death-like coma, making his Kaddim opponent believe he was dead. It wasn't a blow one could learn from a book, but it proved to be a very useful one when conjured on the spot. Perhaps the Majat could start teaching it to their trainees one day?

She knew she hadn't been so lucky with all the Majat. Yet, she found at least marginal comfort in her certainty that she did everything she possibly could.

Raishan's smile widened as he looked at Kara. She blinked. How could he still look at her this way after facing her in battle as an enemy?

"I understand we have you to thank for saving all our lives, Aghat Kara," he said.

She swallowed, her eyes sliding over the bruise that darkened the side of Lance's face. The worst of it was probably be hidden by the hair. It couldn't possibly have felt good. "I wish I could've done better."

"I don't think anyone in your place could've done nearly as well," Lance said.

She shook her head. "If it wasn't for Aghat Seldon's knowledge, Mai wouldn't even be sitting here right now."

Raishan grinned. "Who could have possibly thought that we'd end up feeling so fortunate that Seldon's on our force?"

Kara heaved a sigh. She knew they understood what she meant, even if they chose to maintain this light tone, instead of focusing on the graveness of what they had all lived through. Perhaps she too should take this conversation just a little bit less seriously.

She smiled. "I am just so glad to see you all alive." And this was the truth, the only one that mattered.

• • •

Sunset approached too fast, the biting chill of the mountain wind stripping away the daytime desert heat. The warriors departed in small groups, mounted and on foot, making way to their base camp. Kara felt a new wave of worry as she watched the preparations. Was Mai strong enough to travel yet? Were the rest of the warriors going to recover fully? She used a moment when Mai and Raishan drifted into a conversation to slip off, looking for Egey Bashi.

The Keeper was sitting at the edge of the camp, deep in conversation with Ellah and Kyth. Lady Celana sat beside the Prince, and Kara noted how she was snuggling up to him, and how Kyth kept an arm around her, a display of affection she had never seen in him since the time they broke up. She didn't realize things between Kyth and Celana had progressed so far, but now she felt an unexpected surge of relief as she watched them side by side. At least she no longer had to feel guilty on his account.

She stood in indecision, wondering if she should approach them, break up the conversation, when a rustle of footsteps behind alerted her to someone's approach. She spun around and came face to face with Jamal.

She watched him, with no idea what to expect. During their march, before the battle, they had sunk into formal roles warranted by the proper chain of command, but while Jamal hadn't given her any trouble when it came to following orders, they had a long way to go in developing a warm relationship, let alone feeling like kin. His presence always made her feel guarded. And now, when she felt so wiped out from the aftermath of the battle, she didn't know if she had the strength to face him at all.

She tried to imagine herself through Jamal's eyes right now, still wearing the bloodstained Kaddim robes, disheveled and dirty, swaying with exhaustion that made it difficult even to keep upright. She didn't think this kind of a look befitted a queen. Standing in front of Jamal, she suddenly realized with certainty that becoming a queen had been a mistake for her, no matter what everyone said about the destiny she was meant to fulfill. Now that the war was over, she simply couldn't see herself as a ruler at all.

She looked closer, realizing that Jamal didn't seem all that well himself. The battle outside the fortress had gone better than they feared, but it was definitely a taxing one and Jamal and his men had been right in the middle of it.

"How did the Golden Lions do?" she asked.

Jamal shrugged. "As well as the others, I think. A few casualties, some wounded. The Majat took the main hit, though. We offered to go side by side, but your Aghat Seldon pretty much insisted they spearhead the attack."

*Your Aghat Seldon.* The distancing wording didn't escape her. In Shayil Yara, the Majat would always be seen as outsiders, and whatever else she was, she was one of the Majat too. The Guild was her home – except that now that her lineage was discovered, she wasn't welcome there anymore.

"I'm glad you are all right," she said.

His gaze softened. "I heard what you did. If it wasn't for your strength, we would have lost, wouldn't we?"

Her eyes widened. This was the last thing she expected him to say. "Did you also hear how I nearly became the tool of everyone's destruction?"

He shook his head. "That wasn't you. It was the enemy, using you. I know it must have been very hard. The way you handled it makes you a hero to our people, worthy of all the legends they sing in your name. I just wanted you to know that."

She continued to stare. Illogically, his simple words brought tears to her eyes. She didn't believe crying like this was possible for her anymore, not after years of Majat training, yet as she stood in front of him, tears poured down her cheeks, searing hot like the Reincarnate's touch.

"When Aunt Rajmella found out who you were," Jamal said, "I felt resentful, at first. I wasn't ready for a family reunion, for the knowledge that the mythical sister I was supposed to have had turned up in the flesh. I wanted you gone. I am ashamed of the way I behaved. I'm happy that you are now in my life. No matter what happens, you can always count on having a loving brother."

She wiped her eyes with both hands, but the tears just kept coming, pouring anew when he stepped forward and pulled her into his arms.

As she snuggled against him, she tried to tell herself that this new family she was finding in him could replace her old one, give her a new home instead of the one she was losing forever. The thought was comforting, but she also knew, deep in her heart, that it would never be enough.

After Jamal left, she stood still for a while, composing herself, finding the strength to move again. She nearly forgot her original purpose, to talk to Egey Bashi. By now, walking back to the base camp was beginning to sound unrealistic. She glanced at the group again, noting that Ellah and Celana had departed, and Kyth and Egey Bashi were sitting by themselves.

She was just about to approach them when Kyth lifted his head and saw her. He smiled and jumped up to his feet, walking up to her.

Once again, Kara was amazed at the change in him. After his return from the Forestlands, she didn't have a chance to see him up close – not in a situation when they could just stand and look at each other, like now. She saw the new confidence in Kyth's posture, the inner balance, the power he emanated. Everything that happened at Ayalla's, and afterwards, had made him a man, and seeing him like this brought a smile to her lips.

"You were amazing," she said. "I cannot even think of words that could express my admiration, and gratitude for what you did. But I expect, you're hearing it from everyone, aren't you?"

He smiled. "Yes, whether or not it's deserved. But they also talk about you a lot. Surely you must know this too."

She sighed. However much credit they were giving her, what she did wasn't the same as what Kyth was able to accomplish. It wasn't even on the same scale. But talking about it was useless. There were no possible words that could measure up to the enormity of it.

"You seem happy," she said.

A faint color lit up Kyth's cheeks. "I am. Celana and I..." He paused, as if unsure how she would react.

She reached forward to pat his shoulder. Just a short while ago, this kind of a touch would have been unsettling and awkward, just by the reaction it caused

in him. But now, it felt natural, friendly and easygoing
the way it was meant to be. "I'm so glad for you." She
grinned. "If only because now I can finally stop feeling
guilty."

Kyth grinned too. "You do tend to feel guilty a lot,
don't you?"

"Do I?" She felt genuinely surprised. She never
thought of herself this way. But she supposed there
was some truth to it. By anyone's standards, her
participation in the battle did have a positive effect on
their victory – yet all she could think about right now
was how she nearly killed everyone. She resolved to
become more positive from now on.

"How's Mai?" Kyth asked.

Kara glanced toward the place where she left the
Diamonds, deep in a conversation. Mai was lying
down now, with Raishan and Lance sitting next to him
talking to each other. The sight made her heart quiver
with worry. "He's still very weak. In fact, I was going to
ask Magister Egey Bashi if he's even strong enough to
travel back to the base camp."

Kyth looked too. "I'm sure Mai will recover. But of
course, if you are worried, it's reason enough not to
travel at all. Should I ask Aghat Seldon to set up camp
here?"

She bit back her surprise, suddenly realizing that
this easy solution was indeed within reach. It was just
that if she was the one doing the asking, Seldon would
probably break into a long chain of reasoning that
would ultimately preclude her from having her way.
But in Kyth's new, mature role, she could easily believe
that it would take no more than a simple request from
him for Seldon to comply.

"Let's see what Egey Bashi says." She started to move toward the Keeper, but Kyth stopped her with a hand on her arm.

"Are you all right?" he asked.

She looked up at him. "Yes. Why?"

"You seem... unsettled."

She blinked. Suddenly the tears she thought she had controlled welled in her eyes again. She turned away abruptly, but it was too late to hide.

"It's Mai, isn't it?" Kyth asked.

She slowly looked back at him. "It's... the whole situation, I guess. Nothing important. I'm sure everything will seem much better after a good rest."

She tried to step past him, but Kyth's hand held her in place.

"You're going to be able to marry him now, right?"

Her lips trembled.

Kyth frowned, peering into her face. "Don't tell me anyone can stop you."

She heaved a breath. "Look. I know it's hard for an outsider to understand the Majat rules."

Kyth looked at her in disbelief. "I thought the Guildmaster has absolute power – or at least very nearly so."

"He does, as long as he follows the Code."

"And?"

She shrugged. "You know how important it is for the Majat to maintain full political neutrality – at least officially. Violating this rule would sway the Guild's standing and undermine all the trust people have in the Majat Warriors. How do you think it would look to everyone if Mai put himself above the rules and married Shayil Yaran royalty?"

"Last time I checked, he seemed pretty determined. Is there anyone at your Guild who could stop him?"

Kara swallowed, ignoring the sinking feeling in her chest as she thought through the possibilities. "No one in the Majat Guild is above the Code – not even the Guildmaster. If Mai as much as steps the wrong way, the senior Diamonds will remove him from command. Or worse."

"Just like that?"

"You do remember what happened to the previous Guildmaster, do you?"

Kyth hesitated. "Actually, I never learned what happened to him in the end, not really."

"Exactly."

"But–"

She shook her head. "I know it seems unfair to you, Kyth, but that's the way it is, unfortunately. Besides, now's not the time to talk about it. Mai still needs to recover. Nothing is nearly as important for me as knowing that he is alive and well."

"He'll never be well without you, and you know it."

She heaved a sigh. Somehow, the sight of Kyth's anger made it easier to bear her own grief over this situation. She knew she would probably feel differently later on, but for now she was willing to take it.

"It's useless to dwell on something that cannot happen," she said.

Kyth held her gaze. "Perhaps. But I am finding it hard to believe that after everything you both did, your Guild would hold you to a bloody technicality."

She raised her eyes to him. The change in him was striking. Just a short time ago, she would never consider discussing something like this with him. And now, everything they said came naturally, with no effort at all. "It's not a technicality, Kyth. If he was allowed to marry a queen, all the Majat values would go to hell."

Kyth shook his head. "It doesn't have to be this way. Rules are made to be broken. Personally, I would be very disappointed if things didn't work out the way you want."

*The way I want.* She tried not think about it too much as she stepped forward and hugged Kyth, planting a quick kiss on his cheek.

"I am so proud of the way you've become," she said quietly. "And, thank you. For everything."

## 43

# CHANGE OF RULE

The crowds lining the streets of Tahr Abad chanted Kara's name, throwing flowers into her path as she rode through the city at the head of the Golden Lions, with Jamal by her side. At any other time she would have taken pride in the fact that her people were greeting her return so fervently, but after everything that happened she couldn't find it in herself to rejoice. She felt like a cave dweller, her biggest desire right now to crawl into a deep dark hole and never come out again. This state of mind was so unusual for her. Was this prolonged battle fatigue? Or did the Kaddim link damage her mind beyond repair?

Rajmella and Nelimah waited for them on the palace doorsteps, radiant in their royal robes, surrounded by a select few of their favorite consorts. Kara was surprised at the relief she felt when she saw their welcoming smiles. Like it or not, these women and Jamal were her only family now, and they had previously gotten off to a very bad start. She welcomed the opportunity to put the past behind them and get to know their better sides.

Rajmella enfolded her in a strong embrace, perhaps a bit showy but also seemingly heartfelt. Kara returned it, trying to tell herself that this was what she wanted, that she was content with being accepted as their Queen. Nelimah hugged her too, far more tentative as the Princess kept eyeing the array of blades adorning Kara's formal outfit. But when Mai and the Diamonds of his suite dismounted and strode up to the steps to greet the royal family, Kara saw Nelimah's cheeks light up with color as she spotted Lance among them. Kara felt a little bit better. At least the impression the Majat left in this palace wasn't all bad.

"I need to talk to you," Kara said to Rajmella, watching Jamal and Nelimah exchange hugs and greetings.

The former Queen's shoulders tensed instantly. "What about?"

Kara let out a sigh. There seemed to be no need to drag it out. "This." She knelt in front of Rajmella, then slipped off her bracelets of station and handed them to the older woman. "I am convinced, now more than ever, that these belong to you. You make a far better Queen."

Rajmella's mouth fell open. Around them, all sounds on the plaza died out, all the warriors, citizens, and inhabitants of the palace watching them dumbfounded. For one frightening moment, Kara feared that Rajmella would refuse, that her response would make this change of command impossible to enforce. She held her aunt's gaze, summoning all her strength to appear confident and easy, as if she was giving away a mere trinket for the older woman to adorn herself with.

"Are you sure?" Rajmella said quietly.

"Yes."

"Why?"

"I may have been born for this," Kara said, "but I wasn't raised the right way. I am a warrior. My calling is for battle, not for ruling a peaceful kingdom. Besides," she added, "from everything I've heard, you've been doing a great job as the Queen."

The plaza was deadly quiet now, all the warriors and citizens standing still, staring at the royal group. Just a short while ago, they had all been chanting Kara's name, and now they had no idea what to do as they watched the two women up on the palace steps having a quiet conversation.

"The story of Aljahara," Kara said, "is a beautiful legend that has been alive for nearly two decades. I don't think, with my Majat training, I could possibly do it justice. Sometimes keeping the legend alive is more important than the truth."

Rajmella smiled. "You may be wrong, niece. For certain, you are not giving yourself enough credit as a politician."

*A politician.* Kara had learned politics all right. All Diamonds were groomed for command, for potential situations when they might be asked to overthrow kings and change the course of history. It just wasn't the right politics she learned, not the kind that could maintain peace and prosperity in the land where people had known so little trouble up to now.

She rose and turned to the crowd, holding up her hand to signal that she was about to speak – an unnecessary gesture since everyone within earshot was already so quiet that even the gusts of the gentle breeze rattled like a thunderstorm.

"People of Shayil Yara," she said. "I ask you to hear me out. For a while, we all believed that I am the rightful Queen of your country, but I was able to determine that it was a mistake. Princess Aljahara never existed. I am not her. Today, I am glad to have this chance to restore your rightful Queen to you, the woman who ruled your country justly and wisely for the last two decades. Hail, Queen Rajmella!"

She turned and bowed, low and elaborate, folding her hands in proper Shayil Yaran fashion.

At Jamal's signal the Golden Lions saluted with their swords.

The roar that rose over the plaza this time seemed much more chaotic, no longer a chant, but a disorderly choir that swept through like a storm, swallowing everything in sight. Kara waited it out until the words floating over the crowd took shape, folded into a chant that seemed more recognizable. *Rajmella, Rajmella, Rajmella...* It wasn't as uniform as the chanting of her name had been, but she was sure it would get there in time.

She slipped into the back of the royal group until she was certain she could no longer be seen from the plaza, and rushed up the palace steps.

It was over. The battle was finished, all her duties were done. All she wanted now was to find a quiet place and lie down, so that she wouldn't have to talk to anyone at all.

Kara didn't make it very far when she heard a rustle of swift steps over the marble. She considered speeding up, but quickly decided against it. However little she felt like company right now, she knew she would have to face questions. Perhaps it was best to get this over with.

Her resolve weakened when she saw Mai rushing toward her. He came from a run to a perfect standstill in an instant move that could be achieved only with the top Majat training, his blue-gray eyes peering into her face.

"What did you just do?" he asked.

She briefly lowered her gaze. "I thought it was pretty self-evident, wasn't it?"

"Yes. But why?"

She sighed. "Because I think Rajmella would do a far better job at it."

He shook his head. "This is by far not a certainty."

"I don't want to be the Queen."

"You haven't really tried."

"I tried enough." She met his eyes, trying to recall the resolve she felt just a short time ago. It was much easier to tell herself that she could live without him when she didn't face him like this, when he didn't stand so close.

He reached forward and took her hand.

*Great. Now he will see me cry.* She averted her eyes. "Don't."

"Why?" he asked quietly.

She heaved another sigh, trying to control her twitching lips. "Isn't it bloody obvious?"

"Not really, no."

"There is no way for us to be together. The Majat would never allow it."

He stepped closer. "I love you. Now that the war is over, we can finally be together without the fear of the Kaddim looking over our shoulders. We are finally safe. Do you think I care about rules?"

"But the Guild…"

Mai shrugged. "What could they possibly do to us?"

She hesitated. She could think of so many things the Guild could do to them. In the very least, if Mai disobeyed the Code, he would become an outcast. The Guild likely wouldn't stop until they were both dead. They would have to run forever.

"You can't give up your life," she said. "Not for this."

"Why not?"

She hesitated. It was so hard to think straight when he was standing so close. "We were all trained to put our duty first."

"I've done my duty," Mai said. "We have defeated our archenemy, the one who threatened to destroy us for centuries. All that's left now is dealing with mundane politics and day-to-day operations. The Guild has plenty of capable men to manage a job like this."

She shook her head. She didn't want to cling to this hope, but at least for now she also didn't have the energy to continue this argument.

"Do you still want to marry me?" Mai said.

She frowned. "Is this a trick question?"

"No."

"Yes, I do." She was surprised to see his shoulders sag briefly, as if her answer relieved a serious concern. It seemed odd, but she didn't have the strength to wonder. It was useless to dwell on the possibility too long. Sooner or later, she was going to have to give him up, even if for the moment the Majat Guild may be willing to look the other way.

"If you mean it," Mai said, "perhaps you can agree not to push me away, at least for now?"

"To what end?"

"In the very least, we are yet to hear the Guild's

formal decision on the possibility of our marriage."

Kara's lips trembled. "Isn't it obvious what the decision would be? I am a crown princess, for Shal Addim's sake. I wish I could renounce my bloodlines, but I cannot possibly do that, can I?"

"Would you have wanted to if you could?"

Again, his question struck her as odd. Suddenly she felt so tired that even standing up straight seemed like too much of an effort.

"Can't you just let me go?" she asked.

"Not unless you want me to."

Her eyes filled with tears. Why was he making it so hard?

He kept his eyes on her as he raised her hand to his lips and kissed it. She shivered. How could he touch only her hand, yet make her entire body feel so affected?

"Perhaps," he said, "we can at least postpone the rest of this conversation? You can always send me away later, if you really want to. Right now, though, I'm dying for a bath, aren't you?"

*A bath.* There couldn't be any harm in taking a bath just now, even if she knew exactly what would happen if they found themselves together without any clothes. Thinking of it made her insides clench, a sweet weakness spreading over her body.

"All right," she said.

Mai grinned. "Good. Let's go find your quarters then."

"My quarters?"

"Your royal apartment. Rajmella's consorts were kind enough to tell me where it is."

•••

The royal apartment Rajmella had provided for Kara was as large and luxurious as the one offered to Mai before, when they had first arrived at the palace. It seemed a waste to use only a small part of it, a bedroom that opened into a large bath chamber with its own pool, but at the moment they hardly needed anything else. Well, perhaps food, at some point, but this point seemed distant and vague in Kara's mind as she sank into Mai's arms.

This was goodbye, she was telling herself. It had to be, for there was no way this could ever continue beyond these few last days they had, before the Majat left the palace forever to return to the Guild. Yet, at the moment she felt too exhausted to dwell on the thought, grateful for whatever time they had, determined to make the most of it.

At some point during the evening they heard a knock on the door. Kara didn't feel like getting up, so Mai threw on a robe and disappeared, to return moments later with a large tray of food and some clothes draped over his shoulder. He grinned as he sat the food down on a small table at the foot of the bed and lay out the clothes on a chair at the other end of the room.

"Queen Rajmella asked for an audience whenever you're up to it," he said. "She left a man at the door to wait for your response."

*An audience.* Perhaps Rajmella's intention with this request was to show her how things were going to be for Kara from now on? The fact that she had put it in such a respectful way suggested that Kara was going to be treated according to her station at this court, even if all the prospects of a future here still seemed bleak. She forced the thought away. The sight of the food –

strips of spiced lamb and freshly baked bread, mint and cucumber relish, and a bowl of fresh figs – reminded her that she hadn't had a meal since morning and spent a large part of the day exerting herself in intense physical activities. She settled at the table and dug in, sipping spiced pomegranate cider from a tall goblet.

When they finished eating, Mai collected all the dishes onto the tray again, ready to take it outside. Kara sat back, watching him. She knew she should respond to the Queen's request, probably do her best to see Rajmella today. Yet, somehow, she had the nagging feeling that doing so would put an end to her time with Mai, which had already stretched far longer than she expected. Mai had things to do. They had allowed themselves a brief moment of indulgence, but in the end it didn't change a thing.

"You should go," she said.

He raised his eyebrows. "Are you sending me away?"

*No.* "Yes." She realized as soon as she spoke that it didn't sound convincing at all.

The tenderness in his gaze suddenly seemed like too much to bear. If she had to give up a man, it seemed utterly unfair that he had to be so bloody perfect in every possible way. She turned away abruptly. Mai slid his hand over her cheek, gently turning her face back to him.

"I am not all that anxious to rush the events," he said. "Are you?"

*No. But I'm afraid of how much it would hurt when they force us apart.* Her eyes filled with tears. Perhaps she was indeed being a coward, trying to break things off before time.

It suddenly occurred to her that ever since she and

Mai had found their way into her quarters, the place had been eerily quiet. Normally Mai couldn't take a step without at least some of his Emerald guards. Was something strange going on she wasn't aware of?

"Where are your guards?" she asked. "How come none of the Majat bothered us today?"

Mai's face lit up with a mischievous grin. "After you renounced your throne, you left before you could see all the court ladies rush at our men."

"They did?"

"Yes. Apparently the ladies who were, um, involved last time spread the word. The Majat are officially in high demand at this court."

"And you allowed it to happen?"

Mai shrugged. "It seemed only fair. After everything we've been through, I felt our men deserved a break. I hope they're enjoying it now, even if I wasn't so sure in a couple of cases."

"What about Seldon?"

Mai laughed. "The Queen requested him personally."

"The *Queen*?"

"In her own words, he looked like an experienced man."

"Did he actually agree to it?" She was having trouble picturing it.

"Eagerly, even if he did his best not to show it too much."

Kara looked at him, dumbfounded. At Seldon's age, he was certainly the last man she imagined to be interested in this sort of thing. She hoped the Queen wasn't going to be bitterly disappointed.

"Do you want to grant the Queen her request for an audience?" Mai asked.

She sighed. She really didn't want to leave his arms just yet. "I suppose I should. But what are you going to do in the meantime?"

He grinned again. "From what I've learned of the local customs, the consorts are normally allowed to be present at such meetings, unless otherwise specified."

*The consorts.* She supposed by the local customs she could call him that, a thought that she found unexpectedly appealing. If he wasn't a Majat, he could indeed stay here with her in this capacity, but there was no use to wish for what couldn't be.

She forced away the regrets as she donned her formal outfit.

# 44

# A WARNING

Rajmella looked at Mai with interest as she settled into the divan in the anteroom of Kara's suite. The Queen's two consorts knelt by her feet like watchdogs, surveying Kara with lusty expressions that made her feel instantly uncomfortable. She put her hand in Mai's and he grinned wickedly as he made a show of running his finger down her palm, his touch making her momentarily forget where she was.

"I hope you're finding your accommodations to your liking, Your Royal Highness," Rajmella said.

"Yes, they are very comfortable, thank you very much." *And far too excessive.* Kara guessed that all the extra rooms were necessary to house servants and consorts expected for someone of her station. The prospect of spending the rest of her days in here seemed dreadful, but at least she would now have the memories of her time with Mai to keep her going.

"I wanted you to know how much I appreciate what you did," Rajmella said. "With the way you and I started off, you had every right to execute me for high treason. Giving the queendom back to me – that was the most unexpected gesture I ever imagined. I have to admit, however, that you left me curious. Why did you do it?"

Kara sighed. "Because I truly believe you make a far better Queen."

"Why?" Rajmella's eyes lit up with keen interest.

"You've held this position for nearly twenty years, to everyone's satisfaction."

Rajmella laughed. "There is no such thing as everyone's satisfaction where a whole country is concerned. At any given moment, it is an absolute guarantee that at least some will be disgruntled and a few others will probably hate me and want me dead. It comes with the territory, so to speak."

Kara's lips twitched. "Yes, that too. I hope you'll forgive me if I say that there is nothing about the job that I find even remotely appealing. Not when we have a far better candidate, right here."

Rajmella shook her head. "Why do I have a feeling you are evading the question, niece?"

*Maybe because I am?* Kara met her eyes. Unexpectedly, this direct conversation made her feel much closer with the older woman than she imagined possible. "If you want the truth, here it is. I am not cut out for this. I am too used to deciding everything in battle. My training, my attitude, they're all wrong for ruling a land that has known nothing but peace and prosperity up until now. I know my responsibilities, and I've been taught to always live up to them. In this case, I would be doing ill service to our people by staying in charge."

*Our people.* There, she'd said it. The people of Shayil Yara were her people too. In time, she would learn to come to terms with it. But would she ever truly feel like one of them?

Rajmella briefly inclined her head. "I think I understand. And as I said, I am grateful. I do think I can be a good Queen. It's just that you looked so glamorous when you rode into the city yesterday."

Glamorous. This was the word that always came to her mind when she thought of Mai. Perhaps some of his glamour had rubbed off on her during the time they were close? Or maybe it was true that they did have so much in common – not that it mattered anymore.

"People adore you," Rajmella said. "Even now that you stepped down so publicly, as the name Aljahara is beginning to sink back into the legends and lore, they sing songs about you out there."

"They will forget me," Kara said. "As long as I don't appear in public too often. The songs will help, actually."

Rajmella kept her gaze a moment longer, and Kara had an uncomfortable feeling the Queen understood her much better than she led to believe.

"There's a matter of heirs, though," Rajmella said.

"Heirs?"

"My first daughter, Aljbeda, who is being raised at the northern throne."

Kara nodded. Aljbeda was a spirited and intelligent child, thrown into far too much politics at the age of six. It had been a cruel thing to separate her from her mother.

"Aljbeda is wonderful," Kara said. "And if it was up to me, she would be sent here immediately. I can't influence this decision, though." She glanced at Mai. Perhaps, as the Majat Guildmaster and the man who led their entire army to victory, he might be able to venture the question to the king of Tallan Dar?

"I agree," Rajmella said. "But it's not that. Even though you abdicated, if you ever have any daughters, their claim to the throne would supersede that of mine."

*Daughters.* Kara swallowed. The idea of having children had always been so far from her mind that she was having trouble embracing it.

"I am warded against pregnancy," she said. "All female trainees at the Majat Guild receive a warding spell at a very early age."

"Yes, but if you marry, wouldn't the warding spell be lifted by the priests?"

Marry. Against reason, the word struck her at the core, like a dagger plunged into an open wound. Rajmella knew enough about the Majat Guild's politics to realize that Mai couldn't marry into the Olivian royal house. She also could probably never relate to the joy and sorrow that came with giving all the love you were capable of to only one man.

"Not that it's ever going to happen," she said, "but if, for argument's sake, we imagine that I was allowed to marry Mai, the warding spell would not be lifted. In fact, if it wasn't already in place, the spell would be applied at the mere possibility of such union. Having children, at least legitimate ones, is out of the question for a Majat Guildmaster."

Rajmella smiled. "He is not the only man in the world."

*He is, as far as I am concerned.* Kara glanced away. She didn't think this was something Rajmella could possibly understand.

"If there are any formalities you want me to

go through to ensure that Aljbeda has the right of succession, I will," she said. "Aljbeda deserves it – and from having seen her at the northern court I have no doubt one day she will be an even better Queen than either of us."

Rajmella's face remained solemn, but Kara could see her eyes light up with pride. "Thank you. And now that we have this out of the way, I also wanted you to know that as long as you stay here you will be treated like family. I will personally ensure you never want for anything in your life. Including your share of men, once you are ready." Her eyes hovered on Mai again. "I know this particular prospect doesn't interest you at the moment, but perhaps you would see things differently one day?"

"I won't," Kara said. "But thanks anyway."

Rajmella looked at Mai curiously. "I must admit, the Majat men have something about them that would make your situation almost... understandable. All of our court ladies fortunate enough to get one of them into their chambers yesterday could speak of little else this morning in the throne room. As for your Aghat Seldon..." She paused, her cheeks lighting up with color.

Kara gaped, her own cheeks warming up at the mere idea. Mai's quick grin pushed her thoughts even further, until her embarrassment became nearly unbearable. The last thing she ever wanted to think of was Seldon's sexuality.

"I'm glad you enjoyed yourself," she said.

Rajmella smiled, as if oblivious to the undertones. "I did, and I will again, as long as his duties permit this interlude. The reason I brought this up is to let you know that I think I now understand why, with the

wealth of options our palace has to offer, with the
way all our best consorts are swooning over you, you
choose to lock yourself up with only one man. He must
be the best of them all."

"He is," Kara said, "but as I understand it, we are
speaking from different reference points."

"Yes and no. When I see you together, I also
understand more, something I don't encounter too
often. You truly love him, don't you?"

Kara glanced away. She was trying not to think
about this at all. She knew if she spoke now, she would
probably burst into tears – not something she would
ever want to do in front of the Queen.

"So, what are you two going to do?" Rajmella asked.

Kara squeezed Mai's hand. She didn't feel like
talking, not that she had anything at all to say.

"We'll deal with it when the time comes," Mai said.

Rajmella looked at him thoughtfully. "Like I said,
anything I can do, just let me know. For the moment,
I am guessing I would do best to leave you to your
privacy. Before I go, however, I wanted to inform you
of another reason for my visit. My scouts spotted a large
and very official group that emerged from the forest
at Gard'hal outpost and is now on its way toward the
capital. The King of Tallan Dar is among them. Along
with some other important people, including, I believe,
several members of the Majat Guild."

"The Pentade," Mai said. "They accompany the King
at all times."

"I know that. My scouts report, however, that their
numbers are greater than five the Majat Pentade is
supposed to have, and that some of these men look
very senior."

Mai shook his head. "Impossible. I would have been informed."

"Perhaps they wanted it to be a surprise?"

"Unlikely."

"In any case. I felt it was my duty to tell you this you as soon as I could."

Kara's heart raced as she and Mai exchanged quick glances. This must have to do with the answer to Mai's request for marriage. Their time together was coming to an end.

She tried to tell herself that she expected this, that she was ready for it. She forced away all other thoughts as she looked into Mai's eyes.

"How soon will they be here?" she asked.

"Tomorrow," Rajmella said. "We are preparing a grand reception. I expect it goes without saying that both of you, as well as Prince Kythar, will be the central part of it."

# 45

# NORTHERN EMBASSY

Ellah raised her head from the book she was reading as she heard excited voices and the rustling of footsteps in the hallway outside her room. She carefully set down the volume before rising to her feet. The windows of the chambers she shared with Celana, adjacent to the suite given to Kyth, opened into the courtyard near the palace entrance where people often gathered to gossip about the happenings in the palace. Ellah couldn't hear all the words, but the flares of colors in her mind identified lies and truths, adding up to an interesting piece of information every time. By the size of the commotion right now, this one was going to be noteworthy.

She stepped to the window, but before she could catch anything useful, the doors to her own chambers banged open, letting in Alder. He stopped in the middle of the room, his blond hair disheveled, his handsome face arranged into an expression of nonchalance that made Ellah laugh. Alder was always so adorable in the way he thought he could hide his emotions, so clearly written on his face that it didn't take a truthseer to see through him. Right now, it was obvious that his visit, catching Ellah alone, was deliberate, even if he was trying to pretend he was merely passing by.

"Where is Lady Celana?" Alder asked

"She's with Kyth."

Alder nodded. "And Magister Egey Bashi?"

"In the library." Ellah couldn't stop a giggle. "Are you telling me you ran all the way out here to learn their whereabouts?"

Alder's cheeks lit up with color. A broad grin spread over his face. "No. I hoped to see you, actually."

"Me?" She knew he spoke the truth, even if she hadn't deduced the same information from his body language just now, but she still couldn't imagine why.

He lowered his eyes to fidget with his large hands. Only now did Ellah realize that something was amiss. The three large spiders that normally adorned his shoulder were not there. Her heart raced in alarm. Alder never parted with his spiders.

"Are you all right?" she asked.

"Yes. Why?"

"Where are your spiders?"

Alder sighed. "Ayalla... She no longer needs me."

Ellah's eyes widened. As far as she knew, Alder had sold his body and soul to the Forestland sorceress, who took men as she pleased and did whatever she wanted with them. To the best of Ellah's knowledge, Alder was Ayalla's favorite, the man she was having relentless sex with whenever he was around. Ayalla had named Alder a Mirewalker, one of those men who belonged to her unconditionally.

Was there such a thing as breaking up with all that?

"Just like that?" she asked.

"Yes, apparently so."

"And you are all right with it?"

Alder hesitated. "I think, deep inside, I always knew this was going to happen some day. She is thousands of years old. From her perspective, all her relationships are so fleeting she must feel as if they pass in a blink of an eye."

"Yes, but there is the matter of your perspective too."

Alder looked away. "When Ayalla asked for my pledge, I didn't question it at all." He blushed. "It just seemed natural, as if it was meant to be. But now I am beginning to realize that it felt exactly like being under a spell. As long as it lasted, I could think of no other woman but her."

"And now?" Ellah prompted.

"She can communicate with me," Alder said. "Through the spiders. This morning she said that now that the Kaddim are no longer there, she wants to release me from her service, so that I could lead a normal life. The spiders became dormant after that. They rolled up into balls, just like the others. And I... I felt..."

"What?"

"I felt free." Alder heaved a sigh. "Not that I was feeling forced before – Ayalla is a beautiful woman, don't get me wrong. But waking up today, I suddenly realized that the two of us don't really have much in common, do we? I mean, she is a powerful sorceress, and I... I am just a regular guy."

Ellah stared. She had thought all these things before, when she looked at Alder's relationship with Ayalla, but hearing him say all this just felt so strange.

Alder stepped closer. "Remember how, when we

grew up, your grandma and my dad always thought we should become sweethearts and marry each other?"

*Yes, until Ayalla took you.* Ellah swallowed. When they were growing up, she did always assume she was going to marry Alder some day. This was before their lives got so twisted that she didn't know what was right anymore. Their childhood friend Kyth turned out to be the heir to the throne and one of the most powerful sorcerers in the world. Both Ellah and Alder became instrumental in facilitating historical alliances and fighting a war that threatened to consume the entire land. And now that it was over, her world had just been turned inside out again. Could it truly ever go back to the way it was when she was a little girl?

"I remember..." she said slowly.

"Perhaps," Alder said, "some things we used to have could be picked up again?"

She frowned. It had been so long since she had ever considered Alder from this perspective that it felt strange talking about it. Still, this was the man she had once felt certain she was going to marry. Now that he was saying all these things, the memory of that feeling stirred inside her again, the familiarity and comfort she always felt in his presence – and yes, a bit of excitement too. Alder was very attractive, especially when he wasn't preoccupied with such things as immortal powerful sorceresses and spiders.

"I suppose we could consider giving it a try," she said.

Alder heaved a sigh, his shoulders sagging with relief. "I know it would take a lot to bridge all the gaps that developed between us. And, I would be quite content to remain only a friend. But I... I would never forgive myself if I didn't at least try to see if there could be more between us. All I ask is that you remain open to the possibility, at least for a while."

Ellah looked at him, entranced. She had apprenticed herself to the Keepers, and it was her understanding that if her studies were successful she would devote herself to the work of the Order and give up any hopes for personal happiness. She never even thought of being with a man. But now, looking at Alder's open and honest face, the idea didn't seem so impossible anymore.

She knew there would be a long way for them. Yet, she didn't want to dismiss the possibility altogether.

"Yes," she said. "I will."

His look captivated her, the relief in his gaze bringing a lump into her throat. In some respects Alder was so innocent and naïve, a good and honest man, so different from most. She remembered the times she had hopes of catching Mai's fancy, how every one of her conversations with the Diamond turned into a mind game that left her exhausted and insecure. Alder was the opposite in nearly every way, and that epiphany brought so much relief. She thought of everything they could have together, stemming from the upbringing they shared, and felt warmth spread over her as if she was coming home. Perhaps in the end they would settle for no more than friendship. But exploring the other possibilities seemed like the right thing to do.

She felt her skin tingle as Alder stepped toward her, but at that moment the door banged open again and Egey Bashi rushed in. He paused in the doorway, his dark eyes darting between the two, and Ellah couldn't help a grin as she saw the Keeper's frown of suspicion turn into dawning realization and then surprise.

"I am sorry for interrupting," he said.

Ellah's smile widened. "It's quite all right, Magister." She glanced at Alder who was also grinning and felt a new surge of warmth rush through her. If she and Alder ended up together, things could get so easy from now on that she would probably never have to suffer at all. There were very few people in the world who understood her so well.

"King Evan just arrived," Egey Bashi said. "Along with quite a large party that includes every official I could possibly think about. Father Bartholomeos is with them too – and several very senior Majat."

Ellah raised her eyebrows. She knew Kyth had used the Majat hawk service to send a message to his father about their victory. He might have included a line or two about his new understanding with Lady Celana, a turn of events the King would be bound to feel happy about, since Kyth had been resisting any possibility of marrying a lady of his station for so long. This could possibly explain Father Bartholomeos being in the party. But the Majat?

"The Queen is preparing a reception in the man ceremonial hall," Egey Bashi went on. "We are all invited, of course – and I am guessing this would be our only way to learn what this is all about."

Ellah glanced around the room in search of her official apprentice Keeper's cloak. If things went well with Alder, she might not be wearing that robe for long. But she knew better than to get this far ahead of herself.

"Prince Kythar and Lady Celana are on their way," said Egey Bashi. "We should all get ready by the time they arrive."

•••

Kara looked at the two outfits laid out for her. One, her Majat clothes, black pants and shirt tailored perfectly for action. The other, the royal robes of Shayil Yaran court, a number in violet silks adorned with jewels and gold thread, cut to expose too much skin and make her look like a seductress. She hated the idea of wearing it in public. Yet, this was who she was right now. She turned her back on the Majat clothes and put the royal garb on.

Mai had been called away earlier when the senior Majat arrived. He departed matter-of-factly, giving her only a brief parting kiss, as if confident they would see each other again. She wasn't so sure. They would perhaps be allowed to say goodbye, in public and likely from a distance. But she knew for certain she would never be allowed to spend time alone with him, or feel his arms around her ever again. She tried to tell herself she was all right with it as she opened the door.

Two consorts were waiting for her outside. She was grateful to see that they were older than any of the others ever sent to fetch her, and not the kind that kept undressing her with their eyes and acting provocative and suggestive every time she looked their way. These two were respectful and solemn, striding at a short distance behind her like honorary guards. Perhaps the Queen had sent them as an offering, to start at least the appearance of a new harem mandated by her station, but Kara didn't feel like asking.

She kept to the back rows as she entered the throne room, more crowded than she had ever seen it before. Each party stood in a small group before the Queen's throne, the Tallan Dar nobles dominating the front. Kara had nearly forgotten that the northern court clothing could be just as barbaric and revealing as that of Shayil Yara. The King's tunic fell off one shoulder to expose the left part of his chest. Despite his older age, late forties, he looked fit enough to have some of the Olivian ladies swooning. Kara secretly wondered if this choice of clothes on the King's side was a way of showing off in a place where he knew for certain the display would be highly appreciated.

Her eyes drifted to the group of the Majat. She did her best to keep a cool head as she saw Mai in his full Guildmaster's regalia surrounded by a tight group of Diamonds. Seldon stood by his side, next to several other senior Majat, including the tall elderly man with a long, expressive face – Master Abib, the weapons keeper. Kara frowned. Abib never left the Guild. What prompted him to travel this far south?

She was debating with herself whether to maintain her position in the back or break all rules and etiquette by coming forward to greet the old man who had been such a good friend during her upbringing in the Guild. She almost talked herself into it when the sound of a gong signaled silence, announcing the arrival of the Queen.

Rajmella ignored the guards lined up to clear her way to the throne and rushed forward, extending her hands in greeting. Her voice chimed like a bell, echoing clearly through the hall.

"It brings joy to my heart," she said, "to welcome such important guests to my court. King Evan of Tallan Dar, what a pleasant surprise."

King Evan smiled, squeezing her hands briefly. "The joy is mine, Your Majesty. I thank you for your hospitality." His glance included all the impressive party at his back. "You must be wondering why we are all here."

"I…" Rajmella began, but paused as she met his gaze.

"Please allow me to enlighten you right away," the King said. "I was rejoiced when I learned how my son, Prince Kythar, has played such an important part in our victory over the Kaddim. While we were not acting as a part of any official alliance," the King briefly glanced at the Majat, "I know that many forces, including the elite troops of Shayil Yara, chose to march together against our enemy, and that only their combined effort guaranteed victory. To express my gratitude, and following my son's explicit wish, I would like to present you an offering of my goodwill, one that I hope to become a token of everlasting peace between our kingdoms."

At his signal, the doors at the far end of the chambers opened, letting in a new procession. Kara gasped.

Little Princess Aljbeda walked in front, charming and adorable in her violet gown fashioned in the northern style. Her large suite of Olivian ladies, nannies, and tutors stepped in her wake.

Queen Rajmella clasped her hands to her face. Then she rushed forward and swept the Princess into her arms. She knelt, cradling her for a while, her eyes closed. When she raised her face to the King, tears were brimming her eyes.

King Evan smiled gently. "I feel privileged to be the one to restore things to the way they should be. No parent should ever see their child held hostage and forced into an upbringing different from that entitled by birth. I had suffered this myself, when I had no choice but to raise my son Kythar away from the throne, to protect his identity. In my case, however, this was dictated by considerations of safety and dire need. In your case, I see no good reason to do this at all."

Rajmella's lips trembled, making her look vulnerable and young.

"Thank you, Your Majesty," she said. "I will never forget this."

King Evan nodded. "By restoring Her Royal Highness to her rightful home I hoped to ensure friendship between our kingdoms that wouldn't have been possible otherwise. I wanted you to know that you should consider us your friends, and that my son Kythar, who will eventually inherit my throne, was the one who drove this decision. As a father, I couldn't help but entertain a hope that our families could enjoy an even closer union, to end any possibility of a feud."

His eyes searched out Kara and bore into her, his purposeful smile draining the blood out of her face. The thought had occurred to her before, even though she had done her best to dismiss it. When she had an affair with Kyth, the King had been resistant to it, pushing the Prince to select a bride among the noble ladies whose birthright befitted a future Queen. To Kara's knowledge, this push at least partly drove the decision to include Lady Celana into their traveling party. And now, when her lineage had been uncovered, the tables had turned. There seemed to be no better marriage prospect for the Prince but Kara, the woman he already had strong feelings for, the one at the top of the royal succession line in her land.

She didn't dread the idea of marrying Kyth, especially since Mai was about to leave her forever. But she knew that now, by a twist of fate, Kyth's affections had shifted

ASSASSIN QUEEN

elsewhere too. If marrying Kara would have been an answer to his dreams only weeks ago, right now it was likely going to make him unhappy. She sighed. How did things manage to get so complicated?

She looked at Kyth, who stood further away from the throne with Celana by his side, a determined look on his face. He looked at her too, and she realized from his expression that the topic had already been breached before this gathering. She heaved another sigh. If she couldn't have Mai, she couldn't care less whatever they decided upon for political reasons. But if this meant ripping happiness away from the close friend she considered Kyth to be, she was going to fight this with all her might.

Rajmella noticed these looks too. Despite how flustered she was just now, still clutching her daughter as if afraid the girl would be ripped away from her, she was bound to understand the implications. The King had just handed her the hostage Tallan Dar had been holding against her. They would probably want another one, as a replacement.

Anger boiled in Kara's chest. She was damned if she was going to let them trade Kyth's happiness for politics. She looked at Rajmella and the King in turn and firmly shook her head, then edged deeper behind the rows of the courtiers.

King Evan's eyes followed her thoughtfully. "If I may trouble you with a request, Queen Rajmella, may I have a privilege of a private audience?"

Rajmella's eyes darted to Kara too. "I would be glad to talk, Your Majesty," she said. "Any time."

Kara didn't wait any longer before slipping out of the chamber.

# 46

# MARRIAGE PROSPECTS

Kyth steadied his gaze watching his father pace the room. He wished he had Celana by his side now. It seemed ironic that just a short time ago he wanted nothing else but to marry Kara, while his father pushed him toward Celana. Perhaps it was the nature of things that no one could ever be happy with the status quo? Or was it only true when it came to fathers judging their children's love interests?

"I thought you were in love with Kara," King Evan said.

"I was. But not anymore." Hell, Kyth never imagined he would say these words. He knew he meant it, but voicing this out loud still seemed strange. Kara was gorgeous, and deep inside he would never forget the connection they had. But she was not the woman who dominated his dreams lately. The thought seemed surprising, but true.

"She is a beautiful woman," the King said. "And I know for a fact that you two are very close, even if you continue to insist you no longer have no romantic interest in her. Marrying an attractive woman you have feelings for is far more than any nobleman could ever hope for."

"True," Kyth said. "But I am not any nobleman, am I? I am your heir, and the person whose magic gift was instrumental in winning this war." Saying this seemed strange too. Kyth was never prone to self-praise. Yet, he also knew his words were true. He had gone through hell to win this war. Wasn't this worth at least something in his father's eyes?

"Besides," he added, "Kara is in love with Mai, and Mai is my friend too. I would never come between them." *Another first*. Never, even if his darkest nightmares, did Kyth imagine he would ever call Mai a friend. Yet, he knew it was true now. Outwardly, Mai would probably still swear at him and boss him around, but deep inside Kyth knew that he and Mai were bonded in ways that would probably be difficult for anyone else to understand. Facing certain death together, having a man throw himself on a sword for you, tended to do wonders to people's perception of each other.

"The last thing I heard, he cannot possibly marry her," the King said. "Her royal status absolutely precludes having anything in common with the Majat Guildmaster, even after she renounced the throne — which was a pity, by the way."

Kyth sighed. It was funny how things worked, when someone's status could change overnight to elevate one to immeasurable heights and in the same move shatter one's dreams. If this happened months ago, he would have been overjoyed. But now, all he could think about was the way Kara looked when she had announced her decision to renounce the throne. She seemed so defeated, the look in her eyes full of such fatal resolve that Kyth found himself fearing for her life. If Mai hadn't followed her back then, Kyth would have been the one to run after her. But he knew for certain that even with her shattered hopes, even if Kyth still loved her and no one else, Kara would never be happy marrying him.

And now, he was in love too.

Didn't they all deserve better?

The King tossed his head impatiently. "We don't have much time, son. The announcement will have to be made tonight at the state dinner. I am headed to Queen Rajmella's chambers to negotiate with her now."

"Don't," Kyth said.

"I have to, I'm afraid."

Kyth stepped forward and gently patted his arm. "Look, father. Before this situation arose, you could think of no better match for me than Lady Celana. You and her father have been planning this for a while. You practically pushed her at me. And now, she and I are in love. Shouldn't you be happy things turned out just the way you wanted?"

The King looked at Kyth with hesitation. "At your request, I've given up Princess Aljbeda. Now, if we don't secure alliance to Shayil Yara through a blood bond, our kingdoms could plunge into a war any time, without any leverage on our side. Don't you see this, son?"

Kyth crossed his arms on his chest. "You've done the right thing, father, by restoring Princess Aljbeda to her mother. Queen Rajmella is grateful to you. I see no reason to plunge into a war, do you?"

The King smiled. "You've grown, Kyth. Yet, in some respects you are still a boy. Wars have little to do with goodwill. Proper diplomatic relationships work only if they are backed up by very strong incentives."

"True," Kyth said. "But I'm afraid sacrificing four people's happiness is not the incentive I can possibly accept."

"What do you propose then?"

"Give this up. There has to be another way."

The King tossed his head. "My private audience with Queen Rajmella is about to start. Let's see what she has to say."

Kyth opened his mouth to protest, but the King stopped him with a gesture as he turned around and left the chamber.

Kara hoped for some peace, but messengers simply wouldn't leave her alone. The Queen's consorts came to her doors twice, asking her to join Rajmella in her chambers. When Kara dismissed them, another embassy came along, this time headed by the First Consort himself. She refused to open the door, but had to give in after a while of insistent pounding. When she did, she was surprised to find herself face to face with Jamal.

"You?" She raised her eyebrows. "Did you come here to drag me to the Queen's chambers, brother?"

Jamal shifted from foot to foot, glancing at the First Consort crowding decisively behind him. "No. I came to prevent you from being dragged against your will, actually. Not that I believe for a minute any of our consorts are up to the task."

"You're right in that." She glanced at the five men

standing in the hallway.

Valmir's face folded into the expression of grim resolve. "I was told not to leave until you come with us, Princess Aljahara. If we don't show up soon, the Queen will come here herself."

Kara glanced at Jamal. "And how do you plan to prevent that?"

Jamal sighed. "They are determined to force your marriage to the northern prince. But before any official conversation happens, I wanted to know your wishes in the matter."

*My wishes.* She briefly turned away to control her expression before she spoke again.

"You've traveled with us, Jamal," she said. "You know everything about the situation, don't you?"

Jamal peered into her face. "Is there any chance that you could be permitted to marry the man you love?"

"None."

"In that case, Prince Kythar doesn't seem like a bad choice. He is handsome and gentle, and he cares deeply about you."

"He is in love with another."

Jamal heaved a sigh. "You haven't spent enough time around royalty, have you?"

"I thought I have, more than I ever wanted to." Kara raised her eyebrows. "Why?"

"When your marriage carries so much political weight, being pawned into a male-dominated kingdom means you should feel lucky if your future husband does not repulse you."

She held his gaze. "What if I refuse to be pawned?"

He sighed again. "If you have problems with the idea, you probably shouldn't have abdicated."

Kara shook her head. "You're probably right, Jamal. Yet, I don't regret what I did. Being pawned is still better than being a queen when I feel no calling for it."

Jamal looked at her thoughtfully. "In this case, I see no reason to resist your fate. Believe me, it could be a lot worse. What do you say, sister?"

Kara glanced around the waiting group. She didn't feel like going with them, but Jamal was right. There was no delaying the inevitable. In the very least, going with Valmir meant she would have a chance to tell Rajmella everything she thought about the new plan. Perhaps she could even change the King's mind? Even if she failed, agreeing to marry Kyth wasn't the worst of evils – assuming of course, that the Prince consented to it as well.

"I–" she began.

Just then, clanging of weapons at the end of the hall froze the words on her lips. She turned sharply to see three Majat Emerald Guards rushing toward her, with Lenart in the lead. He skidded to a halt in front of her, breathless, as if he had just run across the entire palace at top speed.

She frowned. What could possibly be the rush?

"Aghat Kara," Lenart said. "The senior Majat are on the way to your chambers. Aghat Mai sent me ahead with this warning. It was all he was allowed to do."

Her heart skipped a beat. Here it was. The Guild's decision. She had hoped she could be spared the necessity to stand there and be told the shattering truth she already knew so well, but she knew how some of the Majat seniors were bent on formalities. Worse, Lenart's words suggested that Mai was aware of the plan and probably could do nothing to stop them.

She threw a restrained glance at Jamal and the consorts. "Please excuse me, my lords. You may tell Queen Rajmella that I will be there as soon as I can."

Valmir frowned, then signaled to the rest of the consorts, who bowed to her deeply and departed. Jamal looked at Kara with question, but she responded with a brief shake of her head. He nodded and left as well, glancing hesitantly over his shoulder as he walked down the hall. Kara looked after him, a turmoil of feeling boiling in her chest. Perhaps she should have let Jamal, her closest kin, stand by her side through the devastating encounter she was about to face? But what would the use of it be? It's not like anyone in the world had the power to change the inevitable.

The group of older men that approached her all wore Diamond-set armbands and full complements of weapons, as if dressed for a parade. They watched Kara solemnly as she led the way into the common room of her suite, taking a space by the far wall, like a queen receiving an embassy. The irony of it made her lips twitch. She was no longer a queen, and these men, more or less in control of the most formidable power in all kingdoms, were not the kind of an embassy royalty normally received. Despite their advanced years, their combined power rivaled that of an elite battalion and played a deeper role in the Majat Guild's operation than anyone ever realized.

She suppressed a sigh as she ran her eyes around the gathering. Nearly every important man from their Guild was here, making Seldon, standing opposite her with an irritated frown on his face, seem like an average, ordinary man. No doubt he hated the feeling, which must be at least in part responsible for his expression. She didn't even want to guess about the others. She had no idea why they all took the time to travel all the way to Shayil Yara, or they all felt it necessary to gather here and oversee her heartbreak.

*Well, let's get on with it, shall we?* She kept her eyes on Seldon, the center figure in the semicircle facing her. Calling in the calmness and balance that came with her training, she assumed a relaxed stance. She would be damned if she would give them the satisfaction of breaking the silence, asking the first question.

Seldon looked uncomfortable as he cleared his throat. "Aghat Kara." He paused. "I know we had our differences before, and you have been among those who questioned our Guild's decision of sending me to accompany Aghat Mai on this trip. I was not at liberty to talk about my reasons before, but as of now I have been empowered by our Guild's seniors to speak openly."

Kara raised her eyebrows. She and Seldon had resolved this before, or so she believed. Besides, he had actually proven very useful in this campaign – not to mention that he was, technically, the person who saved Mai's life by reviving him after the battle. For that alone she would feel indebted to him to the end of her days, no matter how much she wished she didn't have to face him right now.

"In addition to doing my best to assist Aghat Mai in his military campaign," Seldon went on, "the Guild charged me with an investigation that followed up on Aghat Mai's request for permission to marry you."

Her eyes widened at this admission, the small oddities about the way Seldon behaved throughout the trip suddenly clicking into place. *An investigation, eh?* She supposed it shouldn't have come as a surprise that they sent someone like Seldon to do this, the man who always felt negative about any personal interactions involving the Guild's warriors. And now, he was also apparently going to be the spokesman to relay the bad news.

"You may not know this," Seldon said, "but given how serious the implications are of a Guildmaster's marriage for the entire Guild, this type of an inquiry involves far more than a mere investigation into your lineage. The task I was charged with was to observe you two together and determine the likely effect your relationship could have on Aghat Mai's ability to perform his duties. Privately, I must add that I have been one of those skeptical from the start, and that this attitude actually prompted our Guild's seniors to choose me for this task. In a way, we all wanted to know the worst."

*Skeptical. Well, you must be elated now that you know this isn't going to work.* She was surprised she could still feel this kind of anger, careful not to show it as she listened to his words.

Seldon's gaze wavered. "This campaign has not been an easy one. I feel privileged that I was not only a part of it, but able to contribute my skill and knowledge where it was needed most. I want you to know that I felt intensely uncomfortable about this additional role I had to play, observing you and Aghat Mai closely in all kinds of situations, making a judgment even when I couldn't help feeling it wasn't warranted. This war has tested all of our limits in every possible way – and from my side, I can only envy the love you and Aghat Mai have for each other."

*Envy?* Kara's eyes widened. This was the last thing she expected to hear from someone like Seldon. Was he trying to make this hurt even deeper than it should?

"My conclusion," Seldon went on, "was unexpected even to myself. While I do recognize that love in itself could be viewed as a distraction, I am also aware that separating you two would likely cause damage far worse than any danger one can foresee if you are together.

"Aghat Mai is the greatest commander our Guild had in a very long time. He is still young, but we all look forward to the time he develops to his full potential. I strongly feel that without you by his side, he would never be able to achieve the greatness we all know he is capable of. Dealing with this kind of a loss would shatter him. This conclusion, which, as I am sure you know, is very uncharacteristic for me, has driven the recommendation I've submitted to the Majat Guild after our victory."

Kara heaved a slow breath. It was astounding to hear Seldon say these things. It also hurt like hell, as if the older man was probing into a deep wound that hadn't had a chance to start healing yet. She hoped that Seldon was wrong, that Mai would recover from all this better than she did. She was also beginning to regret letting them all into her chamber just now. Seldon spoke the truth, at least where she was concerned. Dealing with the loss would be shattering. Was it really necessary to lay out the wreck in plain view?

Seldon regarded her with an unreadable expression. "I know you may be wondering why I'm saying these things to you now. This is because you are the only one here who hasn't been appraised of my conclusions yet. I had a chance to relay all this to Aghat Mai earlier today, just prior to our arrival here. I also included this in the detailed report I've sent on our return trip back to the Guild."

*Great. So you've discussed our private life with everyone here already.* Yet, she knew this was an unfair thought. The Majat Guildmaster couldn't possibly have a private life. Excluding what went on in his bedchamber behind closed doors, everything else he did was not only widely discussed, but potentially used as material for the chronicles.

"And now," Seldon said at length, "I defer the rest to Master Abib, whose charge was to supervise a team of scholars looking into your lineage. He will relay to you the results of his investigation."

*You know everything about my bloody lineage.* Kara's eyes narrowed. Yet, from the determined faces of everyone around her, she knew she had to listen to this part too. Perhaps it was essential for the Guild's proceedings to relay the details so formally, so that everything could be properly documented. This had to be why so many of the Guild's seniors had traveled all the way down here, wasn't it?

Abib stepped forward and unwrapped a long parchment, bearing an official Guild's seal. "After receiving Aghat Seldon's report and completing my investigation, I hastened to put together this official letter that has been copied and shared with our Guild's seniors, both those present here and those left behind. Our best scholars have done extensive research on your ancestry. Our task was relatively easy, given the fact that you've spent most of your life at the Guild and all your official records were kept in order, but given your Olivian blood, we also consulted with the Shayil Yaran scholars, in case their records contained any additional information. I, and all the Guild's seniors who traveled here with me, did so with the intention of making sure that any decisions reached in response to Aghat Mai's inquiry are irrevocable and protected by the Majat Code."

*Bloody hell.* The Majat weren't only going to trample over their lives, they were going to pile rocks on top, to ensure that nothing could possibly rise again. She glanced at Abib, but could read nothing at all behind his stern expression.

"The Majat Guild," Abib went on, "has accepted you for training after receiving extensive assurances that you are an orphan and an abandoned child, with no lineage or political alliances that could have precluded your Majat ranking. Our archives contain no paperwork or records to the contrary. Many of us have all known you nearly since birth, and closely oversaw your training from the very beginning, all the way until you became one of our very best warriors. While you have been forced to leave our ranks through a set of unforeseen circumstances, I and all my peers can personally vouch that any issues related to that have been addressed. Furthermore, I am personally convinced that despite not being an active Guild member, you, Aghat Kara, remain, at heart, one of us."

Kara's eyes widened again. What was Abib saying? Where could this speech possibly lead him to?

"The Majat Guild," Abib said, "is aware that very recently the Queendom of Shayil Yara has put forth a claim that you are a lost member of their royal house and the rightful heir to the throne. However, our internal investigation, which, as I can assure you, has been conducted in the most thorough way, was unable to find any evidence in support of these claims. According to our records, Princess Aljahara never existed at all. We were able to finalize this conclusion after our arrival here, by comparing these records to Shayil Yara's official chronicles and finding no discrepancies at all."

Kara's mouth fell open. Abib knew what he was saying wasn't true. He couldn't possibly believe otherwise. Those men who participated in their campaign knew it too. Surely they had to. She ran her eyes around the gathering, noticing some smiles now, feeling as if she was asleep and dreaming, for there was no reality she knew in which any of this could possibly be happening to her.

Abib stepped forward and placed the parchment into her hands. "It is my privilege to inform you, that our formal investigation found no circumstances that could prevent your and Aghat Mai's union."

Kara heaved a breath, once again having serious trouble keeping up. Her head was spinning, and she resisted the urge to pinch herself hard, just to make sure she was awake.

"I must apologize to you," Abib said, "for the way we had to relay this information to you in such an official way, without giving you any prior indication of where this was going. Please understand that it is utterly important for the entire proceedings to be conducted strictly following the protocol. If it's any consolation, Aghat Mai was adamantly opposed to this conversation. The only reason he allowed it because we all assured him that this was the only way to proceed."

Kara swallowed, trying and failing to find her voice. She felt numb, as if the events around her were happening in another reality just outside her grasp.

Abib stood up straighter, exchanging glances with the men around him. "Before seeing Aghat Mai again, you must give us a formal answer whether or not you wish to proceed with the marriage."

Kara shook her head, unsure if she heard him right. "Is this a bloody joke?"

"Far from it. If you say 'yes' right now, you will be officially bound to our Guild, and to Aghat Mai, irrevocably and for the rest of your life. Do you truly wish to do it?"

She heaved a breath. "*Yes*."

Abib bowed his head, his face betraying no emotion at all. "Then, follow us."

The guards outside Kara's chambers tried to protest when she directed her steps away from the Queen's quarters toward the suite designated for the Majat. They went as far as blocking her path, but a few whispered words by Seldon sent them rushing down the hallway in the opposite direction. To warn the Queen that something was going on, Kara assumed, even though she didn't give a damn. She focused her entire being on walking steadily, holding her head high, not breaking into a run. This couldn't possibly be happening, she was telling herself. Somewhere, someone was going to catch them and tell them this was all a mistake. Except that every Guild senior she feared the most was walking beside her now, crowding on her, as if determined to prevent her from straying from her path. If only they could know how far she was from this kind of a possibility.

She didn't remember how long it took them to walk down the hallway to the Majat quarters. She barely registered the faces of the Emerald guards, crinkling with smiles as they threw the doors open. Mai stood on the other side, his face pale with determination, and as soon as he saw her he stepped forward and swept her into his arms.

Kara didn't think she would cry, but finding herself in his embrace, something she was sure would never happen again, brought tears into her eyes far too easily. Dear Shal Addim, was she becoming one of those women who cried at the merest excuse? She hid her face on Mai's shoulder, unable to focus on anything besides the fact that she was here, with him, and that if the absurd reality around her was going to prevail she would actually be allowed to keep this place as long as she wanted.

Mai stroked her hair, the strength of his embrace telling her of the mix of emotions inside him.

"Was this bloody necessary, Master Abib?" he asked.

Kara didn't want to turn and look, but by the way the silence stretched behind her she imagined the senior Majat shuffling uncomfortably in place. She heaved a breath and finally disengaged from Mai's arms, finding the strength to stand on her own.

"It's all right," she said. "They had to follow all the formalities."

"Actually," Abib said, "we're not done with the formalities yet."

Kara's heart quivered. In her flustered state she didn't think she could take any more surprises. "We're not?"

"Since you have both, just now, independently confirmed to us that you intend to proceed with your marriage, it must be conducted immediately."

Her eyes widened. "Now?"

Abib shrugged. "There's a negotiation going on in Queen Rajmella's chambers regarding your hand in marriage. To put an end to any further discussion on the topic, you must leave this chamber as Aghat Mai's wife."

She glanced at Mai again. He was grinning, and she couldn't help a grin in return.

"I'd love to," she said.

Abib signaled, and the man nearest the door opened it a crack and spoke to someone outside. After a moment, both of the doors swung wide open, letting in a procession of priests.

Kara stared. Father Bartholomeos, the head of the Church himself, walked at the front dressed in his best ceremonial robes. *Dear Shal Addim, did they have the Holy Father wait out there all the time?*

She felt numb, surreal, as if stuck in a dream so good that she saw no way it could possibly last. Yet, the events proceeded around her like a well-oiled machine. She and Mai faced the priests side by side and were told to kneel, all the Majat kneeling in their wake. Of course, no Majat could remain standing if their Guildmaster was kneeling, an event that didn't happen every century, after all. She held Mai's hand, feeling his eyes on her, swelling with happiness that threatened to burst her apart. The prayer droned on, the smell of the incense going to her head like wine.

She wasn't sure how long it took, minutes or hours, her mind slowly settling into a new world which seemed far too good to be possible at all. She was getting married to Mai. She was back with her true family, going to return to their Guild, the only home she ever knew.

She came back to her senses when she realized that everyone was rising, looking at them with appreciative smiles. Mai pulled her into his arms and kissed her, to everyone's applause. She could only half-register all the congratulations, friendly hugs and pats, laughter and talking around them. The priests were mingling, Father Bartholomeos talking to Abib and Seldon so easily as if he hadn't been mortally afraid of the Majat just a short while ago.

She met Mai's gaze, trying to enfold what just happened. *Married. We are married. He owns me, body and soul. And now, no one could possibly keep us apart.*

# 47

# FAMILY BONDS

A formal train of Emerald guards escorted her and Mai to a private chamber inside the Majat suite. Kara blinked as she stepped inside. All her Majat clothes and weapons were laid out for her, next to a table with refreshments, and a giant bed set with fresh, fragrant sheets. She turned to Mai, who laughed at her stunned expression.

"Formally," he said, "we are expected to consummate the marriage. However, given how little time we have, I suggest you just change into your normal clothes, much as I regret the rush." "The rush?"

Mai grinned. "As I am told, the guards who saw you leaving your chambers with the Majat seniors raised quite a ruckus. Rajmella and King Evan are on their way here. We should expect them any moment."

Kara glanced to the clothes prepared for her, then at her royal Olivian outfit she was still wearing, showy and much too revealing for her comfort. It felt good to know she wouldn't be needing these kind of clothes anymore.

Mai's look sent flutters into her stomach. Happiness

she hadn't felt in a really long time was just starting to settle in, filling the large gap inside her chest that had remained hollow for such a long time. She shivered as she glanced at Mai. *My husband.* This would definitely take some getting used to.

"Did you have any idea our Guild would do something like this?" she asked.

He grinned. "Our Guild is pretty powerful, in case you didn't know."

"Yes, but twisting the chronicles? Changing official birth records of royal families?"

"Not quite, in this case. Officially, the fact of Aljahara's birth is not that well recorded. That made Abib's job a hell of a lot easier."

"Surely not as easy as simply denying your request for marriage."

He shook his head. "I was fairly certain the Guild would find a way. I knew Seldon was supposed to play an important role in making the decision, and if you remember, he owes you his life."

Kara frowned. "You wouldn't have killed him, would you?"

"Probably not, but Seldon doesn't know that. I believe he felt that keeping you around would provide some much-needed good influence on me. Besides, on our return trip through the desert I told him very clearly that it would have to be either both you and me returning to the Guild together, or neither of us. It came down to the question of how much the Majat seniors wanted to keep me in command. Apparently, they do, and are willing to go to considerable lengths for this purpose. Once that question was settled, the rest was all about twisting and reinterpreting the official records, something the Majat are always very good at. I wasn't worried at all – haven't I told you that?"

"I thought you were just trying to make me feel better."

"You really should give me more credit than that."

She swallowed. His tone was light, but his words had inadvertently brought to mind another occasion where she had made the same assumption, the one that nearly led her to ruining everything by committing suicide. That time, her thinking had been partially driven by the Kaddim. And now, with that behind them, she promised herself to change this way of thinking, once and for all.

"I was being foolish, wasn't I?" she said.

His gaze softened. "You were exhausted – not surprising after everything you've been through. I knew that too, so I directed my efforts at keeping you from taking any rash actions rather than trying to convince you that I was right."

She heaved a breath. "How is it possible that you know me so well?"

Mai smiled. "It was just a lucky guess. But I firmly intend to spend the rest of my life learning everything I possibly could about you."

*The rest of my life.* The thought was so overwhelming that she felt tears brim her eyes. He reached over and gently touched her cheek, brushing them away.

"I am dreaming," she whispered.

"Yes," he said. "Me too."

"Aren't you afraid to wake up?"

"I'm not planning to. Are you?"

"No."

He kissed her gently, his tenderness echoing deep

down, all the way to her core. She wanted to lose herself in his embrace. But she knew they had to settle everything else first.

She stepped toward the bed and changed her outfit – quickly, before she could change her mind.

"So, what's the plan now?" she asked.

"We meet Rajmella and present ourselves as the newlyweds."

"Given the situation, I assume she and King Evan may try to contest that."

"Contest the marriage performed by the Holy Father himself?"

"I *am* a princess of Shayil Yara, you know."

Mai shrugged. "One of the reasons we had to delay getting you to the Majat chambers, even at the risk the Queen will get to you first, was because Abib had to make absolutely sure there are no Shayil Yaran official documents that could interfere with our plan. Magister Egey Bashi helped; he knows the royal library quite well by now."

"And?"

"There are no formal records of your birth. Not here, anyway. Admittedly, our Guild does have one or two, but they are now placed into the disputed section of the library, thanks to Abib's work. Trust me, it will all settle down faster than you think. No one wants any trouble with the Majat."

She sighed. "To think that I nearly gave up, while all this work was going on."

"You should have trusted me to handle this."

She stepped closer and nuzzled his shoulder. They were both fully dressed now, with all their weapons on, but it still felt so hard to keep away from him.

"Now that you own me, body and soul," she said, "I will trust you. Always."

He smiled as he leaned closer. "You own me too. You have, all this time. But I expect you already know that."

She grinned. "Oh, yes, Guildmaster – and given the traditions of this court, I can't wait to exercise my rights of ownership." She slid a hand into his hair, pulling him closer, but before they could kiss, a knock on the door interrupted them, gentle but persistent.

"Damn it," Mai whispered. "Time to go."

She nodded, feeling breathless as she drew away from him.

The Majat's anteroom was set up for a private audience, with only a few guards stationed near the doors. As Kara and Mai stepped inside, Queen Rajmella rushed toward them, stopping abruptly when the Emeralds of Mai's escort moved in to block her way. Her eyes widened as she saw Kara's Majat outfit. The Queen had never seen it before, Kara realized.

She briefly glanced at King Evan, who stood very still, his eyes darting from Kara and Mai to the Majat of their entourage. His lowered hand clenched a parchment he must have been reading just before they arrived. The gleam of the official seals, the Church's four-pointed Holy Star next to the imprint of the Majat Diamond token, stood out even from the distance. Pressed into the paper side by side they looked strikingly similar in shape even if different in decorations, the Star printed in glossy black ink, the token filled with ornate lines of the Majat runes. *Our marriage certificate.* Kara hoped it was't the only copy. By Evan and Rajmella's determined looks they were planning to do everything in their power to challenge the validity of it.

"What is the meaning of this, Princess Aljahara?" Rajmella demanded.

"My name's Kara, Your Majesty," Kara said. "Allow me to present my husband, Aghat Mai."

Rajmella pursed her lips, throwing a restrained glance at the armed Majat surrounding the couple, then at Abib standing a few paces to the side. "You just went ahead and *married* him?"

Kara knew she shouldn't be grinning right now – not so widely at least, with everyone's eyes on her. But she felt so happy she couldn't possibly stop herself.

"Yes, Your Majesty."

"With the Majat Guild's blessings?"

"To the extent possible by the Code." Kara glanced at Abib, who bowed his head briefly in confirmation.

Rajmella turned to Abib too. "Are all your Guild's seniors out of their minds?"

Abib regarded her with a stony stare. "Not to my knowledge, Your Majesty."

"Don't act as if we are all idiots here. This woman is a princess of Shayil Yara! Marrying her to your Guildmaster throws away everything your Guild stands for."

Abib held her gaze firmly. "I am aware of the claim your kingdom has put forth regarding Aghat Kara's lineage. I myself led an extended investigation into the matter. According to all available chronicles, Your Majesty, Princess Aljahara is no more than a folk belief. We found absolutely no evidence to substantiate the fact of her existence at all." He glanced at Egey Bashi, who had noiselessly appeared at the door to the chamber and stopped beside him.

"I can confirm this, Your Majesties." Egey Bashi glanced from the Queen to the King. "I've spent days in your royal library and the official record room, and I have also consulted extensively with your court's scholars. On behalf of the Order of Keepers, I fully support Master Abib's conclusions."

"This is preposterous," Rajmella said. "Up until a few days ago she was our Queen, for Shal Addim's sake!"

Abib smiled. "A clever ruse, Your Majesty, to secure your kingdom's forces to our side. Aghat Kara is a brilliant tactician. She knew of Aljahara legend, and she has used it to our advantage. This move, as you know, was instrumental in our victory. But since the war is over now, there is no need for further pretense. You got your throne back, haven't you?"

Rajmella scoffed in disbelief. "Come now, Master Abib, surely you know better than that. All you need to do is look at the back of her neck to see her royal tattoo." She stepped forward and extended her hand toward Kara, but an Emerald Guard inserted himself into her way, while Mai put an arm around Kara's waist and pulled her toward him.

"I must warn you, Your Majesty," Mai said, "that any attempt to touch my wife against her will is a hostile act the Majat will respond to in full force."

Rajmella's face flushed. Her eyes briefly lifted to King Evan, as if seeking support.

"Prior to receiving the news that Princess Aljahara has been escorted to the Majat quarters," the King said, "Queen Rajmella and I signed a formal agreement, pledging her hand in marriage to my son."

Mai's lips twitched. "Since Princess Aljahara doesn't exist, I see no problem in annulling your agreement,

Your Majesty." His arm tightened around Kara and she smiled, relaxing into his embrace. After the long months of downplaying their relationship in public, it felt so good to go along with this open demonstration, a reminder to everyone watching that she now had a lawful place by his side.

"Has your marriage truly been performed by the Holy Father himself?" Rajmella asked, watching the display with a frown of distaste.

Mai grinned. "Would you like to ask him yourself? He's still around here somewhere, I believe. The Guild's seniors asked him to wait, in case questions arise."

*Dear Shal Addim, the Holy Father must be hating the Majat by now.* Kara hid the thought behind a contented smile, watching the complex play of emotions on Rajmella's face. She remembered the way men at this court were expected to maintain secondary roles. Among other things, it was probably difficult for Rajmella right now to adapt to the fact that a man as young and attractive and Mai was speaking to her so openly.

"Has the marriage been consummated?" Rajmella asked.

Mai's grin widened. "I think the Holy Father may be able to attest to that too. He wasn't in the bedchamber with us, of course, but he was present when we were escorted there. I'm sure he would love to discuss the topic with you, Your Majesty."

Rajmella frowned. "You couldn't possibly have had enough time."

Mai's eyes lingered on the Queen with a suggestive expression that made Kara's face flush with heat. Even Rajmella, used to the way men around here looked at women, glanced away in embarrassment, her cheeks lighting up with color.

"I'm sure you can't possibly mean that, Your Majesty," Mai said. "Or else, I would be forced to assume that men at this court are even less capable than I thought."

Rajmella shook her head, taking a visible effort to recover her commanding posture. Still, the way her eyes avoided Mai's direct stare seemed quite noticeable.

"This conversation is not over, Aghat Mai," she said. "If you don't desist, your attempt to steal Princess Aljahara from us will be considered an act of war against our queendom."

Mai's smile remained in place, but his stature changed imperceptibly. He stood taller, his quick glance sweeping over the Majat guards, all armed to the teeth, watching him intently as if waiting for a signal. Kara's skin prickled. This room could turn into a bloodbath so fast Rajmella wouldn't be able to blink an eye.

"Please, Your Majesty," she said. "You don't really want to go to war over this, do you? Not with the Majat. Especially not when so many of our top Gems are stationed right here in this palace."

Rajmella opened her mouth to respond, but at that moment they all heard banging of doors in the outer chambers, followed by voices and rapid clatter of approaching footsteps. Raishan slipped into the room and exchanged a few quiet phrases with Mai, then nodded and departed.

"Prince Kythar is here," Mai said. "With an important announcement, I believe." He glanced at King Evan, who responded with a resigned shrug. Kara had a feeling he knew exactly what this was about. She thought she could guess too, but decided for the moment to keep the guessing to herself. There was too much going on as it was.

Kyth looked solemn as he entered the room with Celana by his side. Once again, Kara marveled at the change in him. Before, he would have stopped humbly in the corner, not to attract too much attention to himself. But now, he held his head high as he stepped into the center of the room, drawing everyone's eyes as naturally as if he was on stage.

"Please forgive me for interrupting this meeting, Aghat Mai," he said. "And allow me to be among the first to congratulate you on your marriage."

Mai's regal nod followed etiquette to the letter, but Kara caught a smile in his eyes that mirrored Kyth, their gazes locked in a private exchange that went beyond words. This was such a change too, from their constant rivalry and near-inability to be around each other, to a friendship that she was sure would last for a very long time. She smiled to Kyth warmly and received a nod in return.

"Thank you, Prince Kythar," Mai said. "This is indeed a joyous day for me. Besides, no matter what business I'm engaged in, you are always a welcome sight in my chambers."

Kyth bowed, then stepped forward and knelt in front of his father, pulling Celana down to kneel by his side.

"Father," he said. "Lady Celana Illitand has just made me the happiest of men by accepting my marriage proposal. We came here as soon as we could, to seek your formal blessing."

King Evan threw a restrained glance around the chamber. All eyes were fixed on him, and Kara was sure that most of the viewers had a pretty good idea what

was going through the King's head. While the news
definitely presented another obstacle to the plans King
Evan and Rajmella were concocting together, it also
gave them all a graceful way out of the standoff that
had reached such a dangerous point just before Kyth's
arrival. Kara could sense the palpably thick silence as
the King ran his eyes from the Majat, alert and ready to
act at a slightest signal, to Queen Rajmella, whose face
showed a visible effort to appear indifferent.

"Congratulations, my son," King Evan said. "And
to you, Lady Celana. This is indeed joyous news and,
as I hope, a happy conclusion to our meeting here. I
give you my blessing and wish you all the happiness
together."

A rustle went through the room, as if everyone had
simultaneously heaved a relieved sigh. Kara smiled
inwardly, watching Rajmella's attempts to compose
herself, which succeeded only after the Queen had a
chance to go through several shades of irritation.

"Congratulations, Prince Kythar," she said stiffly.
"I know that after the crucial role you played in this
campaign you deserve peace and happiness, and I join
everyone here in rejoicing that you have found love.
I hope you and your lovely bride will attend the state
dinner tonight and give us all a chance to celebrate
your engagement."

She didn't wait for a response before she swept out
of the room, the consorts in her wake.

At the state dinner, Kyth's and Celana's engagement
was formally announced and the Prince and his bride
accepted the official congratulations. Since Kara's and
Mai's union was intentionally downplayed – part of

the process that, she knew, would eventually force the fact of this marriage safely out of the openly available chronicles – the young couple became the focus of the gathering. They looking so radiant as they sat next to each other in their best holiday robes.

While Mai made his rounds and engaged in formal conversations with nobles and officials, Kara sat amidst the Majat, chatting with her old friends, laughing at their stories and jokes. It felt like coming home after a long absence, taking her rightful place among them, knowing that from now on she was going to be able to enjoy their company whenever she pleased. This was her true family, and now she was bound to them irrevocably and finally, with no power in the world capable of tearing her away. She couldn't believe her happiness.

After the formal part was over and the general mingling began, the Olivian ladies started drifting toward the Majat, their intentions clear from every seductively curving movement. Princess Nelimah led the way toward the Diamonds, her inviting smile causing Lance by Kara's side to pause in mid-sentence with a distracted look. Raishan was looking too, as another young and beautiful lady in Nelimah's wake beckoned him with her finger. Kara hastily rose to her feet. It was time to retreat.

She glanced around the chamber to spot Mai on the other side, in conversation with Jamal and several other Olivian men. But before she could head that way, another group approaching her table caught her eye. She froze, feeling an unpleasant chill run down her spine.

Rajmella's face held a strange expression, a mix of

wonder and apprehension, as if once again she was seeing Kara for the very first time. The consorts at her sides kept their eyes decisively downward, as if overtaken by an uncharacteristic bout of modesty. Kara watched them in surprise as the Queen approached and stopped in front of her, her violet eyes fixed on Kara intently.

"You surprised me, niece," Rajmella said.

Kara shook her head. "I'm not your niece."

"Yes, you are. We both know it, so why don't you stop the pretense, just between us."

Kara stepped away. "I was just leaving, Your Majesty. Please excuse me."

The Queen's lips twitched. "Very well, if you want to play it this way, *Kara*. I hoped we could be family."

Against reason, Kara felt anger rise in her chest. This was the woman who nearly killed her before, who had just tried to rip the hard-earned happiness right out of her grasp.

"Is this why you tried to sell me into an arranged marriage?" she demanded.

Rajmella shook her head. "A marriage to a good man who cares for you deeply, at the time when I believed that the one you love was unavailable to you."

"Well, you know otherwise now, don't you?"

Rajmella heaved a sigh. "So, do you hate me for it?"

"Do you really care?"

"I do, actually."

"Why?"

Rajmella stepped closer, peering into her eyes. Kara forced herself to keep her place.

"Like it or not," Rajmella said, "you're family. Nothing can possibly change that."

Kara glanced away. She knew the truth of it, but

admitting this openly in front of witnesses right now seemed like a bad move.

Rajmella waited out a pause, then smiled. "Fine. I won't press you into saying anything else. Just tell me one thing. Are you truly happy?"

"I am," Kara said. "More than you can possibly imagine."

The Queen nodded. "In this case, I am giving you my blessing – whatever it's worth for you."

Kara paused, surprised. "Really?"

Rajmella laughed. "What did you expect, that I will chase you up north and storm the Majat Fortress to get you back?"

Kara shook her head. "No."

"Then," Rajmella said, "go to your man and make the most of what you have."

"I will."

The Queen smiled. "Good. I hope he brings stars to your eyes. And now, if you'll forgive me, I have other business to attend to here."

Kara's mouth fell open as the Queen stepped past her into the Majat group, singling out Seldon, whose face dissolved into a very uncharacteristic smile. Rajmella swept toward him, pulling him close, lifting up her face for a kiss.

Kara didn't want to see anymore. She hastily spun around and rushed across the chamber toward Mai, doing her best not to break into a run. Whateven the Queen and Seldon did together, she was certain she would be better off not knowing.

Mai and his companions all paused, smiles playing on their faces as they watched her approach.

"I haven't had a chance to congratulate you yet,

sister," Jamal said.

She bowed her head. "Thank you, Prince Jamal. It pains me to say that we cannot possibly call each other family anymore, but privately it means a lot to me to be able to hear this from you."

He nodded gravely. "I understand. And, while this restriction is painful indeed, I find it a price worth paying for seeing you so happy."

She wanted to hug him, but knew she would never be able to do it in this public setting.

"You are most kind, Prince Jamal." She held his gaze, the approval in his eyes filling her with warmth. She may be losing him after a brief time together, but she knew the bond they shared could never be broken. She saw the same thought reflected in his eyes and smiled back to him, eyes only, before turning to Mai. "I feel obliged to report that our men are becoming quite preoccupied out there."

Mai laughed as he glanced in that direction. Kara followed his gaze, her eyes widening. Dear Shal Addim, were they about to start right here? Was this part of the Olivian custom to end a state dinner with a public orgy?

Jamal guessed her thoughts correctly. "I, um, believe they are all going to retire to their chambers soon. I'm afraid I must also be taking my leave."

"Sound like a good idea." Mai held out his arm to Kara. "Shall we?"

It felt strange to walk back to their chambers alone, without any Majat suite. Yet, Kara knew that with their combined fighting skill, even in a setting far more hostile than this palace, the two of them had nothing to fear. The only challenge right now was to find their way through all the winding corridors back to their quarters.

"The Olivian ladies seem to be quite taken with our men," she said. "I find it surprising, given that they are all used to having their pick of consorts at all times."

Mai grinned. "I guess this just tells you their consorts have something to learn."

Her eyes narrowed in suspicion. "Do you know something I don't?"

"No, actually. It's just a matter of using the knowledge correctly."

"What could you possibly mean?"

Mai's shoulders shook with quiet laughter. "I expect we both had the same combat training in the use of pressure points."

"Pressure points?" She blinked, feeling lost.

"Yes. It takes extensive practice of a different kind to figure out what else they can be used for."

She frowned. Pressure points did provide a range of powerful sensations when touched with different strength. Did the Majat men learn to use them for pleasure? She opened her mouth to ask the question, but at that moment Mai's face brightened as he glanced ahead.

"Here it is, finally. Our chamber. I hope the bath water didn't get cold yet."

*Bath water.* The thought that they were about to share a bath and spend the rest of the night together made her shiver. *Our wedding night.* She still couldn't fully believe it.

"Have you ever used this, um, pressure point technique on me?" she asked as they made their way to the bedchamber and struggled out of their weapons and gear. It had been such a long day.

He grinned. "A bit. I'd love to show you a lot more, but..."

"But what?"

"You will have to give yourself to me, unconditionally."

"Haven't I?"

"Not like that."

She knew what he meant. If she allowed him free rein of her pressure points, she would render herself completely vulnerable to him. There was no counting the ways he could kill or disable her by pressing the wrong way. The thought was thrilling. She had already opened herself to him more than she imagined possible with a man, but this was a new level she never even considered before.

"I'd like to try," she said. "Unconditionally, to do with as you please."

His eyes lit up with a wicked gleam as he stepped toward her and pulled her into his arms.

# ACKNOWLEDGMENTS

Years ago, when I was still struggling as an author and very far from being published, my father once told me: "Believe in yourself. Do what you think is right for you. If you want to be a writer – write, and don't let any other considerations sway you." I found this advice not only very comforting to me at the time, but also very useful, and I still follow it every day, no matter what.

My father passed away just after the first two books in this trilogy came out. Along with the pain of the loss, he left me with so many things to be grateful about. I feel grateful that he could see these publications happen, and know that he carries at least partial credit for making this possible. I feel so very grateful for having him in my life. His support – and challenge, when needed – helped me not to give up. My thoughts will always be with him, and with my mother, his true soul mate.

So many people have contributed to this book by providing their critiques, advice, and overall support. First and foremost, I thank my husband for putting up with a wife who writes at odd hours of day and night, leaves medieval weapons in the trunk of the car, and talks about the fine aspects of martial arts technique at breakfast, dinner, and bedtime. I thank my children for filling my days with joy. I am grateful to my friends and critique partners, especially Bernie Mojzes (who also supplied me with a lot of useful information, and demonstrated various staff and sword fighting styles), AC Wise, Aliza Greenblatt, Siobhan Carroll, JM Sidorova, and Olga Karengina – the people who not only taught me many things about writing but also kept me company through the hardest times of self-doubt. I also thank all my readers and fans, who supported the series by reading my books and spreading the word, by filling my life with their enthusiasm for the Majat Code series.

Writing the series has shaped me as an author and made me realize beyond all doubt that only a combination of fantasy and romance can make me feel truly balanced in my writing. I cannot help but feeling thankful to my characters, who, more than once, took matters into their own hands, to show me what my writing can be.

I am grateful to Alejandro Colucci for doing such a great job with my cover art, that brought my favorite characters to life and made me understand them better than before.

Last but not least, I want to thank my amazing agent, Michael Harriot, and the Angry Robot team – Phil Jourdan, Marc Gascoigne, Penny Reeve, and Michael Underwood – for all their hard work in bringing this book to publication.

I dedicate the Majat Code series to my grandfather, Vladimir Keilis-Borok, who taught me to be a writer and opened my eyes to the fantasy worlds of my dreams.

# PREVIOUSLY —